The Valley of Shadows

Tor Books by Brian Cullen

Seekers of the Chalice
The Valley of Shadows

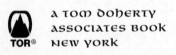

A TOM DOHERTY
ASSOCIATES BOOK
NEW YORK

Brian Cullen

The Valley of Shadows

THE VALLEY OF SHADOWS

Copyright © 2009 by Brian Cullen

A Tor Book
Published by Tom Doherty Associates, LLC
175 Fifth Avenue
New York, NY 10010

www.tor-forge.com

Tor® is a registered trademark of Tom Doherty Associates, LLC.

Library of Congress Cataloging-in-Publication Data

Cullen, Brian.
    The valley of shadows / Brian Cullen.—1st ed.
        p. cm.
    ISBN-13: 978-0-7653-1474-1
    ISBN-10: 0-7653-1474-6
    1. Mythology, Celtic—Fiction.   I. Title.

    PR6053.U372V35 2009
    823'.914—dc22

                                          2008046534

First Edition: February 2009

Printed in the United States of America

0 9 8 7 6 5 4 3 2 1

FROM THE AUTHOR TO THE READER

This is a work of fiction. License has
been taken with Ancient Irish myth
to create a different world.
Anyone trying to make something more
of it will suffer the Ancient Curses.

For Randy

To Cruachan Connor sent the three,
Cucullen, Conall, and Leary,
For Maeve to choose which one
Would be the Red Branch champion.
A cup of bronze with silver eagle
At the bottom went to Leary.
A cup of silver with a gold eagle
At the bottom went to Conall.
But to Cucullen went the champion's
Cup of gold with a flawless ruby
Carved in the shape of a raven
And around its base in Old Tongue graven
"I am made of Air, Fire, Land, and Sea
Only the Just may drink from Me."

—Translated from *Annals of the Red Branch*
   by Aruadh the Wise in the Year 369 Tír Na Og

But I who have written this story (*historia*), or rather this fable (*fabula*), give no credence to the various incidents related in it. For some things in it are the deceptions of demons, others poetic figments; some are probable, others improbable; while still others are intended for the delectation of foolish men.

—Translated from *Annals of the Red Branch*
by Aruadh the Wise in the Year 369 Tír Na Og

the VALLEY of Shadows

PROLOGUE

Rain blanketed the road that Bricriu Poisontongue tried to follow as he made his way from Maeve's fortress at Cruachan Ai in Connacht. Behind him came the Seekers of the Chalice that he had stolen from Emain Macha. The Chalice had been given by Maeve to Cucullen, the greatest of the Red Branch warriors. As long as the Chalice was in Ulster, that country remained at peace. But its theft had unleashed the Dark Forces kept at bay by the Chalice once Maliman, the Dark Wizard, had made his escape from the Great Rift where he had been cast by The Dagda, the king of The Pantheon of Gods in the Otherworld.

Bricriu swore as a trickle of rain slipped under the hood of his cloak and ran coldly down his neck. He touched the pouch at his side where the box containing the Chalice rested. He did not have to open the box to remember its contents: a golden Chalice with a blood-red ruby carved in the figure of a raven at the bottom of the cup. Around the base of the Chalice was the legend

Amatérbaevemethararnécathdiné
Averstanenperthsáitébaeveshné

I am made of Air, Fire, Land, and Sea
Only the Just may drink from Me.

A blood-red ruby carved into the likeness of a raven fell from Ragon's forehead during his fall and was found by Boand in one of the rivers she guarded. Boand gave the raven ruby to Goibniu, who placed it in the bottom of the Chalice of Fire as a talisman to guard the seekers of Truth.

First, the gods drank from the Chalice to become immortal. Then, the Chalice was given to the elves, who lived in the tree houses they built in the forests, and the dwarfs, who lived in the Great Halls they built deep within the mountains. Then the Chalice was secretly buried by The Dagda, the god-king, on the Island of Shadows, where it was guarded by Scathach Buanand, the Woman of Victory. Only the bravest of the brave could reach the Island of Shadows and what lay beyond by making their way through the gray Mountains of Mourne to the Giant's Causeway where they could cross the Misty Sea to the Island of Shadows.

In time, the Pantheon of Gods decided that the heroes of men should receive the Chalice so that they too could become immortal. But only those worthy of drinking from the Chalice would become like gods. Those who were unworthy would enter Dreamworld, where they would walk through the ancient fires of the Fomorians and their flesh would blister from the dreadful heat and the hair be singed from their bodies until only black stubble remained. They would see the fire from the Blood Raven sweep up to the night sky and weep for that which they could not become.

The gods gave the Chalice to Fand, the wife of the sea god Manannan Mac Lir, and directed her to take the Chalice to man. This she did, and in time the Chalice made its way to the Land of Connacht, where it came into the hands of the warrior-queen Maeve. But Maeve could not receive the glory of the Chalice, as she desired power over the land for herself. Still she kept it until the great champion of the Red Branch in Ulster, Cucullen, came to her court in Cruachan Ai. Desiring him for her own, Maeve gave the Chalice to him, but Cucullen ignored her sultry ways meant to seduce him and took the Chalice back to the Red Branch.

The Chalice was to bring peace to the land, but men did not want peace and brought the curse down upon them when they refused to help Macha, a goddess of fertility and the red war-goddess, one of the three feared goddesses along with Baeve, the Battle-Raven, and Nemain, wordless terror, who became the feared Morrigan, during her greatest time of need.

Once, Crunniuc, a wealthy farmer, was mourning the death of his wife when Macha came across a fertile field to become his wife. When she became with child, Crunniuc decided to go to a festival being held by Ulster's king, Connor, where Crunniuc broke his promise to her not to drink and became drunk and boasted that his wife could beat the matched black horses of Connor in a race. Inflamed by Crunniuc's insult, Connor had him arrested and demanded that Macha race his horses to save her husband's head. Despite Macha's plea to the warriors of the Red Branch to intercede for her as she was nearly nine months pregnant, the warriors, too, demanded that she race Connor's blacks. She warned them what would happen if they forced her to do this but to no avail. She raced the blacks, but after crossing the finish line she fell to the ground, writhing in labor pains, and delivered twins. Whereupon she cursed the warriors and all men of Ulster that when they were most needed, they too would fall into the same pain she felt at the birth of her children. For five days and five nights they would suffer, helpless, unable to do anything but writhe upon their beds as if in childbirth.

And then the Chalice was stolen and came into the hands of the servers of darkness.

And although the dark servants could not bend the powers of the Chalice to their will, they could deny the powers to those worthy of the Chalice. And this they did while they quietly searched for one who could be bent to their ways.

Maeve, She-Who-Intoxicates, had betrayed Bricriu after he sought the protection granted him by the Laws of Hospitality given to men by The Dagda, he thought sourly. Yes, he had been given sanctuary, but then the others came and he knew that he had to flee from the comfort of Cruachan Ai and make his way south to where he hoped Cairpre, the King of Munster, would give him sanctuary against the pursuit of the others.

A slight trace of fear touched him as he thought of those coming behind him to regain the Chalice and restore peace to a strife-torn country. From the Otherworld, Cumac, the son of Cucullen, the greatest of the Red Branch's heroes; Fedelm of the Sidhe; Seanchan of the Duirgeals; Bern of the Ervalian elves; Lorgas of the Ashelves; and Tarin the Sword-wanderer, he who was called the Damned and Deathwhisper, who together formed the Seekers of the Chalice.

Grimly, he pressed forward, hoping that somewhere ahead was a dry fortress or even a woodcutter's hut where he might weather the storm.

1

Rain had fallen steadily for two days as the Seekers made their way through the muck that had buried the trail south from Maeve's Cruachan Ai. They rode in single file—Seanchan, Fedelm, Cumac, Lorgas, Bern, and Tarin, huddled miserably deep within their cloaks. A blight had fallen upon the land as Maliman, the Black Wizard, had escaped from his prison deep within the Great Rift and even now had begun building his army of followers—the Grayshawls, the Nightshades, and the Fomorians—from his fortress Dun Darai in the Mountains of Mourne. He, too, sought the Chalice of Fire to bend to his will, for he had once been one of the Duirgeals before turning to the ways of darkness and being cast out of their ways. Yet he took the secret of the Chalice with him.

Cumac listened to the sucking sound the hooves of his horse, the Black of Saingliau, made as he walked through the mud. Water had soaked through the hood of Cumac's cloak and pasted his black hair to his head. Glumly he tried to see through the curtain of rain but saw nothing except more rain and an occasional tree, its dead black arms stretching toward the clouds.

At last he spoke.

"We should stop and wait out this rain. We could come upon Nightshades before we knew it," he said.

Lorgas tried to shake the rain from his cloak but only managed to send a new trickle down the back of his neck. He swore.

"Shelter and a roaring fire and hot ale with salty pork," he said. "This is what we need now. This rain is draining our strength."

Seanchan glanced over his shoulder at the others and said irritably, "Well and good that would be. But where do we find it? It's been two days since last we found a hut and that was deserted, the hearth cold. Where would you suggest we look?"

"What good is a wizard who can't conjure shelter?" Lorgas grumbled.

A hot retort was on Seanchan's lips when Bern spoke, saying, "Stay your words, Lorgas. He cannot bring what isn't there. I would think even an Ashelf would know that!"

"I've seen it worse," Tarin put in from behind them. He hawked and spat. "Many a time I've had to sleep beneath a tree or bush and without a fire in weather like this and was thankful for what I had."

"Complaining won't matter," Fedelm called back. "We'll find a place when we find it. Nothing to do but wait."

"Wait, wait, wait," Lorgas said sourly. "My backside aches and my joints feel rusty. I'll take sooner than later, if you please."

"It would be far better if you spent less time complaining and more keeping an eye out for danger," Seanchan said. "This is a road seldom traveled except by those who mean harm to others."

"I can vouch that," Tarin said somberly. "Cairpre, the Munster king, is careless about keeping his northern borders secure. He is a son of Maeve and relies upon her to protect him here. Not that he couldn't," he added, "but this way he only has to worry about his eastern borders and the sea and only a fool would attempt to land on Munster's coast. There are few places where a landing would be safe."

"I thought Sword-wanderers kept to the forests," Cumac said.

"Most do," Tarin answered. "But there are others who are not Sword-wanderers who prey upon travelers who dare this road. Tinkers and traders travel in large caravans for protection."

"And there are the Nightshades and Grayshawls who may be here as well," Fedelm said. "And we mustn't forget the sumaires either. This gray light is enough for them to attack."

Cumac shuddered and straightened to keep a sharper eye around them. He wanted no truck with the sumaires—vampires, but of the deadliest sort, who traveled not only in dark but in men's dreams as well to drink their blood. They were wraiths with an odor of old blood and rotting meat clinging to them. They rode the Memans, black horses that were also cannibalistic and fed on the corpses left by the sumaires, who did not simply bite and suck blood but, rather, either ripped the throats of their victims with their fangs or, more likely, struck with their swords, which carried a poison within the iron blade that left their victims helpless so the sumaires could feast leisurely. Cumac had had one encounter with the sumaires that had left him wounded and nearly dead.

In fact, he remembered, had not Fedelm managed to get him to the Red Branch, where Seanchan healed him, he would now be wandering Teach Duinn, the Island of Donn, the god of death.

You have to worry about not only the sumaires but the warggads, Cumac thought, the worst of werewolves and nearly indestructible, whose hides cannot be pierced by any man-made weapons. The slightest bite or raking from their sharp claws is poisonous, and one who is wounded must be treated quickly with a poultice of wolfsbane.

And there are also the Truacs, hunchbacked creatures who were created at the same time as hobgoblins. They are incredibly strong. Their skin is gray and their breath as foul as rank meat. They have little value for life, and are just as at home killing goblins and hobgoblins and even the weaker of themselves if they are hungry enough.

Which is worse, I don't know. I would just as soon not meet up with either.

A forest appeared in front of them and Seanchan reined in. He studied the forest glumly.

"What is it?" Cumac asked.

"This is Faindell Forest," Seanchan said. "Much evil is in there."

"Yet the trail leads through it," Tarin said.

"Yes, but I do not wish to go into that forest."

"It is the straightest path to Munster," Cumac said.

"This is the Forest of Bertilgain, who makes his home deep within it. He is not one to reckon with," Seanchan said.

"Well, there's nothing for it but to go through it," Lorgas said grumpily. "Sitting here and moping about it accomplishes nothing."

"Keep watch," Seanchan said, gathering his reins. "Faindell is home to sumaires and warggads along with some Truacs. We must travel through it quietly."

He nudged his horse with his knees and slowly the party slipped into the dark forest. The trees closed in around them but rain still fell, leaving them soaked and cold.

"There must be a shelter somewhere in here," Bern grumbled.

But none could be seen as the party wove their way deeper and deeper into the forest.

"A light," Fedelm said quietly, reining in her horse. "There."

She pointed ahead to a wooded copse. From the dark middle, a light flickered.

The others bunched around her, staring hard through the rain. Their spirits rose in anticipation, yet a caution came with hope. They had not encountered a living soul on the road since leaving Connacht's borders. Only the single burned-out hut. What person would choose to live here?

Cumac glanced down at the silver brooch holding his cloak together. The brooch was set with a blood-red Dragonstone that turned black at the time of danger. The brooch flickered red then black then red. Something there, he thought. Something that my father's brooch is warning me about.

He reached over his shoulder and loosened Caladbolg, his father's sword, in its sheath.

"I suggest caution," Seanchan said needlessly.

"I say we go to it," Lorgas said.

"You would," Bern said sarcastically.

"And tell me if a roof over your head, salty pork, and a mug of steaming ale before a roaring fire would not fit you as well," demanded Lorgas.

"And the others of us," Tarin said. He slid his rune-blade from its sheath and held it loosely across the pommel of his saddle. "But not if we come upon Maliman's mischief instead."

"I say kill them all and let Donn sort out that which he wants to keep and throw the others into the dark," Lorgas said. "And use the hut for ourselves."

"Do not be in such a hurry to kill, Lorgas," Seanchan said. "I do not think any of us has the right to judge others."

"Sumaires and warggads I can judge. As well as the others sent by Maliman," Lorgas said, lifting the ax up and down at his side. "But we won't find out what's there by standing here in the rain."

Wordlessly Fedelm urged her mount forward toward the light. They entered the woods and rode carefully through them, eyes darting to the sides and back in readiness. But the dark and barren wood was silent as they slipped into a small clearing, in the center of which stood the hut.

They reined in front of it and studied it carefully. The hut had been well taken care of, the thatch seeming fresh although drenched with rain and the stone walls gleaming with a lime wash. Lead frames held opaque windows in place but flower boxes beneath the windows held ferns, primroses, and yellow pimpernel. A small corral and stable stood to the left of the hut and their horses stamped their feet and tossed their heads as they smelled the fresh hay and straw tidily stacked in wooden bins.

"Those flowers are out of season," Fedelm warned, slipping an arrow from her quiver and fitting it to her bow in readiness. "This places smacks of magic but good or bad I cannot tell."

Cumac took Caladbolg from its sheath while Lorgas lifted his ax and Bern his sword. Cumac turned Black sideways to the others, staring hard into the rain at the edge of the forest for what might lurk there.

"I sense magic but cannot tell what kind either," Seanchan said, slipping from his horse. "There's nothing for it but to see what awaits us."

He strode to the heavy cedar door banded by black iron braces and knocked loudly with his staff.

The door opened immediately to reveal a beautiful woman standing in the doorway, holding a lantern high to see. She wore her blond hair, which fell to her waist, in tight braids. Her blue eyes were like sapphire. She wore a long white dress with a dark green robe fitted over it. A green leather belt encrusted with gems was belted around her narrow waist.

"Strangers," she said, and smiled warmly. "Welcome! Come in to the fire and warm yourselves. It's a middling evil night to be gadding about!"

Seanchan turned and nodded at the others, who climbed thankfully from their mounts. Tarin took the reins of the horses and led them to the stable as the others crossed the threshold.

"I am Moagin. You are most welcome. Come! Come! Stand by the fire and warm yourselves while I have mulled ale brought to you."

Her teeth gleamed whitely as she smiled. Dimples appeared in each cheek. She turned and left them, only to return shortly with a servant bearing a tray upon which a pitcher of mulled ale and mugs had been placed. The servant placed the tray upon a heavy wooden table in front of the fire and silently took their cloaks from them and disappeared.

"Where are we?" Tarin asked, boldly eyeing her.

"These are the woods of Faindell," she said, pouring ale into the mugs and handing them around. "And this is my house. The woods are mine to keep. Now"—she clapped her hands—"you shall eat and then be shown to your rooms."

"Rooms?" Tarin asked the others softly. "This place is not big enough for rooms. Let alone what we find here."

He did mean for her to hear his words, but she beamed at him and said, "Looks can be deceiving, Tarin. Do not judge everything by what you first see."

"How did you know my name?" he demanded, his hand straying to his sword.

She caught his movement and laughed merrily. "Why, I know all your names. Seanchan, Fedelm, Bern, and Lorgas. And of course, Cumac. Travelers before you told me you would be coming after them. And here you are!"

"What travelers?" Cumac asked. "We have not seen any since we left the borders of Connacht."

"Why, tinkers and merchants traveling toward the fortress of Cairpre, of course. You cannot know who went before you and who comes after you, now, can you? We are not so alone here as one might think."

She laughed again. "Now, I must see to your supper. Will venison and fresh bread and cheese do you? And of course, mushroom gravy."

"Mushroom gravy?" Lorgas repeated, his mouth watering. The Ashelves are greatly fond of mushrooms.

She beamed at him, nodded, and scurried off after the servant, calling over her shoulder, "It will only be a moment."

"It seems that we have come to a haven indeed," Bern said, rubbing his hands vigorously over the fire to warm them.

"I wonder," Seanchan said softly. "There is more here than meets the eye. Of that I am certain. We would be well advised not to make ourselves too much at ease."

"Sticks and stones! You would question the flame of a lone candle in the dark!" Lorgas said. "I say for now we enjoy ourselves of what is offered. This is far better than making a cold camp in the rain."

With misgivings, Seanchan followed the others as they took their places around the table with their mugs of warm ale and waited for the servant to bring the dishes promised.

2

Tarin awoke and yawned and stretched with satisfaction. A warm comforter covered him and he snuggled beneath it, relishing the lethargic feeling that swept over him. He glanced at the room. The fire in the fireplace still flickered, radiating warmth out into the room. The room was simply furnished, with a cedar chest at the end of the bed upon which his clothes, cleaned and neatly folded, rested. A wicker table and chairs stood in the center. On the wall were torches waiting for light in wrought-iron sconces. The curtains were still drawn over the sole window.

He rose reluctantly and padded on bare feet to the window and drew the curtains, wrapping them in iron hooks set into the wall on either side of the window. The glass was opaque and the window sealed so he could not open it, but rain still spattered against the windowpanes and the light seeping into the room was gray and cold. He began stretching and then moved into the various forms of a warrior, concentrating on perfecting each movement until at last he stopped, panting, muscles twanging from exertion, his skin covered with perspiration.

Then he sat cross-legged on the gray stone floor and closed his eyes and brought peace into his mind. He focused on *his* mountain, the peak covered with snow, the valley leading to it covered with trees in autumn colors of burnt red, orange, scarlet, yellow, and brown. A crystal creek ran through the trees, and although he had never been there except in his mind, he knew the creek water would be sweet-tasting, with a hint of tannic about it.

He shivered and left the window, crossing to the chest. He dressed quickly in his black tunic and black leather pants. He slipped on his black knee-high boots and looked at his sword hanging from a hook on the wall. He shook his head, yawned again, and left the bedroom.

He walked down the hall and into the room where a fire was blazing merrily in the stone fireplace. The table had been set with salted pork hot on a platter. Bowls of winter apples had been placed on the table along with two pitchers of mulled wine. He smiled happily as he speared slices of the pork and transferred them to his platter along with a thick slice of bread he cut from one of the fresh loaves shining with butter spread over a golden crust, and ate hungrily.

"Is breakfast to your satisfaction?"

He started at the voice and turned to Moagin standing in front of the fire. Her hands were folded demurely in front of her. She wore a white gossamer gown through which he could see her body outlined by firelight. Above the fireplace a curious stone figure cut from green marble stood in a niche cut from the stone. His eyebrows rose. He had not seen the figure before—a naked woman with her legs apart.

Moagin followed his gaze and smiled, her lips curving into deep dimples.

"She is Sheela-na-gig. She was brought here by the Tuatha De Danann from Murias in Greece during the Fifth Invasion."

"She is, ah"—he cleared his throat—"different."

A strange light began to gleam deep within Moagin's sapphire eyes. She stepped close to Tarin and he could feel the heat from her pulsing against him.

"She is one of the goddesses of love. The most important," she breathed. She touched him lightly upon his cheek. His face burned from where her fingertips had lingered.

"Does she appeal to you?"

Tarin stepped back from Moagin and took his goblet of wine from the table, sipping to cover his feelings.

"She is . . . interesting . . . but she is no goddess for warriors. Especially," he added grimly, "Sword-wanderers."

Moagin pouted and stepped near him, taking a goblet from the table and filling it with wine. Her eyes flickered with bold teasing. She drank and said, "Do I frighten you, Tarin?"

"No, you do not frighten me. But you make me . . . apprehensive," he answered lamely.

"Apprehensive is good," she said, coming closer to him. She held her goblet up near his lips. "Won't you drink from my glass?"

"Ah, I have my own," Tarin said uncomfortably, stepping away from her.

"Don't you like me?"

"Yes, I like you. I like you very much."

"Then," she said, finishing her wine and placing the goblet back on the table, "why don't you come with me?"

"The others—"

"Are still sleeping and will be for a while. We have plenty of time," she said. She turned aside and gestured toward the stairs. Her eyes smoldered with banked fire.

Tarin shook his head and sipped again. "I think I'll wait here for the others. We have plans to make. Not that I wouldn't like to go with you," he hastened to add, "but I must wait here."

"Oh very well," she said crossly, stamping her foot. "I'll go attend to other matters."

She swept from the room, the hem of her gown billowing behind her.

"Whew," Tarin said, mopping his forehead with the sleeve of his tunic. "I know I'm going to regret this."

He heard the others coming down the hall and hastened back to his seat at the table. He shrugged to relieve the tension in his shoulders.

"Morning," Cumac said, entering. Fedelm and the others came in behind him and took their places at the table. Seanchan eyed Tarin curiously, his bushy eyebrows rising in query, then set to his breakfast with relish.

"Morning to you," Tarin answered. He took a deep breath and slowly let it out.

"Tell me: what are our plans?"

Cumac raised his goblet, studying the strange and arcane figures carved on its side.

"It's a bit early for making plans, don't you think?" he said dreamily. "The rain has not let up and we are comfortable here. I say we linger a bit until the foul weather becomes fair."

"I'll agree to that," Lorgas said around a mouthful of salty pork. He washed it down with huge gulps of ale.

"You would agree to anything that pleased your stomach," Bern said. He glanced at the others. "Still, I think we should give great thought to our travel. I do not think Bricriu will be traveling in this storm. We won't lose any time."

Seanchan bit into a winter apple and said, "But we won't gain any, either. Still, I too think we should wait. Better weather will make us more alert."

Fedelm remained silent, studying Tarin carefully. He blushed beneath her scrutiny.

"I would say that there are other reasons for staying, right, Tarin? But, never mind. If that is the wish of you all, then I have no objections to staying until the rain lets up."

And so it was decided and the Seekers turned happily to their breakfast, not noticing the gleam of satisfaction on Moagin's face as she stepped around the corner into the room after listening to their conversation from her hiding place.

"Well," she said brightly, clapping her hands. "I hope you all have slept well. Have you looked outside? Never mind if you haven't. The rain hasn't let up yet. If anything it is coming down harder. You really should stay a bit longer. Nothing *will* be moving in this weather. Take the time to rest fully before moving on. You are most welcome and there is much to entertain you while you are here."

Small wrinkles appeared between Seanchan's eyes as he studied Moagin's guileless face. Something about her words made him uneasy, but he discarded the thought when he glanced automatically toward the opaque windows and saw the rain lashing down upon the panes. He sighed and stretched contentedly, feeling the heat from the fire warm the chill in his muscles and bones.

This *is* much better than sitting in a wet saddle all day, he reflected. And I do not feel danger in this room. Perhaps she is right. Nothing will be moving on a day like this—especially Bricriu Poisontongue. He has always liked his comfort. He will be resting comfortably too against this downpour. Yes, it is better to wait.

"We appreciate your kindness," he said. "And I think we will wait as long as we do not become a nuisance or trouble."

"Nuisance? Trouble?" she cried, then laughed. "No, you will not become a nuisance or trouble. Now, eat! Eat! I like to watch people enjoy my food!"

Again, a small worry nagged at the back of Seanchan's mind, but he pushed it away and helped himself to another winter apple and refilled his mug with ale. At the same time, Lorgas reached for his third helping of everything and even Bern refilled his platter.

Fedelm and Cumac refilled their mugs as well but declined more food. They glanced at each other and saw the concern in each's eyes and both gave small nods acknowledging their feelings. The brooch on Cumac's shoulder was flickering red-black-red steadily. He stealthily slipped a fold of his tunic over the brooch, concealing it from Moagin's view.

"I have a good library which should interest you, Seanchan. And for you, Bern and Lorgas, it is well known that the elves are fond of fidchell, a game like chess. For you, Fedelm and Cumac, I have Brandubh that might entertain you. If you wish, I'll have a servant bring them to you."

Cumac nodded. He had a fondness for Brandubh, or Black Raven, a game that involved the attempt to capture the white king and was played with dice. He had always been very lucky throwing dice.

"And as for you, Tarin," she said, turning toward the Sword-wanderer and giving him a knowing look, "I think we can find something to entertain you. I think you will all enjoy those games."

Fedelm and Cumac caught the quick interchange between Moagin and Tarin and exchanged knowing looks.

"Thank you," Tarin said politely, "but I think I would like to join Seanchan in the library, if you don't mind."

A flicker of annoyance crossed Moagin's face but quickly disappeared as she smiled widely at Tarin.

"Whatever you . . . prefer," she said, placing a slight emphasis on the last word that none there could fail to not understand. "But if you should become bored, come to me and I'll help you find something that will keep you entertained while you wait for clear weather."

And so they spent the first day, entertaining themselves with Moagin's suggestions. Bern and Lorgas played fierce games of fidchell while drinking ale liberally from mugs that they were never aware of refilling. Seanchan and Tarin retired to the library, where Seanchan found a rare copy of *The Temple of Spells*, a book that he had not seen or read from his early days of study with the Duirgeals. He took it to a chair placed before a roaring fire. A carafe of wine and a glass had been placed on a small table beside the chair. He sighed contentedly and sank into the chair, losing himself almost immediately in the ancient tome. He filled his glass from time to time and sipped the tart wine, which had a slight taste of strawberries.

Tarin prowled among the shelves and discovered a book on famous battles in the past and took it down, thumbing through it for a moment before taking it to another chair next to the fire and settling himself to read. From time to time he sipped wine from another carafe, which had been placed on a table near his elbow. The wine had a richness that sent his warrior's soul quickening as he soon lost himself in the stories of ancient battles.

Fedelm and Cumac played Brandubh but refrained from drinking more than a glass or two of the wine that had been made available to them. They spoke softly as they played.

"I do not like this," Fedelm said. "I sense that there is much trickery here."

"I feel the same," Cumac acknowledged, moving a raven piece on the board. "There is something about Tarin for her, I think."

"Think," Fedelm said sarcastically. "What is it men want from a woman or women want from a man?"

"Oh," Cumac said. "That."

"Yes, that," she said mimicking him.

"I hope Tarin is wise enough to understand what she intends for him," Cumac said, moving another piece. "I've captured your king. Would you care for another game?"

"Much little else to do," Fedelm said grumpily, resetting the pieces upon the board.

The day passed swiftly, and soon it was time for supper. The Seekers gathered around the table as a servant set out the dishes. Venison was served along with hot oatmeal and fresh bread and pots of honey. Ale again flowed ceaselessly into mugs as they ate, talking animatedly about the day.

After the meal, they retired to their rooms. Tarin was restrained by Moagin's hand as he sought to walk down the hall.

"Perhaps you would care for a different room?" Moagin said, standing uncomfortably close to him.

Tarin tried to move back but Moagin followed, her body not touching his but close enough that he could feel the heat emanating from her. He swallowed and said, "I thank you but my room is sufficient for my needs."

"Perhaps another would appeal to your other needs," she said.

Suddenly she placed her arms around him and kissed him deeply. When she drew back, she saw beads of sweat standing upon his brow and smiled lazily.

"I thank you," Tarin said, and feigned a yawn. "But I am very tired and would like to sleep."

She pouted and released him and said in a sultry voice, "Perhaps later."

"Yes. Perhaps," Tarin said, and walked quickly down the hall and into his room. He stood with his back against the door, breathing deeply, trying to slow the pounding in his breast and head.

"You'd better watch yourself, Tarin," he muttered as he crossed to his bed. "She says one thing but I think she means another and there will be no good coming from that, I think."

With that, he quickly disrobed and slipped into bed, falling deeply asleep in a matter of moments, his dreams troubled with images that he could not understand.

3

Again the rain fell. Tarin tried to look out the
opaque window being lashed by the storm when
he awakened. Glumly he dressed and sighed
deeply. He made his way down the hallway to
the room where the table had been set for breakfast. Platters of salty pork were centered in the
middle of the table along with pitchers of
mulled wine and ale. Golden brown fresh bread
was on plates next to the meat. Winter apples
nestled in bowls. A fire flickered merrily in the

stone fireplace. Fresh straw matting had been placed over the stone floor.

He glanced at the Sheela-na-gig in its niche on the wall and frowned. He would have to ask Seanchan about it. For some reason, it made him feel uncomfortable.

"Good morning. Did you sleep well?"

He started and turned to see Moagin emerge from the hallway leading back to the kitchens. She wore a deep red shift that slid softly over her breasts and fell down to her shapely white feet. Her gem-encrusted belt cinched the shift at her waist. Her hair was caught behind her by a golden circlet.

"Tolerably," he said cautiously. "I had dreams but when I awoke, I could no longer remember what they were. And you?"

She laughed merrily. "Always. This is my sanctuary and here I can dream safely if I choose."

"You can choose your dreams?"

He stepped casually to the table to put it between them, but she followed and stood closely to him. He smelled honeysuckle flowing faintly from her. It made him giddy.

"Oh yes. My dreams are always of my choosing. I can teach you how to dream, if you wish."

"Thank you," he answered, fumbling for words. "But I think it would be better if my dreams chose me. People say that dreams are foreshadows of what is to come."

"Sometimes," she said, smiling. "Sometimes, however, they are false dreams that can lead you astray."

She stepped closer and placed her arms around his neck, kissing him deeply. Startled, he held the kiss for a moment, then pushed away from her. His face felt hot and a deep disturbance began beating in his chest.

"Afraid to kiss, now?" she asked mockingly. "Where is the brave Sword-wanderer who fears nothing?"

"He is here but hungry," Tarin answered, gesturing toward the table. He glanced down the hallway leading to the rooms of the Seekers but no one appeared yet.

"Then," she breathed, "you should eat. To preserve your strength. Perhaps you shall need it soon."

"Ah, yes. Perhaps."

"Or would you perhaps like to come to my room and I can teach you to . . . dream."

"I have just awakened," he answered defensively.

"Oh yes. But there are . . . other things that need a bit of privacy."

Flustered, he groped for an answer, but was saved by the others emerging from the hall and into the room.

"Ah," Lorgas said, his eyes gleaming as he spied the food upon the table. "Another choice banquet. I could eat a horse."

"That would be about the only thing you haven't eaten yet," Bern said dryly.

Seanchan and Fedelm looked at Tarin and Moagin then exchanged meaningful looks. They came to the table. Seanchan took a seat opposite Tarin while Fedelm sat beside him. Cumac took the chair on the other side of Tarin.

"Well," Moagin pouted. "Perhaps later."

She touched Tarin lightly on the cheek. The spot where her fingers had pressed burned. Hastily, Tarin poured a mug of ale and drank thirstily before filling his plate.

"Rain again," Fedelm sighed. "Will this ever let up?"

"In time," Moagin said. She sat at the head of the table and took a glass of wine from Bern's hand. She sipped daintily and a healthy rose appeared in her cheeks. Her eyes sparkled from the heady wine.

"One can only play so many games," Lorgas said around a mouthful of salty pork. "Then the day begins to bear down upon him."

"Oh," Moagin said, grinning. "I think you can find other things to pass the time. If you look for them," she said meaningfully, winking at Tarin.

Seanchan took a winter apple and cut it in quarters. He speared a slice of pork and added it to his platter. His face remained emotionless.

"There are plenty of books," he said casually. "You could read instead of playing games. Enlighten your mind. Expand your world of knowledge."

"That might be a bit hard for you, Bern," Lorgas said.

"Speak for yourself," Bern sniffed. "It is well known that Ervalians far surpass Ashelves in knowledge. The Ervalians spend their time studying, not chopping down trees."

Lorgas grunted and washed down a mouthful of pork with his ale. He burped contentedly then stabbed another slice of pork with his knife.

"The libraries of the Ashelves are among the largest in the Otherworld," he said. "They were old when the Ervalians came to their forest. In our libraries there are more than one book."

"I think I should care for our horses," Cumac said, breaking into the barbs of the two elves. "Why don't you come with me, Tarin?"

Tarin nodded gratefully at Cumac. "By all means. Right after breakfast. I'm certain that they are beginning to feel neglected. Especially that black of yours, Cumac."

"Your horses have already been taken care of," Moagin said, sipping again her wine. "There is no need."

"Still," Cumac said, "I think I would like to check on them. This rain has to let up sometime and then we will have to be on our way. Not that your hospitality is lacking. It's just that a warrior should always know how his mount is faring."

Moagin shrugged. "As you wish. I have a few things to attend to myself before the noon meal is served."

She rose, smiling at Tarin, and swept from the room. The others paused in eating and looked at Tarin.

"I hope the rain passes soon," Tarin said, mopping perspiration from his forehead with his tunic sleeve. "I think it would be best if we left as soon as we can."

"Yes," Seanchan said. "Yes. I agree. Fedelm?"

"I think our hostess is too eager to have us remain," she answered. "Something is not quite right here. I have never known rain to last so long and fall so heavily. There is something unnatural about it."

Seanchan nodded. "Yes. There is. And I'm beginning to think that we should leave despite the rain. We are *too* comfortable here. Flawless hospitality is seldom found."

"We have only been here two days," Lorgas objected. "What could have happened in two days?"

"*Have* we been here only two days?" Fedelm asked. "Or are we made to *think* that only two days have passed?" She nodded at Cumac's shoulder, where the red Dragonstone no longer pulsed but had become gray. "If things are so normal, then why are we being warned by Cumac's Dragonstone? What do you feel, Seanchan?"

"I am uneasy. I feel as if a web of enchantment has been woven around this house. And why are the windows filled with opaque glass that does not open? Who wouldn't prefer plain glass that would allow more light to come into this house? I think there is more here than meets the eye."

"Well, we'll leave you to sort that out. Come, Tarin, let us check on our horses," Cumac said.

Together they rose and walked to the door. But when Cumac tried to pull the door open, it remained stuck in the wall as if it had become part of the stone. He rolled the muscles in his shoulders and strained but could not budge the door.

"Now we know," he said, coming back to the table. "I think we are being kept prisoner here."

"Let me try," Tarin said and, taking the handles in both hands, threw his weight backward. But the doors remained locked.

"Trickery," Bern said, quickly shoving himself back from the table. "I thought something was not quite right."

"For once I agree with you," Lorgas said. His hand went to where his ax hung on his belt, but it was not there. He frowned. "And when was the last time we saw our weapons?"

Cumac pulled at a lock of his hair and frowned. "I agree with you, Fedelm. Seanchan. But why? What could Moagin want with us?"

A laugh came from the kitchen hallway and Moagin stepped into the room. Her eyes glinted triumphantly. She placed her hands upon her hips and hip-swayed saucily to the table. Lightning flashed and thunder boomed, rattling the plates and mugs.

Seanchan rose, lifting his hands.

"Save the effort, Seanchan," she said mockingly. "Your magic is no good here. The house is bound in a web of fire and ice."

"*Sa il manti bel. Ta ma go ba sal!*" he said. But although sparks came from the palms of his hands, nothing happened.

"I told you," she said with satisfaction. "We serve different schools. Different masters, Seanchan Duirgeal. Within the web, your wizardry is useless. You should know that."

She glanced up at the Sheela-na-gig. For a moment a veil seemed to slip from her and the others saw what lay beneath—a hawk-shaped nose, thin lips with pus leaking from the corners, gray flesh hanging in folds above sagging jowls. Then the mask settled back over her face, leaving it smooth with rosy red cheeks and lips.

"Of course you can play silly little games, if you wish. But you are going nowhere. Not now. In time, perhaps I will release you. Not now, however," she said.

She gave Tarin a wide smile. "You might as well enjoy yourselves. I am in no hurry to undo the web. You will be well treated here—as long as you do not try my temper."

The smile disappeared from her face. For a moment, Tarin thought he could again see the ugliness beneath her mask of beauty, but it appeared in such a time-flicker that he was not certain that what he saw was really there.

She gestured expansively. "Enjoy the library and the games while I play mine."

"The Laws of Hospitality," Cumac began.

"Do not apply here," she said. She shrugged. "And why should they? This place came well before The Dagda handed down the Laws of Hospitality. It was old at the time of the Second Invasion when the Partholonians established the Laws of Hospitality. Bith brought the knowledge with him when he brought his people here from the Old World. It is far older than the Duirgeals and the others."

"Maliman," Bern breathed.

Moagin laughed. "No. Not Maliman. Although he would like to wield this magic here. No, Maliman's magic came with the Fourth

Invasion, as you well know, Seanchan. And no, Bern, your Bisuilglas will not allow you to slip between the weaves of this magic unlike other enchantments. And Fedelm, there is no passage to a Sidhe here either. No, you are mine as long as I wish to keep you. You might as well enjoy your time. Oh," she added as she turned away, "your weapons are being kept safe for you. I shall see you at supper. There are things that I must attend to for the moment."

She winked at them then turned and left, leaving behind the scent of honeysuckle.

"Seanchan?" Cumac asked, turning toward the Druid. "Is she right?"

"Yes. For the moment," he said grimly. "However, all enchantments can be broken if one can find the way. I shall search her library."

Lorgas sighed. "Well, Bern, how about another game of fidchell? There is little else for us."

"We might as well. Although," Bern amended, "too many more and I might go mad."

"Brandubh, Cumac?" Fedelm asked.

He shrugged and followed her to the table where the game had been set.

"And I'll go back with you to the library, Seanchan," Tarin said. "I'll help you if you can tell me what to look for."

"We have little else to do but try to find something. The source for this wizardry must be in the library somewhere. I cannot believe that Moagin would not have a reference handy in case she needed it."

And so the Seekers resigned themselves to what promised to soon become drudgery.

4

On the third day after Moagin's taunting of the Seekers, Seanchan stumbled across an ancient tome lodged behind a book on the Second Invasion in the library. He blew the dust from the book and gingerly opened the cracked leather cover, peering at its contents. Its boards were scarred and musty, the pages yellowed from disuse. The book had been written in a spidery hand that wavered so badly that Seanchan had a hard time making out the letters. And the Ancient Elven language was equally as hard.

Tarin noticed Seanchan's sudden intenseness and asked, "Have you found something, Seanchan?"

"I'm not certain," Seanchan said slowly. "There is nothing about Moagin here but there is something concerning a belt similar to the one she always wears. Green leather with precious jewels and silver Elvish lettering. But I can't make out . . ."

His voice trailed off as he strained to make out the words. His lips moved slowly as he mumbled.

Tarin sighed and turned back to the book he was reading on ancient spells and curses.

Twilight came and went and Seanchan and Tarin left the library to join the others at dinner. Tonight, a large boar roast waited for them, dripping thick gravy, while carrots and onions had been cooked in a marinade made of oil, rosemary, and thyme. The room smelled of cooking scents and mulled wine, and the fire, as always, crackled merrily in the fireplace. Something new seemed to have been added to the room but Tarin couldn't find what was different. Then he noticed the shields on the wall—shields that had been carried by great warriors in the past. He recognized some—Cormac, Fergus, and O'Leary—but others were strange to him.

Somewhere a harp played, a soothing, sensual music that removed worries and concerns from him and, he could tell from the serenity that set on the faces of the others, seemed to lull his senses although he hardened his mind against the music.

He glanced at Seanchan and saw the frown that had settled on his face and the hard set to his eyes.

"Think of something other than that music," he said slowly to the others. "This is another form of trickery that we must guard against."

"Come now," Lorgas said, eyeing the food hungrily. "What harm can a few tunes do? We cannot leave so why not enjoy what we have?"

"Have you forgotten Bricriu already? And the Chalice?" Fedelm asked, although the same peace had momentarily been upon her face.

"It will wait," Bern said. He took a glass of wine from the table and drank half in one gulp. A soft glow came from his face and he sighed contentedly. "Honey and something else. I cannot tell what it is. You should try this, Tarin."

Tarin shook his head and walked to stand beside the fireplace. Heat from the stones warmed him pleasantly. He looked again around the room, noticing fresh rushes that had again been placed over the stone floor. A fir tree, its branches set with scented candles, stood in one corner of the room. Shadows moved around it, and although he concentrated, he could not make them out.

Then Moagin appeared and he blinked his eyes. One minute, he was certain, she had not been there and the next had materialized. She wore a wine-colored dress with ivy woven with green thread around the collar. The green leather belt encrusted with gems was cinched tightly around her waist. She smiled.

"Greetings," she said mockingly. "I hope your day has been eventful."

"As the others," Lorgas said sourly. "These games are beginning to wear on me. And the others as well, I'm thinking. You cannot expect a man to while away his hours with games that do not change."

"Then we shall have to find other games for you," she said cheerfully. "There are many games that will seem strange to you but that is easily remedied. Some of the games can teach you themselves while you play them."

"Well, anything different would be a welcome change," Bern said. Briefly he touched the Bisuilglas, the sacred talisman of Rindale, the Hall of Warriors where Ervalians gather when they are slain, pinned at the shoulder of his cloak. A frown appeared on his face then quickly disappeared.

Casually, he picked up a glass of wine, sipping. He smiled at Moagin.

"Tell me, Moagin," he said. "These games of yours, are they enchanted as well as this hut, building, home—whatever you may call it?"

"Perhaps a little spell to aid you in understanding them," she said brightly. "Should I make them available to you on the morrow?"

"Can't hurt, I suppose," Lorgas said grumpily.

"Then so it shall be," she said. She swept forward and lifted a glass of wine from the table.

"To the day. And the night," she said, casting a meaningful glance at Tarin.

He smiled back at her and walked to the table and poured himself a glass of water from an earthernware pitcher.

"To what happens," he said, and drank with the others.

Moagin's eyes gleamed.

"Well," Seanchan said pointedly, "that aside, I'm hungry."

Lorgas was the first to the table and forking large slices of boar meat onto his plate. He took a large swallow of beer and wiped his mouth on the sleeve of his tunic, belched, and began eating voraciously.

"You could wait for the rest of us," Bern said acidly.

Lorgas made a dismissive gesture. He swallowed and cut another bite of meat and said, "Why? Do you need help in getting to the table? If you do, then I'll wait."

Bern shook his head disgustedly as Cumac and Tarin laughed.

"You're hopeless," Bern said, seating himself.

This time, Moagin joined them but limited her meal to a winter apple and piece of goat cheese, eating daintily while sipping wine. Although she joined in the small talk, her eyes settled constantly on Tarin, who treated her as politely as he could while continuing the table banter with the others.

There wasn't much spoken other than a teasing of each other over the games that had been played that day. Seanchan and Tarin gave brief accounts of what they had read in Moagin's library. But under the talk lay the strain of being held captive and the restless need to continue with their quest. Each there knew that the longer they were held captive, the farther away Bricriu would be moving.

At last, the evening ended and Seanchan announced that he was weary and would seek his bed. The others immediately began yawning as if Seanchan's announcement had reminded them of sleep as well. It was a sleep free from boredom that they sought as they left the hall and stumbled down the corridor to their beds.

Tarin was brought up short by Moagin.

"And tonight?" she asked, purring gently. Her eyes drew him into their depths, and the hypnotic gaze made him restless and wary.

With an effort, he pulled himself away from the haunting want in Moagin's eyes and stammered, "Tonight I am too weary. But I shall do less on the morrow and perhaps then . . ."

He let his voice trail off as a dangerous gleam came from Moagin's eyes as they narrowed.

"I do not like to play this game," she said angrily. "Know that none of you will leave until I am ready to let you leave. And *that*"— she emphasized—"will depend upon you."

Tarin nodded and spread his hands.

"But tonight I am too tired," he said. "Tomorrow night I shall come to you."

"Do not disappoint me this time," she said dangerously, and swept from the hall, leaving him alone.

His hands shook as he poured a goblet of wine and drained it.

"That woman means more than she is saying," he muttered to himself. "Something needs to be done but what?"

He left the hall.

ᴍɪᴅᴅᴀʏ had come when suddenly Seanchan gave an exclamation and lifted his head from the tome he had been poring over.

"I think I've found the answer to our predicament! I believe her magic comes from that belt she is always wearing. It is an old belt and its origin is mystical and appears to have come from the old country our forefathers left to come to Erin's shores."

"A belt?" Tarin asked, his brow furrowing.

"Yes, a belt," Seanchan said. "I have found a reference to such a belt existing before the Tuatha De Danann came to these shores."

"A belt," Tarin repeated, and began thumbing back through the book he was reading. "I read something about a magical belt—here it is!"

He began reading aloud.

" 'A hero in Ancient Times, Hercules by name, was forced to undergo twelve tasks as punishment for killing his wife when the gods had clouded his mind. The task assignment was given to Eurystheus, a king who greatly feared Hercules and sought ways to slay him. When the right to test Hercules was given to him, Eurystheus sought the most dangerous matters for Hercules to perform in the hopes that he might be slain.

" 'For the ninth labor, Eurystheus ordered Hercules to bring him the belt of Hippolyte, the queen of the Amazons, a tribe of women warriors. Now, this was no ordinary belt, as it was given to Hippolyte by Ares, the warrior-god, and when Hippolyte wore it, she was invincible in battle. The belt also gave her strange powers that she could use to entrap those she wished.

" 'The Amazons lived apart from men, and brought men to their island only when Hippolyte decided that certain Amazons who had proven themselves to be mighty in battle should give birth. However, they kept only the females and reared them to be warriors like themselves.

" 'Taken with the mighty warrior, she asked Hercules why he had come, and when he told her, she promised to give him the belt. But the goddess Hera, wife of Zeus, the king of the gods, and jealous because Zeus had sired Hercules with a mortal woman, knew that the arrival of Hercules meant nothing but trouble for the Amazons. Disguised as an Amazon warrior, Hera went up and down the army saying to each woman that the strangers who had arrived were going to carry off the queen. So the Amazons put on their armor and made ready for war.

" 'The Amazons charged Hercules and his small group who had sailed with him to aid the mighty warrior when he needed them. But when Hercules saw the Amazons beginning their charge, he killed Hippolyte and took her belt which he gave to Eurystheus.

" 'The belt gave a strange power and could do the bidding of Eurystheus. But Eurystheus was a weak king and could not manage the power of the belt and the belt was taken from him by Maire, one of the priestesses of Artemis, and then disappeared.' "

He paused and looked up at Seanchan.

"What do you think?" he asked. "Could this be the same belt?"

Seanchan pulled on his beard for a long moment while thinking.

"I think," he said slowly, "that it *could* be the same one that I have here"—he gently slapped the book in front of him—"and the one that is in your book."

He placed his pouch on the table and withdrew a small bottle of dust from it. He tore a piece of a page that had no writing on it from one of the books and carefully wrapped a small portion of the dust within it.

"This is powder from the valerian root," he said. "Tonight, go to Moagin's chamber and when she gives you a glass of wine, slip this into hers. It will dissolve immediately and the wine will disguise its taste. After she falls asleep, take her belt and bring it to us. The others will be waiting in my room. Be careful that she doesn't catch you. I shudder to think of the consequences."

Tarin took the small packet and slipped it beneath his belt.

"I'll be careful," he promised.

ThAT evening when they returned to the dining hall, they were met by Bern, who took them aside.

"I have found a way through the enchantment, thanks to the Bisuilglas despite what Moagin said. I checked on our horses. They have been well cared for."

The Bisuilglas, which Bern wore at the shoulder of his tunic, was the sacred talisman of Rindale, the Hall of Warriors. The Bisuilglas had been fashioned at the beginning of the First Age. It was silver with a large amber stone set into the center. Within the middle of the amber were three pine needles in the shape of a triangle. It allowed its bearer to raise elves from the dead and allowed the bearer to slip through enchantments.

"Moagin is not as clever as she thinks," he said. "There is a slight chink in the enchantment holding us captive that allows me to slip through."

"Unfortunately, the rest of us are not able to follow you," Seanchan said in a low voice as the others joined them near the fireplace.

"*But* it may still be useful. Tarin and I have found the source of Moagin's power. At least," he amended, "most of her power. She may well have worked this enchantment in a manner that will hold if she suddenly loses the source."

He proceeded to tell them what he and Tarin had discovered while reading and of the plan for Tarin to steal the belt from Moagin.

"Now, once we have the belt, we will need to have you slip through the enchantment and ready our horses so when we follow you—*if* we can follow you—we shall be ready to ride fast and shake the dust of this place from our heels. I do not doubt that Moagin has other ways of harming us despite the belt."

Bern nodded. "Give me the time and it shall be so."

At that moment, Moagin entered the hall dressed in a gossamer gown that shimmered warm gold as she walked. She nodded meaningfully at Tarin and greeted the others cheerfully.

"Tonight, a special treat," she said. She clapped her hands, and servants began bringing in the evening meal. A wild boar had been roasted again along with spiced winter apples and grapes still fresh on their vines. A harper materialized in one corner of the room and began to play his harp, singing softly.

> *Bells ring pleasantly on this stormy night*
> *And candles burn softly with a golden light*
> *Where love awaits in the arms of a wanton woman*
> *Who plots a nightly tryst with her chosen man. . . .*

More servants emerged, some carrying pitchers of mulled ale and wine while others bore platters heaping with black and white puddings and bowls of pickled hens' eggs. Bread had been baked with raisins, currants, cherries, buckleberries, and honey. Baked eels lay in a milk sauce and venison rumps had been roasted golden brown.

"Come!" she cried. "Let us enjoy our feast!"

The others moved to their places around the table and began eating as if they were starving. The wine blushed their cheeks and made them merry. Lorgas began singing a bawdy song when the harper paused to drink a mug of ale, and Bern, knowing the song as well, chimed in. Seanchan amused them by conjuring small balls of various colors that he sent bouncing around the room, and Fedelm sung a song from the Sidhe.

> *Four doves flew around the head*
> *Of Aengus, the god of love who led*
> *Young women to their lovers*
> *In the dead of night.*
> *A handsome youth his sight*
> *Would cause young women to swoon*
> *And beg of him to grant them a boon*
> *To spend the night within his arms . . .*

Soon the feast was ended and all went happily to their beds save Tarin, who stayed behind with Moagin.

"So," Moagin asked sharply, "are you ready to fulfill your promise?"

"Ah, yes, my sweet," he answered. "I am no longer muddleheaded with weariness and beg to spend this night in your arms."

Moagin smiled slowly, seductively, and took him by the hand and led him to the hall from which she emerged nightly to greet the Seekers.

This hall was paneled in rich golden oak inlaid with curious letters in black walnut. Upon the floor were mosaics made from tiny colored stones picturing dancing fairies and various flowers—damask roses, alyssum, asters, bluebells, bellflowers, lilacs, and lavender. A deep scent came from them, and Tarin's head swam from their headiness.

Moagin paused and opened a door. Tarin stepped in, and stopped short as his eyes beheld the wonders before him.

A large bed stood against the far wall. Walnut tables gleamed blackly. Upon one table rested a harp. On another, a golden pitcher and two matching goblets. Gaily covered pillows of each color of a rainbow were scattered throughout the room, and in front of the mammoth fireplace from which a fire flickered lay a black bearskin. The walls were festooned with pictures of lovers in various poses.

"Do you like it?" Moagin asked throatily.

"Very nice," Tarin said.

She moved to him and kissed him gently. He tasted sweet rowanberries on her lips. Gently he pulled away and walked to the table with the pitcher and goblets.

"Is there a hurry?" he asked, his back to her, as he lifted the pitcher and poured wine into each goblet. "Let us enjoy ourselves with a cup of wine first."

She laughed and went to the bearskin and sank down upon it, folding her legs beneath her.

"We have all night," she said. "And here, night can last a very long time. As long as we wish."

He slipped the small packet from his belt and tapped the powder into a goblet. He tucked the paper back beneath his belt and, lifting the two goblets, made his way slowly to her.

"Then let us enjoy the night, however long it may be," he said, handing the goblet with the crushed valerian root in it. "To us."

They drained their goblets.

Moagin's eyes took on a smokiness that made Turin uneasy. Gently, he took the goblet from her, saying, "One more glass."

"Enough," Moagin said. She reached up, caught his arm, and pulled him down beside her. She fastened her lips to his and kissed him urgently. Then, suddenly, she gave a tiny gasp and fell across his lap, sound asleep.

Tarin sighed and wiped the sweat from his brow.

That was close, he thought, although it might have been interesting if the root had taken longer than it did.

Gently, he unbuckled the belt and pulled it from her waist. It felt warm in his hands, and for a brief moment, images of former women who had worn it danced in the air in front of him. He shook his head and rose, leaving the room, and hurried back down the hall and to Seanchan's room.

"Here," he said, stepping inside and holding the belt up for all to see. "I have it."

"Give it to Fedelm," Seanchan said when Tarin tried to hand it to him. "I dare not touch it. Through me it would do more harm than good. It is made to be worn by a woman."

Fedelm took the belt and cinched it around her waist. She smiled at the others and said, "I hope I will be able to use it wisely."

"So do I," Cumac said dryly. He looked at Seanchan. "And now?"

"Bern, you slip out through the opening in the enchantment and ready our horses. Now that we have the belt, I may be able to discover how we may follow you."

Bern nodded and slipped from the room.

"Now," Seanchan said, and heaved a great sigh, "let us see what we can do to escape."

But despite Seanchan's efforts he could not unweave the enchantment around the house. Finally he shook his head in despair and dropped into a chair.

"The enchantment is still being held tightly to this house," he said. "There is still magic being worked somewhere."

"Let me try," Fedelm said.

Seanchan shrugged. "Obviously it will do no harm."

Fedelm smiled and crossed to Seanchan's bed and stretched out upon it.

"I will try to find out what it is with the *imbas forosnai*, the sleep of prediction," she said.

She closed her eyes and began to breathe deeply, steadily. Soon her muscles relaxed and she was in a deep sleep.

And found herself in a bleak, barren landscape. The sun was gone and a starless night had fallen, lit only by a blood-red moon. She reached automatically for her weapons, but they were gone, leaving her defenseless. In the distance she could see a dolmen, a gateway into the Otherworld, and began to make her way there. Dead grass crackled beneath her feet as she walked. A cold sweat covered her body.

Then she heard the cry of warggads—the worst of werewolves, as they were practically indestructible. They were vulnerable only through their eyes or being beheaded, but they moved so swiftly that an archer had to be quick to send a shaft into each before the warggads were on top of him.

Her flesh pebbled as she looked for a hiding place although she knew the warggads could hunt by smell as well as sight. She began to run for the dolmen. Perhaps she could escape into the Otherworld. But she knew that warggads could follow her there, now that the Great Rift had been opened and Maliman and his minions were loosed upon both worlds.

A silver mist began to shimmer in front of her and she slowed her steps. Then a Dreamwalker emerged. He smiled grimly at her.

"I am Cathar, the Guardian," he said, drawing a silver arrow from the quiver around his shoulder. "If you can, you must flee this place. I can hold the warggads off for a while, but there are too many for my bow to hold off a long time. Be quick!"

With that, he drew the arrow to his cheek and let fly. A horrible scream followed and Fedelm glanced over her shoulder to see the lead warggad fall to the ground, clawing at the shaft that protruded from its eye.

She dropped to the ground and closed her eyes, concentrating, but the dream would not end. She heard the rhythmic twanging of Cathar's bow. Then she was gripped in a tight hug and felt herself being torn from the dream. She fought for a moment, but the grip was too strong and she relaxed, knowing that whoever or whatever had her was far stronger than she.

She awakened, bathed in sweat, in Seanchan's room.

He studied her carefully as she gave a shaky smile and sat up.

"I could find nothing," she said.

"You were very lucky," Seanchan said. "We could see you were in difficulty as you thrashed about on the bed."

"Seanchan sent a charm into Dreamworld," Lorgas said, his face drawn with concern. "It was that which brought you back."

"I didn't think you could walk in the *imbas forosnai*," she said, swinging her legs over the side of the bed and sitting up.

"I can't," Seanchan said. "I was lucky to find you with the charm."

"Well," she said, giving a weak smile. "That didn't work. What shall we try next?"

The door opened and Bern slipped back inside.

"The horses are ready," he said. He glanced at Cumac. "The Black of Saingliau is most ready to run. I think he would have broken into this place for you if I hadn't been able to soothe him with promises that you would be short coming."

Cumac nodded. "Black is more than any other horse. My father, Cucullen, discovered that when Black appeared from Sliab Fuait, the lake."

The Black of Saingliau was one of Cucullen's horses who emerged from the gray lake of Sliab Fuait along with the Gray of Macha. Black was a magical horse and could only be tamed by Cucullen after being ridden all over Erin while trying to throw Cucullen, his rider. He was a fierce warrior horse and was never beaten in battle, often fighting at the side of his master. Cumac was given the Black of Saingliau by Macha, and Black appeared at Connor's court during the search for the Chalice, going to Cumac and laying his head upon his shoulder. He was a fierce protector of Cumac and seldom tired during long rides. The sight of Black in battle fury often froze the blood of those who meant evil.

"Now what should we do?" Lorgas asked. "We have the belt, but we still cannot leave. Except for Bern."

"There is nothing for it but to wait for morning when the valerian root wears off Moagin," Seanchan said grimly. "Then perhaps we shall be able to persuade her to release the spell."

And so they waited impatiently throughout the long night until false dawn appeared, lighting the opaque windows of Seanchan's room. Rain continued to beat against the panes.

"Let us go to the Great Room," he said, taking a deep breath and steeling himself for what he knew would be coming.

"I do not think I'm going to like this," Tarin mumbled. "She's going to be very angry indeed with what I did."

Fedelm gave him a quick smile. "The fury of a woman scorned should be handled with great care," she teased.

Tarin shook his head despairingly as he followed the others into the room.

The table had not been set for breakfast and the fire was out, the coals still banked for the night. They could see their breath in the cold of the room and pulled their cloaks around them.

"I wish I had my ax," Lorgas complained, looking around the walls for another weapon.

"We all wish we had our weapons," Cumac said grimly. "But we don't. So let us make the most of it."

"The most of what?" Bern said dryly. "There's nothing here to make the most of."

Suddenly Moagin appeared in the room, her eyes glinting angrily, her body rigid with hate. The flesh on her face had tightened until the bones stood out.

"I see that you have taken advantage of my hospitality," she said, looking at the belt around Fedelm's waist. "Give my belt back."

"No," Seanchan said, raising his staff. "But you shall release the spell holding us in this place. This I order you to do."

She laughed cruelly.

"Fool! Do you think your power can match mine even without the belt?"

"This part of your enchantment has been lifted," he said.

She gathered herself and suddenly a flame appeared from her fingers and spat toward Seanchan. He raised his staff, pointing it at her, and the flame blurred and hissed as if striking ice.

"Do not tempt me, woman!" Seanchan roared. "I am from the Duirgeals, Keepers of the Cullasdreu, the Sacred Flame!"

Moagin shrunk in upon herself and threw her hands up protectively.

"Enough! Enough!" she squawked. She tried to run from the room but silver filaments flew from Seanchan's staff and wound themselves tightly around her, staying her.

"Let me go! Let me go!" she screamed.

The others stared in surprise as she began to change before their eyes. The beauty slipped away, leaving an ugly woman behind. Her flesh turned gray and cracked. Her gown fit her like sackcloth. Pus leaked from the corners of her eyes and lips.

"Bertilgain, the maker of my belt, will punish you for this!" she shrieked.

"Release the enchantment!" Seanchan thundered. "By the flame Cullasdreu I command you to release the spell or I shall unleash Cullasdreu upon you!"

"No, no!" she screeched. *"Unth bath sean cuath!"*

Thunder boomed and lightning crackled within the room, leaving a sulphuric smell behind.

"There! Go now! Leave my belt! Go! Release me!" she said, whimpering now.

"No," Seanchan said. "If we give you the belt you will build another enchantment to hold us. Or slay us," he added. "Your belt comes with us."

"No!" she shouted desperately, and began to struggle against the web holding her tightly.

Her flesh began to slowly crumble and she sank to the floor weeping.

"Our weapons!" Seanchan demanded.

"In that room," she said, pointing to a doorway that magically appeared at the far end of the hall. "There you will find everything! Now, give me back my belt. I shall do nothing to detain you. Or harm you."

Cumac and Tarin ran to the room and returned with the party's weapons. They passed them around.

"Bern, Lorgas, go to the kitchens and prepare a food pack for all of us," Seanchan said.

The two elves scampered away and returned shortly, bearing packs.

"You have all that you wish," Moagin said, moaning pitifully. "Release me."

"In time," Seanchan said. He turned to the others. "Now, let us go before Bertilgain comes and Moagin regains her strength."

The party left. Outside, their horses stood, waiting. The rain had stopped but no sun warmed them as they mounted and rode down the trail away from the hut.

"Do not look behind you," Seanchan warned. "This enchantment will pull you back into the house and I will not be able to help you then."

"I still cannot believe that hut had so many rooms within it," Cumac said.

"An illusion," Seanchan answered. "Brought about by Moagin's magic and our wishes to escape the rain."

They crowded close to each other as they rode down the trail. No birds sang, no rustling of underbrush could be heard as they made their way deeper and deeper into Faindell.

5

The cold seeped into Tarin's bones as he rode disgruntledly in Faindell Forest. But he wasn't alone; all of the Seekers were huddled deep within their cloaks against the steady cold rain that fell and dripped from the barren branches of the trees heavy with rain-blackened scabrous bark. Days had passed since they had last seen the sun, long before they had entered Faindell. Their hands were numb and cramped from holding the reins, and their shoulders ached from shivering constantly. A cold breeze came through the trees, and Tarin drew a deep breath, feeling the ache in his lungs from the cold that began to remind him of the last lord he'd served before the Truacs and hobgoblins came in the night to destroy the lord's fortress, leaving Tarin who came to be called "the Damned."

But before he went to Rolfe's fortress, there had been the affair at Ganach's fortress.

Tarin had returned home early to repair a broken trace on his chariot and discovered that his wife, Galata, had left their home at Dun Scathe shortly after he had, taking the road to the fortress of Ganach, where, he learned, she had become Ganach's lover.

Tarin followed her to Ganach's fortress, and what happened there was anyone's guess. A few days later, however, a traveler, seeking hospitality, discovered all had been slain. Blood spattered the walls of Ganach's fortress and Ganach's head along with Galata's had been chopped off and placed on spears bracketing the gate that led into the fortress of Ganach's Great Hall. No one could prove Tarin's guilt when he was brought before the Brehons for trial. Since then, he had been a Sword-wanderer and called "the Damned."

Now he bittterly remembered the good times in the fortress where he had been warm and content when the cold days came and the door of the Great Hall was shut against the cold. Fires had burned merrily and the ale was good and spiced. Grease had dripped sizzling into the fires from large haunches of boar and venison spitted and roasting. Jokes and laughter had filled the room and worries had been carelessly cast aside.

Mumain, the wife of Rolfe Red-Hand, the lord Tarin had served, had eyes for Tarin and always managed to throw a saucy hip his way when she passed him. Her eyes were smoldering black, her hair red-gold falling to her waist. Her breasts were like spring melons as they strained against her low-necked blouse. And Tarin had taken her to bed when the lord was gone boar hunting in the forest. A man could only take so much teasing before his will weakened, and Tarin had taken a lot of teasing before tumbling her into his blankets.

And that, he told himself now, had been the big mistake that set events into motion.

Rolfe's steward—hanged if he could remember the man's name now—had discovered them and told Rolfe about Mumain's betrayal with Tarin. Infuriated, Rolfe had drawn his sword and tried to slay Tarin, but Tarin wounded his lord and escaped from the fortress into the forest.

Enraged at Tarin's escape, Rolfe sent a party of. warriors to kill Tarin. They had discovered Tarin in a flower-scented glade and attacked him. But they were no match for Tarin, who quickly left them dead, their life blood draining into the sylvan pool, turning it red.

The battle had angered him, bringing the bloodlust to him, and he returned to the fortress to face Rolfe in a challenge only to find the fortress in ruins, the timbers blackened by fire, the warriors killed by Deag-duls, ugly beasts of blood-drinking. Similar to vampires, but much worse, they could be killed only by beheading or a hazelwood arrow through their hearts.

The warriors had sold their lives dearly. Dead hobgoblins and Deag-duls were scattered throughout the fortress, but the bodies of the warriors had been butchered for meat. Some warrior bones were charred in cooking fires, and Tarin had almost been sick before he left the fortress for the last time, making his way deep into the forest, searching for Deag-duls and hobgoblins out of a sense of honor to revenge his friends—were they truly friends? He did not know. But he felt a kinship to the warriors.

He had found Mumain in her room, dead after being ravaged by the Deag-duls and hobgoblins. Rolfe lay in front of the door to her room, dead Deag-duls and hobgoblins stacked in front of him where he had made his last stand.

There had been too many to bury, so he had pulled as many as he could into the various buildings and set fire to the buildings. Flames leaped high as he left the fortress, running easily to the forest, not drawing a deep breath until he was well within the deep shadows of the trees.

In his journey through the forest, he had stumbled upon tiny groups of Deag-duls and hobgoblins and had ruthlessly slain them—usually at night when they felt the most secure—dropping as a revenging shadow upon them from the darkness, slashing and stabbing, then slipping back into the night. Time and time again he had done this, and the Deag-duls and hobgoblins began to call him Deathwhisper and frightened each other with tales of his deeds while men continued to call him the Damned.

A thin stream of cold water slipped under the hood of his cloak and trickled down his chest. He swore and glanced up at the lead-gray sky through the branches of the trees. There was no promise of the rain letting up. When he looked down the trail, the faces of the others were opalescent pearls looking back at him in the curtain of rain that separated them.

A strange feeling came over him. He came alert and his hand touched the rune-blade over his shoulder, automatically loosening it in its scabbard. He felt eyes were watching them from the trees, but although he tried to pierce the shadows with his eyes, he could see nothing. He nudged his horse and rode up next to Cumac.

"There is something near us," he said lowly.

"I know," Cumac murmured. "But I don't know what."

Tarin glanced at the Dragonstone on Cumac's shoulder. It was pulsing blackly.

"We'd better tell the others," Tarin said.

Cumac nodded and rode Black up to Bern and Lorgas, talking softly.

The elves looked nervously at the sides of the trail. Bern called quietly to Fedelm and Seanchan ahead of them and Seanchan immediately reined in, sitting on his horse quietly.

"We need to find somewhere we can make a stand, I think," Fedelm said. "I too feel something is out there and I do not like the feeling."

"That is easier said than done," Seanchan said, glancing around. He raised and lowered his staff slightly before gigging his horse onward.

"Well," Lorgas said grumpily. "I don't think we will find another place here. Best we get off the trail, I'm thinking."

"I don't think that would be wise," Bern said. "We don't know these woods. I don't know of any who are familiar enough with Faindell to venture off the trail. I have heard nothing good of Faindell and we have just left the proof of that pudding with Moagin."

"We haven't found any other place where we might seek refuge since we left Moagin either," Fedelm said.

"Not many travelers come this way. There won't be many places where we can make camp," Tarin answered. "Not many Sword-wanderers come this way either. Those that do are those who did not serve their lords faithfully. They would just as soon slit your throat as bid you a good day."

"Well, we are here and here we must make the most of it," Sean-chan said. He urged his horse into a trot. "But you are right, Fedelm. We need to find someplace that we will have a chance of defending. I do not like this place but I have no memory of it either."

"If they are going to do something I wish they'd get on with their business," Lorgas growled. He looked hard to both sides of the trail. "This is one elf that they won't find it easy to take."

They rode in silence for another few miles before the trail opened out into a small clearing. The grass was burnt brown but there was a small pool that looked drinkable and there were blackened embers where fires had been built before by travelers. The trees showed old ax marks where branches had been hacked away for firewood, and small lean-tos had been built for shelter against the weather.

"This is the best I think we'll find," Seanchan said, reining in. "Besides, it will be dark soon and I do not know if we'll find another place farther on. I do not like this place but it will have to do for the time."

The Seekers quickly dismounted and Fedelm and Tarin searched for firewood while the others cared for their horses.

Cumac's Black tossed his head and snorted and stamped his feet as Cumac slipped the saddle from his back. He reached up and rubbed Black up and down his nose.

"I know. I know, fellow," Cumac said quietly. "I too would like to go on but this place is the best we've come across for quite some time. We'll just have to make the most of it. I want you to take care of the other horses. And listen well for us."

Black turned his head and nudged Cumac with his nose, grunting deep within his chest. He shook his head and turned his rump to Cumac, facing the woods.

Fedelm and Tarin returned with armfuls of dead branches, but one glance showed them to be wet and hard to burn. Lorgas took one of the largest and split it down the middle with his ax and worked the punk out of it, making a small mound in the place closest to the middle of the fire pit where fires had been built in the past. He took tinder from a small pouch belted around his waist and struck a small flame, hunching over it to give it the best chance he could to begin burning.

The others took apart some of the lean-tos and brought them closer to the fire and rebuilt them. It wasn't much shelter, but at least the rain would be kept off them during the night, although the ground was still wet.

"I could eat one of those boar roasts Moagin gave us right now," Lorgas grumbled, warming his hands as the fire took hold of a small pyramid of twigs he had made. Carefully he added branches until the fire was burning brightly.

"We have meat," Bern reminded him. "Your share is in your pack."

"I know. I know. But there is something about salty pork and good ale before a roaring fire that we *don't* have," Lorgas said, opening his pack. He peered in it, then made a satisfied grunt. "But this will do. This will do."

He took a small rump roast from his pack and began cutting it into slices while Fedelm and Bern removed loaves of bread.

Tarin crossed to one of the trees and, using his sword, cut a large chunk of bark from the tree to use as a plate. The tree shook in pain and groaned and Tarin jumped back, staring at it carefully.

"These trees seem alive," he said.

"They are," Seanchan said. "They are among the oldest in all of Erin. They were old before Tuan came to these shores."

The others nodded at his words. Tuan had been the first to come to Erin. He had been the sole survivor of the Great Flood that cleansed the earth. He had the ability to shape-shift and exist on land, in the sea, and upon the air. He was the sole survivor of the race of Partholonians and the plague that killed all but him.

"I thought that honor belonged to the Forest of Tuan," Tarin said.

Seanchan shook his head. "No, the Forest of Tuan was begun by Tuan, but there are other woods that are older than that. These are some. I do not think it would be wise to harm any other tree. You can burn the deadwood that has fallen from the trees but do not use your ax on any others, Lorgas. Nor your sword, Tarin. We do not wish to anger them. They could prove to be worse than Truacs or goblins."

"Is there anything in this forest that's good?" Lorgas muttered around a mouthful of meat.

"It doesn't seem so," Cumac said.

He hunkered down inside a lean-to from the rain, remembering the warm days of the Otherworld before his mother, Fand, wife of the sea lord Manannan Mac Lir, had brought his father's sword, Caladbolg the Flaming Rainbow, to him and told him of the opening of the Great Rift that had loosed Maliman upon the earth along with his minions. Since that time, he had discovered he had inherited more than this father's sword. Like Cucullen, he fell into a warp-spasm that left him a deadly killing machine when hard-pressed by the enemy. That day had been warm and lazy. The last warm and lazy day he could recall. From that point on he could number the days of peace when he met the others, most especially Fedelm, the beautiful woman of the Sidhe, who left him feeling odd at times when she was close to him.

"Someone or something evil approaches," Bern whispered.

Instantly Caladbolg was in Cumac's hand. Fedelm nocked an arrow and held it ready while Lorgas slipped his ax from his belt and Bern his sword. Tarin slid the rune-blade from its sheath and stood, facing back the way they had come. The others stood in a rough circle with him, guarding all directions.

A curious light began to glow from the tip of Seanchan's staff when three ruffians stepped into the clearing from different directions. They were dressed in brown leather jerkins and trousers and held their swords unsheathed in their hands. Each sported long greasy hair and a beard and their eyes were black and cold.

"We would share your camp and food," the middle one growled. His voice sounded like a rasp being drawn over iron. "And your shelter. You have more than enough for yourselves."

"And we shall keep it that way," Cumac snapped. "Until you learn your manners."

The leader gave a harsh laugh and glanced at Tarin.

"Well, well. The Deathwhisper. You have come a long way since becoming an outcast."

"Fannell," Tarin said, nodding. "Foill, Tuchell," he addressed the others. "What brings the grandsons of Nechtan Scene to Faindell? The last I heard your lord had thrown you out of his fortress for stealing from his treasury and you were waylaying travelers at the River Boyne."

Fannell's face grew cold. His features narrowed and he took a fresh grip on his sword. Then he relaxed and gave another laugh.

"You always did have a harsh tongue, Tarin. One of these days someone is going to cut it from your mouth. Now, share what you have or we will take it."

"A foolish threat," Tarin said. He gestured at the others waiting nearby, watching the exchange. "There are more here than you and your brothers. Go! You have outstayed your welcome."

"We claim the Laws of Hospitality," Foill snapped. "You have an obligation now."

Tarin shook his head. "Not for grave-robbers and killers. Yes," he said as Foill's face darkened. "I have heard how you open the graves to steal what has been buried with the dead. There is no greater disgrace other than killing one's lord. You are not welcome here."

Tuchell bared mossy green teeth in a smile. His eyes narrowed with a killing light.

"We are not alone," he said. "There are others here as well. Some who would relish the taste of man-flesh."

He gestured and three Nightshades stepped into the clearing

around the Seekers. They were garbed in flowing black cloaks over gray cloth that appeared to be winding sheets for the dead. Their hands and forearms were protected by black gauntlets made of steel and carried black-bladed swords and daggers with poisoned blades.

"Nightshades," Fedelm said with distaste. "Where are your horses?"

Tuchell made a gesture behind them.

"Tied behind us."

On the heels of his words, Black reared, hooves flashing out, and dashed into the woods. Screams of horses came out and the sounds of fierce battle sounded behind the trees following Black's roaring challenge.

For a moment, Tuchell looked uncertain as he turned to the screams; then he grinned and looked again at the Seekers.

"It sounds like your horse has met his end," he said with relish. "Now, give over food and shelter and we may let you live."

"Come and take it," Lorgas snarled, hefting his ax.

Fedelm's bow twanged following his words and one of the Nightshades screeched and fell, clawing at an arrow that protruded from beneath his cowl. His legs thrashed in agony; then he lay still.

The three brothers shouted their battle cry and charged, followed by the remaining Nightshades.

Sparks flew as Tarin's blade deflected the swing of Fannell and nearly decapitated him with a back slash. Cumac struck Foill's sword, Caladbolg singing through the air, while Lorgas roared his challenge and leaped forward, swinging his ax at the legs of one of the Nightshades. Bern struck so swiftly that the second Nightshade had no chance to parry and his head flew from his body, bouncing into the underbrush.

Again Cumac parried Foill's sword, and struck him on top of his shoulder, Caladbolg slicing down and through, nearly parting Foill in half while Lorgas leaped to the side of the writhing Nightshade he had attacked, swinging his ax and splitting the head of the Black Rider.

Fedelm's bow sang again and an arrow plunged into the chest of Tuchell, felling him.

And then it was over and a silence fell deeply over the clearing. A foul smell slipped away from the Nightshades, and the Seekers hastily drew their cloaks over their noses.

The screams from the woods ceased and Cumac ran into the woods after Black.

"I didn't think that we could kill Nightshades like that," Bern said, using one of the Nightshade cloaks to wipe his blade clean.

"We didn't. We've only wounded them," Fedelm said as the bodies of the Nightshades began moving. She bent and took a burning branch from the fire and ran to the Nightshades, thrusting the brand into their clothes. Harsh screams rose, even from the head lying in the bushes, and the Nightshades began to writhe upon the ground as the fire quickly consumed them. Cumac ran to the head and tossed it onto its burning form. It screamed, loud and long, as flames burnt it.

The foul scent disappeared with the burning of the Nightshades, leaving the three brothers alone, stretched out on the ground.

Tuchell laughed and Tarin crossed to him, resting the point of his rune-blade on Tuchell's neck.

"You . . . have no idea . . . what . . . lies ahead . . . for you," Tuchell gasped. He forced a grin.

"Perhaps," Tarin said coldly. "But you will not live to see it."

He leaned on his sword, pushing the blade through Tuchell's neck. Tuchell convulsed then lay still.

Cumac emerged from the woods with Black trotting behind him. He paused and rubbed Black's nose. The great horse's nose was blood-spattered, as were his forelegs.

"You fought a great battle," he said. Black grumbled, pleased, and lowered his head so Cumac could scratch his ears.

"The Nightshade horses are dead as well," Cumac said to the others. "They will not be returning to let others know what has happened here."

"Truly a remarkable horse," Tarin said. He crossed to Black and rubbed his neck. Black eyed him suspiciously for a moment, then relaxed.

"Now, what do we do with them?" Lorgas asked, carefully wiping the head of his ax. He motioned at the brothers.

"Drag them away," Seanchan ordered. "Deep into the forest. Perhaps they shall be a warning to others who would attack us."

"Who?" Bern demanded.

"These were not the only Sword-wanderers," Tarin said. "There will be others, I'm thinking. This forest is ready-made for those who prey on travelers." He glanced around. "Truthfully I have never seen such an evil place."

"It is too late to make our way back," Seanchan said grimly. "We have little choice other than to go forward and hope for the best. We shall have to be constantly on our guard. I'm certain there are creatures out there other than Nightshades who will be waiting for us."

Tarin collected Fannell while Bern and Lorgas dragged Foill from the clearing. Cumac took Tuchell and followed the others into the forest.

"What did you see with the *imbas forasnai*, Fedelm? I know you saw more than what you told us."

Fedelm nodded. "There are others who mean us harm in this forest. I think Maliman has been here and bargained the trees to aid him." She shrugged. "The trees may set us off on a different trail. Or else cause us to wind our way through them until we are lost. We will be hard put to stay to our course."

Seanchan heaved a great sigh. "I may be able to help us there. The Duirgeals have always been the friends of trees. There may yet be some good in this forest among the trees themselves. We shall see on the morrow."

The others emerged from the forest and came to the fire, squatting and warming their hands over the flames. Tarin looked around at the others and said, "There are other Sword-wanderers and many who may be in Faindell. We shall have to always be on our guard. I would suggest two of us take a watch at a time to guard against a surprise."

"I agree," Cumac said. "I do not feel at ease here. And it would be good to have another to share the watch."

"And I shall place a guard around the clearing. But," Seanchan emphasized, wagging a forefinger at the others, "do not rely upon that. Remember that there may be another out there who can pass through the web I will weave. *And* there is Maliman. We do not know where he may be, although I believe he is in his fortress Dun Darai in the Mountains of Mourne repairing it and making ready an army."

"I agree and will take the first watch. What say you, Lorgas, to sharing it with me?" Bern asked.

"Aye," Lorgas said. "My blood is up now and I wouldn't be able to sleep anyway."

"Fedelm and I shall take the second watch. Tarin, you and Cumac the third. And now, let us rest as much as we can," Seanchan said.

Bern and Lorgas readied themselves, huddling beside the fire under a roof they weaved out of sticks while the others took themselves to their beds in the lean-tos. The elves spoke little, their eyes constantly searching the forest wall that surrounded the clearing.

6

The rain still fell when the Seekers, feeling miserable and grouchy, began making their way down the trail again in the gray of morning. The night had passed uneventfully, although rustlings could be heard in the trees beyond the circle of light. As they rode, it seemed the trail twisted and turned away from the south, trying to draw them into the deepest part of the woods, but Seanchan steadfastly refused to part from their way. When the trail turned aside, Seanchan led the way through the trees, constantly veering toward the south despite the seeming attempts of the trees to block their path.

For three days they traveled as eyes peered at them from the underbrush, but no one came forward to challenge their passing. Twice they encountered others on the trail, hard-eyed Sword-wanderers traveling north who accepted their hospitality gratefully without threat or making an attempt upon the lives of the Seekers. They had little news of what lay ahead of the Seekers other than warning them that they should keep a sharp eye out for trouble.

At last they emerged from Faindell Forest and the rain broke, the sun coming out to dry the fields and trail and warm the Seekers. They found a fold in the ground that hid them from others and decided to take a day's rest to dry themselves and relax from the tension that had tightened their shoulders in the forest and left them wary and weary.

They awoke suddenly in the morning to discover that they were no longer on the green plain outside Faindell. The trees had moved around them while they slept, staying just outside the small fold where the Seekers rested. Lorgas, who had been on watch, snored by the fire, hunched cross-legged over his ax.

"What's this?" Seanchan exclaimed as he rolled from his pallet. He seized his staff and stood, eyes sweeping around the fold.

The others rose swiftly, weapons in hand, staring dumbfounded at the trees surrounding them.

"What . . ." Lorgas spluttered as he came awake, rubbing his eyes. "When did this happen?" he demanded.

"While you slept," Bern said bitterly. "We counted on you to keep watch."

"And I did," Lorgas said. "But I do not know how this happened."

"Magic, I would say," Seanchan said. "I sense a spell has been cast."

"Hang the spell," Tarin growled, seizing his rune-blade. "I'd rather fight sumaires and warggads then deal with magic."

"You may well get that chance," a voice said from the forest.

Here you will find those you do not seek
Who prey upon the travelers weak
And slay them one by one
Until their evil work is done.
Passersby should not tarry
Here despite how they are weary
From their journey through Faindell
Where some trees are under Maliman's spell.

They all turned to watch a Forester, one who guarded the forests against harm being done to travelers, step into the clearing. He was dressed in green leather and cloth and carried a heavy bow. A huge ax that couldn't have been raised by two men was on a sling over his back. He bowed to them and said, "I bring you greetings. I am Ballus, brother to Millus, who served you well when you were in his forest. This"—he waved his arm around them—"is part of my forest, Faindell. Maliman has cursed this portion of the forest although," he added, eyeing them carefully, "Faindell is not given to visitors who stray from the given path. Not without permission."

"And who," Lorgas said, holding his ax threateningly, "will give us that permission? I am Lorgas of the Ashelves and this is Bern of the Ervalians. Our forests are far more welcome than this."

"Welcome, Ballus," Seanchan said. "I am Seanchan of the Duirgeals and this"—he pointed at Cumac and Fedelm—"is Cumac, son of Cucullen, the great champion of the Red Branch, and Fedelm of the Sidhe. And Tarin Deathwhisper." He indicated Tarin standing a little away, sword in hand.

"What are you doing in Faindell?"

"We are the Seekers following Bricriu Poisontongue, who has stolen the Bladhm Caillis, the Chalice of Fire, from the Red Branch. He has come through your forest. Did you not know this?" Seanchan asked innocently.

Ballus flushed and shook his head. "I have enough to do to keep the rest of Faindell from falling under Maliman's power. You should not have tarried this close to the forest."

He came to the fire and squatted. He reached into his pack and removed loaves of bread and honeycombs dripping with rich, golden honey.

"Come and eat," he said roughly, "and I will see what I can do to help you on your journey." He looked thoughtfully around him at the trees, grimaced, and shook his head. "These trees may be under Maliman's power, but they still must answer to me who was appointed to Faindell by The Dagda, father of gods. But, Seekers, this is an example of how far Maliman's evil has spread. The roads and the forests are not safe for travelers anymore and inns pay little attention to the Laws of Hospitality. Indeed," he continued, "it would probably be best if you stayed away from the inns. As far as following Bricriu, he has turned from the Forest of Turgain and the Valley of Shadows and gone toward Cairpre's court in Munster. You would be advised to leave this trail which loops its way hither and thither and take the right trail at the fork ten miles distant. That is the more direct route and you may arrive at the same time as Bricriu."

"We thank you for your warning," Seanchan said, touching his forehead and then his breast. "We lost a lot of time back in Faindell."

"I heard," Ballus said grimly. "Moagin. She has overstayed her welcome in Faindell. I shall deal with her later and her lover, Bertilgain, who believes he owns this forest. I will take you through these woods and set you on the right trail to Munster.

"For now," he said, rising, "I will leave you for the rest of the day. We shall travel tomorrow. Do not be afraid," he added, noticing the concern on their faces, "you shall be safe here."

He placed two fingers in his mouth and gave a sharp, piercing whistle. Two wolfhounds emerged from the trees and stood watchfully at the edge of the fold.

"My hounds will keep watch for you while you rest. This is Nuad and Fergma—sons of Dasacht the Fury."

He stared for a moment at hounds. They growled and dropped to their haunches. Then Ballus bid them farewell and disappeared into the woods.

"Well," Lorgas said, wiping his forehead. "I would say that we have been lucky."

"Indeed," Bern answered. "And we could use the rest. Right, Tarin?"

"I agree," Tarin answered. "We should regain our strength. I have a hunch we are going to need it before we arrive at Cairpre's court."

"And we shall," Seanchan said. "Let us put up a couple of lean-tos and build up the fire and dry out. Perhaps tomorrow we shall still have sun instead of the rain."

"I'm for that," Cumac said, and went into the woods, seeking limbs to build rough lean-tos. Tarin followed, while Bern and Lorgas searched for wood that might burn.

Seanchan heaved a great sigh and leaned on his staff as he studied Fedelm.

"And what bothers you, Fedelm?" he asked.

She shrugged and said, "I think we are still wasting time. But I think also that to rush down the trail may be more harmful than following the advice of Ballus."

She removed her quiver of green-fletched arrows and began studying the fletching carefully to see if the rain had ruined the feathers.

"Yes," Seanchan said. "I too would like to hurry but I am tired and my wits may not be as keen as they should be. Yes. It is better to rest."

"Of course," Fedelm said, "this will allow Bricriu more time to build defenses—maybe even recruit Sword-wanderers for a small army—if he decides not to go to Cairpre's court."

"I do not think that he will do that," Seanchan said thoughtfully. "Something tells me that he wants refuge for the moment. But I do not treat your words lightly. He could begin building a small force to aid him. *And* it may well be that Maliman has grown strong enough to send some of his men to accompany Bricriu. There are too many unknowns for the moment. I must think."

With that, he stretched out upon the ground and closed his eyes, placing his staff close at hand. Fedelm watched him thoughtfully for a moment, then returned to carefully study her arrows. One more day wouldn't matter. Bricriu had either reached Cairpre's court by now or would shortly. They had lost much time in Faindell. No, one more day wouldn't matter.

* * *

CUMAC watched the trees carefully as he and Tarin moved among them, searching for deadfall. Constantly he looked back to make certain that the trees hadn't moved once again, blocking their way back to the others.

Tarin noticed his behavior and said, "I think we are safe from more Nightshades. It will be a while before Maliman and the Grayshawls will act. Certainly Maliman will not know that his last attempt at us has failed right away. I am fairly certain we have at least a day before we need worry."

Cumac grunted his agreement. The Grayshawls were spirits who wore gray robes and shawls to hide their faces from all. They were wizards who were descendants of Tuan, the first man who became a shape-changer. Their bodies and souls had become so corrupted that they ceased to be humans and now existed only as spirits. They were the strongest of Maliman's servants. At one time, they were the most powerful wizards among men, but their desire for power left them without form. They could draw the souls from men with deep breaths. Their swords were deadly and were forged from molten steel into which the poison of Rathtrees had been worked.

"I am not so worried about them as I am by the sumaires and warggads. These are the woods that they like best."

"I still don't think we have to worry," Tarin said, nodding at the side.

Cumac turned his head and saw one of the wolfhounds waiting patiently for them to begin their search again. Cumac laughed ruefully.

"Yes, I think you are right. Still, I would rather err on the cautious side than careless. And can that wolfhound keep the trees from moving again as they did last night?"

"I don't think the trees can do that in daylight," Tarin said. "I think they need the night. That is when the most evil is done."

"Then let us hurry and gather what we need and get back to the others before the gloaming falls."

*   *   *

FOR a year Tarin and his wife, Galata, had been happy at Dun Scathe. Or were they? Tarin was. Of this he was certain. But then came the time when Galata walked moodily around Tarin's fortress, finding fault with the servants and reprimanding them harshly for anything that annoyed her. And there was much that annoyed her.

Perhaps he had been looking the other way, refusing to accept the change in Galata that occurred after they were married. Had it been a year? Or had she begun changing weeks earlier?

He no longer knew, and as he sat silently before the fire, his thoughts went back to the early days when he had been happiest. Those days before he became the Damned and Deathwhisper.

He had met Galata at her father's home, Dun Leathe, and had been immediately smitten by her dark-haired beauty and flashing black eyes that boldly held promise within them. Then she had flirted outrageously with him, swinging a saucy hip at him when their paths crossed. But she had refused his first proposal. And the second. But on the third, she accepted and her father, Etorcle, had been generous in his bride-gift.

Everything seemed to be going well until the Askari started raiding the borders of his liege lord, Rolfe, and Tarin had been called away to fight the raiders time and time again to the mountainous areas where the Askari hid after one of their dashing raids on Magslect, the Plain of Adoration, where farms flourished with fields of grain and livestock.

It was the time of the battle at the Pass of Crechen where the landscape was beautiful and rugged with colors that seemed to change daily. Sunlight glistened on the high peaks, causing them to gleam silver in the noonday sun before becoming gray and forbidding as night came. That battle had lasted for three days before Tarin, battered and bloody, returned home to find his wife gone. She returned two days later, telling Tarin that she had been to her father's home to visit her sisters. A tiny alarm went off in Tarin's mind, but he had pushed it away and reprimanded himself for the suspicions that came to him when he saw the satisfied glint in her eyes. Yes, that was when it had started. Of this he was certain now. Then had come the feast held by Culhane, where she had behaved boldly with Ganach, and Tarin had cut their visit short to return to Dun Scathe.

A heated argument developed between them, with Tarin ordering her to remain at his fortress and not to leave to visit anyone during his absences. She had screamed her rage at him but Tarin had remained firm. Then came the time when Culhane called him to his fortress and he had left after warning Galata to remain at Dun Scathe until his return. Three miles from his fortress, one of the traces on his chariot broke. He had returned home to repair it and discovered that Galata had left soon after his departure for the fortress of Ganach.

Red rage had filled him, and he had mounted his favorite chestnut and ridden to Ganach's fortress, where he found Galata and ordered her home. She had laughed at him and placed her arm around the shoulders of the smirking Ganach, telling Tarin that she would come and go as she pleased.

Then the rage descended upon him and he had drawn his sword, the rune-blade of his father, the handle ridged and wrapped tightly in black leather strips and made for two hands. The blade shone brightly and bore curious shapes, and he had seen Ganach's eyes narrow with desire for Tarin's sword.

Ganach's warriors came for him, shouting their battle cries and swinging their great swords. But Tarin was no ordinary swordsman, and after a furious battle, all lay dead, strewn in heaps around him. Then, Tarin left and made his way back to Dun Scathe.

A few days later, however, a traveler, seeking hospitality, had discovered all had been slain. Blood spattered the walls of Ganach's fortress and Ganach's head along with Galata's had been chopped off and placed on spears that framed the entrance to Ganach's Great Hall.

He had been brought to trial for murder but the court of Brehons could find no guilt in Tarin. No one could prove what was said that Tarin had done and he refused to address the court or answer any question put to him by the Brehons. Finally, they were forced to let Tarin go free. But people were certain of the rumors and began to shun Tarin until at last he went to Rolfe's fortress, where he had met Mumain, Rolfe's wife, who seduced him.

The seduction had been easy as not enough time had passed for Tarin to forget Galata and he had fallen willingly into Mumain's arms.

Until they were discovered by Rolfe's steward.

He shook his head and rose, taking the rune-blade from its scabbard, and began the exercises of a warrior, moving smoothly from the Winter Apple Feat to the Scythe Feat, and on through the other dances a warrior practiced constantly if he wanted to be good with the sword. The rune-blade sang through the air so fast that it appeared a blinding blur in Tarin's hands.

"Something is bothering him," Cumac whispered to Fedelm.

"Memories," she whispered back. "Bad memories. All men have them for some things they did in the past. Then they must kill the memories one way or another. That is Tarin's way, I'm thinking. Others will try to blur their memories with drink. But all men have them. The good ones try to keep the bad memories back, while there are others who give in to the darkness and allow themselves to be ruled by their memories. The evil ones."

"Do all men have these memories?"

"All," she said grimly. "That is what makes men what they are. It is those memories that makes Tarin the Damned, I think."

"Then the stories are true?"

She shrugged. "I do not know. Even if they aren't, the true memories of what did happen drive him."

"Do you believe the stories?"

She hesitated then slowly nodded. "Yes, I believe them."

Cumac shuddered and turned his attention back to the black-garbed swordsman working his way through the exercises. Tarin's face held no expression, his features stony, his eyes black anthracite. He moved effortlessly through the exercises, the rune-blade whistling at times in his hands as he brought the blade singing through slashes and counters. A fine sheen of perspiration appeared on his forehead and he began to speed through the exercises to cut

away the memories that pushed hard upon his mind. He concentrated fully on each movement to perfect it, a feat that had taken
him years of steady practice to erase any slightest error.

At last he finished and placed the point of the rune-blade on the
ground, leaning over the hilt to catch his breath. He concentrated
on breathing: one-two-three-hold-one-two-three-release. Soon a
calm came over him and he straightened, slipping his sword back
into its sheath. He wiped the perspiration from his face with his
sleeve and only then did he catch the others staring at him. He
forced a grin.

"An audience," he said. "A long time has passed since I have had
an audience. Or students," he added reflectively. The grin slipped
from his face to be replaced by a gloomy cloud that pulled his lips
into a bitter line.

"Where did you learn how to do the Lightning Feat?" Cumac
asked.

Tarin looked at him guardingly. "It was taught to me by
Scathach."

Fedelm's eyebrows raised in surprise. "Scathach?"

"Who's Scathach?" Cumac asked, puzzled by Fedelm's reaction.

"Scathach, 'the shadowy one,' is a warrior-queen and mistress of
a school for young warriors. She initiates you men—such as you,
Cumac—into the arts of war, as well as giving them the 'friendship
of her thighs.' That is to say, initiating them sexually. She granted
three wishes to your father, Cucullen, because her daughter,
Uathach, being in love with him, told him how to make her do it.
The three wishes were to train him in the arts of war, to marry her
daughter Uathach, and to tell his fortune, which she does by using
imbas forosnai. Scathach is said to be the daughter of the king of
Scythia," Fedelm said. "She does not take students lightly and it is
very difficult for one to become her student." She studied Tarin for
a moment then said, "You were very lucky to have her as your
teacher. But tell me, how did she become your teacher?"

"Garin, my father," Tarin answered. "Scathach owed him a favor."

"Garin," Fedelm said to Cumac's quizzical look, "was one of the
best swordsmen in Erin. He fought—how many duels?"

"Sixty-six," Tarin said.

"And never was defeated," Fedelm finished.

"Once," Tarin said. "He was beaten once."

"How? By whom?" Cumac asked.

Tarin hesitated then said, "Fergus Mac Roich, who fought for Maeve during the Cattle Raid of Cooley against the Red Branch."

A sudden quiet fell over the group as they glanced from one another back to Tarin.

He shook his head. "That is in the past. I bear no blood-oath. My father died as he wished—with his sword in hand. But he took many with him until Fergus used that"—he nodded at Caladbolg on Cumac's shoulder—"in the battle. Still, Fergus was hard-pressed to beat him."

Cumac stepped forward and held out his hand.

"I bear no ill will toward you," he said.

Tarin took his hand and grasped Cumac's forearm with his left.

"I am thankful for that," he said. "I have much to atone for and would wish to be with you on this quest."

"You are," Seanchan said, coming forward to clap Tarin on his shoulder.

"We agree as well," Bern and Lorgas said simultaneously.

"I am grateful," Tarin said, his face softening.

"You have already proved your worth," Fedelm said. "You have nothing left to prove to us. As you said, the past is behind us now."

"And now," Lorgas said gruffly, "that we have this tearful event behind us, let us look for food. My belly thinks my throat has been cut."

They all laughed at the elf's statement and split, each to the chore appointed by Seanchan. Tarin and Cumac searched for firewood while Fedelm took her bow and slipped along the edge of the forest, searching for game. Bern and Lorgas set the fire and began cooking, waiting impatiently for Fedelm to return—which she did shortly, a small deer slung over one shoulder.

Soon, roasts and steaks were spitted and turning slowly over the fire as Bern and Lorgas lightly rolled the spit in turn. Rich smells rose from the venison as fat dripped into a pan into which the two elves placed split wild onions, parsley, and sorrel along with some mushrooms.

The others waited, making small talk, their mouths watering in anticipation, until Lorgas pronounced the food ready.

They fell to with voracious appetites, devouring everything except some strips of venison that Bern pounded thin, working rowanberries into the meat along with pieces of walnut and placing the strips on a drying rack he made that stood above the fire. Lorgas placed a few logs of hickory on the fire below the drying rack, and soon a heady scent wafted into the air while the Seekers slept, watched over by Nuad and Fergma, the sons of Dasacht the Fury.

7

The next day they traveled with Ballus the Forester, who had returned to lead them away from Faindell's reaches until they came to a fork in the road. The right-hand road led down to a small river and a ferry crossing. The river ran a coppery green with white water braiding through a chain of black rocks upstream where the rain-swollen river rushed around a bend. There they paused for a moment until Ballus said that he had to return to Faindell.

"This will lead you to the village of Callyberry. Find Gabha, the blacksmith. He is an honorable man and will give you shelter and protection while you are guests in his inn. But do not linger there. Maliman is searching for you and if he finds you in the village, he will destroy the village to get to you," Ballus said. "I am leaving you Nuad and Fergma to accompany you. They will watch over you while you are resting. They are fierce and deadly.

"Now I must leave you. I wish you well upon the rest of your journey."

With that, Ballus took his leave and disappeared back toward Faindell. The two wolfhounds sat on their haunches and looked quizzically at the Seekers.

"I shall miss him," Cumac said.

"He is a loss that will be felt, I'm thinking," Fedelm said. "But there is nothing for it. He is needed in Faindell."

"Indeed," Seanchan affirmed. "But he left us Nuad and Fergma and I believe they will make up the difference in the loss of Ballus's sword and ax."

"Well," Lorgas grunted. "We are accomplishing nothing here. Let us go on to Gabha's village and inn. Perhaps there we shall find fire and food."

"Do you ever think of anything but your stomach?" Bern asked acidly.

"One must keep up his strength," Lorgas said belligerently.

Seanchan laughed. "Then let us go on. If I am right we should reach the village before nightfall."

He whistled, and the two wolfhounds obediently rose and trotted out in front of the Seekers, questing back and forth at the sides of the road leading down to the ferry, searching for anything that meant danger to the party.

The ferry had been clabbered together and the Seekers paused, studying the makeshift raft under overhanging willow branches from a huge tree whose roots rolled up and over the earth. Across the river stood a thick bank of bullrushes. Black stomped his hooves and shook his head in protest at the prospect of going across the river on the ferry. Cumac soothed him, talking softly and rubbing his neck.

Soon the great horse quieted, although rumblings of misgiving came from him.

"I don't like the looks of this," Bern said doubtfully.

"I don't either," replied Lorgas. "And neither does Cumac."

He pointed to the Dragonstone in the brooch that held Cumac's cloak together at the shoulders. The blood-red stone pulsed darkly.

"Perhaps we'd better look for another crossing," Fedelm said nervously.

Seanchan shook his head. "There may not be another crossing for miles. I do not think we should tarry longer."

He frowned and added, "Although I too feel something is wrong here."

Tarin had started to speak when a huge man stepped from the carelessly built hut next to the ferry. He was slovenly, dressed in gray rags spattered with egg yolk and grease. His hair was long and muddy brown and swung below his shoulders. His grime-cracked feet were as big as shovel blades and his hands almost as big as his feet with knuckles the size of walnuts.

"I 'spect you'll be wanting the ferry to cross over," he growled. His voice sounded as if someone had broken his windpipe in a long-forgotten fight. "Well, it'll cost you a piece of silver each and two for your horses."

Seanchan frowned. "Seems a bit steep for all of us going over together."

The man shrugged and said, "Them's the price. Take it or not. Makes little difference to me. The elves count the same."

Seanchan sighed and reached into a small bag hanging from his belt. Carefully he counted out the silver pieces and dropped them into the man's paw.

"You'll not be stopping halfway over to ask for more," Tarin said, fingering his sword suggestively.

"You are not the trusting sort," the man said. "But there will be no more charges."

Gingerly the Seekers led their horses onto the ferry, talking soothingly to them as they quivered nervously.

Smiling, the man untied the moorings and began hauling on a rope linked by pulleys to the opposite shore.

Suddenly the willow branches snapped out tendrils that seized Bern and hauled him back to its trunk. A huge maw opened in the trunk to swallow him.

"Help!" Bern squawked, twisting and turning violently to free himself.

Lorgas leaped from the ferry, swinging his ax, roaring his battle cry. The ax blade split one of the exposed willow roots. Sap spurted from the cut. The tree shuddered and tried to seize Lorgas, but the elf skipped nimbly out of the way and swung his ax again, chopping through another root. Again sap spurted.

"Release him!" Lorgas roared, swinging the ax again.

The willow quivered and then released Bern. He fell to the ground and leaped to his feet, drawing his sword and hacking at the willow. Branches whipped wildly back and forth, and then a bolt of lightning crackled from Seanchan's staff, striking the willow in the maw.

The willow shrieked and the maw closed.

The two elves leaped back onto the raft.

"Pull!" Seanchan ordered sharply, and the man gave a mighty yank on the rope, propelling the raft to the middle of the river as the willow branches twisted in agony.

"Whew! That was close," Bern said, mopping perspiration from his face. He dropped his hand on Lorgas's shoulder. "Thank you. I owe you a debt."

"It was nothing," Lorgas said modestly.

"It was," Bern said firmly. "And there may come a time when I can return it."

"Perhaps," Lorgas said, wiping his ax head clean of the sap.

Seanchan turned and thrust his staff into the man's belly. "You knew of this!"

The man grunted and then his face went white. He tried to push the staff away but could not and fell to his knees, releasing the rope. Cumac and Tarin seized the rope and began hauling the raft to the opposite bank.

"Explain!" Seanchan thundered.

"Spare me, wizard!" the man cried.

"Explain!" Seanchan said firmly. But he did not withdraw the staff from the man's belly.

"Please," the man begged. "I have done nothing!"

"Explain!" This time Seanchan's voice grew soft and green lights began to pulse along the length of his staff. The man cringed and words burst from him as if he was possessed.

"A Grayshawl! A Grayshawl put a spell on Willow and took a part of me as well! I must do his bidding! Don't you see? Don't you see?" He began to sob.

Seanchan studied him for a moment then slowly withdrew his staff.

"That explains the tree. But what were *you* supposed to do to us?"

"Nothing! Just tell the Grayshawl when you came to cross this ford."

"And how were you to do this?"

"When he visits me at night!"

"Every night?"

The man nodded.

"All right," Seanchan said quietly. "Tonight you will say nothing about us. Understand? I doubt if the Grayshawl has placed a truth spell upon you. I cannot sense one, anyway. But," he emphasized, prodding the man with his staff, "I will know if you do not do this and will return to deal with you."

"I promise!" the man said fervently.

"I say we kill him and be done with it," Lorgas growled. "No sense leaving things to chance."

Seanchan looked at him and said sharply, "Do not be hasty, Lorgas. Are you able to judge who to kill and who to let live? Do not be so hasty in choosing who lives and who dies lest it change you into a servant of Maliman who searches for those who are willing to kill at random.

"And now," he said, turning to the others, "pull us the rest of the way across if you please, Cumac, Tarin."

The two grabbed the rope and began pulling smoothly, sending the raft sliding fast against the opposite shore,

Quickly the Seekers disembarked and the man seized the rope and pulled the raft to the other side so fast the water frothed from the raft's passing.

"Tricked! Tricked!" he shouted. "You are not as wise as you thought, Seanchan Duirgeal!"

Seanchan's face darkened and he raised his staff but the man had disappeared into a dark shimmering light.

"A Grayshawl," Seanchan said and spat. "And to think I let him trick me when I had him for a minute."

"Don't blame yourself," Fedelm said. "He tricked the rest of us too."

"What surprises me is that he didn't act when he could have taken us by surprise. *And* that he could appear in human form," Cumac said. "I thought they couldn't appear as humans."

"An illusion only," Seanchan said. "But another example of how Earthworld is changing as Maliman becomes more powerful." A weak cry came from the bullrushes. The Seekers looked at one another in astonishment.

"That sounds like a baby," Fedelm said. She drew her sword and started into the bullrushes.

"Careful," Tarin warned, drawing his sword. "It could be a trap."

The others followed his lead and started after Fedelm but stopped when Fedelm called, "No! It's a baby!"

She appeared carrying a wicker basket with a baby swaddled in a cloak hemmed in red. She placed the basket on the ground and lifted the baby free. The others crowded around her.

"What on wood is it doing here?" Bern asked.

"I don't know," Seanchan said. "But I suspect that is the real reason the Grayshawl came here. Not us."

"How so?" Tarin asked.

Seanchan pointed to the red lines on the cloak. "Seven lines of red. This is a royal baby."

"And there is this," Fedelm said, pulling back a fold to reveal a gold chain with an amethyst stone around the baby's neck.

"The Ard-ri," Seanchan breathed.

A puzzled look came over the faces of the others.

"The High King?" Tarin asked. "I've never heard of one before."

"There hasn't been one for nearly a thousand years," Seanchan explained. "Not since Eremon was slain and his family nearly destroyed by Feralim who sought the throne. According to the *Annals*, Baeve, Eremon's wife, escaped the slaughter when The Dagda rescued her and put her on Teach Duinn, where she was sheltered and protected by Donn and the Dearg Laochs, Red Warriors, who ride from Teach Duinn to fight evil. This baby is undoubtedly her son. The babe is supposed to be named Cormach."

"How do you come to know this?" Tarin asked.

Seanchan pointed again at the seven red lines along the hem of the cloak.

"Only the Ard-ri can wear seven red lines," he said.

"Anyone could have sewn those lines," Tarin observed.

But Seanchan shook his head. "No. The Dagda would not allow that. And I'll bet there is not a blemish on the child either. Nor wart or birthmark. The Ard-ri must be free of blemish."

"Tonight I'll sleep the sleep of *imbas forasnai*," Fedelm said. "Then perhaps we will know."

"For now, though, I think we would be wise to get as far away from here as we can," Seanchan said.

Swiftly they mounted and rode from the river.

Tbat night they made camp in a small copse of beech trees heavy with early leaf buds. The ground beneath the trees was a soaked golden brown carpet from fallen leaves. The smell of tannic rose from them and a small seep, tasting of the tannic, lay in the middle of the trees. Lorgas took some of the dried venison and made a broth for the baby. Fedelm carefully spooned the broth into the baby's mouth while Tarin took the baby's clothes and washed them in a small pond.

A quiet descended upon the copse except for a slight breeze that soughed through the trees bringing with it a hint of rain or late-spring snow. Cumac and Tarin moved restlessly through the trees with misgivings about the quiet until at last Seanchan told them to relax and wove a protective spell around the copse.

At last night fell fully and the baby slept and Fedelm made herself ready to sleep the sleep of *imbas forasnai.* The others waited impatiently around the fire for her to emerge from her sleep and tell them what she had learned. Seanchan watched her closely. He did not know if he could enter Dreamworld if she appeared in trouble but he meant to try if she showed any sign of distress.

A BLOOD-RED full moon shone over a desolate wasteland. Trees looked burnt and the ground looked ash-covered. In the near distance she saw the ruins of dolmens—the entrances to Otherworld—and the burnt timbers of warrior halls. A single star pulsed blue-white overhead. The air smelled of earth and dead leaves that had been burnt yet still held a trace of tannic. In the distance a golden light suddenly began to glow and grow larger as it moved steadily toward her. Behind the glow a tower built with green stone appeared in a cloud of mist.

Warily she watched the light approach, wishing she could have brought her weapons into Dreamworld with her. But Otherworld or Earthworld weapons could not be brought into Dreamworld and now she was defenseless.

Then the light began to shimmer and widen until at last a young man with golden hair and cobalt eyes stood in front of her. He was clean-shaven and his cheeks glowed ruddily. He wore a white tunic that fell to his well-turned calves and white sandals that laced up his calves. At his side hung a short sword. A soft halo surrounded its black leather grip. He smiled at Fedelm and twin dimples appeared in his cheeks.

"I am Cathlon, Fedelm of the Sidhe. I am a Dreamwalker sent by Coig to guard you and to guide you where you wish to go," he said amiably. "Now, what has caused you to sleep the sleep of *imbas forasnai?*"

"A babe," Fedelm said. Her throat felt dry and she swallowed to moisten it. "A babe we found in the bullrushes. Who is he and why was he placed in a wicker basket and sent into the river?"

"He is Cormach, the next Ard-ri."

"There has not been an Ard-ri for over a thousand years," Fedelm said. "Why now?"

"Look inside yourself, Fedelm of the Sidhe. You know the answer as well as I."

Fedelm closed her eyes, focusing thought. She saw Earthworld being torn apart; armies battling in dark and rain and black clouds laced with lightning bolts snapping like whip lashes overhead. The image slowly disappeared although the cries and clashes of swords remained within her mind. Then a winter apple tree began to slowly bloom, dropping white blossoms tinged with red to the ground, where they instantly became other trees, and grasses and birds began to sing happily. In the center of the scene the Bladhm Caillis—the Chalice of Fire—appeared, glowing goldly and beside the Chalice stood a young man clad in red leather, wearing a golden circlet set with a green emerald upon his brow.

"Who you see is young Cormach, who is needed to unite the kings and become one with the land, which will become fertile once again. *If* Maliman is defeated and the boy lives. Destiny is fickle and changes as the fortunes of man change. Nothing is written in stone that cannot be changed by another.

"The destiny of the land is the destiny of the babe you have found. But whether he will become the Ard-ri of evil or good depends on how his life is formed by those with him who will weave their own ways around and within him, forming him for his future."

"Who will do that?" Fedelm asked.

Cathlon shrugged. "You will have to determine that yourself. I caution you, however, that you do not choose a warrior or a noble. He will learn what he needs to know from a man and woman of the earth. He must learn how to deal with *all* people and not just the select few. They will come with time. First, though, he needs to learn the people he will guard and protect."

He frowned and gripped his sword, looking around him and up into the night.

"What is it?" Fedelm asked uneasily.

"I heard wings. There! Hear that?"

A soft susuring came to her, and Fedelm looked around quickly for the source. A black creature appeared over the moonglow and Cathlon's sword rasped as he slid it from its sheath.

"Sumaires riding Memans!" Cathlon shouted.

A cold settled within Fedelm.

Sumaires. Vampires.

"Quick! End your sleep, Fedelm!" Cathlon shouted. He turned to face the first of the sumaires.

Fedelm concentrated, trying to will herself out of the sleep of *imbas forasnai*. But something held her within Dreamworld. Her flesh pebbled and she grew colder.

"I can't," she gasped. "Something is holding me!"

"A Grayshawl!" Cathlon said sharply. "Run! Go to the Tower of the Guardians! Find Coig!"

Fedelm took to her heels. Her toes barely touched the ground as she ran toward the green tower shimmering in the near distance. Behind her she heard swords clashing and Cathlon's battle roar as he met the sumaires.

She cast a quick look over her shoulder. Cathlon beheaded one of the sumaires and ducked under the neck of his Meman, slicing its neck open as he leaped to engage another sumaire.

But one broke free and was riding hard toward her.

Fedelm increased her speed toward the tower but knew as she ran that the sumaire would be upon her before she could reach it.

The sumaire drew closer and closer and Fedelm could hear him laughing with excitement.

Then a blue and red lightning bolt shot out from the tower, and Fedelm heard a scream as it struck the sumaire and Meman.

Two more bolts cracked overhead and struck the sumaires fighting with Cathlon. Frightened screams of pain flooded back to her as flame encased their bodies, burning them to ash.

Then she reached the tower, and the door, also made of green stone, opened and she slipped inside and leaned against a wall, gasping. She felt the cold of the stone against her flesh and reveled in it. Cathlon slipped in beside her and the door scraped over the stone floor as it slowly shut.

"That . . . was . . . close," she gasped.

"Yes," Cathlon acknowledged. "Closer than I wished. I was nearly finished before Coig sent the cairnfire to help us."

"Who is Coig?" Fedelm asked.

"I am Coig," a voice said from the stairs.

Fedelm looked and saw a white-haired old man leaning on his green staff. He was dressed in white. His bearing was straight and his blue eyes twinkled.

"Coig is the leader of the Dreamwalkers," Cathlon said. He placed his right hand over his heart and bowed.

Coig motioned for Cathlon to rise.

"Barach the Assigner tells me who is worthy of a Dreamwalker and I send him forth," Coig said. "I am the Guardian of the Tower."

"And lucky for us you were watching," Cathlon said with feeling, wiping perspiration from his face with the sleeve of his tunic.

Coig shrugged. "Barach told me that there would be trouble. You should remember to thank him next time you see him," Coig said to Cathlon. He looked again at Fedelm. "Now, let us make you welcome to the Tower."

"I really need to get back to the other Seekers," Fedelm said.

"Alas but that is difficult at the moment," Coig said apologetically. "Barach needs time to unwind the Grayshawls' spell from around the Tower. The same spell that holds you in Dreamworld."

"But I must get back!" Fedelm said urgently.

"I know," Coig said gently, spreading the fingers of one hand. "But there is really nothing we can do at the moment. As I said: such things take time.

"Meanwhile we can make you comfortable here. We are, however, quite austere," he cautioned.

Fedelm nodded glumly and followed Coig as he led her to her room. She entered and looked around. A simple cot with a brown blanket folded neatly at the foot stood against one wall. A washstand and basin and ewer stood next to it. A gray stone fireplace had a neatly laid fire. A chair with a spindly back stood near the fire and a plain deal table and matching chair stood against the other wall.

"Oh Seanchan," she whispered. "Where are you?"

"WHERE is she?" Cumac demanded as they sat around Fedelm's still form. Her face was white and cold. She lay still as death although her breast rose and fell gently with her breathing.

Seanchan shook his head. "I don't know," he said softly. "Somewhere in Dreamworld. I sense a holding spell has been woven around it."

"Can't you do anything to bring her back?" Tarin asked.

"Maybe. I don't know. The weave is tightly woven. I suspect by Grayshawls. If I can unwind it, it will take time and as I told you before, we must not move her. That would be dangerous, for the path of return will be broken and she would wander Dreamworld forever."

Lorgas sighed and rubbed his knuckles furiously over his scalp. "So what are we going to do? We can't go on and to stay here is dangerous."

"Perhaps Deroi and Deiru could help. Together we might be able to break the enchantment," Seanchan mused.

"Who are they?" Bern asked.

"Deroi was my teacher," Cumac said.

"One of the Five who founded my order," Seanchan said. "He sits on the Supreme Council. Deiru is the wielder of Cullasdreu, the Sacred Flame. He is the warrior-protector of the Duirgeals. He awards cairnfire to the ones judged worthy."

"But it will still take time," Cumac said dejectedly.

"It will take time for we must find the weakness of the holding spell. That place where it begins and ends."

"Then summon them and try," Cormac said. "We must not wait any longer than we have to."

"The three of us will have to enter Dreamworld together, as only then can our power be wielded. To go alone is to leave all behind. Alone I would be useless in Dreamworld. And I have a feeling that is what the Grayshawls want."

"Then what are we bandying words about for? Let us get on with it," Lorgas growled.

"It is not as easy as you think," Seanchan said sharply. "So hold your teeth together. I do not need you to tell me the urgency of the matter."

Lorgas glowered but fell silent as Seanchan made himself comfortable with his back against an oak tree. He laid his staff across his knees, closed his eyes, and raised his hands, the thumbs and middle fingers forming an "O." He began to chant in a tongue none there had heard.

Mach an elware draog, Deiru!
Mach an elware draog, Deroi!
Mir bis Cullesdrewu, Deiru!
An fal ba mar fertai, Deroi!

The oak began to vibrate and a mist began to form around Seanchan. The others stepped back hastily as the mist rose and began to slowly swirl. Seanchan repeated the chant and suddenly two figures appeared beside him.

One was a slender old man clad in a white robe and carrying a green staff with a large perfect crystal on the head. The younger one had red flowing hair and was dressed in a scarlet tunic with silver thread around the hem. He wore green leggings and boots that came up to his calves. He had a gold torc around his neck and carried a large sword with a gold blade and black leather hilt. Green fire licked around him but he was untouched by the small flame.

The old man spoke.

"We are here, Seanchan, obedient to your call. What is it you wish?"

Seanchan came erect and the three placed their right hands on the right shoulders of each.

"I thank you for coming," Seanchan said.

"What ails you, old man?" the younger asked.

"One of our party, Fedelm of the Sidhe, is being held in Dreamworld by a spell woven by the Grayshawls," Seanchan said. "I cannot draw her back alone, Deiru. I need you and Deroi"—he nodded at the old man—"to help me. Together we might be able to bring her out. Alone I cannot. The web is tightly woven. I do not think it is Maliman, though."

"The Grayshawls are enough. If they have banded together. You are asking a lot, Seanchan," Deroi said. "It is dangerous for even the three of us to enter Dreamworld with such a spell woven tightly. We could be caught in Dreamworld as well. Do you think this could be a trap for us?"

"This is possible," Seanchan admitted. "Together you and I might be able to break the spell if we channel together. Deiru could stand guard over the two of us. Just maybe that would be enough. But we would have to act quickly."

Deroi mused for a moment then nodded.

"We shall have to use three enchantments. One to find her before we enter Dreamworld. One to enter Dreamworld. One to break the weave so we might leave."

"It is risky," Seanchan said. "But we need her to continue our search for Bricriu Poisontongue. We need her strength and bow."

"All right," Deiru said roughly. "What are we waiting for?"

Seanchan and Deroi smiled at each other.

"The young are impatient and impulsive," Deroi said. "Still, there *is* no reason to wait."

The three joined hands. An orange glow surrounded them for a moment then went away.

"She is with Coig in the Tower of the Guardians," Deroi said. "That is in our favor. We have a destination."

"Very well," Seanchan said.

"Let's go," Deiru said.

A gray mist slowly rose from their feet and beshrouded them.

Then a bright golden flash burst from the mist and they disappeared.

The others looked with bewilderment at each other.

"Where did they go?" Tarin asked nervously.

"Into Dreamworld," Cumac said.

"Let us hope they are successful," Lorgas said.

"Or we will be hard put to continue," Bern observed.

With that grim observation the others sat down to wait, aware of their own helplessness.

TIME has no meaning in Dreamworld and Fedelm had no idea how long she had been in the Tower of the Guardians. Six meals—that she knew—but all else melted into time.

The Guardians took pains to make her feel welcome but still she was restless, wandering around the Tower to find ways of passing time. Could she ever call it "time"? *Being* was a better word, for time past and time present were all one.

After the sixth meal, Coig came and took her to the Tower library and then to an open area where the Guardians practiced with swords and bows.

"You may as well use your time with us wisely," Coig said. "After first meal use our library to study. After second meal, work with the Dreamwalkers to learn the gift of swords. We prepare ourselves constantly for what may be needed."

Fedelm sighed but knew Coig's words were wisdom and began the regimen he had suggested.

She absorbed books, learning many things that she had only heard about in rumors. Soon she could use small magic such as how to conjure fire in wet wood, the language of birds and wild animals (although there were none that she could practice with), and how to bend time in theory as there was no time in Dreamworld.

In swordplay, however, she was drubbed again and again with wooden swords by the Dreamwalkers.

She grew frustrated and reckless until Cathlon took her aside and taught her that fighting with a sword meant that she had to become one with the sword and that the sword became part of her.

"You must learn the mind of the sword," Cathlon explained.

"It is only metal," she said.

"All things are part of all things. Even a pebble has its place the same as you have your place. Learn to listen to the sword. Not direct the sword."

With misgivings, Fedelm tried again and again until suddenly she heard a voice speaking to her and knew at that moment that the sword was speaking to her and becoming a part of her, flickering and dancing through moves that let her hold her own with the Dreamwalkers.

Then after the thirtieth meal, Coig came and interrupted her.

"Quickly," he said. "Come with me! It is time!"

"For what?" Fedelm asked, but she followed Coig as he hurried up the stairs to the top of the Tower. There he pointed down into the gloom surrounding the Tower.

"Look! They have come for you!"

She looked and saw Seanchan and an old man, heads thrown back and arms akimbo as they chanted. Soft green clouds swirled around them. A younger man, bearing a golden sword, fought against three Deag-duls, the blood-sucking beasts that strove to break through the man's defense. But again and again he beheaded one only to have another take its place.

Then a black cloud appeared before them and suddenly opened, revealing green grass and trees.

"It is a gateway!" Coig said. "Hurry! Leap into it as it cannot be held open for long!"

Fedelm leaped and found herself dropping through the opening. Lightning crackled and thunder boomed, hurting her ears with such intensity that she screamed as she fell. Then she found herself back in her body in Earthworld. Seanchan and the others quickly followed and the gateway slammed shut.

Seanchan's face was contorted with pain as he lay panting on the grass. The other two stood, bent slightly forward as they tried to catch their breath.

"That . . . was close," the old man said. He looked at Fedelm. "You appear much less for wear, my dear. I am Deroi and this"—he indicated the young man beside him—"is Deiru. We are of the Duirgeals."

"It took the three of us to bring you back from Dreamworld," Deiru gasped. "I would suggest you do not go in there again if you can help it. The Grayshawls will be ready the next time."

Seanchan nodded, taking deep breaths to calm himself. "We . . . were . . . very . . . lucky."

"Now," Deroi said, "Deiru and myself must return to the place of our order. If we stay too long here we will upset the natural balance of Earthworld."

"Thank you," Fedelm said, and in a twinkling the two were gone.

"What happened? What happened?" the others chorused.

"In time," Seanchan said. "For the moment we must rest. Tomorrow we shall travel to Callyberry and Fedelm can tell you then."

And with that he and Fedelm lay back and rested. Fedelm asked for the baby and Cumac laid it beside her in the crook of her arm as the wolfhounds moved on either side of her and lay down.

Then they slept.

8

True to Seanchan's word, the party arrived at Callyberry village just before the gloaming fell into night. The stars looked like a thick blanket overhead and the smell of sour earth came to them. Sounds of merriment came from the inn in the center of the village. The Seekers moved thankfully to it.

Talk and music ceased when the door opened and the Seekers, followed by the wolfhounds, entered, cold and weary. A crowd of men and women turned from a plain oak table beside the fire. In the corner a fiddler and harpist paused to stare curiously at the newcomers. Mugs of ale stood on the table and in the middle of the table rested a huge rib roast, gravy dripping from its sides. Loaves of bread were piled high. The Seekers' mouths watered and Lorgas took a few involuntary steps toward the table before stopping when a huge, bald-headed man with large sloping shoulders lumbered forward, wiping his hands on his apron. He grinned a gap-toothed smile. Heavy scar tissue bunched over his eyes and his hands were scarred from the many bare-knuckled fights he had fought. A large mole was centered on his forehead.

He glanced curiously at the baby Fedelm carried.

"Welcome, travelers. I am Gabha." He beamed and glanced at the wolfhounds and nodded. "I see you are well protected on your journey. What may I do for you?"

"We appreciate your kindness," Seanchan said. "We *are* tired. Our journey has been long and dangerous. Do you have rooms for us?"

"Well," Gabha said, rubbing the dark bristle along his jaw. "I have four left. Afraid that some of you will have to double up. But that's the best I can do." He glanced again at the wolfhounds. "I don't know about them, now. I suppose I can let them go into one room. Or else they can stay in the stable with your horses. There's plenty of fresh hay and straw there and I have two good bones with meat still on them."

Seanchan sighed and said, "We are grateful for your hospitality. We have come a long way from Faindell."

"Faindell?" a man asked from a corner of the room.

Seanchan turned to him. He was walleyed and dressed in a dirty jerkin that had once been brown and greasy leather pants with boots laced up to his calves. At first glance it appeared that he had no chin but a closer look showed that his chin was drawn back nearly to his throat. Black hair like wires covered his cheeks sparsely.

"Yes," Seanchan said quietly. "Faindell."

"Then," the man said, "you would be the Seekers we have heard about."

"Who are you?" Cumac demanded.

"He is Able, a tinker," Gabha said, folding his thick arms across his mammoth chest. "But I have seen little of his trade."

"I work," Able said defensively. "But there is little work here. You, blacksmith, take the trade from me."

He rose and came toward the group, then stopped as the wolf-hounds moved in front of Seanchan and growled a warning. He turned pale beneath the grime on his face.

"They are not friendly," the tinker said.

"No, they are not. At least not to those who bear the scent of distrust."

He turned to Gabha. "How long has this man been here?" he demanded.

"Came at noontime today," Gabha said, the smile slipping from his face as he studied the tinker closely. "I should say that he *claims* to be a tinker. He does have a wagon out beside the stable but now that I think about it, I didn't see that any of the tools have been much used."

His eyes narrowed. "Just who are you anyway?"

"I told you: my name is Able and I *am* a tinker despite what you think. Times are hard now with the world gone topsy-turvy as it has."

"Uh-huh," Gabha said dubiously. "Well, you are welcome as long as you do not cause any trouble to the rest of my guests. I wouldn't take kindly to that."

Able spread his hands and smiled. His teeth were rotten and mossy green. His fingernails were black with dirt.

"I have no reason to cause trouble. Indeed," he added, eyeing the Seekers, "these men look able to handle any trouble that could be started. I would hate to fall to those swords."

His eyes widened as he looked at Tarin.

"I know you, don't I?" he asked. A louse crawled out of his greasy hair, then back in again.

"We have never met," Tarin said coldly. He eased the rune-blade into its sheath. "I would remember such as you if we had."

"Maybe. But I know you just the same." Fear suddenly flashed over Able's face. "You are Tarin the Damned, the Deathwhisper."

The room grew so quiet the fire could be heard snapping and

cracking in the huge stone fireplace. Fear stank in the room as some shuddered and turned away from the black-clad man.

"I am Tarin."

"And I am Seanchan of the Duirgeals," Seanchan said. "And these are the rest of my party. Cumac, son of Cucullen, Bern of the Ervalians and Lorgas of the Ashelves, and Fedelm of the Sidhe."

He neglected to identify the baby and Gabha looked curiously at him again but refrained from asking any questions. What travelers preferred to keep to themselves he was content to leave be.

"The Seekers of the Chalice," someone whispered and the air in the room turned electric.

Gabha turned toward them, saying, "If you are the Seekers of the Chalice then you are most welcome. There will be no charge for the rooms or food and drink. If there is anything else we can do to help you, let me know."

"We thank you for your hospitality," Seanchan murmured, bowing slightly. He looked again at Able. His eyes became frosty. "That one, however, bothers me if what you say is right."

"We can fix that," Gabha said. He turned to a woman sitting silently in a corner across the room. She wore chain mail over a green tunic, black leggings, and soft black leather boots that came to the middle of her thighs. A silver torc held her long red hair off her forehead. She had gray eyes and a small scar crossed her cheek. Worn leather wrist guards came halfway up her forearms.

"Sirona, would you put this man"—he gestured at Able—"in the cellar and keep him there until morning?"

Sirona rose and took her ivory-handled sword from beside her. She drew it, the steel whispering as it came out of its sheath. The blade was a curious one, slightly curved from hilt to point. The curve was covered with a brass ridge meant to catch blades. Muscles rippled as she moved forward to Able.

"This is not right," Able whined. "I have done nothing to warrant this. I do not like cellars. They are cold and damp and there are large rats in them."

"No rats in my house," Gabha said indignantly. "And there are plenty of blankets down there for you to use to keep warm.

Although," he said sourly, "we will have to wash them thoroughly after your use."

"Move," Sirona said, pricking him in the rump with the point of her sword. Her voice was husky like sand being rubbed over wood.

He jumped and moved toward the cellar, rubbing his rump and complaining about how ill he was being treated when he was only a tinker looking for warmth by the fire. Sirona opened the door and gave him a shove. He yelped as he tumbled down the stairs. She closed and locked the cellar.

"We can guard the door," Seanchan said. He looked at Nuad and Fergma. The two wolfhounds rose and went to the cellar door and lay down, each on a side.

"And now," Lorgas said, rubbing his hands together expectantly. "May we partake of your fare?"

Gabha stood aside and waved them in. "You are my guests. Help yourselves. Will you have warm ale?"

"Ah," Lorgas said, hurrying to the table. "Don't mind if I do."

Bern sighed and refrained from his usual acid remarks toward Lorgas as he followed the Ashelf to the table.

"All of us would be grateful," Seanchan said. "The road was long and cold to here."

Gabha beamed and hurried off to the bar on the far side of the room where two huge kegs rested on trestles. He took clay-glazed mugs and filled them, then brought them to the table. He took a hot poker from the fire and thrust it into each mug. The ale sizzled as he placed one in front of each of the travelers.

"I have fresh butter too," he said. "Churned it m'self early this morning. And goat cheese. I have some fresh milk for the baby as well. I'll get some for you."

"And some broth as well for the baby," Fedelm called.

He disappeared and returned shortly with a crock of butter, still gleaming wetly yellow in the light, and a round of goat cheese that did not crumble when the travelers sliced into it. His wife, a buxom woman smiling cheerfully, came with him, carrying an improvised bottle of milk with a clean piece of white linen to use as a stopper. She set that and a bowl of broth in front of Fedelm.

"Now, dearie, I'll help you with the baby if you like. Been a while since my children were that age. That little one looks as if he'd be wanting a little more attention than you've been able to give 'im," she said. She eyed Fedelm's arms and the gem-encrusted belt critically. "And I daresay that you're more meant for the warrior trail and not keeping a house and husband in line." She gave her husband a bold look and he flushed redly.

"Now if you'll be feeding him right properly I'll make a wee bed for the little tyke in our rooms. He'll be safe there and I don't mind attending him during the night as it looks like you been dragged through an ordeal or two and could use a bit of rest."

Fedelm looked at Seanchan, who nodded and said, "It will be all right. The baby will be safe here for the night."

Thankfully, Fedelm nodded and said, "I'll feed him first."

"That'll be right," the woman said. "I'm Cairin, wife and mother to 'em."

She jerked her thumb at the landlord, who hid his embarrassment by saying, "I'll have m'daughter lay a fire in each of your rooms to warm them toasty while you eat. Now, let's have some music. This is not a night for somber tones!"

Obediently the fiddler and harpist began to play a lively tune that turned men's feet into dance. They whirled around the room, bumping into the wall now and then while laughing uproariously.

Lorgas burped loudly and wiped his mouth with his beard. His eyes beamed happily as he watched the dancers. Bern gave him a withering look and then shook his head and returned to his meal.

Sirona came to the table and dropped beside Tarin, eyeing him boldly.

"And, Sword-wanderer, how fare you on this journey?"

"They are my friends," Tarin said quietly as he cut his slice of roast into small bites. He drank ale from the mug. "I travel with them on this journey."

"And what brought them to you?"

"The way of the road," he answered curtly. "What else brings strangers together?"

"I think I like you," she said.

Tarin's eyes rose in surprise. "Do you always make quick judgments of men?"

"Not always," she said, suddenly serious. "But I can sense a goodness in you that appeals to me."

She looked around at the others, noting their travel-stained clothes.

"You all look the worse for wear," she said.

"It has been a difficult journey," Fedelm answered.

"Yes, if you came through Faindell. I can well imagine. I came through there myself a couple of days ago."

"In search of something?" Cumac asked.

She shrugged. "One thing or another. I'm not hard to please."

She rose suddenly and stood over them.

"Now, I think you need rest. Tomorrow is another day and if I am not mistaken, rain."

Lorgas groaned. "Rain. This foul country seems to always be filled with rain. A few days of sunshine would be welcome." He looked hopefully at Seanchan. "I don't suppose we could rest through the rain?"

Seanchan pulled his white beard and looked at them thoughtfully.

"Rain will slow all men," he said. "We can outwait the rain."

"Ah," Bern said, yawning. "And now, I could use a bed."

"As could we all," Seanchan answered, finishing his mug of ale and standing.

Gabha came forward and rubbed his hands together.

"Your rooms are ready for you. Now, if you leave your clothes outside your doors, I will have them cleaned for you by the morrow. And," he said, looking critically at them, "I think that would be for the best."

The Seekers nodded their thanks and stumbled wearily up the stairs to their beds. Within minutes, they were tucked in, Lorgas and Bern in one room, both snoring loudly, Cumac and Tarin in another, while Fedelm and Seanchan each had a room to themselves.

Downstairs, the gaiety slowly trickled away as the patrons stumbled out of the inn and wended their ways carefully to their homes. The fiddler and harpist went to pallets created for them while Sirona climbed the stairs to her room, pausing outside each of the other doors, hearing the others sleep. She smiled softly to herself and entered her room and soon slept.

9

Tarin awoke with a start, reaching automatically for the rune-blade as he swung his feet out of bed and stood with his back to the wall. Something had disturbed him. Bad dreams, perhaps, but there was something else that made his warrior's second sense come awake quickly.

He scanned the room, then stepped to the small window under the eaves and looked out. Rain came down in a steady fall and the day was gray and gloomy. Something, however, was out there; something that disordered the nature of things; something he didn't like that sent his nerves twanging. He went to the door and discovered his and Cumac's clothes cleaned and neatly pressed. He brought them into the room and dressed quickly before stepping across to the other bed and shaking Cumac awake.

"Get up," he said urgently.

"What is it?" Cumac yawned, rubbing the sleep from his eyes.

"I don't know," Tarin said. "Something."

He glanced at the Dragonstone pinned to Cumac's cloak. It pulsed black and deep red wildly. He pointed at the Dragonstone and said grimly, "There's your answer."

Cumac came wide awake and to his feet in a flash, dressing as rapidly as he could. He splashed water on his face and wiped clean with a towel hanging from a rod on the washstand.

"You'd better get the others up," he said to Tarin, fitting Caladbolg around his shoulder and tightening the large belt around his waist. He slipped his ivory-hilt dagger into the sheath on his belt.

"I'll go down and check the horses," he said. He paused, staring at the Dragonstone. "I think I should awaken the inn as well."

Tarin nodded and stepped out into the hall, moving swiftly to Seanchan's door and hammering upon it while Cumac ran down the stairs. Tarin heard Cumac shouting below as Seanchan opened the door, blinking sleepily.

"We have trouble," Tarin said harshly. "Ready yourself."

He didn't wait for Seanchan's answer but went to Fedelm's room and pounded on the door until the woman from the Sidhe answered.

"Dress quickly," he said. "Something is wrong. Cumac is awakening the inn and checking our horses. We may have to ride fast to get away."

At that moment, Fedelm's gem-encrusted belt that Tarin had stolen from Moagin began to glow a deep emerald color.

"Look!" Tarin said, pointing over Fedelm's shoulder.

Obediently she turned and saw the belt and said, "That's the first time I've seen *that*. Whatever is coming must be very bad indeed. Get the elves."

She grabbed her clothes from beside the door and closed her door while Tarin leaped to the next room, pounding hard to awaken the elves.

"Bern! Lorgas! Hurry! Something's wrong!" he shouted.

"Coming!" Bern yelled through the door.

"I was just having a good dream . . ." Lorgas complained as he tried to disentangle himself from his blankets that wrapped him like a cocoon.

"This is no time for talk!" Tarin said. "Hurry!"

The door next to the elves swung open and Sirona stepped out into the hallway, sword in hand, her long red hair tousled, her gray eyes smoky and hard.

"Trouble?" she asked.

"Of the worst sort, I think," Tarin said quickly, and turned and ran down the stairs. Gabha was up and rudely shaking awake those who had slept by the fire. He nodded at Tarin as he ran across the inn floor and flung the door wide, following Cumac outside.

The air smelled foul and rank and ravens cawed in the near distance.

"Sounds like Donn is warning us," Tarin said grimly. Donn, the god of death and the Underworld, sometimes called "the Black God," ruled his kingdom from Teach Duinn, the Island of Donn, from which his sons, the Dearg Laochs, the Red Warriors, rode forth to aid champions in their fight against evil.

Cumac swung up on Black, the warhorse stomping his hooves, nostrils distended, head up with his eyes rolling wildly in battle fury.

"I'll ride out and see what it is," Cumac said, nudging Black with his heels.

"Be careful!" Tarin shouted as the mighty horse thundered across the wooden bridge over Callyberry Creek.

Cumac didn't answer but waved his arm overhead to tell Tarin that he had heard him.

Tarin turned and went back into the inn. Gabha had readied himself for whatever was threatening his inn, a stained and scarred thick leather jerkin covering his torso, a mighty hammer clutched in his huge hand, his salt-and-pepper hair held back off his forehead with a leather strap.

"What is it? Did you find out?" he asked, his words harsh and clipped, his eyes hard and jet black.

Tarin shook his head. "Not yet. Cumac has ridden out to see what he can. I don't think, however, that whatever is coming is a small force. There is something disturbing in the air. I sense it."

"Good enough for me," Sirona said, stepping off the bottom step and buckling a wide leather belt festooned with daggers around her waist. She drew her sword and held it loosely in her hand. Lights glimmered along its curved blade.

Behind her came the elves, running down the stairs ahead of Seanchan and Fedelm.

"Make ready!" Seanchan snapped. "Warn the rest of the villagers! A mighty force is coming and every man will be needed!"

"As will every woman," Cairin said. She held the infant in her arms. "I shall take care of the babe for you. We have a hiding place deep within the earth out behind the inn. I shall take him there and wait for you. He'll be safe there."

"The tinker!" Bern said suddenly. "Is he still in the cellar?"

Sirona strode quickly to the cellar door and flung it wide. She disappeared into the cellar's depths and just as quickly returned.

"Gone," she said, her lips narrowing into a thin line. "And the door was still locked."

"It seems that a Grayshawl has been making mischief," Seanchan said harshly. He glanced at the baby in Cairin's arms. His face cleared. "And I don't think they are really coming after us."

"The baby?" Tarin asked with misgiving.

Seanchan nodded. "Yes. I'm afraid our tinker has managed to let others know that the baby is here. That may be why a large force is coming. Otherwise, I think Maliman would have sent another patrol to ambush us as we travel, not an army. There is no need for an army for just us."

Cumac stepped through the doorway, his face grim. "And it is an army that is coming and coming fairly fast. Hobgoblins, goblins, Truacs, and Deag-duls led by the Black Riders."

"Nightshades," Sirona breathed. She looked at the others with hard eyes. "And all in daylight. Even those who ride only at night. Great magic is at work. It looks as if our work is cut out for us."

She grinned but it was a grin that no one wanted to wake up to.

"Well, do you want to live forever?" she asked the Seekers, rolling her shoulders to loosen them.

"A little longer would be preferred," Lorgas said, swinging his battle-ax slowly around his head in a wide arc.

"Bern! Go throughout the village and get everyone down to the creek! Now!" Seanchan ordered, his eyes blazing. "Tell them to bring whatever they have for weapons! I do not think we have much time! Tell them to bring wagons and whatever they can to make barricades. We have the advantage of having the creek between us and Maliman's army."

"We don't have much time," Cumac said grimly. "Maybe an hour, two at the most, to make ready. And I think we are going to have a hard time of it. These are farmers, not warriors. How are we going to keep them from running when the dark force attacks?"

"Tarin, you and Sirona take the bridge. We need to hold that at all costs. We'll barricade that as best we can. Gabha"—Seanchan turned to the innkeeper—"give them seven of the best fighters you have in the village. Lead them yourself."

"You stay, Bern. I'll take care of the village. They'll listen better to me than a stranger." He left, mumbling darkly to himself, his shoulders twitching with thoughts of the coming battle.

"Bern. Lorgas. Take the middle of the barricade. Cumac, you go with them. Fedelm, you pick your own place for your arrows."

"I don't know how they found us so quickly," Fedelm said, checking her bow and quiver of green-fletched arrows. An ancient Ogham had been burnt into the front of the quiver: *querfele*—I Am Ever Full. Silver crescents ran down the length of her bow.

"As I said: I don't think that they are searching for us," Seanchan said slowly, his eyes closed, concentrating. "I don't sense that."

"Then what?" Cumac asked.

"The baby," Seanchan said. "I believe they are searching for the baby. If he is allowed to live he is destined to unite Erin, remember? That would not be in Maliman's best interest."

"Then he'll have a hard time getting to the little fellow," Lorgas growled.

He took his ax from his belt and stalked from the room.

Sirona laughed. "I would hate to be the one to come within reach of his ax this day," she said.

"It matters little if we cannot hold," Seanchan said, and led the others from the inn.

The villagers' faces shone with sweat and fear as they heaved wagons on their sides, forming a barrier that ran the width of the village along the creek. Wood stakes were rammed into the ground beside the wagons to prevent them from being tipped over. The women were hastily filling buckets with water and carrying them into the village as a precaution against fire being launched onto the huts.

Tarin eyed the weapons the villagers had brought with them and shook his head despairingly. There were swords, but many of them were rusty from disuse. Hoes and scythes and axes bristled here and there in clumps. But there were a number of bows and quivers and for that he was grateful.

"Keep the barricade close to the water!" he ordered. "Don't let them get a foot on the ground where they can launch an attack. Make them come through the water! It will slow them down and give our archers better targets!"

Obediently the people pushed some wagons closer to the water before staking them down.

"Look at them," Cumac said softly. "It won't take much to make them cut and run."

"You might be surprised," Seanchan answered. "Fighting for one's home sometimes brings courage when all else fades. They are fighting for their homes. That brings out the best in men. And they know what will happen to their families if they lose. No, I don't think we have to worry much on the villagers holding once battle begins. It is the time *before* battle that we must watch. That is the time when imagination runs wild and men lose their common sense and fear takes over."

Bern and Lorgas began to direct the villagers in setting up the barricade by the bridge. Five people, three bearing bows and arrows, began to ready themselves beside the elves. The innkeeper placed himself there as well.

"Oil," Tarin said softly. "We need to spread oil on the bridge. If the battle begins to turn against us here—at the weakest point—we can fire the bridge and make it useless to them."

The innkeeper grunted and placed his hammer carefully against a wagon and slapped the two men without bows and arrows on the shoulder.

"Come! Help me! I have barrels of oil in my cellar. Two should be enough!"

The men willingly followed the innkeeper into his inn. A few minutes later, the two men appeared, struggling to carry a barrel between them. The innkeeper carried another easily. They slipped through a gap in the barricade and Gabha returned for his hammer, smashing the lids of the barrels with two quick blows. The men rolled the barrels back and forth across the bridge, coating it.

Then, they waited. All that could be done had been done. No sound was heard except for a distant rumbling in the distance over the bridge. The rumbling grew closer and closer and then the flags of the army began to appear, each bearing a crimson background upon which various figures appeared—bear heads, black horses, dragons spewing black fire, werewolves—and some with black tridents. The army appeared with armed Truacs, goblins and hobgoblins, men with dead eyes, sumaires riding black Memans, and warggads. Deag-duls, their size dwarfing those nearest them, marched in the center of the army. Behind them came the Nightshades riding black steeds of the night. Black shrouds billowed around the Nightshades.

"Vermin of the night," Cumac breathed. "I did not think they could come out in the daytime."

"There is not enough sun to make much difference between night and day. It is like the gloaming when they would be coming awake," Seanchan said, glancing at the lead-gray sky. "*And* the Grayshawls are working their magic to aid them."

He pointed to six figures standing in a group behind the army.

"There must be five hundred . . . *things* here," Tarin said.

"Likely more," Sirona said from beside him. "Enough to go around. Right, Tarin?" She tapped the flat of the blade of her sword impatiently against her palm.

"More than enough," Tarin said solemnly, drawing the rune-blade. "It will be a hard fight to get out of this."

"You worry too much," Sirona said carelessly, her gray eyes flashing. She grinned. "As I said: Do you want to live forever?"

"Like *I* said: A few more years would be nice," Lorgas growled as he passed her.

A great clamor arose from across the creek as the foot soldiers began banging their swords against their shields. Horses stomped impatiently as war cries rose from the men in front.

"Enough," Fedelm said harshly. "If this is to begin, let us start!"

Saying that, she raised her bow and sent a green-fletched arrow over the barricade. It arched slightly then buried itself in the eye socket of a sumaire, who screeched and tumbled backward from his mount.

"Hold your fire until they come!" Tarin snapped as the villagers nocked their arrows.

A mighty roar came from the throats of the foot soldiers, and then bodhrans began beating. Frame drums two feet in diameter and tacked with goatskin on one side. The sound boomed together like a thousand heartbeats.

The foot soldiers began banging their swords against the rims of their shields. Lances and spears thudded against the soggy earth. A guttural cry rose from a thousand throats.

"Man-flesh! Man-flesh!"

Suddenly the army surged forward, mighty howls coming from the foot soldiers as they charged toward the barricades.

"Fire!" Tarin shouted, and arrows flew from the defenders' bows followed by flight after flight of arrows streaming overhead and falling like hail on the army. Truacs and Deag-duls fell. Hobgoblins and goblins fell with barbs lanced into their throats. A sole green-fletched arrow sailed over the heads of the army and lodged in the forehead of a Grayshawl, who screamed and fell, writhing on the ground. The others hastily retreated as another arrow sailed into their midst, narrowly missing another Grayshawl.

Those in the front ranks screeched in pain and rage as the arrows struck them. They fell to the ground and those behind them stumbled and fell. As they rose, another flight of arrows struck. But it was not enough to stop the charge as others leaped over their bodies and continued the charge.

They came to the creek and tried to run across, but the water was hip-high and they were slowed as arrows lodged in their breasts like hedgehog quills. But some managed to cross the creek and come to the barricade only to be cut down by the swords and axes of the defenders.

A band of Truacs broke free and tried to cross the bridge only to be met by archers and the hammer of Gabha and the swords of Sirona and Tarin, who beat them back.

One Truac managed to clamber over the barricade only to be immediately beheaded by a single stroke from Sirona, who laughed wildly as the Truac's head bounced twice on the bridge then fell into the water.

The foot soldiers suddenly retreated beyond the reach of all arrows except those of Fedelm, who repeatedly found targets for her arrows.

Angry howls and screams of rage came from the foot soldiers, who gathered themselves and once again charged the barricade only to be brought up again by the creek water, which slowed their progress and made them helpless victims for those behind the barricade. But this time, archers sent flights of black-shafted arrows ahead of the foot soldiers. One by one, villagers began to fall.

Then the Nightshades and sumaires came around from behind the foot soldiers and charged the barricade across the bridge, their cloaks billowing like black shrouds around them. Some swung black-bladed swords, others battle-axes, still others maces-and-chains. Memans screamed, their red mouths gaping wide.

"Ready yourselves!" Tarin shouted, crouching close to the barricade. Blood dripped from the rune-blade.

Some horses leaped over the barricade and their riders wheeled them to attack the defenders from the rear, their riders' black-shrouded cloaks billowing around them.

Gabha roared and charged toward the riders, his hammer swinging murderously. It smashed the head of two sumaires and their Memans. One tried to cut Gabha's head from his shoulders but Gabha ducked under the sword and crushed the Truac's chest with one swing then broke the back legs of the Meman he was riding. He waded into the small band of riders, swinging the hammer accurately, ducking and dodging, crushing those in front and at either side of him. His eyes gleamed with bloodlust. His hair dripped blood. His feet sank like fence posts in the mire as he steadied himself and slew two sumaires.

Sirona screamed and ran after him, her long red hair flowing like flame behind her. She darted and leaped, her sword a shining arc that formed a silver circle around her. Heads fell, bowels dropped from bodies.

A few of the Nightshades managed to ride around Sirona and Gabha and came toward the barricade only to be met by Tarin and his rune-blade, which sang a killing song. One Nightshade tried to ride him down but Tarin stepped aside and leaped to the back of the horse, his dagger sweeping across the Nightshade's neck, beheading him. He dropped from the Nightshade's horse as it leaped back over the barricade and galloped across the bridge, the headless Nightshade still astride.

Some of the Truacs and goblins made it to the barricade and clambered over it only to be met by Bern and Lorgas roaring their battle cries and charging from the side. Bern's sword became a blur as he brought it again and again against the Truacs' swords while Lorgas ducked and hacked legs and heads from the Truacs and goblins.

The villagers met those coming over the barricade, chopping with scythes and swords. Blood ran across the ground, saturating the earth. Again and again those Truacs and goblins not slain by archers came over the barricades until small groups of villagers fought desperately, trying to drive them back.

Nuad and Fergma, the wolfhounds, howled and leaped upon the attackers, ripping throats open with their massive jaws. Blood spattered their hair and gobbets of meat dropped from their jaws. Desperately the enemy tried to slay the wolfhounds but they slipped magically away without harm.

A ram's horn sounded and the enemy again retreated, screeching in frustration.

Sirona bent, resting her hands on her knees, panting, as she studied the carnage.

Many villagers lay on the ground, some dead, others wounded. A quarter of the defenders were lost.

She shook her head.

"Another charge might finish us," she gasped.

"They won't come for a while," Seanchan said, leaning heavily on his staff. A sword gleamed bloodily in his hand, his robes were spotted with blood, as was his beard. "We have time to rest and ready ourselves."

"With what?" Cumac said, coming up. He was covered in blood. Caladbolg seemed to pulse in his hand, its blade wet with blood. "Our archers are running out of arrows and we have lost many brave men."

"I say we fire the bridge," Lorgas growled. "That will stop them here. Tarin, Sirona, and Gabha might be able to hold them here with a few archers if those foul creatures don't have a bridge to cross. They'll have to come across the water too."

"Wait until they begin to come across the bridge then fire it. Might as well take some of them with fire," Tarin said.

"Fire." Cumac turned to Seanchan. "Can you use cairnfire?"

Seanchan shook his head. "No. There are too many Grayshawls blocking it. *And* even if I could to use it the result may disrupt the flow of time, which can result in anything happening. It may give Maliman the opportunity to fill the emptiness with his will. I would not use it in a situation such as this. One has to be careful with its use."

"Then," Tarin said quietly, "I fear we are lost. Perhaps it would be best if we cut our losses and ran."

"And leave us to our own?" Gabha demanded. "Alone we have no chance at all. Not at all."

"What do you say, Fedelm?"

The woman from the Sidhe took a moment before answering, then said, "I do not think we can withstand another charge. If we do, the second one will certainly take us. Cairnfire?" She shook her head. "No, I agree with Seanchan. Our deaths would be better than chancing cairnfire against so many."

"You have used it before," Bern said.

"Yes, but that was in the Otherworld, where time is a bit different," Seanchan said, referring to the time he had used it to free them from the Ervalian Throne Room and the Deep when the Seekers were hard-pressed to escape after they encountered Maliman in disguise. "There are too many here to chance it. To use it against them"—he nodded toward the enemy force—"would be to create too many voids in time."

Tarin sighed, wiping his face. "Then we have a quandary. There is little choice left for us."

"Perhaps," Seanchan said thoughtfully. "There *might* be something that I will be able to do. We shall have to see.

"Here they come again!"

The Seekers hurried back to their positions, readying themselves.

The archers again took their toll on the army sweeping toward them. Scores fell from the arrows. The creek became full with bodies and the waters ran red. But there were too many and the dark forces managed to sweep over the barricade.

Tarin was surrounded by three Truacs but the wolfhounds leaped to his aid, each bearing one to the ground and tearing at its throat.

Desperately the villagers and Seekers banded together, fighting furiously to stem the tide that threatened to flow over them. Now they fought more automatically, their swords streaming with blood, their arms aching. But slowly, the enemy began to whittle down the defenders.

Lorgas split the helm of a hobgoblin and his ax lodged in its skull, nearly tearing it from Lorgas's hands as the hobgoblin fell in

the mud. Lorgas swung again and again and then the villagers ral-
lied and slowly began beating the enemy to the barricade. Three
goblins broke from the left and charged Seanchan only to be met
by Sirona leaping in front of them, beheading one and gutting another. A green-fletched arrow lodged in the throat of the third.

Two others came at her, swinging their swords. She met them
with surprising speed, blocking the first and second blows then beheading both and stabbing a third in the belly as he tried to attack
her from the side.

Fire arrows swept overhead. One landed on a thatch-roofed
house, but women quickly pushed a cart to the side of the house
and stood on it to douse the fire that flickered despite the rain.
Some of the arrows struck the barricade but the wood was too wet
to catch and the arrows sizzled and went out.

And then the *riastradh*, the warp-spasm, came over Cumac and
he twisted in fury as his muscles knotted and bulged. His mouth
opened and a battle roar came forth that froze the attackers in their
tracks for a moment. One of Cumac's eyes bulged out of his head
while another slipped to the size of a needle's eye. The hero-halo
erupted above his head and each strand of hair stood out like a nail
tipped with blood.

He charged into the mass, Caladbolg screaming its warrior song
as it bit through three Truacs at once. Then arms and hands and
heads began to leap from its blade as Cumac roared again and became a fighting frenzy.

The enemy force hesitated, then began to buckle.

Thunder boomed and lightning cracked.

And then a thunderous boom sounded, causing all to pause.

Red Warriors, led by a huge horseman dressed in red armor,
swinging a sword that four men could not lift, rode forth down
from the cloudy darkness, their swords and battle-axes gleaming,
their horses snorting fire.

"The Dearg Laochs!" Cumac shouted, and renewed his attack,
Caladbolg singing a murderous song as it sliced into sumaire and
goblin flesh. Blood spattered and filled the air with a fine mist as
he hewed his way through the attackers. Bits of flesh fell, heads

rolled in blood-soaked mire. A huge hobgoblin leaped to attack Cumac only to have his blow blocked with such force that his arm went numb just seconds before it flew from his body. A goblin raised his sword high to cut Cumac down but a searing pain stabbed into his belly as Cumac buried Caladbolg hilt-deep in the goblin's stomach.

Then the Red Warriors from Teach Duinn, the House of Donn, the King of the Dead, rode down in fury upon the enemy.

Red lightning flashed from their swords as they hacked their way through the enemy, driving them back amid screams of terror and pain. The Nightshades and sumaires wheeled their horses to gallop away from the barricade but the horses of the Red Warriors leaped over the barricade. Their hooves lightly touched the surface of the water as they raced after the Nightshades and sumaires.

The battle began to turn and the villagers and Seekers drove the enemy back to the barricade and then over it. A few Nightshades tried to cross the bridge to flank the defenders, but Seanchan's staff crackled and streams of fire laced the bridge, sending it into flame that quickly swept the black figures as they tried to turn away.

Black lightning crackled around the Dearg Laochs from the Grayshawls who desperately tried to drive the Red Warriors back, but the bolts of lightning bounced from the Red Warriors' shields and laced their way through the dark forces, killing them in bursts.

Shrieks of pain and fear sounded as the dark army turned and took to its heels, the footmen sprinting away, throwing away their armor, shields, and weapons as they tried to lighten themselves. But the Red Warriors rode them down, their horses' hooves stamping them into jelly, the Red Warriors' swords halving them.

The red horses screamed as they seized Truacs and goblins and hobgoblins with their teeth, shaking them once, then throwing the lifeless bodies from them.

A huge sumaire in black armor managed to weave his way through the Red Warriors and came again against the barricade. He leaped his Meman over the wall and began laying about him with his black sword.

Then Tarin leaped to front him, ducking again under the murderous swing, cutting the legs from the Meman with his rune-blade.

The sumaire tumbled over the head of his Meman as it fell forward. He tumbled over and came to his feet, swinging his two-handed sword.

Tarin came in to meet him, blocking blow after blow, the rune-blade dancing a weave of death as he drove the sumaire back. Helplessly, the sumaire tried to stop Tarin. The sumaire's left arm suddenly dropped from his trunk and black blood spurted high into the air. He shrieked from pain and renewed his attack, trying to drive Tarin back, but the Deathwhisper was already inside his guard and the rune-blade sang viciously as Tarin swung it in the Lightning Feat, cutting the sumaire in twain.

And then the battle was over and the defenders stood, panting, in their tracks, some dropping to their knees and gasping, as the Red Warriors halted their charge and rode slowly back to the barricade.

"We thank you and your lord," Seanchan said, bowing to the leader.

The Dearg Laoch nodded and leaned over his saddle, ripping a tunic from a Truac and using it to wipe his blade clean before sheathing it. His mount danced restlessly but was held firmly in place by its reins.

"You are welcome. I am Balfur," the Red Warrior said. His voice rasped like steel over a file. "Donn sends his greetings." He leaned over his saddle, his words meant for Seanchan's ears alone. "Is the Ard-ri safe?"

"He is," Seanchan said.

Balfur nodded in satisfaction. "That is good. But you cannot stay here. You must leave as soon as possible before Maliman can raise another force and throw it against this village."

"I understand," Seanchan said.

"Stay the night to rest but when the sun first comes, be on your way. I do not know how much time remains before Maliman sends others against you. If you are gone, this village will be spared."

"And the Ard-ri?" Seanchan asked.

"That you will have to decide. But if he is not with you, Maliman will not find him. With you, all Maliman has to do is search for you. And then the child will be lost. It was good that you found him and saved him from the Grayshawl, but now you must leave the child and shake the dust of this village from your heels," Balfur said.

"So it shall be," Seanchan said, bowing his head again.

Balfur nodded and wheeled his horse. He raised his sword above his head and the other Red Warriors followed him as he galloped from the earth again into the darkness of the clouds and disappeared.

"They certainly did not wear out their welcome," Lorgas observed, cleaning his ax head.

"No," Seanchan said. "But we and this village would have been finished without them. And you, Cumac," he added as the youth came up to him, panting, his face pale, perspiration dripping from him as the warp-spasm left him. He dropped to one knee, hanging his head. His hands trembled and he nearly dropped his sword.

"Are you all right?" Fedelm asked anxiously.

Weakly he nodded. "I am cold."

"That is the warp-spasm," Seanchan said. He crossed to Cumac and laid a hand on top of his head and closed his eyes, murmuring softly.

Cumac drew a deep shuddering breath as Seanchan removed his hand. He rose and stood shakily for a moment, then nodded his thanks to Seanchan.

"Better?" the Druid asked.

"Much," Cumac said. "But I still feel weak."

Fedelm took his arm and placed her other hand around his shoulder, steadying him.

"That will soon pass," Seanchan said. "But you must be careful about using the warp-spasm. Too much use will weaken you to where I will not be able to help you. It will burn you out. I think I have told you this before."

"Yes. But sometimes it just seems to happen without me willing it," Cumac said.

"And that is its danger," Seanchan said. "Your father also could not control it and that aged him each time he used it."

"I'll try harder," Cumac promised.

"And now," Gabha said, coming up to the Seekers, "let us repair to my inn. I have a barrel of mead that has been aging for three years and waiting for a time such as this to be opened."

"And salt pork?" Lorgas asked anxiously.

"And salt pork," Gabha said, laughing. "And before the day is finished, there will be fresh bread and venison turned on a spit."

He looked at the wolfhounds. "And there will be plenty for you as well. You have earned it as well as the others."

The wolfhounds sat on their haunches, tongues lolling.

Lorgas rubbed his hands together with relish, beaming at Gabha's offer.

"Then, since I don't wish to give offense, let us retire to your inn."

"And rest," Bern said wearily. "Although I too will welcome a mug or two of mead and food."

"As will the rest of us," Seanchan said.

"And a rest?" Lorgas asked hopefully.

"We leave tomorrow," Seanchan said firmly. "At first light."

"Then we have no time to lose," Lorgas said, hastening toward the inn.

The others laughed and followed him into the inn and the merriment that comes after warriors are victorious.

10

"Oh, my head!" Lorgas complained, pressing his palms against his temples and rocking to and fro. "My mouth tastes like a Meman galloped through it."

"You drank enough," Bern said, although his head too was pounding.

The Seekers were gathered in the front room. Dirty dishes cluttered the tables. Cold venison lay on platters, grease congealed around them. The floor was sticky from spilled mead but sometime during the night the Seekers' weapons had been cleaned, as had their clothes, although that made little difference to the elves.

"Tarin and Cumac are making the horses ready," Seanchan said, finishing a mug of tea. "And first light is showing. It is time we leave."

Fedelm nodded and rose, readying her pack. The elves sighed and began fumbling with their packs reluctantly.

"I don't see why we can't stay the day," Lorgas complained. "My bones feel like they've been trampled."

"As do mine," Bern admitted.

"We will stop at the gloaming," Seanchan said firmly, rising. "We do not dare stay here any longer lest we bring Maliman's forces against the village again."

Cairin came forward, bearing the infant. Her face was somber as she started to hand it to Fedelm.

"I shall miss him," she said regretfully. "He is a good baby."

"And would make a good son," Gabha said roughly.

Seanchan looked at Fedelm and nodded.

"These would be good people to raise him, don't you think?" he asked.

For a moment Fedelm hesitated, then handed the baby back to Cairin. An ache appeared in her heart. She had not had the infant for long but it had been long enough to waken the mother within her.

"Our road is treacherous and he will be better off with you. Raise him carefully and wisely. Teach him everything you know. And what the others in this village know."

Cairin and Gabha beamed as Cairin took back the infant and looked gratefully at Fedelm.

"We shall raise him as we did our others," Cairin said firmly. "He will want for nothing that we can give."

Seanchan nodded and opened the child's blanket to reveal the amethyst. He touched it with a forefinger, closed his eyes, and muttered to himself. Then he opened his eyes and said, "Hide this and keep it safe until he comes to manhood. Then give it to him. He will know what to do with it at the time."

Gabha frowned slightly at Seanchan. "This is not just a baby, then, is he?"

Seanchan smiled. "For now, he is. And that is all that is important. Protect him, Gabha. Keep him from harm."

"Nothing will happen to him while I live," Gabha said quietly. He flexed his hands and the muscles bunched along his arms and shoulders and Seanchan knew that he and Cairin would follow what he told them.

"And do not tell others from whence he came," Seanchan added. "Especially the rest of the villagers, for tongues will be wagging after this battle when the ale and beer flows too greatly. *And*," he emphasized. "Do not let travelers see him if at all possible. You do not know who they may be."

"We will," Cairin and Gabha chorused.

"Come," Tarin said roughly. "If we're going, let us go. The sooner we get on the road the farther away we will be when the gloaming sets."

"Yes," Seanchan said.

He bade the couple farewell and led Tarin and Fedelm outside to where Cumac and Tarin stood with their horses. Black stamped his feet impatiently as if he knew there was distance to be traveled before night fell.

Seanchan's eyebrows rose quickly as he saw Sirona sitting easily on a chestnut gelding, a pack tied behind her, her sword showing above one shoulder.

"I've decided to go with you," she said, laughing gaily. "If you do not mind." She eyed Tarin and he blushed deeply to the roots of his black hair.

"I have no objection if the others do not," Seanchan said. "Your sword will be welcome."

The others glanced at each other and nodded.

"Then ride with us," he said, mounting his horse.

The wolfhounds, their coats gleaming from a scrubbing by Cairin, took the lead, trotting in front of Seanchan. The others fell behind them, Sirona falling in place beside Tarin as they followed

Seanchan through the village and out onto the road leading south-west toward Munster and Cairpre's court.

THEY rode in silence, adjusting to the step and sway of their horses. The rain halted but the sky stayed dark and overcast and a cold wind blew from the south. The brome looked damp and gray, no green to the stalks. The sedge along the various ponds they passed looked sodden brown and the road was slick with wet clay. The trees still had no leaves upon them and appeared dead, with long black limbs reaching toward the sky.

The horses moved along the trail, heads hanging low except for Black, who tossed his head and shook his mane as he continued to look left and right of the trail. The wolfhounds patrolled around the party, one going in a right circle, the other in a left so at all times one covered what the other left. Their riders huddled within sodden cloaks, Tarin and Sirona sniffling from the cold and trying to warm their hands by blowing on them and slipping them beneath their tunics to warm them against their stomachs.

A raven landed on one branch and looked beady-eyed at them until Seanchan reined in and sat, silently watching the bird until it shook its feathers and rose and winged its way to the north.

A wolf started to parallel their travel but suddenly ran away as the wolfhound Fergma went out to meet him.

They entered some woods and traveled more slowly as the road twisted and turned and narrowed between the trees. A deeper chill hovered in the forest and the only sound heard was the sucking sound of the horses' hooves as they lifted them from the muck. There was ancient wisdom in these woods and a foul force seemed to try and pull them deeper into the woods. But Seanchan held a steady pace and the force soon disappeared like a disgruntled prayer.

A man in a red shirt appeared and slipped through the woods, appearing and disappearing. For a moment he was there and the next moment he was not. But he made the Seekers uneasy and they automatically gripped knives inside their cloaks, feeling the security of their weapons and becoming more comfortable if watchful as they rode.

Night came quickly upon them in the forest although not fast enough for the two elves, who complained constantly how their horses were stomping over the road leading from Callyberry, making their heads pound. The others ignored them except for once when Tarin told them he had little sympathy for them for the amount of drink they had taken. This drew a glare from Bern's bloodshot eyes but he said nothing and sank into grumpy silence.

"I hope we don't have to make a cold camp tonight," Tarin said. "I feel rain may fall."

"We'll go on a little farther," Seanchan said. "I'm certain that we will find an inn shortly. Although," he added, "we'd better be on our guard. I have had a bad feeling ever since we crossed Munster's borders."

Cumac glanced at the Dragonstone pinned to his cloak at the shoulder and again at Fedelm's belt. Both retained their color.

"Perhaps you are whistling in the night," Cumac said. "I see no danger. At least, not at the moment," he amended.

"That doesn't mean it isn't there," Seanchan said, annoyed. "Not all evil is foretellable. Sometimes evil slumbers only to be awakened when the opportunity is ripe. I have a feeling that may be what I am sensing although I cannot make it out."

"A light!" Sirona sang out cheerfully. "Straight ahead. Perhaps the gods are smiling on us now. With luck, it may be an inn. Or a house with a stable we might use for a silver piece."

The Seekers quickened their pace and soon they halted before an inn with a faded sign reading THE ROSE AND THISTLE. The rose was a vague outline and the thistle had long disappeared. The door was weathered gray and cracked down the center plank, hanging in its frame with old leather straps. The windows were so grimed that the light shining through them appeared a weak orange glow. The thatch roof was badly in need of new sheaves. Pigeons nested beneath the eaves. A few stones had tumbled from the top of the chimney and lay carelessly in a rubble around the foundation.

Rats scurried along the outside of the walls, staying under the eaves that swung down close to the windows.

"I don't like the look of this place," Cumac said lowly.

"Any place in storm or night," Tarin said. "But I do agree. I too do not like the look of this place. It has a feel of . . . malice about it. Something sleeping but ready to awake."

"There are others inside," Fedelm observed.

"I can hear them," Tarin said. "But there is something wrong. That I know."

"Be cautious," Seanchan said, dismounting. "And stay together. One always near another. It may be nothing but the look of the place that is making us uneasy. And looks can be deceiving. There is nothing wrong with being cautious while giving someone the benefit of doubt."

They entered the inn and paused. A gray smoky pall hung over the room from the fireplace that drew badly. The tables were stained from gravy and beer and ale spills and gray from careless scrubbings that appeared to have come later and later as time passed.

The men sitting around the tables were shabbily dressed and all talk ceased as the Seekers came through the door and fanned out on either side. Feral heads swung to regard them and study them. No one smiled a welcome or bade them to warm themselves beside the fire. A smell of meat just turned came to them, causing Lorgas and Bern to wrinkle their noses in disgust. The floor was hard-packed earth with dark stains from long-dried puddles scattered on its surface. Somewhere the Seekers heard water dripping.

A shunted staircase stood at the far end of the room and the Seekers could see the steps were cracked and worn, one missing. A wooden and scarred bar ran the length of one end of the room. Dusty bottles stood on a shelf, slanting toward the floor, behind the bar. Two old oak kegs had been placed in the center of the bar with empty wooden mugs banded in iron stacked beside them. A fire flickered, sending cheery warmth out into the room but it seemed false and artificial, unable to drive the earthy chill from a fresh-opened grave that lingered in the room. The silence rested heavily upon the Seekers.

"Innkeeper!" Seanchan said loudly.

A burly man with a large paunch covered by a stained gray apron spotted with grease and what appeared to be blood stepped away from a small group of men at the far corner of the room near the fireplace. He wiped his hands, surprisingly small with the knuckles disappearing into the pudge.

"What do you want?" he asked rudely.

His rudeness caused Tarin to stiffen and he stepped forward, muttering darkly, his hand going to the haft of the rune-blade canted over his right shoulder. But Seanchan placed his hand upon Tarin's shoulder, halting him. Sirona stepped up beside him, her hand fiddling with the dagger at her waist, her face darkening, lips curving into a dangerous grin.

"Hospitality," Seanchan said. "That which should be given without surliness."

The innkeeper glanced around the room at the others, who were silently watching. He smirked and said, "Hospitality, eh? All right. What is your pleasure?"

"Shelter and food," Seanchan said. He glanced at Fedelm's belt, which glowed a soft emerald green and Cumac's Dragonstone, which gleamed black agate on his shoulder. He straightened, his hand tightening around his staff.

"I have two rooms left," the innkeeper said. "You'll have to make do with them. Which means"—he leered at Sirona and Fedelm—"you'll have to share, dearies. With some of the men."

Sirona regarded him coolly. "What I share is none of your business, innkeeper. Keep your teeth together or lose them."

The innkeeper's eyes went cold and he wiped his hands again on his apron. "Well, that's how it is and such. Food can be had. As can ale. Don't have nothin' else. You'll have to make do with that or go hungry and thirsty."

"We'll manage," Cumac said.

"And well," Lorgas growled, lifting his ax meaningfully.

The innkeeper laughed at this and waved contemptuously at a table in front of the fire.

"Then take a seat. You there," he said to four men sitting at the table, "take another place. These folk are fair drenched and likely chilled. You've spent enough time there to warm your innards."

Obligingly the four rose and silently took their places at other tables, their eyes constantly fixed on the Seekers.

"I'll bring what I got. Which is all anyone could do. Mind you it ain't food for kings and such."

He disappeared through a doorway behind the bar as the Seekers warily took their places in front of the fire. Small tendrils of steam rose from their clothes. Cumac and Bern rubbed their hands together vigorously, working the stiffness from them. Lorgas rested the head of his ax meaningfully on the floor while Tarin and Sirona eased their swords up and down, loosening them in their sheaths.

The innkeeper appeared, carrying a trencher with a cold leg of mutton on it. He plopped it down in the center of the table. He went to the bar and took seven wooden platters and dropped them carelessly on the table along with knives and two-pronged iron forks.

The Seekers looked with distaste at the dirty platters and the mutton lying in a puddle of cold grease on the trencher. The innkeeper went back to the bar and returned with mugs of ale. Then he went back to the group he had stepped from when the Seekers first entered the inn.

"Think maybe that innkeeper needs a lesson in manners," Lorgas growled. He looked at the mutton and grimaced. "If I wasn't so hungry I'd stuff that mutton down his throat."

He took a knife and cut the mutton into slices, placing a piece on each plate.

Cumac took a taste of the ale and grimaced. "This tastes like dirty water."

"Indeed," Seanchan murmured, taking a swallow. "This is an evilly run place. I have no doubt about that."

"Your Dragonstone," Tarin said to Cumac.

The others glanced at the Dragonstone and back to those in the room. A large man stared at them, his black eyes glittering. For a moment the Seekers thought they saw his face slip, revealing a dark evil, but then his face cleared and what they thought they had seen was again covered.

"Pah!" Lorgas said, spitting the piece of mutton he had stuffed in his mouth into the fire where it sizzled and turned black. "As foul as fish from a black mere."

He glowered at the innkeeper, who smiled at him.

"If this is the best meat in the inn then I say we would fare better with the dried venison in our packs."

Seanchan frowned and took a small bite and immediately spat it out.

"Leave it!" he ordered the others sharply.

He rose and put his back to the fire, raising his staff slightly. His face was stone with fury.

"Man-flesh," he said harshly.

The Seekers leaped to their feet, drawing their weapons and facing the room.

The innkeeper laughed and the others rose from their chairs, the masks covering their faces slipping, their bodies changing, becoming large, and their lips pulling back from their teeth, revealing long fangs and sharp teeth with filed points.

"Sumaires and warggads!" Sirona yelled.

"The night of the full moon," Seanchan said, bringing his staff to bear.

A manic laugh filled the room as the vampires and werewolves launched themselves at the Seekers, foam appearing at the corners of their mouths, loud howls filling the room.

Grimly the Seekers fought to keep their backs to the fire so they would not be surrounded. Tarin attacked with the Lightning Feat, splitting a sumaire open. Sirona went through the Thunder Feat, gutting the innkeeper, who gave an unholy shriek and fell to the floor, trying to push his intestines back into his body. Heads flew from hairy trunks as Lorgas and Bern hacked away at those trying to press them against the fire.

One sumaire snarled and leaped toward Fedelm only to find himself on the floor with a wolfhound's fangs sunk deeply into his throat. The other wolfhound launched himself at a warggad, ripping his throat open before continuing on to a sumaire. He grabbed the sumaire by the leg and gave a savage shake of his head, the bone snapping loudly. The sumaire howled and fell to the floor, writhing in pain.

Cumac danced in and out of the sumaires and warggads, Caladbolg a blur in his hand, a bright rainbow springing from its blade. The rune-blade sang in Tarin's hands, cutting off arms and heads, while Sirona's curved blade whirled in her hands, slicing into rotten flesh.

A mist rose in the center of the room and a face appeared, floating above the floor. Anthracite eyes gleamed malevolently. A carefully trimmed black beard covered lean jaws, and long black hair fell to the nape. He smiled and pearl-white teeth gleamed.

"Maliman!" Seanchan shouted.

A fire blazed from the end of his staff, piercing the head. A bellow came from the thin lips and the face disappeared.

Again, fire burst from Seanchan's staff, and shrieks filled the room so loud that they hurt the ears. The sumaires and warggads burst into flame and crisping bodies fell to the floor, writhing in agony.

Then, the inn was quiet and filled with a foul stench that rose from the blackened bodies.

Lorgas kicked one and it fell apart into ash.

"Maliman's minions!" He spat and rubbed his lips vigorously with the back of his hand. "I say we leave this place. Better to sleep under a tree than here."

"No," Seanchan said slowly. "We will stay here but we will mount a watch. These sumaires and warggads cannot be the only ones in this forest. Where two are there is another and we cannot sap our strength fighting them through the night. Far better to board the doors and windows and wait till morning."

And so the Seekers sealed the inn from the inside and mounted a watch throughout the night although their bellies rumbled with hunger and their parched throats wettened slightly with tiny sips from the water bottles they carried.

Dawn came cheerfully and when the sun came up above the trees, the Seekers mounted and left, quickening their pace down the road that wound through the trees, hurrying to leave the forest and its loathsome creatures far behind.

11

On the second day they emerged from the dark woods into a bright and sunny spring day. Flakes of frost still clung to leaves of grass and the day was still cool enough that the Seekers kept their cloaks wrapped around them. But Seanchan still didn't stop, electing to continue on well into the night to place as much distance from the woods as possible before halting.

Wearily Lorgas and Bern made a fire from a pile of dried dung and the Seekers fell gratefully into their blankets after a meager supper. Sirona and Tarin took the first watch. Both fought to keep their eyes open. Overhead the stars shone brightly, the moon looking as if one could reach up and pluck it from the sky. Tiny rustlings came from the grass around them as mice foraged. A lone wolf came near the fire but quickly disappeared when the wolfhounds growled a warning.

"I would think the wolfhounds would be good enough sentries," Sirona muttered, yawning.

"Maybe. But why chance it? All that is lost is a little sleep," Tarin answered.

Sirona nodded and fell silent for a moment before speaking.

"What causes you to be with them?" She nodded at the sleeping others.

Tarin remained quiet before answering. "I guess it's because I feel I belong here. The life of a Sword-wanderer is a lonely one. Geld-lords are hard to find nowadays and for me even harder. My reputation precedes me wherever I go," he said wryly.

"I have heard stories," she admitted. "Tell me, though: are they true?"

Tarin sighed and rubbed the heels of his hands under his eyes. "Does it really matter?"

She shook her head. "I suppose not. Even if it were not others would still believe the stories rather than the truth. It is the nature of man to prefer stories to the truth. Mankind relishes the flamboyance of lies rather than the dull truth."

Tarin remained silent for a long time, then said, "There is always some truth to the stories. That makes them believable or else enough to convince others that they are true. A little truth in stories suggests that all stories are true."

"So what is the truth?" Sirona asked.

"I have never killed a woman in my life," he said. "That much is true."

"Then what—"

"Crom Cruach. And my wife was a firstborn."

Sirona moved uneasily at these words. Crom Cruach was an ancient golden god who made his home on Magslect—the Plain of

Adoration—surrounded by his stone disciples. He was a cannibal who welcomed travelers to his home, then fed them flesh from humans after making them unaware of what they were eating with huge mugs of nut-brown ale. Those who lived near him were required to give him their firstborn each of the feast days: Samain, Imbolc, Beltaine, and Lughnasa. Some travelers he pressed into service until they reached late middle age, when they were slain and butchered. To even mention his name was enough to summon him if a person wasn't careful.

"Then you did not go to the fortress of Ganach."

Tarin shook his head. "No, I did go to his fortress. And I did kill him and his warriors who tried to stop me. But I did not slay any of the women."

"How do you know it was Crom Cruach who came to the fortress after you left?"

Tarin smiled grimly, a haunted smile, and within that smile Sirona could read the anguish that Tarin felt and the hopelessness that had followed him before he joined the Seekers.

"A tinker," Tarin said. "A tinker hid in a well when Crom Cruach attacked the fortress and slew the rest of the men and all of the women. He knew who are the firstborn and he knew about . . . my wife. It was Crom Cruach who placed their heads upon spears, knowing that doing such a thing would make others believe it was me."

"Why?"

"I drove him back into his fortress on Magslect when he tried to raid a village that was left for me to defend."

Sirona's eyebrows shot up in query. "*You* defeated Crom Cruach?"

"No. But I did hold the borders against his forays, leaving him to raid the east and south and north but not the west. That was enough to earn his ire and when I went to Rolfe's fortress to pledge my sword to him, the borders were left free for his anger. And that is when I became 'the Damned' and 'Deathwhisper.' And when I returned to Rolfe's fortress after he sent warriors to slay me in the forest, I found that Deag-duls, led by Crom Cruach, had been there before me and slaughtered everyone. I became a Sword-wanderer because no other chieftain wanted my sword."

An ululating howl came from the darkness and Sirona and Tarin stiffened, sliding their swords from their sheaths and coming to their feet to study the night.

"A wolf?" she asked, straining to peer through the darkness.

"I don't think so," Tarin said. "I think warggads. They are not close, now, but they may find us before morning."

"Should we awaken the others?"

Tarin hesitated, then said, "No. Not yet. We'll listen to them talk and if they get closer then we'll awaken the others."

Another howl slipped through the night and Sirona shivered.

"I do not like this," she said. "Sound is misleading at night."

"If they come, sumaires will come first as their horses, the Me-mans, can scent a trail as well as our wolfhounds. They will lead the warggads to us."

"Perhaps we should move camp," she suggested.

"Now, that is an idea," Tarin said. "We would put more distance between us and them."

"Let us leave it to Seanchan to decide."

Tarin walked to where Seanchan, wrapped in his cloak, slept. He bent and shook the Druid awake.

"Warggads and sumaires have found our trail. At least I *think* they have found our trail. Should we move camp?"

Seanchan rose and shook himself, rubbing his eyes awake. He sent a thought into the night, then nodded.

"Waken the others," he ordered. "We'll travel through the night. Tomorrow near noon we shall come to the inn of Da Derga. There we'll find shelter and rest. It would be foolish for the sumaires and warggads to attack his inn. Unless," he added, "they are a large enough force. He owns two inns, one in the west and the other in north Munster. He is a fierce warrior whose cousin, Balfur, leads the Red Warriors. Da Derga had an enchantment placed around each of his inns that keeps dark forces at bay. If the enchantment fails, Balfur will lead his Red Warriors from the Island of Donn to aid his cousin. Maliman is not stupid. He knows that his armies are not strong enough to attack Da Derga's inns. At least not yet. In time perhaps. But not now."

Tarin and Sirona nodded and quickly moved to the others, shaking them awake, ignoring Lorgas's grousing at being awakened so early. They repeated what Seanchan said and all protest was forgotten as the others hurried to ready themselves and their horses for travel.

"Leave the fire," Seanchan said. "That will give the sumaires and warggads pause as they will be slow in determining if we are sleeping or not."

He whistled and Nuad and Fergma rose and trotted out into the night. Seanchan followed, raising his sorrel to a ground-gaining lope. The others came close upon his heels with Cumac, astride Black, taking the rear. Fergma moved out of the darkness to trot beside Black, occasionally slipping away to check the back trail for followers while Nuad coursed back and forth in front of the party.

The sun had reached its meridian when the Seekers arrived, weary and dusty, at Da Derga's inn. Their horses were nearly done in by the ride throughout the night and morning, and a boy came out to collect them and take them to the stable, where they would be washed and curried and fed before resting.

Black tossed his head, tearing his reins from the boy's hands, then led the way to the stable. Nuad and Fergma sat on their haunches, tongues lolling, in front of the Seekers while the door opened and a jolly, red-faced man came out to greet them, wiping his hands upon a spotless apron that shone whitely in the sun.

"Welcome! Welcome! I am Eogan the innkeeper, the cousin of Da Derga," he cried, beaming at them. "By the looks of you you have come a long way and could use a good washing and dusting and a hearty meal. I have rooms for all of you and a bard to cheer you with a few songs. You'll find no better ale than my nut-brown in all of Erin and fresh venison on the fire along with fruit from my own orchards and vegetables from my garden. Carrots and peas and turnips. Brown gravy is made from fresh mushrooms and wild onions. I have fresh leek soup as well."

"I'll take it all," Lorgas said, stumbling toward the inn door.

"As will the rest of us," Seanchan said. "We have been traveling a long way. And sumaires and warggads are on our back trail."

The smile disappeared from Eogan's face to be replaced with a grim visage.

"Then we shall ready for them. Maliman cannot break our guard, so you are safe here. There is no reason to place your own guard. We are well guarded."

He glanced curiously at Nuad and Fergma.

"Fine wolfhounds," he said. "They are welcome too. I shall make a pallet for them in the hall outside your rooms. Or within a room if you prefer. And I have food for them as well. Meat with gravy. Unless you want something else for them?"

"That will do and thank you," Seanchan said gratefully. "It has been a long ride to here. We rode throughout the night and half-day after leaving the woods and trying to make camp on the plain."

"Banwood?" Eogan turned his head and spat. "That is a foul place indeed. You are lucky to have come through it without harm. I refuse to even burn wood from that place. You never know what you might release from such a foul wood and there are many things that would like to be brought within the enchantment to attack us.

"But," he added, clapping his hands, "let us forget that for a while. Come in! Come in! The fire is built and the inn cozy and warm! Tonight, leave your clothes outside your doors and one of my servants will wash and ready them for your travel."

Obediently the Seekers entered the inn and stood at the entrance to the main room, studying it. The floor was wood and the joints tightly fitted. The floor had been scrubbed as had the chairs and tables until they looked bone white. A sweet scent filled the air from burning sage and rosemary. A walnut and oak bar stood next to a door to the kitchen, from which depths came the smell of roasting venison that made the Seekers' mouths water. Even the fireplace stones had been scrubbed free of ash and smoke, and in a niche beside the fireplace sat a bard playing soft songs on his lap harp.

A few guests sat at the tables with pint mugs, wooden with curious carved figures, foaming from nut-brown ale. Four guests were playing fidchell in fiercely contested games.

"Sit! Sit!" Eogan said, gesturing at the table closest to the fire.

With a sigh, Seanchan took a chair and stretched out his hands to the warmth. The others quickly followed suit. The chairs had been carefully built with slightly slanting slatted backs to make the most comfortable chairs available.

Eogan came to their table, bearing three platters of soda and raisin bread along with pots of honeysuckle honey and fresh butter.

"Now, this might hold you for a bit until I can prepare the rest for you. Soup and such all around?"

A chorus of "ayes" came from the Seekers' throats and Eogan grinned with pleasure and disappeared back into the kitchen.

Lorgas took a deep breath and let it out slowly. He propped his feet on the hearth and wiggled his toes with pleasure.

"About time we found a good place," he said, then straightened and looked anxiously at Seanchan. "This *is* a good place, isn't it?"

Seanchan smiled and nodded. "As I told you: Here we are perfectly safe. We shall rest here for a couple of days before continuing on. Enough time has passed that Bricriu has reached Cairpre's court and is taking advantage of the Laws of Hospitality given by Cairpre. We will have difficulty getting Bricriu to leave there once we arrive. He is not a stupid man and knows that Munster is an enemy of Ulster and the Red Branch. He will feel safe and remain there until Maliman takes him. And there is nothing we can do to force Bricriu from there—unless we are very clever."

"You have seen this?" Cumac asked.

"Yes. Maliman will move against Munster and soon. There will be a great battle and I fear Cairpre doesn't have the army to defeat Maliman. Munster is well off from the rest of the Four Provinces and the people have grown fat and lazy, since Maeve is not building an army to invade Ulster's borders and summons them. Remember: They owe their allegiance to Connacht, Ulster's mightiest enemy."

Cumac remained silent, remembering the stories of his father's prowess. At the age of seventeen, Cucullen had single-handedly defended Ulster from the army of Connacht during the Cattle Raid of Cooley. The men of Ulster were disabled by a curse, so Cucullen prevented Maeve's army from advancing by invoking the right of single combat at the many fords the army had to cross in order to move into Ulster. He defeated champion after champion in a stand-off lasting months. When Fergus was sent to face him he agreed to yield, so long as Fergus agreed to return the compliment the next time they met. Finally, he fought a grueling three-day duel with his best friend and foster brother, Ferdia, at a ford that was named for the battleground.

"I think Maeve might force Munster into honoring our request of Cairpre to give us Bricriu despite the Laws of Hospitality," Cumac said. "She is aware of the danger if Maliman manages to get the Chalice of Fire."

"I don't know," Seanchan said doubtfully.

"I could ride to Connacht and ask Maeve to have Munster honor our request," Tarin said.

"No," Seanchan said. "It would be too dangerous for one to make that journey."

"I could go up the coastal road and avoid Faindell and the rest," Tarin argued. "*And* it will be shorter than going back up the road we have just traveled. I could cut across country and intercept the road. Four, five days at the most and then I could rejoin you."

"I'll go with him," Sirona said. "Two are better than one and have a greater chance of making it through Maliman's men *if* we even encounter them."

"I like the idea," Fedelm said. "I too don't think Maliman has been able to seize the coastal road. At least I don't sense it. It would be good to have Connacht as an ally in this. And I think Maeve is shrewd enough to know that she cannot withstand an invasion by Maliman's forces alone. I think she will begin to raise an army.

"In fact," she continued, "I think all of the provinces know that they should raise armies to fight against Maliman. If one province falls, the others will quickly follow like tumbling blocks."

"I agree as well," Cumac said. "Although I think it should be me who goes."

"No, that's out," Seanchan said. "It is your father's Chalice that we seek. You have the greatest claim upon it if we have to challenge Cairpre. *And* you represent the Otherworld, as do Fedelm and Lorgas and Bern. We need to keep you four together here, as each of you represents most of the Otherworld."

"Then the two of us are the likely choice," Tarin said. "You represent the Duirgeals *and* the Earthworld. As does Cumac in a way."

"That is a long way," Seanchan said. "And your horses are tired."

"Perhaps we can get new ones here," Sirona said. "The better innkeepers usually have good mounts available for emergencies. Perhaps Eogan can supply us with two. Or know of someone who can. We will need light packs as well. Food and water only and that enough for only four days as we will not want to stop and hunt."

Resigned, Seanchan sighed and gave in. "All right. Let us question Eogan. He will have knowledge of how the coastal road runs now and whether there are beings that you need to be wary of."

Sirona and Tarin exchanged glances and gave a brief nod to each other.

"Come back to us whole," Lorgas said gruffly.

"And don't dally," Bern said. "We shall have need of your swords."

"And remember," Seanchan said, "we have a better chance slipping through Maliman's search if we keep a small party. Unfortunately, that makes us extremely vulnerable. But seven is far better than five. Yes, we will have need of you."

"We'll hurry," Tarin promised. "We should be able to rejoin you at least within ten days."

"Meet us at the Pass of Adene. We shall wait no longer than five days for your return. We do not dare tarry too long, for the pass is deadly and the home to hobgoblins and goblins and Swordwanderers," Seanchan said. "But there is an abandoned citadel there which will give us some safety as it is cut into a niche of the west wall. There we shall be safe for a time."

"We'll hurry," Sirona promised. "We'll leave tomorrow."

Seanchan nodded. "I'll speak to Eogan about fresh horses for you. Meanwhile, I suggest you eat and drink then retire for the night. You will need all your strength to travel so quickly."

Tarin and Sirona nodded.

Eogan returned with the promised dishes, beaming as the Seekers dived into the meal and ate with the relish of a starving man. The bard in the corner began to play and sing.

I sing about men of glory
And what made them a story
Of bravery and honor foretold.
One day they rode forth in bold
Pursuit of mad Bricriu who took
The Chalice of Fire. Look!
This means that peace is gone
From the land and strife
Has spread to any life
And has giv'n evil Maliman
A place within our land.
We sing of Cumac the son
Of mighty Cucullen the son
Of Lugh the god of light
Who gives all men the sight
That pierces the evil night.
We sing of wise Seanchan
Who leads the Seeker band
Across the strife-torn land. They
Try to keep the evil at bay.
We sing of Fedelm of the Sidhe
Who brings hope for you and me
We sing of Lorgas of the Ervalians
Who together with his elf friend
Bern brings the skill of the elves
To all the Seekers themselves.
We sing of mighty Tarin
The Deathwhisper who has been
A mighty swordsman for the band
The protecting anchor of the band.
We sing of Sirona whose sword

Is the equal of Tarin's sword.
And this is all of the tiny band
Who seek to bring peace to the land.
Who will ever forget their story
And stalwart feats of glory?
Together they stand
Against evil Maliman . . ."

"Already we seem to have become the songs of bards," Tarin said. He gave a wry lopsided grin. "I hope we don't disappoint them in the end."

"So do I," Cumac said. "But I think it would have been better if they hadn't made this song. It draws too much attention to us."

"I agree," said Seanchan. He took a sip of ale and wiped his mouth with the end of his beard. "But perhaps we will be lucky and this song will not have spread as far as we must travel. Of course in the long run it means little. We have had those adventures that all men wish they could have to become immortal in song and story. All men wish to bathe in glory but only a few are called to perform such feats."

"So what will be the end of the story?" Tarin asked.

"I don't know," Seanchan said. "I simply do not know."

12

When false light began to glow in the east, Tarin and Sirona came down to the common room, where Eogan had breakfast waiting for them. Two large saddlebags had been readied for them with meat jerky that could be eaten without a cook-fire. Fresh bread had been carefully wrapped in clean linen. Winter apples were in the bottom of each bag.

Their clothes had been washed and mended

while they slept and their boots cleaned; the boots gleamed from fresh oil that made them waterproof.

They sat and ate with gusto and Eogan beamed at their appetites.

"Stuff yourselves," he said. "That way you will not have to stop until dark. Two miles up this road you will find an old road forking to the northwest. Take it and ride carefully, for it will weave its way through the Marsan Mountains until it reaches the coast. You may encounter bandits and some Sword-wanderers who have fallen upon bad days. It is also home to goblins and hobgoblins although I haven't heard of anything else 'cept wolves. But it will cut a full day and a half off your journey.

"I have saddled two of my best stallions for you. Bain and Borun, twin chestnuts who can run all day without pause. Their mother was Besfallen, the horse of Anu. They will also defend you while you sleep. There are no better horses in southeast Erin. They will carry you through safely."

"We thank you for your kindness," Tarin said, rising from his breakfast. Sirona followed and silently took the saddlebags out to tie behind the saddles on the horses.

"Your search affects us all," Eogan said gruffly. "I will do what I can for you."

Tarin smiled and gripped Eogan by the shoulder, then went outside. Sirona was already mounted, holding the reins of Tarin's horse, Borun.

Seanchan put a hand upon Borun's neck and said, "Remember: The Pass of Aden within ten days at the most."

The two nodded solemnly. Together, they wheeled and cantered down the road toward the gray and dark brown Marsan Mountains.

They made good time the first day, arriving at the coastal road just as dark fell. They made a dry camp and rolled into their blankets after picketing their horses. When they arose, the sky was clouded over and black thunderheads began to roll in from the sea. Hastily they ate breakfast and saddled their horses but rain began to fall as they swung into their saddles and pointed the horses' noses toward the north.

"Why is it that we always seem to get rain when we need clear days to travel fast?" Sirona asked.

"I don't know," Tarin said. "But I fear that our foes may have learned of our intentions and journey. There were many ears back at the inn and not all may have been friendly. Even though Eogan said the inn was safe, that doesn't mean that one who serves Maliman couldn't have slipped through under disguise. Remember the Grayshawl back at the ford? We took him for a man until he revealed himself. And to complicate things, a Maliman follower could be only a man who has sworn himself to Maliman. No one drew attention to themselves with the exception of the bard. Ah, maybe I'm just whistling in the wind, looking for trouble everywhere."

"I think that is safer than taking peace for granted. Far better that we keep our wits about us and view everything with a jaundiced eye."

"You're right," conceded Tarin. "And now we are on the coastal road, where we must be extra careful despite what Eogan says. We do not know for certain what lies ahead. *And* I am getting a bad feeling. As if we are being watched. I will be glad when we are out of these foothills."

They rode in silence for a long moment, and then Sirona said slowly, "I too feel something but I do not know what. Something."

Her horse moved sideways restlessly and she brought him back under rein.

"Even Bain senses something."

Tarin reined Borun in and Sirona rode a few paces before halting Bain. She turned to look curiously at him.

"What is it?"

He pointed at Borun's ears, pricked forward, and the trembling along Borun's neck muscles as he shook his head.

"Something. I think we may be right," Tarin said lowly. "There is something ahead of us. And I really don't want to ride down that."

He pointed to a narrow rocky gorge through which they had to pass in order to come down out of the foothills and reach the level road.

Sirona turned her head and studied the gorge. Large boulders teetered on the sides of the gorge and lined the way along the road so narrow that they would have to ride single file in places. Alarm moved within her and she shivered. Two ravens suddenly leaped into the air and wheeled away toward the north. No birds sang. The rain let up.

"We have no choice," she said softly. "We do not have enough time to go around. Whatever is there we'll have to chance it. Although I too don't like it. And neither does Bain."

Bain danced sideways back and forth, his head up. Borun followed suit and Tarin and Sirona had a difficult time holding them back.

Sirona laughed and unpinned her cloak, rolling it and securing it behind her saddle. Tarin followed her lead, and together they nudged their horses forward, eyes darting to possible hiding places, the hair on the back of their necks prickling.

Tarin took the lead through the gorge. Shadows from the high walls threw the gorge into a gray light. A quarter way through, a figure leaped from behind a boulder and slammed into him, knocking him off Borun. The stallion squealed, eyes flashing, rearing as another figure darted around from behind another boulder and tried to seize the reins. Borun's hooves crushed his skull.

"Goblins!" Tarin shouted, throwing off the one who had leaped at him. The rune-blade hissed as he drew it from its scabbard and quickly placed his back against the gorge wall.

As he spoke, another figure launched itself through the air, trying to unseat Sirona. She drew her blade in one swift motion and sliced it across the goblin's throat. He screamed, the sound bubbling through black blood that gushed from his throat. His weight carried her off her horse. She leaped to her feet, delivering a back stroke that felled another goblin. Then she ran to put herself at Tarin's side as goblins seemed to pour like foul hail down the sides of the gorge.

Grimly they fought but more and more goblins emerged until

the gorge was crowded with them and Tarin and Sirona found themselves hard-pressed to keep the goblins at bay.

Then their horses screamed and barreled to them, stomping goblins under hoof, bared teeth savagely ripping through goblin flesh. The goblins screamed in pain and fury.

"To horse!" Tarin shouted, and leaped to Borun's back, the rune-blade gleaming blackly with goblin blood.

Sirona followed him, and their horses slammed through the goblins while Tarin and Sirona slashed furiously on either side.

A goblin blade sliced through Tarin's thick leather jerkin. Another glanced off his saddle. Behind him he could hear Sirona's battle cry as she followed him through the gorge.

And then they were on the other side, galloping down the hill and onto the road leading across a plain, leaving the goblins behind.

They gave their horses their heads and let them set their own pace. Wind sang by Tarin's ears and he leaned over Borum's neck as the mighty stallion raced along the road, thick muscles bunching and releasing.

After five miles had flown behind them, the horses slowed and slipped into a canter and then stopped, necks and chests heavy with sweat.

Tarin slipped to the ground and patted Borun on his shoulder.

"Well done!" he cried. "Well done!"

"We were very lucky," Sirona panted as she dropped from Bain beside him. A long scratch stretched over her forehead and her jerkin showed several rips from goblin blades.

"Yes," Tarin said. "Very lucky indeed. Eogan was right: These are by far worthy horses."

He took his cloak from his saddle and used it to rub Borun dry. Sirona followed suit with Bain.

"I think we need to rest the horses," Tarin said. He took Borun's reins and began walking him to prevent him from cooling too fast.

Sirona moved up beside him. "Are you hurt?"

"No. You?" he asked.

"I don't know how we managed that," she said. "I was certain we were dead there for a while."

Tarin nodded. "As did I. We were very hard-pressed to get through that ambush."

"Maliman?" she asked.

Tarin shook his head. "No, I don't think so. I think that was an isolated band that preys upon travelers. If it had been Maliman, I think there would have been others with them."

"I hope that's the last of them."

"So do I."

Rain began to fall again. They stopped and remounted, letting the reins drop across their horses' necks, allowing the horses to set the pace as they began following the coastal road, which wound its way along the cliffs and through the red and brown brome, bearing steadily northward toward Connacht and Maeve.

13

Waves crashed against the face of the cliffs and sleet was slowly changing to snow as Tarin and Sirona bowed, huddled inside their cloaks. They had been riding wet for the past three days now and were beginning to long for the warmth of the Great Hall at Cruachan Ai and the hospitality of its red-haired queen. The trip had been uneventful save for the cold since they had left the gray gorge. They saw nothing; not a bird, not a wolf, not even a rabbit as they rode along the road that was beginning to change from muck to a hard and frozen surface.

Bain and Borun seemed not to mind the weather, keeping a steady pace that ate up the miles swiftly. For this, Tarin and Sirona were thankful, as it drew them closer and closer to anticipated warmth. Two days had passed since they had been able to light a fire, and they rose each morning cramped and stiff from sleeping on the cold ground.

Their food was nearly gone and their stomachs had begun to tighten with hunger. They spoke little, lost in their own thoughts.

For the first time in a long while, Sirona reflected on the warmth of the hearth of her home with her parents and three brothers. It was the day that did this, as her home had always been snug and warm despite the storms that howled outside, coming in off the sea on the southeast coast of Erin. Her father had worked as a butcher for the small unnamed town comprised of a small huddle of huts and cottages and a tavern where the villagers would gather on an evening for song and talk. Sirona went along with her father when he visited the tavern, liking its smoky taste of peat and the occasional sip from her father's tankard and crisp smoked pork skins that the tavern keeper put out for them to nibble on while they drank. Always there had been a glass of fresh buttermilk for her and she pretended that it was ale as she drank with her father and his friends.

Outside the house had been a seasonal garden where her mother grew herbs and vegetables, neatly planted in lines, carefully weeded each day. On the other side of the house, away from the sea, stood a small apple orchard, and her mother would gather the apples and store them in an underground cellar in baskets covered to keep the mice out. Seldom did they have oatmeal for dinner, as her father always brought home the choicest cuts of whatever he had butchered during the day. Her mother always cooked them just so and served them piping hot, aswim in a bowl of good brown gravy.

Life had been good except for the few times when her brothers teased her but she quickly set them right, brawling into them with a savagery that caused them to flee after receiving a thumping from her fists. Her broad shoulders had the set of a man's as she grew to a man's height.

Then came the longships as the Norsemen came out of the sea down upon the village, slaughtering her mother and father and brothers while she hid in the woods up in the hills and watched the massacre. A huge man with beard and hair in braids and wearing a leather jerkin with a red dragon on it killed her family with his huge, two-handed sword.

She had gathered the bodies of her parents and brothers and placed them neatly on the floor in the house before firing it and burning it to the ground. Then she had set off with a meager pack of clothes and what food she had been able to scrounge from the Norsemen's leavings, making her way inland away from the coast.

On the sixth day of travel she had come upon the small fortress of Eber Mac Roich, a blade warrior, and his wife Bodua. They had taken her in and treated her kindly. They had no sons or daughters and Eber began teaching his skills with the sword to Sirona, much to the tongue-clicking of Bodua's disapproval.

"Watch the belt buckle," he repeatedly warned her during their swordplay. "A man can twist and turn for all he's worth but you will know which direction he is going to move by watching his middle. The middle always tells the movement.

"And don't grip your sword so hard. You need to hold your sword loosely so your arm won't tire. And it gives you more feats you can use when you fight. Don't drop your guard so often. The sword is only one thing that you use in a duel. You need to learn footwork and rely upon your legs and feet to avoid low cuts while you keep your blade up. When a swordsman tries to go low to cut your legs from under you, you can make him miss and return his stroke through his neck or split him from shoulder to stem, as he is helpless then.

"Remember to keep swordplay to a minimum. The longer you spend fighting someone the more you reveal to him and the wiser he becomes in fighting you. Swords are meant for quick ends, not dallying with parry. Defend yourself, of course, but remember that you are trying to kill him as quickly as possible and not play with swords."

She was happy at his fortress but knew the time was coming when she would have to leave and search out the Norseman who had slain her family.

Eber knew also that the time was soon coming and tried to keep her with him as long as possible by teaching her every trick he had learned and some he invented. But then came the day when he finally halted his teaching and smiled wryly at Sirona and said, "That is all that I can teach you. You are better with the sword than I or any other I have seen except the three great champions of the Red Branch—Cucullen, Conall Cernach, and Leary. I wish you would stay but I know that is not to be.

"I have a present for you," he said. He left and quickly returned bearing an ivory-handled sword in a leather scabbard with a curious silver design. She drew the sword and studied it. The blade curved slightly from hilt to point and was covered with a brass ridge meant to catch blades.

She swung it, testing it, and was surprised at how it seemed to mold itself to her hand. The blade made a slight whisper as it cut through the air.

"Thank you," she said gratefully. "It seems as if it was made for me."

"It was," he said gruffly. "The steel has been folded twenty times and forged through three fires, the blade quenched in wolf oil each time. It is hard enough to carry an edge despite its use and will cut through armor as a hot knife through butter. Now, let us see what Bodua has prepared for supper."

He reached out and ruffled her hair before turning and leading the way into the great room.

The next day she had left, feeling a lump in her throat as she turned to wave at Eber and Bodua as they stood in the gate to the fortress and watched her until she had moved out of sight.

For six months she had traveled the eastern coastline, searching for the Norseman and finally finding him on the Cooley Peninsula, where she waited secretly until he went into the woods to hunt. Then she had fought him for nearly half a day before splitting him down the middle. His sword had given her the scar across her cheek and she had taken the silver circlet that had held his hair off his face for her own.

Since that time she had made her own way the length and breadth of Erin, halting for a brief spell at various fortresses, where she earned her place among the skeptical warriors and joined them in brief forays against the enemies to earn silver.

But in time, the restlessness would descend upon her and she would take her leave despite the entreaties of the chieftains to stay. Usually this came right after warriors began taking an interest in her that was not in admiration for her bladework. Only once had she been forced to fight and kill a warrior who had proved too persistent and suddenly tried to take advantage of her. The fight was over within a minute and the warrior was left on the floor, bleeding profusely from a slit throat.

Bandits and Sword-wanderers had repeatedly come upon her alone in the woods and had paid dearly for their impertinence with their lives. Her reputation began to slowly build, so the times that she encountered one who saw her only as a woman became rarer and rarer. Especially when they learned her name. Still, there were always some who wanted to test her skills and she willingly obliged them.

Suddenly Tarin reined in, drawing her from her memory, as a squad of six warriors rode out from behind a small stand of trees.

Quickly they drew their swords then sat patiently on their horses while the squad came up to them.

"Who are you and why do you cross Connacht's borders?" the leader demanded, a large man with a heavy beard and long hair held off his brow by a red leather strap crisscrossed with never-beginning, never-ending golden lines. He wore a heavy black leather jerkin and matching trousers tucked into boots that came up over his knees. A short sword hung at his side and Sirona wondered if that was because he had long arms or whether he was not skilled enough with a long blade.

The others, dressed in Cruachan colors of red, silver, and black, stopped on either side of him.

"We have crossed Connacht's borders?" Tarin asked.

"So you have been told," the leader said rudely. "Now state your business."

"Our business is with Maeve, not a message boy," Tarin said, his eyes growing bleak.

The leader flushed and moved his hand toward his sword but stopped when Tarin said, "That would be the biggest mistake of your short-lived life. Take us to Maeve. Now!"

An ugly smile crossed the leader's face as he shifted his gaze from Tarin to Sirona and eyed her with bold lust.

"Now, that's a pretty thing you have riding with you," he said, licking his lips.

"More than you could handle," Tarin said. "Now, do I have to repeat myself? I am Tarin the Damned, the Deathwhisper. This is Sirona."

"I have heard of Tarin but who is this Sirona? And why does she hold a man's blade? I have half a mind to take it and spank her with it for thinking she can take a man's place in the world."

Tarin shook his head. "Then be it on your shoulders. Not mine. You have been warned."

The leader glanced at the other riders beside him and smirked. He started forward toward Sirona, drawing his short sword, then gasped as the sword suddenly leaped from his hand when Sirona's blade flashed twice in the gray light, returning on a back stroke that neatly sliced most of his beard from his face.

He gawked stupidly at his sword lying beside the road while the other men with him roared in laughter.

"Serves you well, Darin," one called out. "It seems you have met your match. If I were you, I wouldn't press it any further."

Flushed, Darin swung down from his horse to retrieve his sword. For a moment he stood undecided but a quick look at Sirona's grim face turned intent into jelly and he quickly mounted, wheeling his horse around and saying, "Well, come on then! It is not far to Cruachan Ai!"

He set a swift pace. The others swung in behind Tarin and Sirona as they rode in a near-gallop along the road.

Within an hour they sighted Cruachan Ai on a bluff above the plain and slowed their pace as they neared its gates. A sentry stepped forward to meet them.

"What business do you have here?" he demanded.

Tarin glanced behind him and saw others ready to come to the sentry's aid if needed. Frowning, he looked at Darin, then at the others riding behind them. Misgiving slipped over him.

"I am Darin, guard of the southern road," Darin said impatiently. "Open the gate! We have two who wish to see Maeve."

"Darin?" The sentry looked confused as he took a firm grip on his lance. "I know of no Darin at the southern road. That is usually held by Lugaid and his men. And Maeve is gone hunting to the northwest so she cannot vouch for you."

"And if the man is sick then who rides for him?" Darin said impatiently. "Stop being insolent before I pare your ears from your head. These are Tarin the Damned and Deathwhisper and Sirona. Never heard of her but she rides with Tarin. Now, is that good enough for you?"

The sentry blushed and said, "Now, there's no sense being surly. Pass through. Pass through."

Darin grunted and rode past the man, brushing him aside with the shoulder of his horse, with the others following.

The sentry growled and said in a low voice after Darin had passed, "And may The Dagda spit in your drink tonight."

Stablemen came forward quickly to take the horses and lead them to the stable. Tarin and Sirona shook water from their cloaks and tried to make themselves respectable before climbing the stairs to the door leading into the Great Hall.

Servants came forward to greet them and took them to the baths, where they stripped their clothes from their bodies and submerged themselves thankfully into the slightly perfumed hot water. Their clothes were taken away but they stopped the servants when they tried to take their weapons, laying them close at hand near the edge of the tubs in which they lay.

"I thought we'd never get here," Sirona sighed, wiggling her toes happily.

"Neither did I," Tarin said, ducking his head under the water and coming up, hands smoothing his long dark hair back over his shoulders.

"I wonder where the guards are," she asked, looking around the room.

"They are there. Never fear. We are being watched and watched carefully. I'm sorry that you have no privacy," he said apologetically.

She laughed. "Think of me as a warrior and not a woman."

"That is impossible," Tarin said, ducking his head again.

They stayed a long time in the baths while fresh clothes were brought to them. Tarin's were black and hers green with two red lines around the hem of her tunic. The clothes had been made from finely spun wool woven so tightly that they would shed water.

"At least they haven't forgotten us," Tarin grumbled, dressing.

"I wonder what's next now. Do you think we'll see Maeve?"

"Not until the evening meal," Tarin said. "Meanwhile, I believe we are going to be given a room to rest until then. For which, I must confess, I am grateful."

"As am I," Sirona said, suddenly feeling the weariness set upon her shoulders.

They followed the servants as they silently led them down a long hall to a room with windows on two sides. Two beds were in the room and a fire roared in the fireplace, radiating warmth out into the room.

They needed no further urging but slipped their weapons from them and, stretching out on the beds, fell instantly asleep.

14

They had slept no more than four hours when suddenly they were awakened by Darin's men surrounding their beds. Tarin reached for his sword but halted when the tip of a sword touched his neck. Slowly he sat up and glanced over at Sirona. Her eyes flashed with fury but she too was helpless with swords drawn and fixed upon her.

"And now, Tarin and whore Sirona, we shall see how you like Cruachan's dungeon," Darin said, and smirked at them.

"I demand that we see Maeve!" Tarin snapped. "This is a breach of the Laws of Hospitality! And if not her, then her husband, Ailill!"

"Now, that," Darin purred, "would be difficult. Both are gone. You will have the dungeon to reflect upon your manners. And as for the Laws of Hospitality, well then know that Cruachan is not mine but hers. The Laws of Hospitality do not apply to me. Or my men. Get dressed!" he added harshly.

Silently, Tarin and Sirona slid from bed and dressed. The men leered at Sirona as she slipped into her clothes.

"Now, then, she's a tidy figure of a woman," one of the guards said. "She's sure to be a wonder in bed, I'm thinking."

"Yes. And perhaps she will be willing to talk to us between the bedclothes in place of the cell that awaits her," another added. He jabbed her lightly with the point of his sword in her belly.

"Place a hand upon me and draw back a stump!" Sirona snapped.

"Ah, a feisty one, eh?" the man said, and pricked her again, and then gasped and doubled over in pain as her booted foot landed in his groin. His face turned a dirty white and he fell to the floor, grasping himself against the shards of pain that pulsed through him.

The others laughed at him but did not relax their guard.

Quickly Tarin and Sirona were bundled from their room and forced down three flights of stone steps to the deepest cells. The limestone walls dripped niter and laid white streaks over the walls and torches threw a dim yellow light to guide the way. Thicker and thicker smells of urine and feces rolled up like waves as they descended.

They came to a cell and Darin pulled the door open, the hinges squeaking like a thousand bats in flight. He grinned at them and then shoved them in and slammed the door shut. He opened the check door and grinned at them standing in the faint twilight.

"Enjoy yourselves," he said. Then his voice dropped to a whisper. "You will not be alone. Not here but in a sense as Maliman knows who you are. And who the others are. They will be well welcomed at Cairpre's court."

"Maeve . . ." Tarin began, but was cut short.

"Is not here. And will not know *you* are here when she returns.
Nobody knows you are here except for me and my men. Others
who have seen you will know only that you left Cruachan suddenly.
Impatient for her return. It will matter little to her. If you are not
here, that is. And few will ever know you are here. Until Maliman
calls for you."

The door slammed shut and the light disappeared, leaving them
standing in total darkness. A rat scurried around the edge of the
wall, its nails scratching on the stone. A faint squeal came from
somewhere. Then, there was silence.

"Sirona?" Tarin asked in the blinding darkness surrounding
them. He placed his back against the wall and started feeling the
walls of their prison. His feet moved through sludge and he could
feel tiny pricks from the bites of insects that lived in the muck and
climbed the walls. Hard-shelled, scabrous creatures.

From the edge of his vision he had the sensation of movement although when he strained to see, his eyes met nothing but blackness.

"Here," she said.

She felt along the walls of the cell but could find nothing that
would allow them a chance at escape. At last her fingers touched
his sleeve. He jerked away reflexively, then calmed and slowly put
out his arm, touching her hair.

"Did you find anything?" he asked.

"No," she said. "But that doesn't mean there isn't something. I
can only feel wet stone."

Tarin sighed and ran his free hand through his hair, pulling hard
on the strands, trying to awaken sight.

"Neither did I," Tarin said. "But there are things in here with us.
I can feel them."

"I know," she said. "Did you find a bench or something where we
can sit?"

He shook his head, then remembered that she couldn't see him.

"No. I think all we have is the floor. And I really don't want to sit
there."

"We will have to in time, I'm thinking," she said.

"Later. Let's try again. You go my way, I'll go yours. Perhaps we can find something the other missed."

Again they worked their way blindly around the walls of the cell but met again having found nothing.

"So? Now what do we do?" Sirona asked.

"Wait. That's all we *can* do: wait. And hope that Maeve returns and discovers where we are."

"I don't think those were Darin's own men. Not any of the Connacht warriors. She may never discover where we are. Or even if we *are* here. Those are Maliman's men. It seems that he is beginning to become stronger and stronger if he can send some of his men around the country."

"I think that is what he has come to, what with losing the battle at Callyberry. Instead of massive armies, he is sending small groups out to weasel their way into the courts of the kings and chieftains while he continues to build up his armies from his citadel, Dun Darai, while he remains safely in Asarlai, which can be easily defended. Attackers have to cross the Criostal Droichead, the Crystal Bridge, to get to him. And that is a formidable crossing. I've seen it once after Maliman was imprisoned and the fortress laid bare. Only one person at a time can cross that bridge. The keep can be held by a small band unless," he added thoughtfully, "they can be crushed in a rush. Of course, I'm certain that Maliman has an enchantment placed on the bridge as well to prevent people from crossing unless he wills it."

"We could do it," Sirona said firmly. "That is *if* we can get out of here."

"Perhaps. Right now, it is a small matter, attacking the keep. As you say, if we can get out of here. And at the moment, that doesn't look very promising."

The thought of staying in the cell sobered them and they fell silent, standing together with backs to a wall, shoulders touching, taking a small relief in the presence of the other.

15

The day was bright and warm—a false spring day—as the Seekers made their way toward the court of Cairpre. Nuad and Fergma, the wolfhounds, trotted ceaselessly in wide circles around the small party, ready to warn them if danger appeared. And knowing this allowed the Seekers a certain ease as they rode along the mud-hardening road bearing ever southwest. In the near distance loomed the Pass of Adene, where Seanchan had promised to wait for Tarin and Sirona to return from Cruachan Ai.

Birds sang and wheatears, blue-gray above with black wings and white below and an orange flush to the breast, and corncrakes, giving a rasping call of alarm, their chestnut wings and trailing legs showing brightly in flight, scattered from the tawny grass alongside the road ahead of the Seekers along with grasshopper warblers. Overhead golden eagles flew in widening gyres searching for prey. Occasionally a rabbit, ignored by the wolfhounds, would spring from the grass and hop frantically in a zigzag route ahead of the Seekers.

They rode steadily, letting the horses set their own pace although Black flung his head restlessly, wanting to gallop ahead of the band, causing Cumac to gently tighten the reins and whisper softly to the mighty warhorse to calm him.

The sun's rays coming down upon their shoulders made them drowsy along with the steady rhythm of the horses. Lorgas dropped asleep and fell from his horse, causing brief merriment among the Seekers as he climbed red-faced back upon his horse, saying that the fall was no accident but planned by him to awaken the group from their lethargy, causing the others to laugh even harder at his lame excuse.

"We elves don't ride much," he said, miffed by the laughter. "We are at home in the trees."

"You have ridden long enough now to be used to it," Fedelm teased. "Besides I always thought elves were agile enough to adjust to anything."

"Tell them, Bern," Lorgas growled. "Tell them how we elves are strangers to horses."

"You fell asleep, Lorgas. Face it," Bern said, halting his laughter to gasp out the words.

"Small thing when an elf refuses to stand with another elf," Lorgas said, nudging the sides of his horse with his heels. "Now, if you all are finished braying like jacks, let us move on."

"He's right," Seanchan said, trying to restrain his smile. "We need to travel. I should like to get to the mountains and find a suitable place to wait for Tarin and Sirona before dark. Someplace easily defended if the need arises. I am certain that there are Sword-wanderers in those mountains and I won't be surprised if goblins and hobgoblins make their home in the rocks there as well."

Sobered by Seanchan's words, the little party fell silent and nudged their horses into a ground-gaining lope that pleased Black greatly, his muscles bunching and contracting eagerly.

Then in the distance between them and the mountains a pillar of black smoke stood up against the deep blue sky.

Seanchan drew rein and sat on his horse, studying the smoke as the others gathered around him. He closed his eyes, concentrating. His lips thinned and he opened his eyes, hard as hazel wood.

"A village has been torched," he said harshly, and lifted his horse into a faster pace, his cloak billowing behind him like a white cloud.

They rode hard toward the smoke, coming to what had been a small village within the half hour. The wolfhounds immediately coursed through and around the village, searching, then came back to stand beside Seanchan's horse.

Slowly the Seekers moved into the blackened village, their hands warily near their weapons.

The stench of burnt bodies filled the air. Men and women lay sprawled in their death struggle around the village. Some had been felled by arrows, others gutted and throats slit by hooked swords. One woman lay with the body of her unborn child that had been hacked from her womb. Even the dogs had been slain. The huts smoldered from blazing fires. Ravens stood on blackened timbers, watching the Seekers approach with beady eyes. Some of the vil-lagers looked as if they had been butchered for food, flesh cut reck-lessly from their bodies as they died in agony.

But no enemy bodies lay anywhere, although dark pools of blood that had soaked into the ground marked where some had been slain.

"Who did this?" Cumac whispered in the hush that lay over the village like a blood-soaked blanket.

Fedelm slipped from her horse and pulled an arrow from a body.

She studied its barbed needle tip for a second, then threw the arrow from her with loathing.

"A goblin arrow," she said. "They came in the night. Without warning." She looked up at Seanchan. "This was no impulse raid. This was well planned."

Lorgas and Bern dropped from their horses and began to circle the village, looking for tracks. The ground had been torn by galloping hooves from around the village.

"They came from all directions," Bern called.

"Sword-wanderers too," Cumac said, slowly riding Black around, leaning from his saddle to study the wounds. "No goblin blade made all this slaughter."

"And they stayed for a banquet," Fedelm said from the bonfire in the center of the village. Blackened bones and spits for holding meat lay carelessly thrown around the edges of the fire.

"They left toward the mountains," Lorgas called from the far end of the village. "A hundred at least."

"Has this place a name?" Cumac asked Seanchan. "Have you been here before?"

"This is a village of farmers," Seanchan said. "It had no need of a name."

"Not even an inn," Lorgas said as he and Bern rejoined the others.

"Or alehouse," Bern added.

"I see no weapons other than hoes and sickles and wood axes," Cumac said.

"What shall we do with the bodies?" Fedelm asked. "We cannot leave them here for the carrion birds. Or wolves," she added.

"Too many to bury," Seanchan said. "We do not have the time for making cists." Cists were small stone structures in which the dead were buried.

"Pile them up in the center over a set fire. We will have to burn them."

The others remained in an uneasy silence for a long moment. Burning the bodies went against tradition. Some people even believed burning the bodies also incinerated the souls and spirits of the dead.

"I don't know," Cumac began doubtfully, but was interrupted by Seanchan.

"We must make the mountains in daylight," he said. "And if we do stay and bury them, that will take at least a week. We would be at the mercy of roving bands. If we do bury them, any who come along after us will know that someone rides ahead of them. It wouldn't take much guesswork for them to discover we are the riders."

Silently they gathered the bodies and neatly placed them on top of a huge pile of kindling. Then Cumac lit a torch and walked around the pyre, lighting it in several places. Soon the smell of sizzling fat and burning meat hastily drove the Seekers back from the flaming pyre where they stood and watched until the pyre had burned down to charred bones and ashes.

"I think we may go now," Seanchan said quietly, and the Seekers mounted their horses and rode from the village, each disgusted over the turn of events, following the trail of the raiders, which led straight to the mountains.

They had just crossed a small marsh and the sun had fallen into the gloaming when Seanchan discovered a site that looked defensible from anyone or anything that might attack them during the night.

It wasn't a good place as far as the others were concerned. The night clouds were gathering as high and dark as the mountains over which they loomed. The humid air had suddenly cooled, and the smell of fish spawning in the marsh and marsh gas rising was unpleasant. The wind came up and began to ruffle the grass and carried with it a hint of rain to come punctuated by lightning flashes that unleashed brimstone into the air. A dead and bone-white tree lay on the ground like a giant's thighbone, and bullbats swept out of the mountains and wove complicated patterns in flight over the marsh to catch the fireflies that rose from the marsh grass and lit the gloaming with tiny bits of light like a farmer's candle seen in a window from a far distance.

Lorgas and Bern climbed down from their horses and went to

the tree and began hacking wood from it to make a fire for roasting the marsh hares brought down by Fedelm's bow as they had ridden along the road that narrowed and led through the marsh. Enough rabbits had been slain that each of the Seekers would have a complete one for supper.

Seanchan dismounted stiffly and walked around the site, rubbing his lower back, which had stiffened during the day's travel. Cumac and Fedelm picketed the horses behind the camp next to the wall, where they would be safe from attack. By the time they had finished rubbing each horse down with handfuls of brown grass, the elves had a fire burning cheerfully between two boulders that would reflect the heat to the Seekers as they skinned and cleaned the rabbits and spitted them over the fire with stiff branches cut from a small willow tree.

Each one made his and her own pallet as close to the fire as possible as the rapidly approaching night carried a chill to them.

A mist rose from the marsh and clung close to the ground like a roiling gray blanket, carrying with it the smell of dead beings. They heard twites singing, a nasal "tzeeip" like a jangling linnetlike song of "chi-chi-chi-chi." From somewhere a fox barked and fell silent. The wolfhounds sat at the edge of the fire, intent on the night.

"Well, we could have picked a better place but I suppose this is as good as any if it weren't for the marsh," Lorgas said grumpily.

"I think you would complain if you were snuggled between the covers in a bed in Cairpre's fortress," Bern said. "But for once, I agree: This place is as good as any if we have to defend it. We have our backs against that granite wall and only a small passage between the boulders if it should come to that."

"Our enemy could drop down upon us," Cumac said, looking up.

"Only if they sprouted wings," Bern answered. "A jump from up there would break a leg at least. Even goblins can't be that stupid. What do you say, Seanchan?"

"Never underestimate your enemy's intelligence. Goblins aren't any different from man in that regard. Jumping from up there, I mean. There are always some who would throw caution to the wind and leap without thinking. Sometimes hate too can cloud their minds to danger," he said.

"I think we'd better keep a close watch tonight despite Nuad and Fergma," Fedelm said. "Better safe than sorry. I'll take the first watch."

"I'll take the second," Cumac said.

"Lorgas and I shall take the third and fourth," Bern said.

"Always volunteering me," Lorgas growled. "I can choose for myself."

"All right, then which watch would you prefer?" Bern asked.

"The third or fourth," Lorgas answered.

The others chuckled and turned their attention to the roasting hares. Cumac drew a knife and gently prodded one of the rabbits.

"A bit longer, I'd say. Not too much or they will taste like leather." He took a small sack of spices and salt from his pack and carefully sprinkled some on each of the rabbits. "There, that should make a difference. It isn't much but it will make the flesh a bit more tender. I don't like stringy rabbit."

"And we appreciate your thoughtfulness," Seanchan said. "You make life so much easier."

Cumac glanced swiftly at Seanchan to see if the Druid was pulling his leg, but Seanchan looked innocently back at him. Mollified, he prodded the rabbits again, watching closely that they did not char.

Lorgas sighed and leaned back on his pallet, stretching his booted feet toward the fire. He wiggled his toes with pleasure.

"I think we'll sleep well tonight," he said. "Wish we had some autumn ale, though, to wash those rabbits down. It's a good time for the last making which, as you know, is the best ale you can drink."

"Autumn is far behind us now," Bern observed.

"Not entirely," Lorgas admonished, wagging a finger at Bern. "A good brewer always holds back some autumn brewing for this time of year." He sighed. "A good malt beer would be satisfactory as well."

"Or even cold stream water," Fedelm said, making a face after a drink from a water bottle. "This water tastes stale."

Seanchan sighed. "Why dwell on something you do not have instead of being thankful for what we *do* have. We could be stuck out in that marsh if night had fallen faster as we would not be able to see the road to ride through it. *Or* we could be roasting on spits over a goblin fire. *Or* Fedelm might have missed the rabbits she shot"—this latter drew a dark look from Fedelm—"*or* we might not have found this place where it is warm and safe even if the ground is a bit rocky. *And* if you take close consideration of the wall behind us you will notice that it slopes inward, providing a bit of a roof if it does rain. Which," he added, lifting his head to sniff the air, "is coming now even as I speak. If my nose is still correct."

"I can feel it coming," Fedelm said. "And I never miss with my arrows with rabbits or deer and seldom men."

"There is always chance," Seanchan said pleasantly. "We cannot always be a guardian to our wishes."

"Enough of this jibber-jabber," Lorgas growled. "Are those rabbits ready yet?"

Cumac lifted one of the willow spits from the fire and tossed the rabbit to Lorgas, who caught it, then dropped it with a yelp and began frantically blowing on his fingers.

"I guess they are ready," Cumac said pleasantly, his eyes twinkling. He handed the others their rabbits, cautioning, "Be careful. They're hot."

The latter drew curses from Lorgas and laughter from the others as they watched the elf trying to pick up his rabbit from his lap and yelping again as the heat made its way through his trousers. He jumped up and began dancing upon his pallet, blowing on his hands and slapping against his thighs then blowing on his hands again.

"Hee hee hee," Seanchan laughed, wiping tears from his eyes.

Fedelm collapsed with laughter as did Cumac while Bern guffawed at the antics of Lorgas.

"I'll remember this!" he fumed, glaring at the others. "See if I don't! The next time someone else can fetch the wood and make the fire and *I'll* do the cooking. See if you like my fare."

"That's all right," Cumac gasped. "I really don't mind the cooking. I think your rabbit has cooled enough by now that you might eat it."

Gingerly, Lorgas picked up his rabbit with the tips of his fingers, blowing furiously on the meat, his heavy mustache waving like tiny butterfly wings as he blew. He took a small bite, lips spread back from the meat, and chewed quickly, sucking air to cool the meat on his tongue.

"More salt," he said gruffly, dropping cross-legged to his pallet, where he pulled the meat from the bones.

"Be thankful for what you have," Cumac said, imitating Sean-chan's words. "You can always give it back if you do not want it," he teased.

"Yes. Yes. I am. Grateful, that is. Delicious. Very," Lorgas said, taking quick bites between his words lest Cumac snatch the rabbit from his hands.

"How far to the pass you reckon?" Fedelm asked Seanchan.

He shrugged. "Hard to say as I don't know the road between here and there. But I should think we will reach it by midafternoon. Then we shall have to wait for Tarin and Sirona although I shouldn't think that the wait will be longer than two, three days."

"Unless something has happened to them," Fedelm said.

Cumac looked up sharply. "You feel something?"

She hesitated, then spread her fingers, saying, "I'm not certain. More of a misgiving than anything else. It's probably nothing."

"Learn to trust your instincts," Seanchan said.

They ate in silence; then, after a little small talk, each rolled into his blanket, leaving Fedelm alone and staring into the fire, wishing she could see beyond in the dancing flames and glowing embers. But whatever it was that seemed to gnaw at the back of her mind remained elusive, leaving her only with a feeling of dread despite the comforting knowledge of Nuad and Fergma resting nearby.

16

The tiny door at the bottom of the cell door slid open. A small shaft of light came through the door, piercing the utter darkness. A hairy hand pushed two bowls through the door, then slammed the little door shut.

Tarin and Sirona groped their way through the dark to where they had last seen the bowls. They hurried as fast as they could as they had learned—over the past week, which they could not know had passed—that if the food was not taken quickly, it would draw bugs and mice like iron to a lode-stone.

They had no spoons and ate the oatmeal with a greedy hunger despite wishing that the contents of the bowls were something else. Each longed for a piece of meat, vegetables, fruit, whatever. Anything but oatmeal.

And fresh water too. The water in the bucket in one corner of the cell had grown stale and tasted like bronze, and bugs had to be swept aside by hand before one could drink from it. By common assent they limited their use of water, as they had no idea when fresh water would be given to them. They no longer paid any attention to the insect bites over their bodies from when they had to lie down in the filth of the cell. One could, Tarin wryly said to Sirona in the blackness, become used to anything over time.

Tarin heard Sirona sigh in the darkness and say, "Oh for a piece of meat."

It didn't matter that Sirona would say this after each meal or that he agreed with her. It was enough that it was said, as it would provide something to talk about in the darkness, which could press in upon a person and drive him mad when he began to imagine that others were in the cell with him.

"Yes," he said, subscribing to the daily ritual. "It would be good for a piece of meat. But it appears that none will soon be forthcoming."

"How long do you suppose we will have to be here?"

"I don't know. It will all depend upon whether Maeve or Ailill, her husband, learns about us and how we were denied the Laws of Hospitality. Or even if they become interested in us after they discover our whereabouts."

Silence reigned for a moment, and then she said, "Surely a wise person would not wish to attract the judgment of the gods."

"Some do not care a whit about what the gods proclaim or do," he answered. "Some have lost faith in the gods and have determined that life on earth is simply an accident and that when you are dead you are dead and done with life. They believe that life should be lived to the fullest and then die and be done with it."

"Do you believe this way?"

He hesitated with the new question added to their routine. Did he believe that the gods accepted a man or not after he had died? And what was that acceptance based upon?

"Tarin?"

"Yes," he said slowly, "I do, although at times I wish the gods would step in and help out when we have our backs up against the wall."

A quiet chuckle followed his answer.

"Perhaps we are supposed to find our own way."

"From here? If you can find it, let me know."

They fell into a silence that was growing longer and longer each day as the impossibility of their escape became greater and greater.

But, Tarin reminded himself, it would be extremely difficult for their imprisonment to be kept quiet for long. Someone would discover that they had been imprisoned in defiance of the Laws of Hospitality during Maeve's absence and work to release them.

On the heels of his thoughts came the sound of keys jangling outside their cell. Then the grating of a key turning in a rusty lock and the door being forced open against rusty hinges.

A light pierced the dark, hurting their eyes, and Tarin and Sirona held their hands in front of their faces until their eyes slowly adjusted to the blinding glare.

Slowly Tarin opened his eyes and saw a man standing in front of the cell, outrage plain upon his face, his shoulders quivering with anger as Tarin and Sirona slowly exited from the cell. The door was forced shut again, the grating sound harsh upon their ears.

"I am Curan of the Guard. How long have you been here?" the man asked, looking at their clothes with disgust.

Tarin and Sirona shrugged simultaneously.

"We have no way of telling," Tarin said. "Time ceases to exist in there. Certainly longer than one or two days," he added ruefully.

He nodded at the cell and scratched his head with a dirty finger. His scalp felt alive with lice. He looked down at his clothes hanging with thick mud. He shook his head wryly and looked at Sirona, her long hair stringy with filth, her clothes covered with sludge, tiny bite marks upon her face and arms.

"Long enough," Sirona answered. "How did you discover us?"

"Through the kitchen," Curan said. "One of the cooks complained on how they had to prepare oats each day for the past two weeks for a couple of prisoners in the lower level. No one is allowed to be imprisoned here without the permission of Maeve. That's what brought you to my attention. I decided to find out who had been imprisoned here and, well, here I am and there you are."

"Good of you," Tarin said.

"Come," Curan said with embarrassment. "Let us provide you with baths and clean clothes. I don't know about your hair," he said to Sirona. "You may lose it."

"We shall see," Sirona said firmly in a voice that prohibited objection.

"What about the man who imprisoned us?" Tarin asked. "Darin, he is called. I want him."

"I can imagine you do," Curan answered. "But he is not here. He has been sent to the northern borders for a week to relieve the men stationed there. He will return, though, and I am fairly certain that Maeve will allow you to deal with him."

"As long as I have the chance," Tarin growled. "And our weapons?"

Curan shook his head. "They may be hard to find. Whatever can be taken from a prisoner goes as a prize to the one who has captured him. Your weapons may be with Darin or he may have given them to someone else as a gift or to curry favor. Perhaps someone in Cruachan Ai will be carrying one of your weapons, and that you may have for having been taken illegally from you. You may be challenged, however, and if so, well, there is nothing that I or any other of the queen's men will be able to do for you. You will have to fight the challenger."

"Willingly," Tarin said, his eyes gleaming.

Curac took a step back from the cold death slanting from Tarin's eyes and swallowed deeply. He was glad, he thought, that he was not one of the men who would be searched out by Tarin. Or Sirona, for that matter, he thought after glancing at her.

"Let's make you more presentable," Curan said roughly, turning his eyes away.

He led the way up the long granite stairs that wound like a gyre upward to the door leading from the dungeon itself.

ıt took longer and longer for Tarin and Sirona to regain their strength and many baths to remove the filth and insects from them. One of the maidens attending the baths produced a lotion made by her mother from sour wine, melted butter, honey, and egg yolks that eventually killed the lice that infested their hair and bodies after three days during which time they burned their clothing each night and bedding each morning until lice disappeared from their hair after long combing with a lice comb and the red spots disappeared from their skin.

The fifth day of their release they were summoned to Maeve's court. Her eyes flashed fire as she listened to the account of their capture and imprisonment, and hard white lines appeared around the corners of her mouth.

"Who is this Darin? Why have I not heard about him?" she demanded from her court of advisors.

"We cannot tell," said Allaid, her Druid, who lived in a cave near her court and appeared only when sought. "Perhaps it is because he is not from Connacht but from the Mountains of Mourne, where he serves Maliman."

"And why have I not been told this?" she asked icily. Many in her court quailed from the sound of her voice, knowing that frequently when Maeve reached this point she would become ruled by her rage, lashing out in all directions at once.

But Allaid refused to be cowed by her. "You have been gone. Among our lakes in the north where certain warriors who have gained your whimsy live. Darin came after you left, from what I have been able to discover. Had you remained here in Cruachan Ai where you are sorely needed, given the happenings of this world, this would not have occurred. It is as much your fault as any other's fault that such a man could gain a bit of power in such a short period of time. Do not blame others for your doings. You have only yourself to blame."

He stood, looking calmly at Maeve while she fought to gain control of her temper. At last she drew a deep, shuddering breath and said, "Then give us your advice, Allaid. What should we do?"

"There is not much you can do," Allaid replied. "Tarin and Sirona are entitled to rewards from you for your negligence. They are entitled to challenge Darin upon his return. They are entitled to five cows each and the length of your left arm in white gold and the length of your right arm in red gold. They are also entitled to one plowland of one hundred and twenty acres of arable land each. This is not a minor infraction of our laws but one of the gravest consequences. You must pay this penalty as you left no one to govern in your absence while you plied your charms on the warriors in the north, Maeve of the Friendly Thighs. Your lust clouded your judgment and now you must pay."

Maeve took a deep breath and let it out slowly. Her penalty was enormous, but the breaking of laws handed down by the gods was not to be considered lightly. The penalty for ignoring the penance was too harsh to even consider.

She twisted her neck, the tendons cracking, and said, "Then it shall be paid. And the challenge to Darin, which will be fought in this hall. Those who accompanied him during this breaking of the Laws of Hospitality will be imprisoned where Tarin and Sirona were imprisoned until I deem their punishment has fulfilled their crime against our court. Or, they may choose to fight a champion instead and if they win, be sent out swordless and weaponless into the wild to make of themselves what they can. The choice shall be theirs to make.

"Send messengers to recall this man Darin to my court but do not tell him why I am desirous of his attention. Only that I wish him to present himself before me."

Mac Chect, her herald, bowed and left. His black hair gleamed in the torchlight and small rays danced off his dress. Yet no one would ever have called him a fop, for his skill with the short sword by his side was legendary despite the golden wand he carried that marked him as a messenger of the court and free from harm although, many privately said, the ways had been challenged now by Maliman, who more than likely would ignore tradition. But then

Maliman was Maliman and Maeve was Maeve and one did not lightly throw away her orders in favor of those of Maliman. Disobedience was not something to be mocked by either one.

tʜʀᴇᴇ days after Mac Chect left, Sirona fought a duel with one of Maeve's warriors.

The duel probably would not have come about except that Sirona, an oddity in that she was a woman warrior, which shouldn't have been the subject of humor by Maeve's warriors in that women were frequently taught the ways of the sword, was constantly besieged by taunts and teasing that stopped just short of becoming offensive to Sirona's honor. But that couldn't last as the warriors grew bolder and bolder and more reckless in their attitude toward her.

At last the day came when one of Maeve's younger warriors out to make his reputation, named Ercrin, crossed the line between common sense and insult.

The day was bright and warm, one of those days that made men lazy and given to telling bawdy stories and stories of their own prowess in battle.

"Ah," Ercrin said, when Sirona and Tarin walked into the Great Hall. "Here is the answer for men. A woman warrior excellent with a sword. Tell me"—he leered—"do you need a sword to play with? I have one that is the hope of all women." He was big and burly with gray eyes and perfumed black hair.

"And why is that?" Sirona asked quietly, but had Ercrin been paying attention to matters other than his own words, he would have caught the sudden flash of anger in her eyes.

"Come to my bed and I will show you," he said, bringing guffaws from others who witnessed the exchange.

"You have gone far enough," Tarin said sharply, and started for Ercrin only to be brought up short when Sirona placed her hand on his shoulder.

"This is for me alone," she said softly to him, then loudly, "I have seen many men who have a high opinion of themselves but stumble when they walk with their sword by their side. Unless, of course, that it is a small sword more given to carving beef than a warrior."

Ercrin turned crimson as the warriors laughed at him. He glared at Sirona and said, "The place of a woman is not playing men's games but learning to sew and embroider and serving men. I cannot see where you are any different than other women. Comb the rats out of your hair and give up a warrior's garb for a dress and you would be where you belong."

Sirona gave a smile that one would not like to wake up to and crossed the floor to stand, hands on hips, before Ercrin. He grinned insolently at her and said, "Serve your function and bring me ale."

"My function?" Sirona purred. "Then here it is."

With that she delivered a blow that sent Ercrin head over heels out of his chair. For a moment silence reigned in the Great Hall, and then laughter erupted as the warriors grasped their sides and gasped for air.

Ercrin leaped to his feet and tried to land a blow, but Sirona swayed easily out of his reach and landed another blow that knocked him flat.

"I can do this all day if you can take it all day," she said. Then she spat. "Now, why don't you join the other children and play with hurley sticks—if you can find one small enough."

Ercrin again stood and said, "If you were a man—"

"I give you leave," Sirona said contemptuously. "Say what you will."

He laughed and said, "I will not waste my time on you. It would be like dueling with an unarmed person."

Another blow felled him and Sirona's eyes blazed.

"Get your sword," she said sharply. "That is, if you are brave enough to face me."

"A challenge!" someone shouted from the group of warriors. "You'd better get your sword, Ercrin. If you can find it!"

"In the courtyard. Within the hour!" Ercrin said, and stalked from the room.

Sirona turned to Tarin and smiled. "It seems that it is time for a little exercise. Would you watch my back?"

"Gladly," Tarin said.

Together the pair left the Great Hall and returned to their rooms. There, Tarin buckled his sword diagonally across his chest while Sirona slipped her leather jerkin over her head and buckled leather guards around her wrists. She shrugged her shoulders, trying to settle the hang of the jerkin.

"I wish we had our old clothing," she said wistfully. "But the new that Maeve has given us will serve. As soon as they are supple enough."

"Be careful," Tarin warned as they made their way down to the courtyard. "You have ridiculed Ercrin and he now must prove himself to his words to regain his honor and place with the others. Do not play with him. End it as quickly as possible."

She shook her head. "No, I must show the others my swordplay or else someone else will take up the challenge. Men do not want to see a woman best them in what they think are men's games. No," she added grimly, "I will play the sword-game with him."

They emerged into the courtyard. Word had passed quickly through the fortress, and the sides of the courtyard were three deep with onlookers who were curious about Sirona's alleged skill with the blade and curious about the outcome.

Ercrin swaggered to the middle of the courtyard and swung his sword around his head, loosening his muscles. Then he went through a few simple feats designed to show Sirona what she could expect.

Sirona smiled thinly and rolled her shoulders, then did the Lightning and Thunder Feats flawlessly, moving into more complicated feats, dancing and twirling her blade in moves too fast for the eye to follow except as a blur. The warriors considered the odd blade she used, slightly curved with a brass guard.

A murmur of interest rose from the ranks of warriors and wagers began to be made. Most, however, favored Ercrin, as Sirona's slim figure appeared too frail compared with Ercrin's broad chest and thick arms.

"Well, little one," Ercrin said. "Are you ready for your lesson? I shall take it easy on you but you will learn to respect your betters by the time I am through."

"Then let us begin before the day grows hotter," Sirona said.

She stepped forward, flowing like a cloak in the wind, her blade dancing, flickering in and out of Ercrin's guard.

Ercrin laughed and swung a hard overhead slash toward her, but his blade caught only air and struck the paving stones of the courtyard, sending sparks high.

Sirona laughed and slipped in and made a tiny cut on his cheek and danced out of the way as he tried to counter her stroke.

Again he lunged and again she darted away. This time her blade slashed through his heavy leather jerkin, making an "X" that left the four pieces of his jerkin flopping like a long-eared dog facing into the wind.

The laughter slowly slipped away as the warriors watched her skill as her blade sang in her hands, slicing bits of clothing here and there until Ercrin stood bare-chested, panting, in the middle of the courtyard.

"Marvelous!" a voice cried from a balcony overhead, followed by the clapping of hands. Sirona glanced up and noticed Maeve smiling. "Perhaps I should have you teach my warriors!"

Sirona stepped back and stood easily, waiting for Ercrin to recover his breath, taunting him with, "Out of shape, eh, Ercrin? Not a wise state for a warrior to be in. You could retire, you know. The kitchen could always use another person to scrub pots and pans."

Ercrin roared and rushed her but stumbled with his blade slicing through air. A loud *splat!* stung his buttocks as Sirona struck with the flat of her blade as if she was spanking a child. Startled, he leaped into the air, a hand automatically rubbing his backside.

Laughter came again from the warriors as Ercrin spun around, pushing his hair back off his forehead and wiping the sweat from his face with his large hand. He gripped his sword hard and came at her again, vainly working through feat after feat, trying to find a way through her guard. But Sirona's blade kept slipping between his sword's slash and attempted parries, nicking pieces of skin from his chest here and there, shaving the hair from his head.

Desperately Ercrin rushed her, trying to pin her against the wall with his bulk, but Sirona danced away, this time her blade cutting his beard from below his chin and a good patch of hair from his head.

Taunts began to rise from the watching warriors as Ercrin stumbled awkwardly over the paving stones, trying to catch the elusive Sirona but to no avail. His breath burned in his lungs, but Sirona appeared to still breathe easily. Sweat flowed down his face, but Sirona appeared to have barely broken a sweat. His sword seemed to weigh fifty pounds in his hand, but Sirona's sword appeared light as a feather in her hand.

It was now that Ercrin began to feel the first faint signs of fear. He gritted his teeth and changed his way, coming forward slower and slower, ignoring Sirona's flashing blade as he concentrated on killing her. But each time he thought he saw an opening, his blade found nothing but air.

The sun moved over the courtyard, leaving half in shadow as Sirona continued to play with Ercrin. The crowd had grown silent as the warriors realized that Sirona was mocking Ercrin with her swordplay. The warriors began to watch more closely the attack and defense of Sirona, admiring her skill but also feeling the same helplessness of Ercrin, knowing that they too could be in the center of the courtyard, facing her blade, and being treated with contempt by her. And knowing as well that she could have ended the duel anytime she wanted against the hapless Ercrin.

Another piece of hair flew from Ercrin's head, sliced cleanly away without touching the skin. Another nick appeared on his chest. Then Sirona moved through the Rolling Feat and Ercrin found himself standing naked with his warrior's apron and pants lying in a puddle around his ankles.

He stared stupidly at his naked self, then raised his eyes to meet Sirona's cold stare. She laughed and said, "I think it is time you dropped your sword and retired to the kitchen. You have little skill with your sword to call yourself a warrior. This is child's play."

And Ercrin roared and leaped toward her, his sword swinging wildly around his head. But no one saw Sirona's blade as it struck his head from his shoulders, sending it rolling toward the center of the courtyard, where it lay, mouth agape, the eyes bulging in a death mask.

Sirona walked to where his clothes lay in a pile and bent to pick up a piece of Ercrin's shirt. Carefully she wiped blood from the blade before slipping it back into its sheath over her shoulder. She smiled at the warriors and instinctively they tensed, hands moving toward daggers. She laughed.

"Stay your hands," she said. "I am finished. But know this," she added, her voice hardening. "I will not tolerate wagging tongues anymore. It all ends here. Unless some of you wish to play swords with me."

She turned and nodded at Tarin and together they left, reentering the Great Hall. Maeve had gone before them and lay now on a couch, her burgundy dress showing the tops of her large breasts. Her eyes had a smoky look to them. She raised a glass and toasted Sirona.

"To the woman who bested a man," she said. She gestured to them to sit.

They drank, and Sirona and Tarin took their places at the head of one of the tables closest to Maeve's throne, causing some men to grumble but they took their places below the pair without voicing complaint. Servants appeared bearing platters of meat and fruits and bread. Others brought mugs of fresh ale along with pitchers to the tables. A bard began singing, improvising a song about the duel that would make the rounds of bards across the country.

But for now, the feast was eaten with little talk above a whisper while Tarin, Sirona, and Maeve ate calmly, talking about Sirona's skill with the blade. Tarin told Maeve about Sirona's part in the Battle of Callyberry. Maeve looked curiously at Sirona, then laughed, and slowly the tension dissipated from the Great Hall as the warriors began to dissect Sirona's skill, some enviously, the grizzled ones recalling other duels they had witnessed in the past with someone whose skill with the blade was if not better, then at least equal to the skill Sirona had displayed.

17

Suddenly Seanchan came awake and sat up. Something had moved in the darkness, something foul and deadly. A foul stench slowly rolled up out of the marsh mist and hovered over the sleeping Seekers. He glanced over at the watch and saw Bern and Lorgas sleeping, contented smiles upon their faces. A small black cloud hung over them, casting soft black rays slanting toward them as would sun if it came through wisps of straw. Fedelm slept curled against

Cumac for warmth. But the wolfhounds stood, hackles bristling, staring out into the marsh, growls rising threateningly from their throats.

Seanchan rose and took up his staff, trying to pierce the darkness with his eyes but catching only glimpses of a shape that seemed to shift from one edge of his vision to the next. He crossed to Cumac and Fedelm and shook them awake. They sat up, rubbing the sleep from their eyes.

"What is it?" Fedelm asked.

"Something. I don't know," Seanchan said, keeping his eyes on the marsh. "I feel it more than I see it."

Cumac stood, slipping Caladbolg from its sheath. He looked over at the sleeping elves and frowned. He started toward them but stopped when Seanchan held up his hand.

"Leave them," he said softly. "That something seems to be holding them in sleep. Best not disturb them until we know what it is."

"I don't like this," Cumac said, gripping his sword tighter. He glanced at the Dragonstone turning black on his shoulder. "Maliman?"

"I don't think so," Seanchan said. "But I too don't like it."

A soft emerald glow came from Fedelm's belt. She fitted an arrow to her bow and held it ready.

Seanchan closed his eyes and sent out a tendril of thought, searching.

Out in the marsh, yellow will-o'-the-wisps appeared above the mist, darting like swallows; then they began to change to fire and gather slowly into a form.

Then Seanchan's eyes snapped open and he said harshly, "A Bamulae. A creature from an ancient world. This is not Maliman!"

The Bamulae rose roaring from the mist, a body of fire with streaks of blackness writhing snakelike on its body. It clutched a chain of fire with a ball of black fire at its end that crackled and snapped. Flames licked from its mouth, above which only a gaping hole served as a nose.

Fedelm loosed an arrow but it burst into flame when it struck the Bamulae.

They ducked as the Bamulae swung the fiery chain at them as it began to lumber toward them. Hot sparks dropped upon them as the chain passed overhead. The mist coiled around its legs and turned to gray serpents with large fangs.

"Watch out!" Cumac yelled, and leaped forward, swinging his sword.

Caladbolg struck against the fiery chain and bounced back. Cumac gritted his teeth and took Caladbolg in both hands and struck savagely at the Bamulae's belly. But the blade passed through without harming the creature.

The wolfhounds sped beneath the Bamulae, snapping at its legs. Then they looped back to stand snarling defiantly beside Seanchan.

Again the Bamulae swung the chain at them, narrowly missing Cumac, who leaped back next to Fedelm. The woman from the Sidhe nocked two arrows and sent them whistling at the creature but again the shafts burst into flame when they struck.

Fedelm dropped her bow and, drawing her sword, leaped forward, darting under the massive chain as it swept overhead. She struck at the Bamulae's legs and drew a howl from the Bamulae's gaping mouth.

"He's vulnerable!" she shouted, and struck again, but a massive paw deflected her sword and threw her back against one of the boulders, where she crumpled senselessly to the ground.

"Fedelm!" Cumac cried. Then the *riastradh*, the warp-spasm, took him. He shook uncontrollably from head to foot and revolved within his skin. His face become blood-red, one eye growing almost Cyclopian in size while the other became as tiny as the eye of a needle. His mouth stretched into a grotesque form and sparks leaped from it. His heart boomed in his chest like a huge drum and a shaft of blood-red light leaped up from his head in a hero's halo. Caladbolg vibrated like living steel in his hand and the Dragonstone spat blood as he performed the salmon-leap above the Bamulae's head, striking down with a mighty blow.

The blade split the top of the Bamulae's head and fire belched upward, nearly striking Cumac as he landed lithely behind the creature and struck a hard two-handed blow against the monster's back.

The Bamulae arched backward from the blow, the roar turning to an earsplitting shriek. It turned toward Cumac but again Cumac leaped like a salmon over the top of the Bamulae, striking a blow at its neck as he passed.

The Bamulae screeched in rage as its head tilted to one side.

Cumac feinted another leap and, when the Bamulae threw up its hands to block him, darted in beneath the Bamulae's guard and savagely drew Caladbolg across its middle.

Streams of black fire slipped out of the Bamulae's belly as Cumac leaped back. But still the creature came forward.

Then a blue-white streak of fire, harsh to the eyes, bolted past them and struck the Bamulae. The creature roared, then suddenly burst into tiny will-o'-the-wisps that fluttered away across the marsh, disappearing into the mist, which slowly began to dissolve.

"Come back!" Seanchan commanded as he turned toward Cumac.

But Cumac continued to vibrate in the warp-spasm.

Seanchan raised his staff and muttered a spell.

"Mith a'rac dae maern ta seiboth!"

A cloud gathered quickly over all and rain poured down, soaking everyone immediately.

Cumac shuddered and the warp-spasm slipped away. He fell to the ground and lay still. Fedelm and Seanchan took him by the shoulders and dragged him to a boulder, propping him against it.

He took a deep breath.

"I . . . am . . . tired," he said. His eyes fluttered, then closed.

"Will he be all right?" Fedelm asked anxiously.

Seanchan nodded. "For now. But he cannot continue using the *ri-astradh*." He shook his head. "But I don't know how to teach him to control it. It comes on its own. Unless he learns how to control it, one day, he will not come out of it and will burn to ash."

"Something must be done," Fedelm said desperately. She smoothed Cumac's hair back from his forehead.

"I'm afraid that he may be destined to go that way," Seanchan said. "Perhaps in the Otherworld he would be able to control it but I doubt that. It is a both a gift and a curse. Time only will tell what will happen."

"What's going on?" yawned Lorgas, sitting up and scrubbing his hands over his face. He looked sleepily at the others.

"Did you have a good sleep?" Fedelm asked, annoyed.

Bern shook himself awake. "What's going on?"

"That's what I'm trying to find out," Lorgas said.

"Well?" Bern asked.

"Well?" Lorgas echoed.

"Later," Seanchan said. "We must rest for a bit, then leave. We have tarried here long enough and should be on the road."

Cumac shook his head and slowly rose. He swayed and Fedelm again steadied him.

"Do you think you can sit Black?" Seanchan asked.

Cumac nodded and stumbled back toward where the horses stood against the cliff. The wolfhounds trotted at his heels.

"What's wrong with him?" Lorgas asked.

"Later," Seanchan repeated. "Now we had better go."

"Go?" Bern asked, frowning. "It's still night."

"You have slept enough," Seanchan said. "Now saddle your horses and ready yourselves for traveling."

"No one tells me anything," Lorgas grumbled, following Cumac and Fedelm to the horses. "You'd think I was a servant or something."

"Oh shut up!" Fedelm said crossly.

Lorgas looked in surprise at her and opened his mouth to speak, then snapped it closed and meekly continued on to the horses.

Within the hour the Seekers were mounted and again headed west, following the old road as it looped around boulders and stunted firs. The wolfhounds again took their positions, one in front, the other in back.

18

The days passed slowly as Tarin and Sirona grew stronger and stronger and waited impatiently for the return of Darin and his soldiers. The Connacht warriors moved warily around them, keeping Sirona in the corners of their eyes so often that Tarin chuckled occasionally when three or four passed together, studiously studying ahead.

"You seem to have made many of the warriors uneasy," Tarin said.

Sirona laughed. "Warriors? Well, perhaps. I

think, however, that those who shy away are those who are too un-
sure of themselves. The older warriors, you notice, do not look
away. They have nothing else to prove. The young ones, however,
some of those would like to build their reputation by fighting us.
We need to be most wary of them. You especially. They have seen
me fight and that is the first they have heard about me. You, however, the Deathwhisper and the Damned, are well known. Mark my
words: You will undoubtedly have to show yourself before we leave
here. *And*, if you remember, Maeve sent her herald to summon
Darin back to court. She has already declared that a challenge will
be issued on your behalf. *Our* behalf, that is."

"Speaking of which, we are long overdue to join our friends."

She frowned. "Yes. But look."

She nodded at two men who were standing half hidden in the
shadows of columns, making a study of ignoring them.

"I think that Maeve doesn't want us to leave yet. But why, I don't
know. Unless it is because she wants to see your swordplay and is
waiting for Darin to show himself. I can't think of what else it
could be."

They walked in silence across the gray paving stones, content in
each other's company, enjoying upon their shoulders the feel of the
sun, which warmed them and brought a feeling of contentment to
them.

They made their way down to the stables to see if Bain and
Borun were being well taken care of, then strolled around the
fortress, watching silversmiths and blacksmiths at work, weavers,
stopping to watch a game of hurley being played by boy warriors.

As the sun began to dip over the walls of the fortress, they made
their way back to the Great Hall, where Maeve's warriors were beginning to gather for the evening meal. Servants were setting out
huge platters of roast pork and fresh-baked bread and bowls of hon-
eyed carrots and lentil soup. Pitchers of foaming October ale had already been placed down the center of the long tables and platters
and goblets arranged for the diners.

The room appeared washed in a golden light as they walked into
it. Heavy crossbeams glowed warmly with a golden sheen. Their

supporting wooden pillars had been carved in intricate sworls and circles with no beginning or end. Large platens carefully laid with oak bundles burned a steady flame, casting light into the most distant recesses of the hall. Warrior shields hung around the hall, and in niches made in the pillars rested the heads of some of the greatest warriors Maeve's champions had met and defeated.

Tarin looked with distaste at the heads. Although the head of a warrior was considered to have special powers when taken in a duel, Tarin did not hold with that custom. Heads were heads, he thought, and once detached were only heads without special powers that had ended once the warrior was slain. The geld-lord he had last served had believed in the powers of the heads but Tarin could never remember words falling from the mouths of the slain let alone prophecies.

Maeve, dressed in a sheer red gown with a gold circlet holding back her mane of red hair, entered the hall and took her place upon the dais at the far end of the room. Allaid sat beside her on a black wooden chair while young soldiers gathered discreetly behind her, armed with swords and spears.

No sooner had she seated herself than a trumpet sounded, followed minutes later by the door to the Great Hall crashing open and Darin swaggering in followed by his soldiers. He ignored the warriors seated and strode up to the bottom of the dais. Mac Chect discreetly took his place to Maeve's left.

Darin was dressed in a stained leather jerkin and cape, his boots muddy, his face still covered with a fine film of perspiration. He stared insolently up at Maeve and said, "Well? You have called me away from the defense of our northern borders. This is carelessness on your part, Maeve. Now they are guarded by young boys seeking to make a name for themselves as warriors. They are little prepared to keep our enemies at bay."

A bright flush appeared on Maeve's face and her eyes blazed at Darin's effrontery. Her full lips drew themselves into a hard straight line. The soldiers behind her moved restlessly, sensing the fury building within their queen.

"You are forgetting yourself, Darin," she said. Her words carried an iron edge to them. "Is this how you greet the queen of Connacht? With arrogance? Mind well your manners if you do not want to scrub pots and kettles in our kitchens!"

Darin smiled smugly and gave an exaggerated bow that stopped just short of insolence.

"Forgive me, my . . . 'Queen.' I have been riding hard to obey your . . . command. I'm afraid that my manners were left behind my horse's hooves."

Maeve's lips grew even tighter.

"And you dared to show yourself in my Great Hall dressed like a slovenly boy? As do your soldiers?"

Darin spread his hands and smiled again. "I hurried to obey your command that I appear before you. You made it clear that my appearance here was of the greatest importance."

Maeve leaned back in her chair and eyed him, her eyes glinting dangerously, her face drawn and cold.

"It has come to my attention that while I was hunting you took it upon yourself to imprison two who had come to my gates claiming the Laws of Hospitality. Is this true?"

"I placed two who appeared to be assassins in custody," Darin said. "That is my privilege as it is any of your warriors' privilege if they feel that a threat is possible against Connacht."

"And you hid their presence from my Druid and others who I had left to govern in my stead."

Darin bowed and said, "I did what I thought was best. You can ask no more from any man."

"Yes, I can," she said icily. "I demand my men follow my orders when I am not upon the throne. *All* my men."

"They spoke discourteously of you as well," Darin said. "And . . ."

He had no chance to finish his words when Tarin leaped from his place at the table in front of Darin. His eyes were black flint. White lines appeared down his cheeks, tightening the skin until his face became a death's-head. His body vibrated with tension.

"You are a liar," he said harshly. "You are a liar and a coward who brought us here to Cruachan Ai under the guise of duty only to send men in the dead of night to capture us and take us to the dungeons. And for that, you will pay!"

His fist exploded on Darin's chin. The captain fell backward and sprawled dazed upon the stone floor. Chuckles came from around the room. Darin flushed and struggled to his feet, holding on to the edge of a wooden table as his knees threatened to buckle again. His hand swept down to the pommel of his sword, half-drawing it, then froze as Maeve's voice cracked like a whip throughout the hall.

"Stay your hand, Darin! Unless you wish to lose your head!"

Five warriors sprang forward, swords drawn, points within a foot of his throat.

Slowly Darin's hand opened and his sword slipped back into its sheath. He stood white-faced, staring at Maeve, anger hard in his face.

"You will be conducted to the baths, where you will be allowed to bathe. Then to your rooms—all of you," she said, indicating the others who had entered with Darin. "On the morrow, you will face Tarin."

"I do not duel with Sword-wanderers," he said, glaring at Tarin.

"You will fight any I put before you," Maeve said. "The challenge does not come from him but from this court. Be happy that I do not place you in the cell where he came from. Take their weapons!" she snapped.

Obediently warriors rose from the tables and came forward and collected the weapons and took them to a corner of the hall, where they dumped them carelessly.

"Tomorrow, you will face the Damned," she said. "Deathwhisper, who you seem to hold in such contempt. Now take them from my sight!"

Her last words thundered through the Great Hall. Obediently the warriors came from behind her and surrounded Darin and his men.

White-faced, Darin turned and strode swiftly from the hall, his men hard upon his heels. When the door slammed shut, a loud sigh echoed from the walls and ceiling of the hall as the warriors expelled held breaths.

Maeve seized a goblet of wine and drained it, her hand trembling with rage. A servant leaped forward to refill the goblet from a pitcher he held, then retreated back out of her sight. All there knew that when the fury was upon her, no one was safe from her anger. Far better to stay tactfully away.

With a visible effort she brought herself under control, the tension slowly easing from her shoulders and disappearing from her face. She nodded at Tarin.

"Tomorrow. At noon in the courtyard," she said. "You will have your wish fulfilled. Now"—she clapped her hands—"let us relax and eat and drink merrily!"

But it took a while before laughter began to be heard in the hall, as the warriors kept casting wary glances at Tarin, who took his seat once again beside Sirona, his face a stony mask that chilled the others who caught his eye by accident.

A few warriors tried to make halfhearted wagers, but Tarin's reputation was well known. Only the young warriors were willing to take Darin's side, and they did not have the money to make worthwhile wagers.

The bard began singing from his place at the foot of the dais, strumming his harp in accompaniment.

> *Of swords and fools I sing*
> *For the battle that will bring*
> *Death to Darin the Unwise*
> *Who failed to realize*
> *The feared Deathwhisper*
> *Whose mighty blade whispers*
> *Past duels and battles*
> *That ended with death-rattles*
> *In the throats of the unwary . . .*

A GRAY dawn spilled over Cruachan and remained unchanged to the noon hour, when Darin was brought to the courtyard and given his sword. His men arranged themselves along the walls on either side, their swords hanging from their belts nearly scraping the ground.

Darin wore a brown leather jerkin layered with twelve skins. His feet were clad in boots that came up to midway on his thighs. A leather band wrapped around his forehead kept his hair out of his eyes. Leather bands also covered his wrists and forearms.

He took his sword and began to stretch, swinging it easily around his shoulders and slashing and stabbing to loosen his muscles. He spread his legs and twisted and turned, pulling the muscles taut then releasing them.

Then Tarin slipped into the courtyard like a shadow. For a moment he wasn't there; then he was, as if magic had suddenly dropped the scales from the eyes of the onlookers. A quick intake of air whispered over the courtyard at the sight of him.

He was dressed all in black—leather jerkin, boots to midthigh, a soft linen shirt covering his arms and anchored with leather wristbands. His hair was clubbed behind his neck. His eyes glowed like black sapphires with flames lurking in their depth. His face was marble-white. He held the rune-blade loosely in his right hand.

He stood quietly, watching Darin go through his exercises, slipping over the gray slate paving of the courtyard. He smiled to himself as he watched Darin's feet slip now and then—just a little that would not have been seen by any other warrior.

At last Darin, finished. A fine sheen of perspiration covered his face. He leered contemptuously at Tarin and grounded his sword, waiting.

From a balcony above the courtyard, Maeve dropped a red scarf and Darin charged, swinging his sword around his head for a great slash at Tarin's head.

Tarin moved slightly and Darin's blade whispered past his head, barely missing it. As he slipped Darin's attack, his sword danced lightly around Darin's chest, slicing through his jerkin, barely touching Darin.

Again Darin charged and again Tarin danced away from the attack, his blade slipping inside the other's guard, slicing though the jerkin again.

Again and again Darin rushed Tarin, bellowing his war cry, and again and again Tarin slipped past Darin's defenses. Soon Darin's jerkin hung in tatters around his hairy chest. Tarin stood on the opposite side of the courtyard as Darin leaned over his sword, panting from exertion. Steel had yet to meet steel despite the vain attempts by Darin to engage Tarin.

Darin glared across the courtyard at Tarin. Perspiration dotted the gray slates but Tarin stood quietly, showing no exertion, his breathing regular and his muscles loose and relaxed.

"Is this a dance or are you going to fight?" Darin growled.

Tarin shrugged. "You need a little lesson with your sword. So far, you have shown me nothing but the hack and slice of a young boy first learning swordplay. You treat your sword as an ax. Not much technique in that," he said, taunting.

Laughter rose from the watchers around the edge of the courtyard. Darin's face turned the color of old liver. He bared his yellow teeth in fury and came again at Tarin, working his blade through the Thunder Feat, but Tarin slipped away again and again. This time the rune-blade cut small gobbets of flesh from Darin. Soon, blood trickled down his chest and arms, making his sword difficult to hold.

Again he tried the Thunder Feat and again Tarin slipped through his defenses, his sword flicking in and out, not meeting the other's blade.

Admiration rose among the onlookers at the demonstration Tarin was giving. Indeed, some warriors murmured to each other, this was a master at work, and more than one whispered that they were glad they didn't stand in the courtyard against Tarin.

"I can see that you are not learning anything," Tarin said, slipping through the other's defenses for the uncountable time. "And I'm tired of teaching. Defend yourself."

And Tarin moved in toward the other, moving through the Lightning and Thunder Feats as his sword struck ringingly against Darin's sword, sliding down the his blade to cut larger and larger chunks of flesh from Darin.

Once Darin managed to close on Tarin and while they stood, nearly nose-to-nose, Darin said, "You will lose, Deathwhisper. Know that I not only fight myself, but with Maliman's skill as well."

Then Darin's breathing returned to normal and a new strength washed over him. He began to stalk Tarin, his blade probing Tarin's defense as Tarin moved slowly back away from Darin's attack.

Darin's blade slipped through Tarin's defense and nearly decapitated him but Tarin slipped away, spinning like a child's top back into the center of the courtyard. Darin smiled and swung his sword in a figure eight as he moved toward Tarin. His sword began slicing and stabbing with renewed vigor, faster and faster, and Tarin was hard-pressed to defend himself from the other's attack.

Then Darin gave a mighty roar that echoed around the courtyard as he attacked furiously. Tarin gave a hard laugh and this time moved in to meet the other's attack. Faster and faster his sword moved, slowly driving Darin back. Doubt began to appear in Darin's eyes as Tarin's attack grew harder and harder to keep from reaching through his guard.

In desperation, Darin tried to defend against Tarin's attack but could not. He began to falter, his sword beginning to feel like an iron weight in his hand. He clutched the hilt with both hands, swinging wildly.

Suddenly Darin's head flew from his body, bouncing against the walls of the courtyard, as Tarin's blade slashed crosswise from Darin's shoulder, splitting him nearly in half. The onlookers gasped in wonder. No one had seen the blow, so swiftly had Tarin delivered it.

Darin stood for moment while blood spouted in a crimson spray. Then he toppled and lay quietly on the slates.

"This is truly a sword-master," a grizzled warrior breathed. "Surely a gift granted by Lugh, the sun god. First Chair at Maeve's table belongs to him."

Murmurs of agreement came from the other seasoned warriors around him. The First Chair belonged to the greatest of champions among a gathering of warriors at the tables in the Great Hall and he who sat in that chair was known as one to be given a wide berth.

"Come, Tarin!" Maeve cried from the balcony. "Come all! Let us drink to the greatest champion in some time to walk through Cruachan's gates! Not since Cucullen have I seen one dance the sword-dance as well as this Tarin the Deathwhisper! Let us honor him and show Cruachan's famed hospitality for one who has earned that right!"

A roar of approval came from the throats of the warriors. Sirona grinned at Tarin and said, "It seems you have made your mark too!"

Tarin nodded. "There comes a time when a fool must be taught how foolish he is and how foolish his minions are. But"—here he lowered his voice—"he was more than just a foolish warrior. He was one of Maliman's men. He told me that during the duel."

Sirona bit her lip and said, "Then Maliman's sending spies out to infiltrate the courts of kings and chieftains." She glanced across at Darin's men shifting their feet and standing uncertainly in a group. "I'll wager my sword that those men are Maliman's as well."

"Uh-huh," Tarin said. "I think it's time we voiced our thoughts to Maeve and her guards. It's as certain as the shamrock that they were sent here to assassinate Maeve and seize control of Cruachan."

Tarin lifted his arm, calling for silence. Slowly the uproar died and when he could be heard, he lifted his voice to Maeve, saying, "My queen! Gladly do I accept your kind offer. But first, I must inform you that those"—he pointed at Darin's men—"are in the service of Maliman! Darin admitted as such to me during our duel!"

Maeve's eyes flashed anger that made the courtyard blaze with fire fury. She stood and pointed at the warriors Tarin had accused.

"Take their swords and put them into the hell-pit!" she thundered. "They are Maliman's men!"

Instantly swords rang as they were drawn from their sheaths, and before the accused could draw their own, they were surrounded by Maeve's warriors. One grizzled warrior struck one of Darin's men with a heavy gauntleted fist that crushed the bones in his face and dropped him to the ground. In a twinkling, the others found themselves disarmed and being pummeled. They tried to defend themselves, but the numbers were too great for them and they were beaten from the courtyard and driven down to the dungeon's lowermost recesses, where there were no cells, only a deep pit from which one could not climb. No light came here in the hell-pit and those thrown there knew that death would be their only release.

"It is time that we ask Maeve for our favor with Cairpre," Sirona said softly as she and Tarin made their way into the Great Hall. "We are long overdue to meet the others at the Pass of Adene. I do not think they are waiting for us any longer and have probably gone on to Cairpre's court."

"You are right," Tarin said. "We have tarried here long enough. Our words must be spoken and we must leave despite how long Maeve wishes to keep us at her court."

"Then let us attend to it," Sirona said, and stepped aside to allow Tarin to enter before her in the place of honor.

Maeve's warriors followed them, laughing and swearing and animatedly describing how they saw the duel fought as they took their awarded places at the feasting tables. Maeve herself appeared almost as soon as they had made themselves comfortable and seized a goblet of wine, raising it high.

"A toast!" she cried. "To one of the greatest swordsmen! Tarin the Damned, the Deathwhisper!"

A roar of approval came from all throats as goblets were lifted and drained. Then Tarin stepped forward and said, "Maeve, Queen of Connacht, listen to my words!"

The noise trickled away to silence as attention turned to Tarin.

"Speak, Tarin. Ask what you wish to half of my kingdom! For that you may not have as you are not Connacht-born."

"Of gifts I wish only one. You have seen for yourself that Maliman has been or is now present in your court. And if he is in the mighty fortress of Cruachan Ai, where else might his followers be among the other courts and fortresses in Erin? It is time that Connacht start gathering armies to protect her borders against Maliman's soldiers and ready her defenses regardless of old enemies and alliances against those chieftains and kings who willingly break alliances to serve the Dark Forces. Connacht is one of the mightier kingdoms along with Ulster and to have one or the other slip away to Maliman could mean disaster to all of Erin.

"Still, we, the Seekers, must retrieve the Chalice of Fire from Bricriu and to do that, we need your intervention with Cairpre of Munster. We ask that you inform Cairpre that it would be wise to suspend the Laws of Hospitality so the Seekers may take Bricriu and the Chalice and return both to Ulster."

Maeve sank back in her chair, eyeing Tarin as she thought. Then she leaned forward and said, "Suspending the Laws of Hospitality is not something to be done lightly, Tarin. We cannot predict the ways and means of the gods and to openly challenge The Dagda in this way may not be wise. And what sign or proof do we have that once the Chalice is returned to Ulster that Ulster will honor a peace between us? The Chalice may bring peace to Ulster but it also is a mighty weapon that can be used against one's enemies if one knows how. The Chalice, especially in the hands of Connor's Druid Cathbad, would make Ulster invincible in battle against Connacht. There is no love lost between Connacht and Ulster. We are bitter enemies and have been for thousands of years. Once I was wife to Connor but soon discovered that he wanted a wife to do his bidding and tried to keep her from being herself. It is no secret of my love for men. But Connor would not allow me that. Or," she reflected, "*tried* to not allow me that. My leaving his bed was enough to bring up old hatreds and angers between Connacht and Ulster.

"As for Cairpre, he's a fool and worse, a lazy fool who lives for pleasures and pleasures alone. His army has grown weak with their indolent ways and many no longer wear warrior's dress but silks and fine mantles and spend their time with delicacies and good wine and women. But the dangerous thing about such a fool as Cairpre is that he believes himself to be a powerful warrior. He disillusions himself by equating his throne with the throne of Connacht or Ulster. A fool is like that, you know. Filled with misguided self-worth. I believe you could take Bricriu if you wish to do so from Cairpre's court with little trouble."

She shook her head. "No, this I will not do. Ask of me anything else but not this. I will not place Connacht in jeopardy. I gave you permission once to take Bricriu from my court and that is enough. The gods could have punished us for that violation of the Laws of Hospitality. It is not for me to force Cairpre's hand. Some things must be done on one's own. Cairpre himself must judge whether to suspend the Laws of Hospitality or not. Or for you to disobey them and take Bricriu and the Chalice deliberately from Cairpre's court. I am sorry, but there it is."

Tarin's face turned grim, but he managed a respectful bow and said, "Then there is nothing for it but for me and Sirona to return to the others. We thank you for your hospitality toward us and regret having brought difficulties to your court. Now, if you will excuse us, we must make ready for our journey to join the other Seekers."

"Stay," Maeve urged. "There is no hurry. Surely you can enjoy a day or two with us."

Tarin shook his head. "I thank you for your offer and regret that we must be on our way. Time is a luxury that we no longer have."

He bowed and turned away from Maeve and nodded at Sirona. Wordlessly she rose and followed him from the hall despite protests from the warriors.

Outside the Great Hall, Tarin glanced at her and said, "We need to hurry. Maeve is temperamental and could well decide that we have insulted her court and detain us."

"She is a fool," Sirona said, matching his stride. "Surely she knows that Maliman has no alliances and would recognize none even if he had some. I don't see the reason for someone to deliberately place themselves in the path of danger when it could be so easily avoided."

"It is the old hatred between enemies," Tarin said. "For Maeve, the threat is not Maliman now but Ulster. Darin and his men should have been reason enough to sway her to our cause but old traditions often betray one or the other."

"She is a fool."

"Perhaps. But this is no time to dwell on that. Gather your things and meet me by the stable immediately. We can still put a good number of miles between us and Maeve's court before the gloaming."

"Bain and Borun are fresh and so are we," Sirona said. "We could ride on through the night."

"We'll come to that bridge when night falls," Tarin said. "But for now, let us ride."

Within a half-hour Sirona and Tarin had packed and made their way to the stable, where they quickly saddled their mounts. A bare five minutes later they were at the gate and through it, galloping along the coastal road, heading due south toward Munster.

19

The Seekers reached the Pass of Adene as the sun began to drop over the tops of the mountains and fall toward the sea. Seanchan called a halt just outside the pass where a small cutback filled with alder and willow and oak trees and a bubbling spring provided the Seekers with an ideal resting place. Stone walls were against their backs, and the entrance into the cutback was a narrow defile easily defended by two against any who tried to attack their camp. Wood had been cut and carefully stacked at the back by a thoughtful fellow who had camped here before, and a fire pit had been laid with stone against the back wall where the fire would reflect out and warm those lying beside it.

The wolfhounds disappeared as soon as the Seekers began unsaddling their horses and reappeared a quarter-hour later, each with a hare dangling from its huge jaws. Meanwhile, Lorgas gathered some branches and carefully laid a fire in the pit and slowly stoked it until the flames flickered cheerfully. Cumac and Bern began to ready the evening meal, while Seanchan rested, leaning his back against the wall. Fedelm swiftly climbed to the top of the cutback to study their back trail. She could see no one following but did spy a small herd of red deer feeding at the end of the marsh grass. She dropped lightly to the ground.

"We could use fresh meat. There's a small herd of red deer feeding at the edge of the marsh."

"I'll go with you," Cumac said, rising.

"There's no need," Fedelm said, sliding a piece of beeswax along her bowstring.

"There is always need here," Seanchan said. "Let Cumac come with you. Four eyes here are better than two. And be careful. There are others in the area beside us.

"Along the way, to the right of your path you will find a salt lick. Bring some salt back for us."

"And some wild thyme, onions, and rosemary. If you should stumble across any," Bern added.

Cumac laughed. "Let's go Fedelm before these folk think we are going to market. You have seen the deer. You lead."

Fedelm trotted off, relishing the movement of her thigh muscles as they stretched the weariness of saddle riding away. Her feet barely touched the ground before she was springing forward, moving effortlessly, quartering their trail.

Cumac laughed and matched her, stride for stride, feeling the good air fill his lungs as he watched Fedelm's hair stream behind her in auburn waves. Yet he kept his eyes shifting from one side of their path to the other and back over his shoulder, guarding against surprise should a threat be launched at them.

Then Fedelm slowed and came to a stop behind a huckleberry bush. She motioned with the flat of her hand for Cumac to crouch and join her.

In front of them an unwary herd grazed peacefully, unaware of Fedelm and Cumac.

"The wind is in our favor," Fedelm whispered to Cumac. "When I rise to shoot, they will turn and run toward the west where they can find safety in the hills and mountains. You go down that way"— she pointed to a small fold in the ground—"and turn them back toward me. I will drop one over there as they turn."

"Why not here?" Cumac asked.

"Too close to the path. If any are following us, they will find the pool of blood and know we are very close and continue searching during the night. But over there, in the fold, they may miss the blood and stop for the night before carrying on."

"Makes sense," Cumac said, and backed away from the bush, then moved on a slant to slip into the fold.

Fedelm stood and the sentry immediately snorted and led the herd leaping away from Fedelm. Then Cumac rose and the deer paused for just a second before turning toward the south. But in that pause, Fedelm loosed an arrow that sped true to its mark and felled a yearling.

By the time she had made her way over to Cumac and the yearling, Cumac had gutted the deer and stuffed the cavity with handfuls of dried grass to soak up blood. He rose, lifting the deer across his shoulders, carrying it easily.

Fedelm nodded and turned and led the way back toward the Seekers. They stopped twice; once to pick wild onions and mushrooms, again to gather a bit of thyme. Of rosemary, they saw none, but Bern was satisfied when they returned and dropped their gatherings to the ground.

"Lorgas, you can do the butchering," Cumac said, panting a little.

Lorgas's eyebrows shot up. "Why do I get the dirty job? Let Bern do it!"

"Bern is cooking," Fedelm said patiently. "And we gathered the food. That leaves you to butcher."

"Unfair," Lorgas muttered, but gathered his knife and moved to the side of the deer, skillfully skinning it.

"Did you see anything?" Seanchan asked.

They shook their heads.

"No," Cumac said. "No one followed our trail as far as we could see. But that doesn't mean there aren't any beyond our sight."

"I feel troubled," Fedelm said, moving her shoulders uneasily. "But I do not know why. Perhaps it would be better if I backtracked a few miles to make certain that we are safe. Temporarily, that is."

Seanchan shook his head. "No. If someone or something is following us, that would make you vulnerable. There is more safety in our numbers here in this place, which is very defensible. The cliff hangs over our little campsite so none can drop in to surprise us. And only two at a time can come to us through the niche. We are best served here. Tarin and Sirona will easily be able to find us here at the mouth of the pass and the wolfhounds can easily guard us tonight so we may get a good night's sleep for a change. No, this is for the best."

"I'm not certain I can agree with that," Lorgas said, bringing two roasts to the fire so Bern could spit them with willow branches.

"Nor I," Bern echoed. "Goblins can easily scratch their way down that wall and Nightshades can come down from the sky as well. For that matter, sumaires themselves could surprise us. Truacs . . ."

"Yes, yes," Seanchan said impatiently. "But we will still have plenty of warning from Nuad and Fergma. No, we shall rest here and wait for Sirona and Tarin to join us. They should be here within five days. We can wait that long."

"I think Seanchan's right," Cumac said. "We are as safe here as anywhere and perhaps better so. We have food and water. The horses have fodder and this place better lends itself to defense than some of the places where we have camped before. Even better, perhaps, as if you recall Callyberry still had one of Maliman's men within it when we arrived. What town or village or inn or even court can boast itself to be free from Maliman's servants? No, here we have no fear of that. No doubts that this person or that person is in the employ of Maliman."

"Perhaps," Lorgas said grudgingly, pulling his fingers through his beard. "Still I have misgivings. Oh, I know what you say makes sense, Cumac, but I can't help feeling that the longer we remain in one place the more we set ourselves up to be trapped. This place offers good defense but it also offers a trap as well. Our food is not limitless. A band of warriors could encamp just outside our defenses and wait us out. They would not have to hurry one way or the other and still we would be forced to eventually go out to meet them."

"*After* being weakened by our fast," Bern added. "I agree with Lorgas. This may be a fine place for the moment but it could still be our death trap if we decide to wait here for Tarin and Sirona."

"Five days . . ." Seanchan began

"May be too long," Lorgas said. "Perhaps on the other side of the pass there is another place that we could wait as well. Two days here and two days there and leave on the fifth day. At least we have some movement with our party. *And,*" he added as an afterthought, "we could be ambushed as we move through the Pass of Adene. Have you thought of that?"

Cumac exchanged looks with Fedelm and shrugged.

"We could have been ambushed anywhere along the road we have traveled," Fedelm said. "Nowhere we travel is there any guarantee of safety. Our safety lies better in keeping hidden and here we are pretty well out of sight. We shall use hardwood for the fire as that gives off little smoke. We shall limit our coming and going to that which is absolutely needed and, I think at the moment, that we do not even need to do that. Tomorrow I shall slay another deer and between the two we should have enough food to last five days. There is a small ledge up there under that outcropping"—she pointed and the Seekers craned their necks to see—"where we can mount a hidden watch on the coastal road. I say we spend the rest of our time resting—which we all could use."

Lorgas and Bern exchanged glances, then both shrugged and squatted on their heels by the small fire flickering cheerfully.

"In the long run, Bern," Lorgas said, "one way or the other is an equal choice. Whether we stay here, resting on our heels, or go back and forth through the pass. We can be caught either way. This place offers a certain comfort that we can only guess at on the other end of the pass."

"By m' tides," Bern said, shaking his head. "You're right, of course, Lorgas. I guess I'm becoming an old woman in my age, blinking and shifting at shadows. Given the state of the times now one place is surely as good as another. We can only take time when it is given. Can't make it into anything else. So, yes, I'll go along with the rest of you and hope for the best."

"That's all we've ever had, Bern," Seanchan said mildly. "Hope."

"Aye, but I still like a little certainty around me," Bern said. "And now"—he raised the roasts from the fire with a flourish—"our food is done and the gravy made. So I say, let the ashes fall where they may: let's eat."

"And high time," Lorgas said, taking his bone-handled hunting knife from his belt and slicing off a generous hunk of roast and dropping it onto a chunk of deadwood cut in the rough shape of a platter. He heaped onions and gravy on it and set to with relish.

The others followed and soon the food and the soft night soothed them and they lay contented upon the pallets they had made and slept while the wolfhounds Nuad and Fergma kept watch.

The four days passed serenely enough, although a few small parties of Truacs and goblins made a night passage through the pass, but the Seekers remained hidden and free from attack. Once a Meman ridden by a sumaire tried to turn in to the small cul-de-sac, but the sumaire brutally yanked its reins and goaded it through the pass. The rest of the time, the Seekers rested quietly, keeping watch from the ledge that Fedelm had noted cut into the granite wall above them.

On the morning of the fifth day, Seanchan stirred himself and said, "I do not believe that Tarin and Sirona are coming. Or, if they are coming, they have been detained. We have waited here long enough and now must move. Although we have been safe here for the past four days, we cannot leave much to chance anymore."

"Where to?" Cumac asked.

"On to Cairpre's court," Seanchan said. "Although I fear that we will not be welcomed as we wish, we will at least be granted the Laws of Hospitality."

"*If* Cairpre does not lift the Laws for others to attack us or take us prisoner," Lorgas pointed out. "We asked Maeve to help persuade Cairpre to lift the Laws for us against Bricriu. There is no reason that the Laws couldn't be lifted for Maliman's men against us."

"Yes," Seanchan said. "We will have to be watchful once we are in Cairpre's court."

"Do you want to send others to Maeve?" Bern asked. "Lorgas and I could travel up there."

Seanchan shook his head. "No. We can't risk losing any others. If Sirona and Tarin made it, then we should have an answer when we get to Cairpre's court. If not, then we are no worse off than we were in the beginning when we left the Red Branch."

"They still may come," Fedelm said. "They may have only been detained. Maeve is pretty mercurial—she washes warm and cold at whim. We do not know that she hasn't decided to keep Tarin and Sirona at Cruachan Ai for one thing or another. If you remember, Cumac, she has already agreed to let Connacht's armies be led by Scathach Buanand, the Woman of Victory, who lives on the Island of Shadows, if Ulster will allow the same. And, she did relax the Laws of Hospitality after you entered the Cave of Cruachan and faced the three lions of Connacht and slew them. But Bricriu had already left Cruachan Ai by the time that was accomplished."

Cumac nodded. He well remembered the fight with the three great lions. Each had been as tall as the mast of a ship at the shoulders. Their teeth had been yellowed spikes and their claws like pounded steel. Scales had seemed to cover their bodies, with tufts of fur sticking out from around the edges of the scales. Their eyes flashed green fire, and Cumac shivered now as he recalled how close that battle had been.

"Yes, I remember," he said. "How could I forget? They nearly finished me."

"We cannot count on Maeve interfering with Cairpre's court. Certainly she could, but I feel now that she is waiting to build her armies for the coming battle and that is her worry as of now. That plus waiting to see if Connor will agree to allow Ulster's armies to be led by Scathach Buanand. We cannot continue to ask more of her at this time," Seanchan said. "I feared that before we agreed to let Tarin and Sirona attempt to enlist her help with Cairpre.

"Now I feel we must take matters into our own hands and travel to Cairpre's court and see if we cannot find a way to get the Chalice from Bricriu and Bricriu from the court."

"Even if Maeve refused to help, I wish Tarin and Sirona were here," Cumac said.

"As do we all," Fedelm said. "But if wishes were horses . . ."

"I know, 'beggars would ride,'" Cumac finished. "We accomplish little sitting here and playing what if and for. Best we continue making our way to Cairpre's court and there we shall see what may be done. Perhaps we can frighten Cairpre enough with Maliman to enlist his help."

"I do not hold much hope for that," Seanchan said. "Cairpre lives for pleasure alone. A man like that is reluctant to take a path that will take pleasure away."

"I have little use for his sort," Lorgas growled, fingering the haft of his ax.

"As do I," Bern said, slinging his sword over his shoulder. "But we can do little here. Better we seek new ground rather than continue growing fat and sassy here. I say we ride."

"As do I," Fedelm said.

In no length of time the Seekers made ready for their travel, rolling their blankets and tying them securely behind their saddles. They checked their weapons, and when satisfied, they mounted their horses and moved into the pass, Black eagerly stepping high as he led the way, happy to once again to be moving and not standing listlessly in the wooden copse of the cul-de-sac.

The Seekers rode into the ambush just as they started leaving the boulder- and rock-strewn Pass of Adene. They had ridden cautiously while coming through the pass and for a brief moment had relaxed their watch, but only briefly, when Truacs and hobgoblins rode down on them from behind a pile of boulders that had fallen freely from the cliff during the time of Tuan and the Great Flood. But Nuad and Fergma had time to bristle and growl menacingly, bringing the warrior's sense back to the Seekers.

Two Truacs, riding Memans, rode hard against the elves, but Bern and Lorgas leaped high above their saddles, drawing sword and ax and decapitating them as they rode by. The elves dropped nimbly to the ground and put their backs against a cliff wall side by side. Fedelm's bow sent arrow after arrow into the attackers, each shaft finding its mark. But soon the attackers came too close for her to use her bow and she was forced to draw her sword, leaping to stand near Seanchan's back as a Truac leaped and unhorsed him.

Caladbolg rang sharply as it sang from its sheath into the hands of Cumac, who dropped Black's reins and let the warhorse find his own attack. Black's hooves flashed and a he bugled his war cry as he leaped into the foray.

Blood spattered and filled the air with a fine spray as the Seekers fought, but the numbers against them slowly began to tell as they were forced back to the cliff wall.

Then a sword stroke sliced into Lorgas's shoulder, staggering the elf. Another found Bern's arm when he tried to help his friend.

Seanchan's staff spat blue sparks as he wielded it against a pair of hobgoblins who kept trying to get behind him.

And then Cumac's back arched and all there heard his bones crack and his muscles grew into huge knots. His hair stood on end with a drop of blood on each hair and a hero's halo rose from him and hovered around him as his battle cry roared, sending terror into the hearts of the enemy. One eye shrank to the size of a needle and the other bulged with red-veined fury. Throwing caution to the wind, Cumac charged into the middle of the enemy force, sending Truac and goblin heads flying from their shoulders to ricochet off the walls and bounce down into the pass.

"The Beast! The Beast!" shrieked the hobgoblins as they tried to flee Cumac's wrath. But there were too many of them and the ones in front caused a jam when they tried to flee only to be met by the charge of their brothers.

"The Beast!"

Bodies dropped, cleaved in half, gobbets of flesh flying from them, blood fountaining high into the air to spatter against the cliff walls. Tiny rivers of blood began to flow to the south and still Cumac roared and hacked his way through the wall of attackers.

A huge Truac, easily half again Cumac's size, roared as he charged on stumpy legs, swinging a mace-and-chain high overhead. Cumac ignored him and gave the salmon-leap, soaring over the Truac's head to fall lightly behind him. A single stroke struck the Truac's head from his shoulders. The head flew high, arching over a pile of boulders, nearly striking a pair of ravens perched on the top boulder.

Then Badb's shrill war cry, the cry of the Battle Raven, sounded along with the bellow of Neit the Terror, the war god, whose roar over the battlefield struck fear into the hearts of the enemy. They milled in confusion and another dozen were slain in an instant by Cumac wielding Caladbolg.

"Away! Away!" the Truacs and hobgoblins in front shrieked. "The Beast! The Beast!"

The tide gave way and Truacs and hobgoblins ran howling back through the pass, heading toward the marsh and darkness.

Cumac roared and charged after them only to be knocked senseless by a bolt from Seanchan's staff.

"Seanchan?" Fedelm panted, frowning at the Druid.

Seanchan shook his head as he gasped, "I . . . had to . . . stop him. Somehow."

She nodded as Seanchan took a deep breath then found a seat on a boulder and leaned back against the cliff wall.

"Lorgas? Bern?" she asked, concern deep upon her face as she came to the elves to attend their wounds.

"Just a scratch," Lorgas said, then his eyes rolled up into his forehead and he pitched forward onto the ground.

"Just like an . . ." Bern started, then followed his friend to the ground.

"They've lost a lot of blood," Seanchan said, forcing himself erect. He crossed to Fedelm who was busily washing blood from their wounds. "Hmm. That one on Lorgas is a nasty one. You'll have to sew it, I'm afraid. Now, Bern"—he turned to the other elf and examined his wound—"I think we can close this with a poultice of wolfbane. Be sure you sprinkle some wolfbane into Lorgas's wound too. No telling what that Truac blade had been used for last. Better to be safe than sorry. You'll find fresh linen in my bag." He pointed behind him as he walked to Cumac and bent over him. He placed the pads of his fingers on Cumac's eyes and closed his own, chanting softly, so softly that Fedelm could not hear the words. A soft blue glow grew into the size of a water lily from beneath his finger pads and slowly Cumac's muscles relaxed and the warp-spasm disappeared.

Cumac's frame shuddered and his eyes opened as Seanchan removed his fingers. He tried to sit up only to fall back against the ground, gasping for breath. Pain etched deep lines into Cumac's face only to disappear as his breathing slowed. But there was a new small silver streak running through his hair and his eyes looked bruised.

"Rest," Seanchan said softly. "Rest."

He pressed his fingers again against Cumac's eyes. This time a soft green glow appeared, and Cumac's breathing slowed as he fell into a deep slumber.

Seanchan sighed and rose, his knee joints popping from the effort. He frowned as he studied Cumac and shook his head.

"The warp-spasm is beginning to tell on him," he said. He pointed to the slash of silver in Cumac's hair. "This is the beginning. Each time he uses it, he loses time from the end of his life. To make matters worse, the warp-spasm is beginning to come unbidden on its own. Cumac seems to be losing control over it."

"Can't you teach him?" Fedelm asked as she laid out the contents of her bag in search of wolfbane. She found some and crushed it and began mixing it with some bittersweet to create a poultice.

Seanchan shrugged. "Perhaps. Now that I know a little more about it. Once we reach Cairpre's court perhaps we'll have some time. It isn't something to be learned overnight. But," he added grimly, "I imagine that we may have time before Bricriu decides to leave Cairpre's safety. *If* we can convince Cairpre of the importance of suspending the Laws of Hospitality for Bricriu. As I've said before: Cairpre enjoys his pleasure and does little to upset that pleasure. For example, coming through that pass"—he nodded toward it—"puts us within Munster's borders. And yet we see no guard or patrol."

"They could have been slain by the Truacs and hobgoblins," Fedelm pointed out.

"True. But I doubt it. We may encounter them as we travel south and if we do, it might be wise if I do the talking. Agreed?"

He looked at the others, who wearily nodded in agreement. The battle had taken much from them and they were in no mood for argument. Indeed, what would be the point? One spokesman would be enough for all. It would be enough to have an escort to Cairpre while they recovered from the wounds and aches and pains of battle.

"Now," Seanchan said urgently, "I think it would be in our best interest to ride away from this foul place. The hills here will be crawling with Truacs and hobgoblins and such once darkness falls. We need to continue on as fast as we can."

"We could always go back through," Bern pointed out.

"And be forced to come through the pass again later? No. We have put the pass behind us and I do not wish to retrace our steps. There will be something farther on. Of that I am certain." His eyes twinkled. "And who knows? We may even find an inn with a roaring fire, malt beer, and salted pork fresh off the bone for you, Lorgas."

The elf's eyes lit up and he tried to rise to his feet but was forced back as Fedelm applied the poultice to his wound. He winced and glared at the woman from the Sidhe.

" 'Tis enough I have the wound," he complained. "Let alone causing me more grief."

"Oh hold still!" Fedelm said crossly. "The sooner I get your wounds dressed the sooner we can ride and the sooner we might get to that inn you want."

With that, Lorgas fell silent, although he squirmed a little as the poultice began to burn. True to her word, however, Fedelm quickly dressed their wounds, and within the hour all were mounted and following the road away from the pass, lifting their horses into a ground-gaining lope heading ever south.

20

A blood-red sunset appeared in front of the
Seekers as they came over a small rise on the
coastal road and saw the lights of a small village
and an inn ahead of them. A cold wind blew in
off the sea, chilling them, but a spark of hope
ran through them as they rode through the small
town of Adene and hurried toward the inn. A
creaking sign overhead made from burnt ash
named the inn the Anchor and Plough and although the inn was obviously an old one, it

seemed neat and well kept, the hedges and trees pruned and the grass scythed. They smelled fresh hay in the hayloft as they rode into the hard-packed dirt courtyard and wearily dismounted. A smiling stableboy came out to collect their horses. Cumac went to the well and dipped an oaken bucket with water, drinking. He sighed.

"Water always tastes better from an oaken bucket," he said. "Better still if the water runs through an oak stump but this is good enough for thirst."

Fedelm and the others drank from the bucket, and Lorgas splashed some of the cool water on his face, blubbering as he ran his hands across his lips.

The half-door opened and a smiling innkeeper came out, wiping his hands on a nearly spotless apron. He wore well-mended pants and half-boots and his huge shoulders threatened to split the seam of his butternut shirt.

"Welcome! Welcome!" he cried. "Fresh boar is on the spit and I've just split a barrel of Imbolc malt beer." He sang heartily:

> *Thig an grainneog as an toll*
> *La donn Brigid,*
> *Ged robh tri traighean dh' an t-sneachd*
> *Air leachd an lair.*

> *The hedgehog will come from the hole*
> *On the brown Day of Brigid,*
> *Though there should be three feet of snow*
> *On the flat surface of the ground.*

"Ah," Lorgas sighed, rubbing his hands together and flinging droplets of water to the ground. "We have come to the right place."

"That you have! That you have!" the landlord said gleefully. "And good clean rooms with nary a tick or louse on the fresh linen."

"How far to Cairpre's court from here?" Seanchan asked.

A frown immediately replaced the smile on the innkeeper's face. "A good day's ride. Not far. But you'll be better off here than there. Outlandish prices for thin ale and ticky mattresses and greasy food. Not a place for honest folk just as I think you are," he said. "The court is no place for good men and women," he added, bowing toward Fedelm. "It has fallen upon bad times since Cairpre became king. And I don't care who hears me saying that," he said lifting his chin high. " 'Tis become a place for wild pleasure despite marriage vows and oath-takers. Swordsmen have grown fat and lazy and the forge lies cold and unlit. The streets are filled with dung in the market square and brazenly painted fishwives and hags hawk their wares."

"We shall rest here for two nights and a day," Seanchan said. "We are expecting two others. Will you have room?"

"You are the only guests I have so far," the innkeeper said, then smacked the palm of his hand against his forehead. "And where might my manners be? I am Fergus, your host."

"And I am Seanchan Duirgeal. This is Fedelm of the Sidhe, Cumac son of Cucullen, Bern of the Ervalians, and Lorgas of the Ashelves. We indeed seek your hospitality."

"Then enter and welcome!" Fergus beamed.

He scurried ahead of them into the inn. The others followed and paused inside the door, looking around them at the freshly whitewashed walls, the plank floor white from many scrubbings, the fireplace ash-free with a huge boar on a spit in the fireplace. The skin of the boar had been seared quickly so the juices would remain inside, although a catchpan sat beneath the boar to catch drippings for brown gravy. To their left was a shunted stairway, the steps as white as the floor planks. To their right was a ringed counter with wooden-spigoted dust-free barrels of beer and ale resting on a backboard. The smell of freshly baked bread and meat pies filled the air and their mouths watered in anticipation.

"A welcome surprise," sighed Lorgas as he walked to the bar and took the mug of beer the landlord drew for him. The others came on his heels and took their mugs and went to the fire, where they sat on wooden benches in front of the fireplace to warm themselves. The landlord set out some bread and fresh goat cheese and apologized that it would be another hour or two before the boar was ready.

"But here is a bit to curb your growling stomachs until the meal is ready," he said. "I've had my daughter go to your rooms to open windows and freshen them up. O'Leary will be coming soon for his evening pint and I expect he'll bring his fiddle to set your toes a-tapping. His son may come too and never was a man who could lift a song with a sweeter voice. He'll have a story or two to tell. Others too will be here soon for food and drink. But there's a storm brewing from the sea and that will keep some away, I'm thinking."

Hard on the heels of his words a loud thunderclap sounded, threatening to shake the very beams of the inn. Then came the rain lashing against the windowpanes like tiny trip-hammers working iron on a forge.

A collective sigh went up from the Seekers. Seanchan waggled his toes in front of the fire and said, "We're lucky to be here, I'm thinking. It would have been a cold night along the road otherwise."

He glanced at the others, who nodded in agreement; then he stopped and frowned as he studied the Dragonstone on Cumac's shoulder. It pulsed a soft black in the flickering light from the fire. Fedelm caught his frown and followed his gaze to the Dragonstone.

"Something's wrong," she said softly. She nodded at Cumac's shoulder. Lorgas and Bern followed her look. Then her belt began a soft emerald glow.

"Too good to last," Lorgas sighed. "Ah me! So what is it now, Seanchan?"

The Druid closed his eyes, concentrating. Shadows appeared in a murky fog but just as the figures began to become visible, they fled from his sight. He concentrated harder and twin frown lines showed between his eyes. Then he shook his head and said, "Something but I can't find it. I feel it more than see it."

Lorgas sighed. "Will we ever come to a place where we can eat and drink and sleep in peace? One fight each time we're facing."

"Maliman's reach is getting farther," Fedelm said.

"Yes, yes. We've known that since we began the search," Lorgas said. "But surely he cannot be reaching this far yet. You've said as much, Seanchan. He has to gain more strength before he can spread his minions."

"Callyberry is not that far behind us," Seanchan reminded him. "And if Maliman managed to reach Callyberry with his men, then we must assume that he could have made it this far."

"And you forget the pass yesterday," Bern said to Lorgas. "Truacs and hobgoblins were there."

"They might not have been sent by Maliman, though," Cumac said.

"But we can't be certain," Seanchan said. "Remember when Ulster had the Chalice the world was pretty much at peace. It's only since the seals holding the Great Rift closed began to collapse that we are seeing Maliman and his men beginning to surface into Earthworld. *And* I am uncertain if the last of the seals holding the Great Rift shut hasn't broken and still holds."

He sighed deeply and ran his fingers through his beard, pulling the knots from it. His eyes clouded with worry. He chewed the ends of his mustache for a moment then said, "If we are finding these . . . things . . . this far to the west, then we have to assume that Maliman is at last completely free from the Great Rift. We already know that he has ordered the rebuilding of his stronghold in the Mountains of Mourne and that the Grayshawls and Nightshades are free—although not all of the Grayshawl powers have grown to what they once were. Still, they have enough to wield an influence upon Earthworld now."

"Cairpre's court?" Cumac asked.

Slowly Seanchan nodded. "Yes, we shall have to assume that *something* is there. Even as pleasure-loving as Cairpre has become, I don't think he still wouldn't have patrols along his borders. *And* we haven't run across any yet."

Fergus scurried to their table, bringing bowls of apples and plums. He plunked them down in the middle of the table and beamed again at them. Then he plunged an iron fork into the boar carcass on the fire, twisted it, and smiled.

"I think it is ready," he said. "But first, we must make the gravy. I make it rich brown with garlic and onions and rosemary and thyme. It won't take long."

"Has another man passed through?" Seanchan asked. "A tall man dressed in black and green? Black hair and eyes with a face like a hatchet head? He would have kept a pouch with him all the time."

"Bricriu Poisontongue," Fergus said, and nodded. "He left for Cairpre's court a few days ago." With that, he scurried off into the kitchen.

Bern frowned. "How did he remember Bricriu's name? He wouldn't have used 'Poisontongue.' Bricriu, yes, he would have given. But not the other."

"Something else," Cumac said suddenly, breaking into the quiet left with the exit of Fergus. "Did you see anyone when we rode through the village? I didn't."

Lorgas and Bern looked at each other and shook their heads.

"Come to think of it," Fedelm said, "neither did I."

"Nor I," Seanchan said, frowning again.

"What can it mean?" Cumac asked.

"Bad, bad," Bern said sadly, shaking his head. "I don't know what but I have a feeling now that it is bad."

"This inn may be intended to lull us into relaxation in order to make us unwary," Cumac said.

"Perhaps," Seanchan said.

At that moment Fergus's daughter Wane came down the stairs. She was as thin as a rail with a ghost-white face and hair the color of ripe spring wheat. She wore a black shift with a curious red design on the front. Her fingers were long and slim, as were her bare feet. She gave the Seekers a closed-lip smile, but the smile, never touched her dark eyes. She nodded at them and disappeared into the kitchen.

Nuad and Fergma rose, growling, their hackles stiff on their backs, their eyes glowing as they watched Wane.

"What is wrong?" Cumac asked.

Seanchan shook his head. "I don't know. But something. Of that I'm certain. And I have a strange feeling that it bodes ill for us."

The door banged open, and a man in gray with black hair and eyes that glittered entered. He clasped a fiddle and bow in one hand. When he saw the Seekers he beamed and said, "Ah, visitors to fair Adene! Welcome! Welcome! I am O'Leary the herdkeeper."

"And I am Seanchan Duirgeal. This is Fedelm of the Sidhe, Bern of the Ervalian elves and Lorgas of the Ashelves. And Cumac, the son of Cucullen, the Hound of Ulster."

"Noble guests!" O'Leary cried. "I shall play you a tune that will liven the blood in your veins. As soon, that is, as I have a pint to loosen my throat. Landlord! Fergus! Where are you and why don't you greet your guest?"

Fergus came from the kitchen, saw O'Leary, and shook his head in mock dismay as he went behind the bar and pulled a pint of beer for him.

"Now, you'll be minding your manners around these good folk, O'Leary. None of your shenanigans once you're into your beer. You will find yourself cleaned to the skin and tossed out upon your ear, I'm thinking, if you become the wee bit belligerent toward them."

He raised a bung stopper threateningly.

"I've had enough of your antics to last me a lifetime."

"Ah, sure, I'm a mellow man to be here and have me nightly pint."

He raised the mug and drained it and slammed it back onto the bar. He wiped his mouth with his sleeve and beamed at the Seekers.

"And now for your tune." He plucked the strings, listening with a critical ear, tightened two pegs, then announced, " 'The Fox and the Hounds.' "

Immediately he began sawing away at his fiddle. Notes spilled wildly from the strings that strangely sounded like horsemen riding furiously after the fox. Up and down the scales he played until the Seekers' faces blushed red from the song that seemed to fire their blood and put their toes a-tapping.

O'Leary finished and immediately swung into "Hunter's Moon," and when he finished that, "The Ride of Boand" poured from the strings.

The door opened and others entered and shouted encouragement to O'Leary, who began to play even more vigorously. Another pint appeared at his elbow and he paused to drain it and played again, songs that made some of the villagers dance and clap their hands. Shouts of laughter came from their throats.

Cumac leaned over to Seanchan and said, "They're all white as ghosts. If these are farmers, they should be as brown as autumn oak leaves."

He glanced down at the Dragonstone. It glittered blackly in the firelight. Seanchan nodded as he looked at the Dragonstone and motioned at it for the others to see.

Low growls crept from the throats of Nuad and Fergma. They crouched, ready to spring.

The Seekers' hands crept toward their weapons as they watched the leaping and cavorting of the villagers.

Fergus came from the kitchen carrying two bowls of thick rich brown gravy. He weaved his way through the dancers and placed the bowls on the table.

"And now, for the meat!" he cried. He took a large curved knife from his apron and began sawing off chunks of boar and dropping them on wooden trenchers for the Seekers.

"Eat! Eat!" he cried. "Feast yourselves and make merry. The night is young!"

He tossed two meat-heavy bones to the wolfhounds, then went behind the bar and began pulling pints for the villagers as O'Leary paused, wiping the perspiration from his face with his sleeve and burying his nose into another foaming pint.

The villagers panted from their exertion as they seized the pints and drained them and clamored for more, which Fergus obliged, drawing the pints as they appeared empty on the bar.

"Something to calm the blood now!" one villager cried.

O'Leary grinned then his fingers pressed the strings. The mellow and mournful "Song of Calleach" came from his bow. The others fell silent and listened as he played, fingers moving slowly and skillfully along the strings. A melancholy mood fell over the room and the Seekers felt their eyelids growing heavy and struggled to keep awake. Then suddenly the kitchen door banged open and Wane appeared. The sound startled the Seekers and they came instantly awake as O'Leary's fiddle abruptly ceased.

"Something is wrong," Cumac whispered. "Nuad and Fergma have not touched their bones."

The Seekers glanced at the two wolfhounds, silent now, but crouched and ready to spring.

The villagers turned as if one to the Seekers. Their mouths opened in blood-red grins and their eyes glowed redly. The Seekers stopped eating and wiped their fingers clean as they stood, eying the villagers watchfully. A black mist seemed to gather in the inn and hovered overhead against the high ceiling.

"You are more than welcome," Wane said softly.

Fergus grinned and said, "Did you not wonder why no one appeared in the village when you rode through?"

"Vampires," Fedelm breathed. She looked at Fergus. "I cannot understand how you came outside."

Fergus shrugged. "Someone has to be the greeter. And I am not one of them." He nodded at the others in the room. "I simply do their bidding."

Caladbolg sang as Cumac drew it from its sheath. Fedelm nocked an arrow. Bern's sword slipped smoothly from its scabbard while Lorgas lifted his ax from his belt.

"This is one elf you won't gnaw on easily," he growled, holding the ax in front of him.

"Nor this one," Bern said.

"Leave us in peace," Seanchan said, taking a firmer grip on his staff. "We ask for the Laws of Hospitality."

Fergus laughed, an ugly sound, and said, "These are the damned. Do you think that the Laws mean anything to them? Come now! Surely you are not that dense!"

"Take them," Wane said, gesturing comtemptuously.

A bright light shone from Seanchan's staff as the vampires moved toward them. Then they shrunk back, shielding their eyes and screaming as the light swept up and over them. Cumac leaped forward, Caladbolg shimmering like a rainbow as he cut through necks, beheading those within his reach. Fedelm's arrow sped through the air and struck a vampire in his heart. The vampire shrieked as the wooden shaft pierced his heart and flames erupted around his body, consuming him to ashes.

Nuad and Fergma howled and leaped forward, each knocking a

vampire to the floor and ripping his throat apart with one savage bite. They spun on their hind legs and leaped at two others.

Lorgas ran to bar the door and windows with thick timbers then roared his battle cry as he leaped on top of the table and swung his ax, striking the head off the nearest vampire. Black blood fountained high and the vampire fell to the floor.

Bern's sword sliced again and again, matching Caladbolg's murderous singing, and the vampires began crowding back away from the Seekers.

"Take them!" Wane shrieked again.

The vampires gathered themselves and launched themselves at the Seekers, howling in fury, hands shielding their eyes as they started through the light. But the Seekers had cut a swath in front of them that allowed them room to swing their swords and ax. Fedelm's shafts struck the hearts of vampires who shrieked as flames burnt them to a crisp.

Still the vampires pressed forward grimly, making their way through the light that began to blister their flesh. Black blood ran across the floor in small rivers. Then Bern leaped from the table and seized a burning limb from the fire. He lunged at the nearest vampire, igniting his clothes. The vampire screamed in pain and ran for the door. Again and again Bern danced nimbly through the crowd, swinging and stabbing his torch into one vampire after another.

Lorgas shouted angrily and swung his ax furiously. Heads flew like bouncing balls from shoulders. But the vampires pressed closer and closer, threatening to overpower the Seekers being backed slowly and slowly toward the fire.

Then a vampire leaped to Bern's side and sank his fangs into Bern's shoulder. Bern dropped the torch and staggered away toward Seanchan as Cumac's sword split the vampire in half. Bern fell to his knees at Seanchan's feet then slowly toppled to the side as blood drained from his face, leaving it chalk-white.

"Close your eyes!" Seanchan shouted, and the others immediately turned, placing their hands over their eyes as blue-white cairnfire leaped from the end of Seanchan's staff and swept over the room, torching the vampires, turning them into ash immediately.

Then the room was quiet. Wane alone stood with her father near the kitchen door as the cairnfire died. Seanchan slumped weakly on the bench. The others leaned on the table, panting from their exertion.

Wane screamed then shouted, "You have won the inn, but others gather outside its doors! You will never escape!" Her flesh was covered with blisters and the ends of her hair were scorched but otherwise she was unharmed.

An arrow sped across the room and buried itself to its feathers in her breast. Another scream burst from her mouth as flames licked hungrily at her clothes and flesh. She batted her hands wildly at her clothes and flesh.

"Daughter!" Fergus shouted and beat vainly at the flames, trying to slap them out. But the fire burned relentlessly, turning her to ash. He sobbed as he knelt and scooped up a handful of her ashes and pressed them against his chest. Tears rolled down his face.

"You will pay! You will pay!" he shouted at the Seekers.

Lorgas jumped to his side. Fergus looked up fearfully as the elf swung his ax high and said, "You reap what you sow!"

Fergus screamed as the ax descended and split him nearly in half. His hands groped wildly at his wound; then he pitched forward and fell to the floor, eyes glazed in death, mouth gaping wide as red blood poured from it.

"The horses!" Cumac shouted, and ran through the kitchen, pausing to slice the head from a cook, then throwing open the door to the stable. Fedelm and Lorgas rushed after him and formed a semicircle around him as vampires began to stream through the stable door. Grimly the Seekers fought on but the vampires were many and slowly forced the Seekers back.

Seanchan drew upon his reserve, and bright shimmering light streamed from his staff, forcing the vampires through the door. Cumac leaped forward and slammed the door shut, barring it with a huge thick oak plank that they dropped into the iron hooks on either side of the door. Immediately the door resounded from the pounding of many fists but the door held firmly. Nuad and Fergma took up stations in front of the door, intent upon the pounding, threatening growls coming from their throats.

"That should hold," Seanchan gasped weakly as he collapsed onto a sheaf of hay.

"Lorgas, you and Fedelm take the inn! Shout if they manage to break through the door! We'll take the stable door."

Obediently they ran into the inn and took up positions next to the bar.

"All we have to do is keep them out until the sun rises," Cumac said.

Seanchan panted as he looked at him and gave him a lopsided grin. "All? Well that seems easy enough. It's hours to first light. A lot can happen between now and then."

"Do you have another plan?" Cumac asked.

Seanchan shook his head. "No. Unless we turn them all into flames. And I can't. I must regain my strength."

"All right," said Lorgas, kneeling over the fallen Bern. "Bern's been bitten. What can you do, Seanchan?"

Seanchan shook his head and said, "We need a poultice for the wound." He turned to Fedelm. "Look in my bag for monk's hood root powder. Use a little powder and make a mash with water. Wrap it in a clean white cloth and tie it to the wound. Quickly! The venom spreads rapidly!"

Obediently Fedelm took the powder from Seanchan's bag and prepared the poultice. She made a small cut over each of the fang marks then pressed the poultice firmly in place.

Bern convulsed and Cumac held him down firmly by his shoulders until the spasm passed. A small blush appeared in the elf's cheeks and Seanchan sighed.

"Find garlic in the kitchen now and shave it thin. Remove the monk's hood and make another poultice with garlic and place it over the wounds."

"Will he be all right?" Lorgas asked anxiously.

"Yes. I think so," Seanchan said. "We will have to stay here two days. When day comes and the vampires are gone, tie garlic bundles and hang them from the doors and windows. That should keep the vampires away."

"Let us take the horses into the inn," Fedelm said. "We can bar the kitchen door! Pile hay against the door. If they threaten to break through there, I'll send fire arrows to light the hay."

"So far the door seems to be holding," Cumac said. "We may get lucky."

"We could use some," Fedelm said grimly.

Together they untied the horses and took them from their stalls, leading them into the inn. Seanchan tottered after them, leaning heavily upon his staff.

Lorgas and Bern turned to watch them come in as Cumac said, "We've decided to stay in the inn. That gives us a stronger band than splitting up. It will be far easier to defend the inn than the stable and inn."

Lorgas nodded and walked to the table. He placed his ax on the table and sat. He pulled a trencher to him and began eating. "Then let us eat and regain our strength," he said around a mouthful of wild boar. "So far we are safe."

"That would be for the better, I'm thinking," Bern said joining him.

The others followed and ate in silence, listening to the furious pounding on the doors and windows, keeping a sharp eye out should one splinter and give way. They spoke little as they ate, each lost in his or her own thoughts.

21

Two days passed without incident although the Seekers could hear the vampires moving around the inn, cursing.

Bern awoke at noon of the second day. His face was wan, but he still managed a weak smile at the Seekers.

"How do you feel?" Seanchan asked, checking Bern's wounds. They were closed but an angry red blush appeared around each wound.

"Tired. Weak," Bern said. He looked around. "The vampires?"

"They can't get in thanks to the garlic we placed around the windows and doors," Fedelm answered. "Right now we're safe."

"I think we've pushed our luck far enough," Seanchan said. "Do you think you'll be ready to ride tomorrow?"

"I think so," Bern said wearily. He closed his eyes. "Sorry that I've kept you here."

"Say nothing more about that," Lorgas said gruffly. "If you hadn't charged into them with that torch we would have been hard-pressed."

A smile came over Bern's lips as he slipped into sleep.

Lorgas looked inquiringly at Seanchan.

"He'll be all right now," Seanchan said. "He's very lucky."

"He's an elf," Lorgas said. "What do you expect?" He took a damp cloth and wiped Bern's face.

"I say we should all rest now," Seanchan said. "We will mount a watch tonight in case the vampires find a way in. We'll leave at first light."

The Seekers turned to their pallets in front of the fire and within minutes, all were asleep.

The third day rose sunny and warm, one of those early false spring days that teases one into believing that the hard, cold winter has passed. Wrens sang beneath the eaves of the Anchor and Plough and squirrels chattered, scampered, and played along the ridgepole at the top of the inn as the bleary-eyed Seekers cautiously opened the windows then the door. All was quiet and the elm in the middle of the courtyard near the stables had begun to bud out although the day was cold with a hint of weather-change in the air.

Wordlessly they saddled their horses and led them out of the inn, mounted, and lifted the horses into a ground-gaining lope to put Adene as far behind them as possible. The road was soft but not muddy, and a green furze covered the land on either side of the trail. Isolated clumps of blackthorn came and went. They rode through a small boulder-bolted pass without incident and without stopping for noon.

"We will be in Cairpre's fortress by midafternoon," Seanchan said, hunched tiredly in his saddle. "We should be relatively safe there."

"Good," Bern said. "I can use a bath."

His face appeared strained from the ride.

"I would be obliged if you took one," Lorgas said.

Bern glared at him and said, "I'm not the only one."

"Cut it out," Cumac said wearily. " 'Tis enough has happened to put up with your grumbling."

The elves looked as if they wanted to retort but a look from Fedelm made them fall silent. She gigged her horse to ride next to Black and Cumac.

"I think we've had enough sour words all around," she said. "They are easing the tension they've been carrying since we left Adene. As have you. And I. And Seanchan."

Cumac nodded and turned in his saddle to say to the elves, "I'm sorry. I meant nothing by my words. I spoke out of turn."

"That's all right," Lorgas said graciously. "We are all tired. Sometimes it is good to let others know how you feel. We have been through a lot together. Enough so we cannot take offense at words among friends."

Cumac nodded and straightened in his saddle to ease the stiffness in his back.

"I can still smell the stench inside the inn," he said.

"We were very lucky," Fedelm answered. "Without Seanchan's cairnfire we would have been hard-pressed indeed. But I wonder what has happened since its use. Remember that cairnfire not only kills but erases everything that was from the world as if it had never been here at all. We do not know the full extent of what has happened in Earthworld since he used it. There has been change somewhere."

"I hope it has erased a lot of vampires," Cumac said fervently.

"Everything has a place in Earthworld. Something was linked to those vampires and that something has been destroyed as well. It is a never-ending river and where it stops nobody knows. We may have lost some supporters."

Cumac wrinkled his forehead in thought for a moment then said, "I cannot think that any good would be eliminated by destroying those vampires with cairnfire. They destroyed everyone they could. Night is the watch-hour for such things and whatever and whoever was not like them would not be erased from Earthworld. No, I think Seanchan's use of cairnfire burns evil from Earthworld."

"We shall see," Fedelm said doubtfully. "I hope you are right. But . . ." Her words trailed off and they rode together in silence.

"Remember," Cumac said suddenly, "what happens in Earthworld is also reflected in the Otherworld."

"I remember," she said.

"And now," Seanchan called back to the others, "if you are finished with your bickering I call your attention to Cairpre's fortress just ahead of us."

He pointed and the Seekers straightened in their saddles and quickened their pace.

As they neared the fortress, the Seekers noted how the fortress wall had fallen into neglect. The wooden stockade in front of the wall was splintered in many places and rotting in others. Stones had slipped from the wall and lay nearly covered with grass and lichens, leaving gaping holes behind.

"This wouldn't hold a child out," Lorgas said softly. "Not even watchers on the walls or decent guards at the gate."

"It has taken time for this fortress to fall into near-ruin," Bern acknowledged.

"I do not think Cairpre is worried," Seanchan murmured. "This is the southernmost fortress and I think he feels secure in that. Or else he simply doesn't care. Sometime he will receive a rude awakening."

The gate to the fortress stood open with four guards lazily sitting on stools and lethargically waving people on through the gate. Their spears leaned against the gatepost and later Bern would swear that he saw spiderwebs between the spears and the gatepost. The oak gate bar hung splintered from one iron hook.

They rode through the gate and entered the lower village beneath Cairpre's main house perched high on a knoll above. The streets were a quagmire and had not been cleaned for a long time. Manure and sludge lay everywhere. The stench almost gagged the Seekers and they hurried through it, ignoring the cries of the merchants in stalls with multicolored shades on either side of the main thoroughfare. Flies buzzed in clouds around the Seekers and children wrestled in the mud of the streets, oblivious of the muck. Warriors lolled on stools by small wooden tables outside small inns, drinking thin ale. They watched curiously as the Seekers rode by but no one stood to challenge them. Whores flaunted their wares as they leaned out of inn windows and called coarsely to the Seekers as they passed.

The road leading to Cairpre's court wound around the knoll and the stench lessened as they continued up although there was still a hint of it in the air. They dismounted in front of the court and two stableboys dressed in dirty clothes with bits of straw hanging in their hair came forward to take their horses. They were surly and indolent until Lorgas threatened to bash their heads together at which point they hurriedly gathered the reins and left at a trot for the stable.

"I'd hate to see the stables if this is what the village looks like," Bern muttered darkly as they carried their own bags through the door and dropped them by a support post before continuing on to the Great Hall.

Cairpre greeted them from his chair set on a dais at the far end of the room. Warriors sat at the long tables, eating and drinking. They eyed the Seekers curiously as they made their way to the three steps leading up to the dais. Halfway there, they saw Bricriu Poisontongue sitting to the left of the champion. He grinned sourly as they paused in front of him. Nuad and Fergma growled from beside Seanchan and for a second fear crossed Bricriu's face then disappeared.

"We meet again, Bricriu Poisontongue," Seanchan said flatly.

"It took you long enough," Bricriu said. His features were narrow and dark. Black hair hung limply to his shoulders. His nose was narrow and pointed above red thin lips. His chin weak and his eyes black agates.

"Why don't you simply give us the Chalice and be done with it?" Lorgas growled. "Save us killing you."

Bricriu gave a brittle laugh and said, "I'm under the protection of Cairpre. Here, I am untouchable. And you know that."

Seanchan nodded and turned to address Cairpre. His face was meaty and shiny. His brown hair hung in oiled ringlets. His lips were full and fleshy. His eyes were brown and buried deep above suety his cheeks. He wore a blue tunic edged with gold thread and matching pants.

"Welcome," he said, smiling broadly. His eyes nearly disappeared into his cheeks. Stains showed on the front of the tunic where gravy had spattered.

"We seek shelter," Seanchan said abruptly. "I am Seanchan Duirgeal. This is Fedelm of the Sidhe, Cumac the son of Cucullen, Bern of the Ervalian elves, and Lorgas of the Ashelves."

"And what brings you to my court?" Cairpre said, lifting a silver goblet with ring-laden fingers. He drank and replaced the goblet at a small table beside him. He blotted wine from his beard with his thick fingers.

"We seek Bricriu Poisontongue," Seanchan said, half-turning to indicate Bricriu. "He has stolen the Bladhm Caillis, the Chalice of Fire, from the Red Branch. We ask for its return."

"The Chalice of Fire," Cairpre mused. "You must know that I have granted Bricriu protection under the Laws of Hospitality. I'm afraid there is nothing I can do for you except give you the same privileges I have extended to him."

"The Chalice is needed to help the people of Erin defeat Maliman from spreading his evil across the land. He has been released from the Great Rift, as I believe you know, and even as we speak is building armies to conquer all of Erin. Already his people have made their way westward. At Callyberry his armies sought to take the village and us but were defeated. But that was before his armies come to full strength. Our way has been dangerous as his people have sought many times to kill us."

"Yet you are here," Cairpre said.

"Yes, but we have been hard-pressed to make our way here. The Chalice must be returned to the Red Branch. If not, Bricriu will take it to Maliman, who will be able to use its power for his own purposes. Again I ask that the Chalice be given to us. We will not abuse your hospitality by taking it by force, for that will violate the Laws which we all must attend."

"Nor would you be allowed," Cairpre said. "But Bricriu and his possessions are all under my protection. Surely you understand that."

"We understand that you won't help us," Lorgas growled. "Even though it would be in your best interests."

Cairpre's eyes narrowed. "Be careful. You are overstepping your bounds."

"Be quiet before you make matters worse," Seanchan said quietly to Lorgas. Then aloud, "Then we will accept your hospitality with many thanks."

He turned toward Bricriu, his eyes cold as winter. Bricriu squirmed under Seanchan's gaze but there was still a defiant lift to his chin.

"Be aware, Bricriu, that your safety is not forever in this court. Maliman reaches far even as I speak. I do not think there are many who will grant you hospitality once their borders are threatened by Maliman's armies. And they are coming. Like a dark wave across the land, scorching the land as they come, killing all in their way except those who may be willing to swear allegiance to Maliman."

"I tremble before you," Bricriu sneered. He lifted a pouch from beside him and held it high. "Here is what you seek. Why don't you take it now?"

"In time," Seanchan said. "In time."

Bricriu started to speak but the sarcastic words froze on his tonuge when he looked into Seanchan's ice-blue eyes.

Seanchan turned back to Cairpre. "We accept your hospitality with thanks. But know that the Laws of Hospitality are not endless. They do not last forever. Even The Dagda, leader of the gods, will not extend his grace forever."

"That we shall see," Cairpre said. He gestured at servants standing patiently against the walls. "Take them to our best rooms and provide for them whatever they wish." He turned back to the Seekers. "We eat when the gloaming falls. I hope our fare is to your liking."

Seanchan bowed his head and, turning, led the Seekers and the wolfhounds from the hall, following the servants appointed them.

Cumac hesitated, looked at Bricriu, and said, "I fought the lions of Connacht to win the right to take you from Maeve's Cruachan Ai. But you were too cowardly and fled like a thief in the night. Do not make that mistake again. We *will* find you, Bricriu, if you leave this court. And then, I will kill you."

Bricriu's face went white as Cumac turned on his heel and followed the others from the Great Hall. Shakily Bricriu lifted the goblet in front of him and drank deeply, then laughed falsely and said, "Some people just do not know when they are beaten."

"Perhaps," Cairpre said thoughtfully. "But I wouldn't want to be the one that they seek. The Chalice has protected you this far. They have come on their own despite what has stood in their path. And Seanchan is right. The Laws of Hospitality are not endless. But you are welcome here under my protection as long as I can allow it."

Bricriu blanched and refilled his goblet, drinking deeply. Fear twisted its way through his belly and his legs trembled beneath the table.

SURPRISINGLY the Seekers' rooms were bright and airy and clean. Fresh linen had been placed upon the beds and the wood shone with a soft golden glow from being rubbed with beeswax. New clothes had been laid out for them and servants scurried to fill the baths at the end of the hall. Small tables and cushioned chairs had been arranged in front of the fire that took the chill from the room. Wordlessly servants brought mulled wine to their rooms while the Seekers bathed and dressed in clean clothes. Their travel-stained clothes were discreetly taken away to be washed and fresh bread and jars of honey waited for them when they returned to their rooms.

But Seanchan had them wait and they gathered in his room to make plans. Nuad and Fergma lay on a rug in front of the fire, gnawing on meaty bones that had been brought for them by the servants.

"I for one say we just take the Chalice and go," Lorgas said, reaching for a goblet and filling it with wine. He tore a chunk of bread free and dipped it into a pot of honey.

"You know we cannot do that," Seanchan said sharply. "Bricriu would like nothing better than to have Cairpre place us in his cells."

"From what I have seen we would have little trouble fighting our way clear," Lorgas answered around a mouthful of honey-laden bread. "Come on. We can take them."

"We are a long way from the gate and the warriors would surely be upon us before we could leave this fortress," Fedelm said.

"Then let's steal it back," Bern said, accepting a goblet of wine from Lorgas, sipping. "We could slip out before anyone becomes wise. From the looks of the guards, I do not think we would be hard-pressed to go by them."

Seanchan shook his head. "Bricriu would like nothing better than for us to try that. And I have a hunch that Cairpre will have guards posted to prevent just that from happening. No, we shall have to bide our time and wait for Bricriu to make a mistake."

"That cur will not make a mistake, I'm thinking," Cumac said darkly. "Maeve had a challenge for us that if we should win Bricriu would be turned over to us. Perhaps Cairpre has one as well."

"Perhaps," Seanchan said grudgingly. "But what Maeve did was in defiance of the Laws. Cairpre is content to remain within the Laws—unless," he added thoughtfully, "we are attacked. Then we would have the right to protect ourselves. If only we could arrange something to have Bricriu break the Laws first. Then we would be within our bounds to take him and the Chalice. *But* I say we wait until Tarin and Sirona make their way here before we try to force Bricriu's hand."

"You are sure they are coming?" Fedelm asked.

Seanchan nodded. "Yes, I feel that they are. If all goes well with them, they may well be here within a few days. Then we will be stronger and something may open up for us."

"With Tarin," Cumac said.

"Yes," Seanchan said. "Tarin, I think, is the key right now. He is a Sword-wanderer and the Deathwhisper. I think he may receive a challenge to show his swordplay. And I have no doubt that he will win if it comes to that."

"I can work a challenge as well as he," Cumac said.

"No. That worked once but this time I think we shall have to depend upon Tarin."

"What about Sirona?" Fedelm asked.

Seanchan shook his head. "No, I am certain that it will have to be Tarin. And I do not think Bricriu will be so foolish as to challenge him."

"Then how—" Bern began.

"By pushing Cairpre's champion into a duel," Seanchan broke in. "But something else may happen as well. The Laws of Hospitality only extend as far as Cairpre's court. If Bricriu steps outside the court walls, then he is on his own. The village is not a part of the court."

"That's a technicality," Fedelm said. "And I don't think Cairpre will fall for that."

"Fall or not, it is a technicality and one that we can use without fear of retribution," Seanchan said.

"The trick is to get Bricriu outside the wall," Cumac said. "He is not a stupid man. He knows the limits of the Laws, I'm certain. And I don't think that Cairpre would allow his champion to fight Tarin."

"A challenge is a challenge," Lorgas said, reaching for another chunk of bread. "I think that is the way to go. So, why don't I work out a challenge? Then we'll be done with this whole mess."

"Because you are unknown," Seanchan said. "The champion would not rise to your challenge. Another would take his place."

"Then I'll hack my way through them until he is forced to challenge me," Lorgas growled.

"I have no doubt that you could do that," Fedelm said. "But I agree with Seanchan. Let us wait and see if Tarin and Sirona make their way here. A few more days won't matter much. As long as Bricriu doesn't run again."

"He won't," Seanchan said firmly. "This time we shall keep a watch on him ourselves. If he goes, then he is ours."

Lorgas sighed and drained his goblet, refilling it. "Well, at least the food is good. And I think we could all use a rest. All right. I go with Seanchan. We'll give that a try. But if Tarin and Sirona do not come in a couple of days, I will force the challenge."

"Agreed," Seanchan said, raising his bushy eyebrows at the others. "And what say you all?"

"Yes," they answered in chorus.

"We'll wait," Cumac said. "There is nothing lost by waiting a couple of days. Meanwhile, let us rest. I think that once we leave, we shall need it. We still have to get the Chalice back to Ulster. And to do that, we shall have to go through land controlled by Maliman."

22

Their horses were blowing hard by the time Tarin and Sirona halted for the night in the jack-pine woods of a small cove near the sea. They dismounted, stretching to remove the tiredness from their muscles, then stacked their horses out on a grassy hummock before gathering driftwood for a small fire. They removed dried pork from their saddlebags and warmed it on willow sticks over the fire. A small stream back within the woods provided them with fresh water. The silver orb moon hung over the sea as they spread their blankets.

"I'll take the first watch," Tarin said. "I'll awaken you when the moon is half gone."

Sirona yawned and said, "Do you think that we will catch up to them tomorrow?"

Tarin shook his head. "No, I don't think we will find them until we get to Cairpre's court. That's two good days' ride from here. And we shall have to be careful going through the Pass of Adene. I would like to make it by midday. It will be safer going through the pass in daylight. A lot of goblins and hobgoblins live in the hills and mountains around the pass and we will have less problems, I'm thinking, during the daylight hours."

"What's after the pass?"

He frowned. "I'm not certain. The village of Adene before we hit Cairpre's border. That I know. And I have a bad feeling about that village. Don't ask me why," he continued as Sirona started to speak. "I just have a bad feeling. I haven't been this way in a long, long time and much has changed since then. Including, I feel, the village. Fact is, I would like to go through the village during daylight as well. I think that if we camp before we reach the village and go through it the next morning we will be better off."

"And how far is Cairpre's court after the village?"

"If I remember correctly, not quite a day's ride. We should be able to make it within two days if we hurry. And I will be more comfortable if we ride hard and take our ease in Cairpre's fortress."

"Then let's leave at false light," Sirona said. "Sleep now. I'll take the first watch instead. The night will pass swiftly and we shall need our rest if we are to ride hard."

Obediently Tarin rolled in his blankets and within moments was sound asleep as Sirona kept watch. Overhead the moon slid a ghostly galleon over the cloudy sea. Owls hooted and nighthawks circled high overhead, looking for an unwary field mouse or perhaps even a rabbit. Crickets chirruped and Sirona pinched her cheeks to keep herself awake.

Strange sounds came from the woods and Sirona quickly drowned the fire and rose, alert, sword in hand. But whatever or whoever it was passed without finding them and she relaxed.

She watched Tarin sleeping, noticing the fine line of his jaw and how his features settled into a mask as he slept. His legs twitched now and then, and twice his hand found the hilt of the rune-blade and squeezed it comfortably before he fell back into Dreamworld. A strange feeling filled her breast and she frowned, trying to isolate it and understand it. But it was too fleeting and although she tried to bring it back, it remained elusive.

She shook Tarin awake when the moon started to slip away. He came awake instantly, his hand gripping his sword as he sat up.

"Something or someone passed," she said as she prepared to slip into her blankets. "I don't know what it is but I don't think we should have another fire."

He glanced at the cold ashes and nodded. "Better safe with a hare than hunt for a deer. I'll wake you at false light."

She nodded and closed her eyes, slipping unconsciously into a dreamless sleep.

"Fedelm!"

She came awake with a start and looked bewildered around her at the bleak landscape. The earth appeared to be ashes and dead trees beckoned her forth with black limbs. Black clouds bunched like palaces in the sky and she heard the thrumming of bat wings overhead that pounded within her skull. She winced and sat up, pressing her thumbs against her temples to relieve the headache. She felt grimy and her clothes looked filthy, as if they had been dragged through an unclean barnyard. Yet, her senses warned her that danger welled all around her and she rose, if a bit unsteadily, to her feet, looking around her wildly, seeking the cause of her feelings.

"Come! Quickly!"

She felt a hand upon her forearm and quickly shook it off, spinning around and recognizing the young man with golden hair and cobalt eyes, wearing a white tunic that fell to his calves. He held his short sword in his hand.

"Cathlon," she said warmly.

"We do not have much time! Come, now!"

"Where? To the Tower of the Guardians?"

He shook his head, his eyes turning to blue ice.

"It will have fallen by the time we are there, I fear," he said harshly. "The Deag-duls, sumaires, and other filth serving Maliman have besieged the tower. Coig sent me out through a portal to get you to a safe place. *If*," he added grimly, "such a place can be found."

"I thought the Tower was impregnable," she said.

"Nothing is impregnable," Cathlon said impatiently, pulling at her arm. "Now we must hurry."

He jerked her forward into a hard run, leading her down into a stone-strewn gully and weaving around the large fallen stones around horseshoe bends and dry oxbows. He kept glancing over his shoulder as if he heard pursuit hard on their heels but no one followed.

Fedelm brushed a clod of dirt with her shoulder and narrowly missed being covered as a side of the gully caved in behind her. The air smelled dank and of burned flesh.

"Where are we going?" she asked after Cathlon slowed his pace.

"To the Valley of Shadows," he said grimly.

"Send me back," she said. "You can do that, can't you?"

He stopped and drew a deep breath and gave her a hard look.

"When your friends come to gather you in the morning, they will not find you in your room."

"What do you mean?" she asked, alarmed.

"You have been pulled body and spirit into Dreamworld."

"But," she asked, "how is that possible? What magic is this?"

"Maliman's!" He spat as if the very word itself left a foul taste in his mouth. "With the help of his Grayshawls. I do not know how this is possible but apparently Maliman has found a way of creating a portal *around* a person and drawing them into this world."

Fedelm shook her head and suddenly dropped to her knees, her hands clasped hard against her head.

"What is it?" he asked.

"I don't know," she said in agony. "Something is squeezing my head tightly like a wooden clamp."

Suddenly she vomited again and again until nothing was left in her stomach.

"Cathlon!" she moaned.

His lips thinned. He stabbed the sword into the ground and squatted beside her. He pulled her hands from her head and placed the palms of his hand on either temple. A soft gold and silver glow appeared around his hands, quickly building into a mist that surrounded them. He muttered strange words, an ancient incantation that had been lost before time began.

The pain disappeared, leaving Fedelm weak and shaking. The glow disappeared and Cathlon pulled her roughly to her feet and said, "Now! We must run! The Grayshawls will know that you have been freed from their hold and will be searching for you. Come!"

He jerked at her arm until she began to run, staggering at first, then eventually sliding into a fluid step that matched his stride-for-stride.

"Won't they be able to find me anyway?" she gasped.

"Perhaps. Perhaps not. Remember: You are no longer dreaming. You are here. Awake. They have to find you as a being, not a dream. Now enough talk! Save your breath!"

He increased his pace as they ran through the gully. The sides of the gully slowly came together, ending in a steep slope that led up to the top. In the distance, she saw gray cliffs drawing nearer and nearer. Then, they were within the cliffs, running through narrow defiles until they reached a yawning cave where Cathlon ran inside and stopped. She fell, exhausted, to the floor of the cave. Her mouth tasted vile, coppery, as if licking dried blood from one's hand.

"Where . . . are we?" she gasped.

"In the Cave of Tuan," he said. "Here, we will be safe. For now. We can rest."

He threw himself to the floor and leaned back against a wall. His chest rose and fell rapidly and she realized that the run had taken as much out of him as it had her.

Slowly her breathing eased and she levered herself up against the wall opposite him.

"Explain," she demanded.

He sighed and ran his fingers through his golden hair and shook his head.

"Well, this is the cave where Tuan, the first of people, took refuge during the time of the Great Waters when they covered all of the world. They did not cover this, however, as Tuan created an island out of space and time that was away from Earthworld. This is the place of the Beginning. Where Dreamworld was born."

She nodded, recalling the story of Tuan, the sole survivor of the race of Partholonians and the plague that killed all of them. When he metamorphosed into a salmon, he was caught and eaten by the wife of Cairill, who gave birth to him in human form so he could recite the early history. After reciting this, he used his power to slip back into the memory of what he had been. She remembered Cernunnos, the Horned God of the Forests, singing the Song of Tuan when she and Cumac had entered his forest in the Otherworld:

> *I am Tuan*
> *I am legend*
> *I am memory turned myth.*

"I am the storyteller. Warriors and young boys creep away from the hearths of wine halls to hear me. Greedy for tales of honor and history, they watch my lips with bright eyes, for I give them what is more precious than gold: treasure unlocked from my heart.

"My words burn like flame in the darkness. I speak and hearts beat high, swords warm to the hand; under my spell boys become men.

"But I know both the pain as well as the brightness of fire. I am the storyteller who cannot find rest. The peace of death will never be mine. I am condemned to watch and to speak; my hand reaches in vain for the warrior's sword.

"Once I, Tuan, was a man, the chieftain of a great race, the Cesair. My warriors sat on wolf skins. They raised golden chalices to me brimming with wine. Neither evil nor harm dared cross the threshold where I sat, my throne studded with jewels, inlaid with ivory.

"But the gods envy the happiness of men. Flood and sword combined to destroy my people. Now the wine hall stands empty, ruined; doorway and roof gape wide to receive the beasts of the earth and the birds of the air. It was ordained that I alone should be saved to bear witness to my people's fate. I watched helpless while the fair land of Èireann was ravaged by the scavengers and foes. The golden cities I once loved lay fathoms deep beneath gray seas.

"For many years I wandered as a man seeking shelter in caves and the depths of the forest. But when at last the noble race of Nemed came to reclaim their homeland I was barred from greeting them as either chieftain or warrior. Another fate was mine: to watch unseen, keeping the secrets of time close in heart and brain. The gods had singled me out for a strange fate, unfamiliar pains and pleasures, for as the years passed, they bound me within the bodies of beast and bird so that I might watch and keep the history of Èireann, unnoticed by men.

"The first transformation came upon me unaware. I had grown old as a man. The years had left my body naked and weak; my joints ached and my hair fell gray and matted over my bowed shoulders. One day a great weariness came upon me. I sought shelter in my cave, certain that death had claimed me. For many days and nights I slept. Then at last I awoke to the sun. My limbs felt strong and free. My heart leapt up within me for I had been reborn as Tuan, the great-horned stag, king of the deer-herds of Èireann. The green hills were mine, the valleys and the streams.

"As I ran free across the heather-covered plains, the children of Nemed were driven from their homeland. Only I remained, grown old as a stag, their story locked in my heart. Then the great heaviness of change again weighed me down; again I sought shelter in my cave. Wolves eager for my blood and sinewy flesh howled to the moon. But I slept, floating loose in dream-time. Through the heaviness of sleep I felt myself grow young again. When the low rays of sunrise touched me I awoke.

"The wolves still sniffed about the entrance to my cave. But now I was young and strong, fit to face them. I, Tuan, with joyful heart, thrust my sharp tusks out of my lair, and the wolves fled yelping like frightened dogs. I was fresh, lusty with life. I had been born again, a black boar bristling with power, thirsty for blood. Now I was a king of herds. My back was sharp with dark bristles; my teeth and tusks were ready to cut and kill. All creatures feared me.

"But while I had lain locked in dreams a new race of men had come to disturb the silence of mountain and valley. The were the Fir Bolg, and they belonged to the family of Nemed. These I did not chase, and when they chased me I fled, for their blood was mine also. The Fir Bolg divided the island into five provinces and proclaimed the title Ard-ri, that is High King, for the first time in Èire-ann.

"As I roamed the purple hills I would often leave my herd, gaze across to the High King's hall, remember with sadness the time when I also had sat in council, with warriors at my feet and the bright eyes of women gazing upon me.

"Once again the ache of change drove me back to my lonely cave in Ulster. After three days fasting, another death floated me beyond dream-time. Nights circled from summer into winter until one morning I woke and soared high into the clear sky.

> *I was reborn*
> *I was lord of the heavens*
> *I was Tuan, the great sea eagle.*

"I, who had been king among the heather and scented woodlands, became lord of the heavens. From the highest mountain I could see the field mouse gathering wheat husks. Nothing escaped my sharp eye.

"Motionless, feathering the air, riding the wind, I watched the children of Nemed return to Èireann. Now known as the Tuatha De Danann, they sailed down over the mountains in a magic fleet of skyriding ships, led by Nuada, their king, until they came to rest among the Red Hills of Rein.

"Rather than fight their own flesh and blood the Danann offered to share the island with the tribes of the Fir Bolg, but on the advice of his elders Eochadhi, their High King, refused, and the battle lines were drawn up.

"I, Tuan the eagle, watched that fratricidal struggle; that terrible slaughter of kinsmen known as the First Battle of Moytura. I saw the same green plain, across which I had, as a stag and boar, led my herd, drenched in blood. There I saw for the last time the Fir Bolg in their fullness and their pride, in their beauty and their youth, ranged against the glittering armies of the Tuatha De Danann. The battle was fierce and ebbed and flowed like waves on a sea of fortune and price.

"The circles of my eyes were rimmed with bitter tears as I watched that dreadful carnage of kinsmen, for all who fought were bound by a common bond, the blood of Nemed the Great. The battle raged for many days; death cut down the flower of the youth on both sides.

"At last the Tuatha De Danann took the sovereignty of Èireann from the Fir Bolg and their allies. But in that First Battle of Moytura, Nuada, King of the Dananns, had his hand struck off, and from that loss there came sorrow and trouble to his people, for it was a law with the Danann that no man imperfect in form could be king. So it happened that Nuada, who had led his people to victory, had to abdicate his throne and hand the royal crown over to the elders of his race.

"I, Tuan the sea eagle, wept secretly with Nuada over the loss of his crown, for he was a noble king and a just ruler who had won back the land of Èireann for his people. His mutilation and his loss were the result of his bravery in battle. For he was a great warrior, skilled and courageous and as one with his god, the Sun.

"When the noise of battle and the wailing of women had faded into silence, when the earth had soaked up the blood, when the plain of Moytura had become a sad spirit-haunted place marked by pillars and cairns, I, Tuan, still sailed high above it. I knew that that same force of history that governed the fortunes of men had made me the winged bearer of myth. I knew that the pattern of change is never completed until the world's end. Still I would have to bear the burden of man's triumph and grief.

I am Tuan
I am legend
I am memory turned myth.
I have lived through the ages
In the shape of man, beast, and bird
Mute witness to great events,
Guardian of past deeds.

"You are remembering," Cathlon said.

She nodded. "Yes. I remember. But where is this place, the Cave of Tuan?"

"In the Valley of Shadows," he said.

And she felt a cold descend upon her flesh, pebbling it, and a fearful dread swept through her.

"What are we to do?" she asked.

He shook his head and said, "Nothing. Here we shall wait. We are no longer in Dreamworld. We are now in Earthworld. Coming through the gully, we crossed the boundary separating Dreamworld from Earthworld. Here, in this cave, we are at the Beginning and the End. You will be safe here for a while as long as you do not go farther into the valley and do not go out of the cave very often."

"And you? What about you?"

He shrugged resignedly. "I will have to go back. Soon. But not for a while. I will hear Coig's call and then I must return." He smiled wryly. "The war in Dreamworld is still being fought and I will be needed in the Final Battle which shall come when it comes in Earthworld. Before I go, though, I will leave food and water for you. Later, if you wish, you can travel to the West."

"I have no weapons," she said in despair, showing him her empty hands.

"I know," he said. "You were brought directly into Dreamworld and then back into Earthworld. I shall try to get your weapons to you but do not count on that. It may prove too difficult or impossible to accomplish. In fact, I think Coig has the only power strong enough to transport things from Earthworld."

"Then I'll be defenseless," she said, alarmed.

"For a while," he said hastily. "You will have to use your wits until something can be done."

"And how long will that take?"

"I don't know. Now, I'd better see about gathering food and water for you." He rose, gave her the best smile he could summon, and left.

Fedelm turned slowly to look at the back of the cave. A curious light flickered in the back, and she frowned and walked toward it. As she neared the light, she saw that it was a small flickering fire casting shadows upon the wall. The figures of men and women danced in the flickering light, but there were no men and women other than their shadows on the wall. Other figures appeared chained on the opposite wall with a low wall separating them.

A quick chuckle came to her, and one shadow moved off the wall and slowly became a wasted man. He was still a shadowy figure, but skeletal features appeared.

"What do you want here, Fedelm of the Sidhe?" he asked hollowly.

"Identify yourself," she demanded.

The shade shook his head. "No names are here. Only shadows. Once there were men. But no longer. Now only shadows of what once was."

"And you? Surely you have a name," she said.

"I am called 'Speaker' but it has been a long time since I have spoken. No one comes here anymore. They are afraid. And we are afraid. That is why we stay here as shadows. Light hurts us and if we come into the light and then come back here, our eyes are bewildered and others regard us suspiciously until our eyes once again become used to the darkness."

"I do not understand."

He shrugged. "It is not so difficult. When we came here, we were afraid of the world. Wars and battles flared up across the land and we knew that sooner or later we would be forced into a war or battle. So we fled. To here. And here we remained until we wasted away into shadows. Yet, we miss the light and the sun and would like to go out into it. Only we cannot. We are the Unforgiven."

"I would imagine your masters are long dead."

"Indeed."

"So what do you fear?"

"Everything that is not with us here."

"I pity you."

Speaker bristled and tiny black flames flickered in the hollows where his eyes once were.

"Do not pity us! *That* we do not have."

"Then you are why this is called 'Valley of Shadows.' "

The shade rolled his head. Fedelm heard bones cracking.

"No. There are more here than just us. There are other caves. And one in the middle of the valley where our court sits."

"Why are people afraid of the Valley of Shadows?"

"Because once they enter here they stay here. They become one like us. There is no escape once you enter the valley. As you will find out."

"I can go back the way I came," she said angrily.

"Can you? Try. There is a way in but there is no way out. Unless the king allows it and he has not allowed it in centuries. There is a circuitous road that winds just below the rim of the valley and along that road people are permitted to pass if they entered the valley through the Pass of Angau between the Paps of Anu. No other entrance is allowed."

"Bricriu, he who stole the Chalice of Fire, will be coming through here, I'm thinking, if Cairpre does not allow the Seekers to take the Chalice from him."

"He may enter but that does not mean he will be allowed to leave. Here we all are prisoners. Shadows and life as well."

23

They almost made it to Cairpre's court without conflict, having come down the coastal road from Connacht and through the Pass of Adene before running into danger, but danger found them as they came down from the pass and made their way through the village of Adene, silent, ghostly, unnerving.

"What is this place?" whispered Sirona, looking around her nervously. She drew her sword and rode with it lying over the pommel of her saddle.

"I don't know," Tarin whispered back. "But I sense there is much evil here. Evil that is not necessarily that of Maliman. Something old and rotten from another time. Something of earth and night. I think it would be best if we shake the dust of this village from our heels as quickly as possible."

"We need rations and our horses are spent," Sirona noted.

Tarin bit his lip. True, he had overestimated the time it would take to travel to Cairpre's court from their last camp, and the sun was dropping toward the sea edge. Still, there were enough daylight hours to put a few miles behind them before they were forced to stop when night fell. The problem was that he was traveling a strange road. Oh, he *knew* the road well enough—everyone knew about the coastal road even if they hadn't traveled it—but that was all. Everything else was new and unexpected.

They halted in front of the Anchor and Plough. Its sign was creaking in a faint sea breeze blowing inland. The smell of salt was fresh and clean, and Tarin breathed deeply of it, but there was also a tiny taste—a hint, really—of something vile beneath the salt air. He looked around him, then decided.

"Hold my reins," he said, dismounting and flipping the reins to Sirona. He drew his sword. "I'll have a look around before we decide."

She nodded and turned the head of her horse so she could see what might be coming toward the inn's courtyard. She held the reins in her left hand, bringing Tarin's horse around behind her to her left side so her sword arm would be free.

Tarin moved cautiously into the stable. He noticed the door half-hanging on its hinges. The floor of the stable smelled dank and sour, and the walls just inside the door had been splattered with something, but he could not tell what it was. He stepped to one and ran his finger down it and tapped the end of his finger against his tongue. Immediately he spat again and again. Vampire blood. Or warggad or sumaire. It didn't matter. It was not human; that much he knew.

He walked carefully over the floor, stepping to avoid dark puddles, and found the door to the kitchen. Something or someone had tried to break through the door, but it had held, and still held when he put a shoulder to it. He gave up and returned to the courtyard and went to the inn door. It opened but sagged halfway through the turning as an iron hinge gave way. Slowly he entered the inn. No fire burned in the fireplace and the room was dark and cold. The same foul smell held in the air as it had in the stable. Two piles of horse dung were in the middle of the room, and he frowned. For some reason, the Seekers' horses had been brought into the main room of the inn. He walked slowly around the main room, keeping his back to the walls. Piles of gray ash lay scattered on the floor. The beam holding the kitchen door closed was splintered but still held.

He felt someone behind him and turned quickly as Sirona came through the door, sword in hand.

"I feel something," she said. "Something evil is here. I thought you might need someone at your back."

"And what about your back?"

She smiled grimly.

"You watch in front of us. I'll watch in back."

He nodded and crossed to the shunted stairway and slowly climbed, walking on the balls of his feet close to the edge of the steps, ready to spring away if something came suddenly out of the gloom.

At the top of the stairs, he slipped quietly over to the first room and tried the door. It was unlocked. He entered the room swiftly, sliding against the wall, sword ready. Little light shone in the room. But it was enough for him to see. A long box stood upon two sawhorses. He crossed to it and squatted beside it. A small pile of dirt was beneath the box.

A chill swept through him. He rose hastily and backed away from the box, holding the rune-blade ready in front of him. He glanced around the room and out the door and back down the hall, his nerves twanging like the strings of a bard's harp too tightly pulled.

He returned slowly to the box and, taking a firm grip on the rune-blade, struck one of the sawhorse legs off at a slant. The sawhorse gave way and the box fell to the floor, canted awkwardly with the foot of the box still held by the sawhorse. The lid slipped off the box, revealing a vampire slumbering. He began tossing and turning in the faint light. Hurriedly, Tarin picked up the sawhorse leg, struck the end of the leg with a sharp blow from his sword, creating a point, and plunged it into the vampire's breast.

The vampire's eyes opened wide and his mouth gaped as a scream came from deep within his throat. He clawed desperately at the stake but Tarin held it fast. Blood erupted from the vampire's mouth, and then a brilliant flash of light burned across Tarin's eyes and the vampire burst into flames. A scream that pebbled the flesh poured from the vampire's mouth, and then it was over. A fine sheen of dust covered the bedding of earth inside the box.

"Well," Tarin said. "This might not be the best place to spend the night."

Sirona went to a window and looked out. She shook her head in disgust.

The gloaming had fallen upon them and shadowy figures were beginning to move on what had been a deserted street. The blood-red moon began to creep up from the horizon, and the first faint stars twinkled in the deep purple of the sky. A small wind rolled in from the sea, bringing with it a hint of sea spray along with the odor of decayed bodies.

Sirona spat in disgust.

"I don't think we have any choice," she said grimly. "I say let's bring in the horses and barricade ourselves as well as we could. *And* check the other rooms and the root cellar for more of that." She pointed toward the ash covering the inside of the box.

"I agree," Tarin said, after casting a quick look over his shoulder. "I'll bring the horses in and barricade the front and stable doors. You check the other rooms for more of these."

He ran down the stairs as Sirona, sword in hand, her face set in a hard mask, made her way down the hall, throwing open doors.

The vampires were almost upon the horses when Tarin ran outside and gathered their reins, pulling them back into the great room. An enraged howling came on his heels as he slammed the front door closed and dropped a big timber in the iron braces on either side of the door. He grabbed two benches and braced them against the door too before running to the kitchen door and bracing it. He checked the windows, but they still held strongly.

A shriek came from upstairs and he ran back to find Sirona battling two vampires. He roared his battle cry and drew the rune-blade and neatly decapitated one as Sirona gutted the other before slicing off his head. The bodies stood shuddering for a moment, then collapsed to the floor, twisting and turning in agony before bursting into flames.

Tarin gathered their heads by their long greasy hair and ran downstairs and threw them into the fireplace. Quickly he piled wood on top of them and lit a fire. A screech came from the chimney as the flames roared up through the stone and mortar. A figure fell down, writhing in pain as the relentless fire burned him. Sirona cut off his head and turned away as the fire began consuming the body. She kicked the head into the fireplace and turned to Tarin.

"The root cellar?" she asked. "There's surely a few down there."

"The door to the cellar is inside the kitchen. I blocked the kitchen off, so it doesn't matter."

A steady pounding began at the front and kitchen doors. The horses whinnied and stomped their feet nervously, looking around wild-eyed, their sides sweating from fear. The doors began to shudder as timbers were driven against them. A deep thudding came from the roof, and Tarin and Sirona looked at each other, their faces hard planes.

"I don't think the roof will hold," Sirona said calmly, drawing her sword. "The timbers are strong enough but the thatch will give. I'm surprised they haven't thought of that before now."

"Yes," Tarin said grimly, slipping the rune-blade from its scabbard. "It'll be a hard fight to get out of this one, I'm afraid."

She nodded and started toward the stairs. "The hall is narrow enough that they won't be able to come except one or two at a time. I might be able to hold them there."

"It's a long time until morning," Tarin said. "The doors and shutters seem to be holding well enough. We can fight together, one resting while the other holds the hall from them."

Sirona shook her head and gave him a crooked grin. "They'll get us in a rush, you know."

"Maybe," Tarin said grimly. "But they'll pay a price for that."

"That they will," she answered, mounting the stairs two at a time, taking a firm grip on her sword.

A crack of thunder sounded and rain began to fall heavily.

"Fire!" Tarin said suddenly. "The hallway is mainly stone with wood covering it. We can fire the hallway, and the thatch may be thick enough to burn slowly. The rain will keep it damp enough. I hope."

"Risky," she said. "If it catches, the entire roof may go."

"Do we have a choice?" Tarin asked, crossing to the fire and picking up a flaming brand.

Sirona shrugged. At that moment, a screech of triumph came from the hallway and three vampires tumbled through the hallway and leaped down to the floor of the great room.

With a sinking heart, Tarin realized that entry had been made. The vampires rushed toward him as Sirona ran to the hallway to keep the others at bay. She screamed her battle cry as she met the vampires at the beginning of the hallway, her sword a blur in her hands. Tarin caught the first vampire lunging toward him with the brand, setting its ragged clothes on fire, the rune-blade slicing through another's neck. The third one leaped, his weight bearing Tarin back. The brand fell from his hand as he grappled with the vampire. A triumphant cry came from the vampire as he bore Tarin to the floor.

24

For the third time Cumac banged on Fedelm's door before opening it. He stepped in and looked around, but she was not there. Frowning, he left the door open as he walked down the hall to Seanchan's room and entered without knocking. The Druid looked up from his seat by the fire, a frown appearing between his bushy eyebrows at the sight of Cumac's grim features.

"Fedelm's gone," Cumac said. "I knocked

on her door and entered when she didn't answer. She wasn't there."

Seanchan's eyes narrowed as he rose, taking a firm grip on his staff.

"Get Lorgas and Bern!" he snapped as he left his room and strode swiftly down the hallway to Fedelm's room. He entered and looked around: the bed was unmade and the room empty, the fire flickering just above the bed of coals. A cold dank smell filled the room. He shivered and walked to Fedelm's bed and placed his hand upon the blankets; they were cold. She had been gone for a while.

He turned as Cumac entered followed by Lorgas and Bern, rubbing their eyes sleepily.

"What's wrong?" Lorgas asked.

"Fedelm's gone," Seanchan said harshly.

"Gone? Where?" Bern asked.

Seanchan shook his head. "I don't know. But wherever she is, she didn't leave voluntarily." He pointed at her weapons carefully laid on the table. "Otherwise she would have taken those."

As he spoke a silver mist formed around the weapons and then opened. The weapons slipped through the mist and disappeared.

"What . . ." Lorgas asked, mouth agape.

"They have been taken to her, I think," Seanchan said. "At least she is in Earthworld. Somewhere. Otherwise that could not have happened. But where she is, I don't know. I cannot feel her but that may be because we are separated by a great distance."

"Maliman?" Cumac asked.

"I don't think so," Seanchan said slowly. "No, not Maliman. He would not have armed her. She may have been drawn from Earthworld but she is back in it now. I do not know if she has been harmed or not but I do know she is in Earthworld. How, I do not know. But she is."

"Then she is safe?"

Seanchan shrugged. "Perhaps. I *feel* she is, but there is distance and"—he frowned—"something else between us."

Cumac folded his arms and stared at Seanchan. "Cairpre has a Druid. Perhaps he?"

"Maybe. But I doubt it. He is not of the Duirgeals. That I know.

He may—" Seanchan slapped his hands together in disgust. "Of course. How stupid of me."

He pushed by the others, who clamored for an answer, and stormed down the hall. They fell in behind him and followed him to the Great Hall. Cairpre lounged on his throne. His robe had been changed. A platter of sliced pork was on a table next to him along with a goblet of wine and sweetmeats. He popped one into his mouth as the Seekers came into the hall and said, "Ah! Our guests! I trust you slept well?"

Seanchan strode up to the three steps leading to the dais where Cairpre sat. He folded his hands around his staff and looked sternly at the king. The others spread out on either side of him, watching Cairpre's men as they stuffed their mouths with meat and bread and rich brown gravy, carelessly throwing bones over their shoulders to the floor, where fierce dogs fought over them. The floor was spotted with gobbets of fat, and dark stains were spattered where grease and gravy had been carelessly spilled. One, however, dressed neatly in leather jerkin and pants, sat at the head of the long table. He ate fastidiously, moderately, and eyed the Seekers curiously. His long black hair had been freshly washed and a long scar slid down the right side of his face from his temple to the corner of his mouth. His eyes were black but no animosity shined from them.

Next to Cairpre sat a Druid in gray robes on a highly polished walnut chair with arms that curved around him like a stag's horns. His staff—ash wood—leaned against the back of his chair. His eyes narrowed at Seanchan's approach, and he took in the ends of his mustache and chewed automatically on them.

"We slept well," Seanchan said. "But we seem to be missing one of our party."

Cairpre's eyebrows rose. "Missing one? Now, why would that be?"

"Perhaps we should ask your Druid," Seanchan said dangerously. Then extended his staff as the Druid's hand reached for his staff. "No! Do not touch your staff!"

The Druid's hand froze, then slowly returned to grip the arms of his chair as his black eyes stared malevolently at Seanchan.

Cairpre sat up, frowning at Seanchan.

"You forget yourself, Seanchan Duirgeal. This is *my* court. I give the orders here!"

"Seanchan is known for forgetting his place," a voice said from behind him, and Bricriu stepped into view, his lips curved into a malicious smile.

Slowly the boisterous talk slipped away in the room as the warriors looked suspiciously at the Seekers.

Lorgas dropped his hand to the head of his ax and glowered at the warriors. Bern gave a faint smile and tapped his sword pointedly with his fingers. Cumac, however, drew Caladbolg and held it negligently by his side.

"You dare to draw your weapon in the presence of the king?" the Druid growled.

"Be silent!" Seanchan said. "And name yourself!"

"I am Braken of the Caorthanns, the Ash Druids," he said loftily. "And you are no longer welcome here."

A thin smile spread beneath Senachan's beard and his voice sank so quiet that the others had to strain to hear him.

"Careful, Braken of the Caorthanns. Do not anger me more. You know what happened the last time the Caorthanns came against the Duirgeals."

Braken flushed and started to his feet only to slowly sink back into his chair as Seanchan moved his staff slightly.

"That was long ago," he said angrily. "That would not happen again if you tried!"

"A challenge!" Cairpre said happily, clapping his hands. "How exciting! This should be interesting! Relieve the boredom and all. Shall we say this afternoon in the courtyard?"

Seanchan shrugged and grounded his staff. "I accept," he said, inclining his head toward Braken.

The Caorthann blanched, but his words had been spoken, and he dared not take them back in front of the others lest he lose face in Cairpre's court and become the subject of jokes and snickers behind his back.

He rose, bowed, and took his staff, straightening himself to his full height.

"And I accept," he said. He stalked down the steps and out of the Great Hall as a great babble arose from the warriors around the table.

"And what do we need for a Druids' contest?" Cairpre asked cheerfully.

"The courtyard," Seanchan said dryly. He turned and left the hall, followed by the Seekers, who cast careful looks over their shoulders as they exited the hall.

Cumac caught up to Seanchan and said, "Are you certain about this?"

Seanchan glared at him and said, "The day I cannot handle a Caorthann I will retire to the Duirgeals and spend the rest of my days teaching. Besides," he added, "we were looking for a challenge and now we have it."

"I thought we were waiting for Tarin and Sirona," Cumac reminded.

"One challenge is as good as another. We will have our show of strength, and we will be able to demand Bricriu's deliverance for this breach of the Laws, as Cairpre allowed the challenge."

"If Cairpre recognizes it as such," Cumac said. "The challenge is not between men but between Druids. Do the Laws of Hospitality extend to that?"

"The Laws are the Laws," Seanchan said, stopping to poke Cumac in his chest with a hard forefinger. "You would do well to remember that in the future."

"I don't trust that Druid," Lorgas growled. "Come to think of it, I don't trust Cairpre either."

"For once I will agree with you," Bern said. "There is trickery here, I'm thinking. We will have to be on our guard."

"I'm counting on that," Seanchan said gruffly, and increased his pace toward his room.

BRAKEN walked quickly to his rooms. A chill began to work its way up from his stomach as he thought about the coming duel, and doubt began to worm its way into his mind. He breathed deeply, trying to still the sudden pounding of his heart, and his hand grew slippery with sweat around his staff.

"Can you beat him?" a voice said, and Bricriu fell in beside him, matching him stride for stride.

Braken gave him an irritated look. "I can. But it will not be easy." His mouth grew dry as he spoke, and Bricriu caught the sudden cracking of his voice.

"You know he is one of Connor's favorites," Bricriu said. "And the rest of the Red Branch as well. He is not one to treat lightly."

"I know. I know," Braken said, a hint of desperation creeping into his voice. "But I have little choice in the matter."

"Once words are spoken they cannot be brought back," Bricriu said. "You should have thought of that before you challenged him."

"I didn't," Braken said. "My words were twisted by Cairpre. Now I am committed."

He stopped suddenly and sagged against the wall. He used the sleeve of his robe to wipe the sweat from his forehead. He took a deep ragged breath and said, "I have heard of Seanchan and what he can do." He bit his lip. "I don't know. I don't know."

"If the Seekers lose Seanchan then their strength will be halved," Bricriu said. "You need to defeat him. Better yet, kill him."

Braken nodded wordlessly.

Bricriu laughed. "And many things can happen in a duel. If Seanchan should lose his concentration, say, then he will be vulnerable."

A light appeared in Braken's eyes and he said, "You have a plan?"

"Anything can turn a man's attention," Bricriu said, his lips turning up in an evil smile. "A bird flying too close, a sudden noise, a pebble thrown at his feet, anything."

"I see," Braken said, straightening. "A sudden noise. That might do it."

"It might," Bricriu said. He turned and retraced his steps, disappearing back into the Great Hall.

Braken walked to his rooms, his step lighter, the fear lessening in his stomach. Then he laughed and took a fresh grip on his staff.

25

Tarin rolled desperately, trying to escape the vampire as it clawed at him. The vampire laughed and bent his head, but Tarin managed to get a knee between them and thrust hard, throwing the vampire from him.

He leaped to his feet as the vampire rushed him again and, taking a two-handed grip upon the rune-blade, slashed diagonally. The rune-blade cut through the vampire's head and through his torso, severing both. The vampire teetered for a moment, then fell as black flames licked around his body.

"Tarin!" Sirona cried from the balcony above him.

Tarin looked up and saw Sirona hard-pressed. He seized the flaming brand and ran up the stairs, the rune-blade in hand. He charged into a vampire, gutting him, then thrust the brand against his clothes. Flames leaped high, and the vampire shrieked and tried to retreat, but his burning clothes quickly caught the clothes of the others on fire.

The vampires danced around, trying to slap the flames from their clothes, but the wood of the hall caught on fire and howls became screams of agony as the flames consumed the dark evil.

"Back!" Tarin gasped as the flames licked hungrily up the wall to the roof. The thatch caught fire, and fire raced back and forth in the thick thatch. More screams came from the hall, and from above, on the roof, Sirona and Tarin heard the vampires leaping to the ground to escape the cleansing flame.

Sirona and Tarin made their way downstairs and leaned, gasping, against the table to catch their breath. They watched as the flames roared, then diminished into a small fire that smoldered in the wet thatch.

Tarin heaved a sigh of relief. "That will give us a respite."

"For a while," Sirona said.

But no sooner had she spoken when a window's shutters gave way and vampires crowded together, each trying to climb into the inn. Together, Sirona and Tarin ran to the window, hacking and stabbing at those trying to enter, driving all back amid cries of pain and fury. Again and again the vampires sought entry, and again and again they were driven back. Grimly, Sirona and Tarin fought, their limbs growing weary as the night crept slowly toward dawn.

A scream from behind them spun them around. A vampire had braved the flames and, clothes burning, leaped from the balcony to the floor. He landed catlike, but as he rose, Bain, Sirona's horse, lashed out with forehooves, smashing his skull.

The horses' eyes rolled in madness, and they screamed their

fright and fury, rearing as two other vampires leaped from the balcony only to meet the hooves of Bain and Borun.

"The fire is fading," Sirona gasped. "What shall we do?"

Tarin wiped the sweat from his brow with a quick swipe of his palm. He looked at Bain and Borun and said, "Ride out."

"Ride out? Are you crazy? That is the way to sure death."

"Maybe. Maybe not," Tarin panted. "We may take them by surprise. Bain and Borun are ready to run," he added grimly. "If we can make it through the crowd, we should outrun them. Or at least stay in front of them until Lugh brings the sun from the sea."

Sirona swung her blade, decapitating a frothing vampire.

"It's better than staying here, isn't it?" Tarin demanded.

She shrugged and gave him a sudden reckless grin. "Why not? We're damned if we stay here. We're damned if we go out there. I'd rather be out there than staying here and moaning our fate like weaklings."

"Hold them, then!" Tarin said, and ran to saddle the horses. He grabbed a coil of rope from a hook beside the kitchen door and tied it around the timber barricading the door. He threw the other end of the rope over a beam, caught it, and climbed up on Borun.

"Let's go!" he shouted.

Sirona gave one last swing of her sword and ran and leaped upon Bain's back. Tarin gave a yank on the rope and the timber slipped from its hooks. The door opened suddenly, and vampires, caught unaware, sprawled inside.

"Ride!" Tarin shouted, and clapped his heels to Borun's sides. The chestnuts needed no further urging. They leaped for the door, trampling those vampires who lay on the floor. Tarin and Sirona ducked as the horses galloped out the door. A crowd of vampires milling on the outside fell back as the broad and powerful chests of the horses drove into them, scattering them. The swords of their riders sang as they hacked their way free of the crowd and galloped down the road. Bain and Borun, free from the flames and vampires, stretched their long legs as they ran, their hooves a blur in the pale moonlight.

Behind them, Sirona and Tarin heard the vampires howl angrily and cast a swift look over their shoulders at the crowd racing after them. But to catch Borun and Bain the vampires needed the speed of bats in flight, and soon they disappeared behind the racing pair into the night.

The riders loosened their reins and crouched over the necks of the horses as they galloped tirelessly down the road, hooves throwing clods of mud behind them as the rain hammered against the riders' backs.

The moon sailed a ghostly galleon on the cloudy seas as Tarin and Sirona reined in Borun and Bain, letting them cool down as they loped along the road. Sirona looked over at Tarin and laughed and said, "A good idea but I don't want to try that again."

"Nor do I," Tarin answered. "We were very lucky. Surprise did it. They were expecting us to stay inside."

They pulled their horses to a walk, giving them a breather.

"Do you want to stop?" Tarin asked.

"No," Sirona said. "I say we keep riding. Bain and Borun look ready enough to go a while longer. How long to Cairpre's court?"

Tarin shook his head. "I don't know. A half-day at least, I'd say."

"Then let's ride through the night. We should be there by mid-morn if you're right."

"Probably a wise choice," Tarin admitted.

They lifted their horses back into a ground-gaining lope, riding through the night, trusting to luck that nothing further waited ahead for them.

26

Tired and dusty, Sirona and Tarin rode through the gate into Cairpre's fortress. They drew curious looks as they made their way to the Great Hall. Sullen servants came forth to take Bain and Borun, drawing a sharp rebuke from Tarin.

"Not exactly what I expected," Sirona said, slapping dust from her clothes. She crossed to a water trough and plunged her head in, drinking deeply. She rose, flinging her long hair back. Beads of water sparkled in the sun as they flew from her tresses.

"Nor I," Tarin answered, following her to the trough. "This man is looking for trouble and I have a hunch that it's not far off."

"Do you think the others are here?"

He nodded, pushing back his wet black hair. "I'm certain of it. We would have come upon them otherwise."

"Unless they met with trouble," she said.

He frowned. "I think we still would have come across something that would tell us that they didn't make it to this place." He looked around him. "Although I don't think I want to stay here any longer than necessary."

Sirona wrinkled her nose in distaste. "You'd think they would at least clean the streets. And," she added as a rat ran across the dirt in front of her, "do a little fumigating as well."

Tarin didn't answer; he didn't need to. The obvious was the obvious.

"Let's see if things are different inside the court," he said, turning and leading the way to the doors, which stood ajar with guards loafing, leaning against the walls, sharing a flagon of wine. Their spearheads were pitted with rust, and mold grew along the edge of the wall on either side of the door. As they watched, one of the guards turned and, pulling down the front of his trousers, urinated in the dust, unconcerned about any others.

"By the gods!" Sirona swore and gave the guard a hard look as they passed. "This is a place waiting to be conquered."

"And Maliman will probably be the one to do it," Tarin answered grimly.

They had turned to make their way down the corridor to the Great Hall when a shout brought them up short.

"Sirona! Tarin! Where have you been? What has taken you so long? We had about given up on you!"

The words came in a rush as Lorgas ran down the corridor from the apartments and rooms to embrace them.

"It is good to see you!" he said, then wrinkled his nose. "Although I think a trip to the baths is needed."

Tarin clapped him affectionately on the shoulder and gave him a lopsided grin as Sirona embraced Lorgas.

"And it is good to see your ugly face," Tarin said. "How long have you been here?"

"Two days," the elf answered. "Come! I'll take you to Seanchan and the others. Hey! You!"

A passing servant paused, hands on hips, and looked insolently at Lorgas.

"What do you want?"

Lorgas stepped close to the servant, his nose scant inches from the servant's, and said, "A civil tongue in your mouth or by the gods I'll take it from you." He wagged his fist under the servant's chin. The servant's eyes crossed as he looked down his nose at the threatening fist. "Now bring water to rooms for these two and be quick about it."

The servant drew himself up and said loftily, "That can be ordered only by Cairpre."

Lorgas's fist cracked against the servant's chin, sending him tumbling down the stairs. He landed, dazed, in a pile of fresh manure at the bottom.

"There are two rooms vacant on the other side of mine!" he thundered. "Bring bathwater and fresh clothes or I'll haul you into the Great Hall before Cairpre by your ears!"

He turned, smiling at Tarin and Sirona. "Sometimes you just have to learn to speak the right language," he said.

They laughed and followed him down the hall.

"You're just in time," Lorgas said, lowering his voice. "Fedelm has gone missing and Seanchan has been challenged to a Druids' duel by Cairpre's Druid, Braken. That'll be this afternoon in the courtyard."

"Fedelm's missing? Any ideas where?" Sirona asked.

Lorgas shook his head. "No one knows. Not even Seanchan, although he has tried to find her."

"That is bad news indeed," Tarin said. "And this challenge? How did that come about?"

"Well, Braken got a little wordy with Seanchan. Took on a bit too much, he did. Seanchan told him that he needed a lesson in manners—more or less what was said, you understand—and Braken got mad and challenged him. That will work out anyway," Lorgas added, waving his hand carelessly. "Seanchan said we needed a challenge in order to force Cairpre to suspend the Laws of Hospitality. Braken, being Cairpre's Druid and all, put his foot in his mouth when he brought words against Seanchan. He is bound by the same Laws that Cairpre is. Or," he amended, "that's the way Seanchan explained it. More or less."

"Then Bricriu is here," Tarin said.

"Aye, he's here," Lorgas said grimly. "And as poison-tongued as ever. I still say we should just take him from here and bring him back to the Red Branch."

"And the Bladhm Caillis? The Chalice of Fire?"

"It's here. Bricriu made a big show of having it in his possession. Taunted us, he did. I wanted to settle his meat then but Seanchan said no. That we had to work within the Laws. Though I don't see why when Bricriu stole it in the first place. A thief is a thief, after all."

"And entitled to the same Laws as are we all," Sirona said.

"Ahh," Lorgas growled derisively, waving away her words. "All twigs and brambles anyway, I suppose. Seanchan's duel should settle the issue quite nicely anyway and then we'll be on our way back to the Red Branch and away from this dung heap."

"Don't think the eggs are in your basket before you put them there," Tarin cautioned. "There's many a slip between what will be and what happens. I don't like the look of things here. There's not much here to lend itself to respectability, and when a bunch of warriors gather in a place like this there's no telling who among them you can trust. This careless living lends itself to deceit and bad doings."

"And someone will have to keep a watch on Bricriu. Remember how we were distracted in Maeve's court and Poisontongue managed to slip away? We don't want a repeat of that here," Lorgas said.

"I FOR one do not think that Cairpre cares one whit about the Laws of Hospitality when they do not meet his whim," Cumac warned after the two returned, refreshed from their bath. "Seanchan's win over Braken doesn't necessarily mean that Cairpre will bend to the will of the Laws. I have a hunch that he is keeping Bricriu to play him on and off against us. This is all a game to him, I'm thinking. The Red Branch is far enough away from here that Cairpre doesn't worry about it. *And* he also has the pledge of Maeve to come to his aid if he needs help. No, Cairpre doesn't worry about anything; he thinks his army is as good as Connacht's army so why should he worry about anything? Keeping the Chalice from the Red Branch means the land is no longer at peace and that appeals to Cairpre's cruelty. Frankly I think he'd as soon slit our throats as let us be his guests. If it gave him another moment of pleasure. This is a man who feeds on the discomfort and dismay of others. Maybe it would be better if we cut his throat in the dark of night."

"That would make us no better than the others who live here," Seanchan said. "We do not want to fall into *that* puddle. Traditionally the victor of a duel can request a boon from the ruler, be it king or chieftain. I will request the return of the Chalice. Cairpre can keep Bricriu. They deserve one another."

"The hour grows near," Bern said, looking out the window. "It is time. Are you ready, Seanchan?"

"Always," Seanchan said, gripping his staff firmly. "Now, let us be to this unpleasant business."

"And the rest of us to see that the duel is an honest one," Tarin said. "Let us split up and mingle with the crowd and keep a sharp eye out for false dealings. I cannot think that Bricriu won't try something. Or Braken."

27

The Dagda looked around at the Pantheon of Gods that had gathered to his call in his fortress. Fand sat aloof beside her husband, Manannan Mac Lir, the sea god. Lugh, grandfather to Cumac and the craftsman and the sun god along with Bile, lounged in his chair, as did Aengus Og, the love god, softly strumming his harp, which made irresistible music. Aine, a woman of the Leanan Sidhe, a daughter of Manannan whose stone, Cathair Aine, made whoever sat upon it lose his wits, sat to Manannan's left. She had a quick temper and took offense easily. Danu, the mother goddess, sat to The Dagda's left. She held her beauty despite being the ancestor of all gods. Scathach, the shadow self that walked the mists as the supreme warrior, sat silently, apart from the other gods, her face and arms showing scars that she had received in battle. Boand, the river goddess and mother of the love god, Aengus, and The Dagda's consort, winked at him. Badb, Macha, and Morrigan, three feared battle goddesses, waited impatiently for The Dagda's words. The others made small talk until the last god, Cernunnos, the god of the forests and protector of the wild, arrived, late as usual.

The Dagda stirred himself and rose. The others fell silent, looking at him expectantly.

"You all know by now that Cumac, Fand's son"—a nod at Fand—"has been sent into the Earthworld to get the Bladhm Caillis, the Chalice of Fire, away from Bricriu Poisontongue, who stole it from the Red Branch, and return it to Ulster so peace might well be regained. We agreed at our last gathering to allow this to happen, as our Otherworld mirrors what happens in the Earthworld. But so far, Bricriu has managed to elude the Seekers—Seanchan, Cumac, Fedelm, Bern of the Ervalians, Lorgas of the Ashelves, and the mortals Tarin Deathwhisper and Sirona—who have been formed to regain the Chalice. Bricriu is bending our Laws of Hospitality by seeking shelter from kings and chieftains in the Earthworld, which means that when the Seekers catch up to him, their hands are tied by the Laws. They cannot force Bricriu to give up the Chalice or harm him. This is clever indeed but I question such use of the Laws. I suggest that we allow the Laws to be suspended in this case to allow the Seekers to obtain the Chalice and return it to its rightful owners."

The gods looked at each other as The Dagda fell silent. Then Tuireann, the god of thunder, rose and said, "I do not think this should be allowed. For if we do allow Bricriu to be slain by lifting the Laws of Hospitality for the deed, then that sets a precedent and would allow the Laws to be lifted again and again by whim or need. No, I believe we should keep the Laws as they are. The Seekers are going to work their wiles against Bricriu or capture him when he is not under the Laws' protection. If we lift the ban once, we open the door to lifting them again and again. Far better, I say, to allow Bricriu protection."

"Maeve lifted the Laws when Bricriu claimed them at her fortress Cruachan Ai," Fand pointed out, rising.

"Yes," Tuireann said doggedly, "and placed herself and her land in jeopardy. Had Bricriu not made his escape, we would have been forced to deal sternly with her. The lifting was, in part, due to her own arrogance. She comes closer and closer to abandoning our ways as it is. Now Bricriu claims protection under the Laws at Cairpre's court, and although I do not like this 'king' "—he pronounced the word with distaste—"he does obey the Laws. We cannot abandon the Laws. That is the path to no Laws, and man needs something to govern himself. He must have rules that he cannot bend without suffering punishment from us."

Badb rose and glowered at the others. "I agree with Tuireann. We cannot lift the Laws at whim. We must obey the Laws as much as we demand the mortals to obey. This may be the time for the end of the Otherworld. You all know the prophecy."

She recited:

> *There will come a time*
> *For summer without flowers*
> *When in their bowers*
> *Cows no longer give milk*
> *When women become needy*
> *And men become greedy*
> *And morals and valor*
> *Are lost to all time.*
> *And there will be no kings*
> *And the woods become bare*
> *And birds no longer fill the air*
> *And the sea will become barren*
> *As will the earth become barren*
> *And all will be lost for all time.*

"And that will give sway to you, Badb, and your sisters Macha and Morrigan," Oghma, the god of love and wisdom, said harshly. "We know how you three love war. You feast upon death and put fear into the hearts of men. No," he continued, shaking his golden locks, "I say that we end this now before Earthworld falls into ruin. We have enough on our hands with Maliman and his minions. But Earthworld can unite itself against Maliman *if* the Chalice is returned to the Red Branch. Peace will then reign and in that peace the bonds of war will be forged but for good, not evil. Prophecies are only prophecies. If gods and men refuse to recognize them, then they no longer exist and are no longer a threat. Remember: We are a mirror to Earthworld. What happens there will happen here. If Earthworld is destroyed, then we too will be destroyed. Or," he amended, "at least the Otherworld as we know it will be destroyed. I say the Laws must be lifted in this instance. We do not necessarily have to allow another lifting even though we have done it once.

"No, our only hope is to hold to the Laws we have given the mortals. We too are bound by them. The Seekers must be left on their own and what comes shall come without our meddling in the affairs of the mortals."

"There is the problem of Maliman," Boand began, then was interrupted by Oghma.

"And that we will deal with when the time comes," he said firmly. "But we cannot meddle in the affairs of mortals. They must be left to their own ways and means. Do not fear, Badb, Macha, and Morrigan, your time will come and there will be much left on the field of battle for you. *That* we know as Maliman will not rest until both Earthworld and the Otherworld are his."

"I think . . ." Boand began, only to be interrupted again by Oghma.

"We must . . ." he said.

"Oh shut up," Boand said. "Others have words as well as you, and I for one would like to hear them."

Oghma turned red-faced and started to speak, but The Dagda raised his hand, calling for quiet.

"You have had your say, Oghma," he said. "Allow Boand hers."

Boand cast a smug look at Oghma and said, "As I was saying before being interrupted, there is the problem of Maliman that all will have to face sooner or later. If those in Earthworld are to be united to fight against Maliman and his evil forces, then the Chalice must be returned to its rightful place. Otherwise, we will have petty kings and chieftains fighting among themselves, which Maliman wants. When that happens, then he will pounce upon all like one of Cernunnos's wolves. It is easier to handle individual slices of bread rather than the whole loaf. One slice is not strong enough but a whole loaf may be. One king by himself is no match for Maliman. All kings and chieftains together will have a chance. I say that we lift the ban provided by the Laws and allow the Seekers to take the Chalice from Bricriu and return it to the Red Branch."

"I say let the Laws stand," Lugh said, rising. "We can *still* help Earthworld when the time comes . . ."

"As you did when you helped the Red Branch and your son Cucullen when Connacht invaded their lands," Boand said pointedly. "And you did that without our permission."

Lugh flushed brightly. "Yes, as I did before and will do again if needed. There is no reason for us to lift the ban at this time. Men must stand by themselves. If we continue to meddle in the affairs of men then men will become dependent upon us to solve their difficulties. Maliman is one problem that will help strengthen men if they are allowed to deal with him by themselves. And, as I said: We can *always* help later."

"Later may be too late," Boand said.

"Maybe. But that has been and should stay the will of the two worlds."

"I agree," said Donn, the god of death, rising to his feet. "We can always help the mortals *if* it comes to that."

"In the meantime, your land, Teach Duinn, the Island of Death, will gain more and more souls," Boand said acidly.

"Teach Duinn will always have its shadows," Donn said. "Either way, there will be dead. So there is no reason to use that as an argument, Boand. We can have Goibniu, our blacksmith, begin to prepare weapons so we will have them if and when we need them.

We all know that the final battle is coming, but we do not know when. This could well be the time. I say we leave things as they are."

"All right. All *right*," The Dagda said as arguments broke out among the gods. "Then let us put it to the vote."

But when the vote came in, it was dead even for either lifting the Laws or leaving them be.

"So," The Dagda said, sighing. "We are to that, are we? Very well. Then I must say we leave the Laws as they are. It has long been our way that when such voting is held and accounted for we do nothing but leave things as they are. Still, I will allow any god free will if he or she wishes to exercise it. But be aware that to meddle too much in the Earthworld will be dangerous."

"But . . ." Boand began.

"That is my will, my order," The Dagda said firmly. "Now, this gathering is over. See to your own business. I shall be watching, however, that any of you decide to take advantage of the new freedom I have granted. Do not anger me. Be wary of what you do and when you do it."

He rose from his throne and left as the gods began to argue among themselves.

28

The Seekers appeared a somber group as they made their way down the hallway and out into the courtyard. Bright sunlight dazzled their eyes for a moment. First their eyes watered and they smelled the filth in the courtyard—rotting apple cores, rancid fat, puddles of dried urine and feces—and then their eyes cleared and they noted the small piles of bones and garbage that had gathered along the edges of the courtyard where the pavement met walls. A couple of beggars made their way through the crowd that had gathered, holding out their wooden bowls and pleading for money. Silk tunics, dyed many different colors, showed in the crowd. Near the entrance to the courtyard, common merchants had gathered, while along the sides, warriors had gathered, some holding cups of wine, others gnawing on chunks of meat still on the bone. The windows overlooking the courtyard had small balconies that were crowded by those eager to see the duel in hopes of bloodshed. At the north end, the balcony was much larger, and Cairpre rested on a fine velvet-covered couch, eyes sunk in meaty cheeks, waiting impatiently for the duel to begin. His favorite warriors and women stood clustered around him. He raised a silver cup to drink rich Falerian wine, the knuckles of his hand disappearing into fat, leaving dimples behind.

Beneath the balcony Braken stood, glowering as Seanchan took his place against the south wall and leaned on his staff, staring at Braken with a slight twist to his lips as if he was contemplating a secret joke about his opponent.

Nervously Braken ran his hand up and down his highly polished staff. A dog sniffed at his toes and received a kick for its effort. The dog yelped and ran around the courtyard and disappeared through the south gate.

Bricriu walked closely by and murmured, "It has been done. Watch for Seanchan's attention wandering, then strike. But strike well. You will only have one chance."

A dark smile wreathed Braken's face and he straightened his shoulders as he stared across the courtyard at Seanchan with new confidence. He would have to hold his own only until whatever Bricriu had arranged came to happen.

"I have a bad feeling about this," Sirona said suddenly. "I think Tarin is right; we must split up."

"What is it?" Cumac asked.

She nodded at the Dragonstone pulsing on Cumac's shoulder.

"Something wicked is coming," she said. "I do not know what it is but I do know that it is coming. Your Dragonstone warns us as well. If this were to be a fair fight then your Dragonstone would not be warning us. But it is. I feel it has already been put in motion."

Cumac frowned and gestured to the others to join him. Nuad and Fergma trotted to his side and sat on their haunches, intent upon the crowd before and around them.

"Sirona feels that something is amiss," he said. "Spread out among the crowd and keep a sharp watch." He glanced across the courtyard and saw Bricriu smiling evilly at them.

"And I think that what is going to happen is the work of Bricriu," he added. "Keep your weapons handy."

"Let it come," growled Lorgas as he lifted his battle-ax up and down on his belt. "I'll split whoever tries to meddle like a ripe melon."

"Do not hesitate," Sirona warned. "For when it happens it will happen suddenly. You will only have one chance to stop it."

The others nodded and slowly began to work their way through the crowd, taking a stand here and there among the people looking on expectantly as Seanchan leaned on his staff, his eyes fixed on Braken at the north end, under Cairpre's balcony.

"Well?" he demanded. "Should we begin?"

Without answering, Braken sent a bolt of lightning streaking across the courtyard toward Seanchan. With a disdainful wave of his staff, Seanchan blocked the bolt and sent it back at Braken, who was forced to leap hastily out of the way. He looked shaken but wove a small gray cloud of writhing serpents and sent it out. Again Seanchan blocked and sent the cloud back at Braken, who disintegrated the cloud and sent flaming balls of fire back at him. This time, however, Seanchan sent them back and then sent an ice cloud, which struck Braken in the chest, staggering him. A length of rope followed the ice cloud and wrapped itself around Braken, but he managed to break the tie.

Braken felt his strength ebbing, and dots of perspiration covered his face and appeared under his armpits. Desperately he materialized a hunchback cat with foot-long curved fangs. It leaped toward Seanchan, but a fog of red smoke began to curl around Seanchan, and then a red dragon appeared from the fog, spitting fire. The cat screamed as fire rolled around it and burnt it to a crisp. The onlookers screamed in terror and cowered back against the walls. But the dragon ignored them and lifted itself into the air and hovered over Braken. The Druid desperately constructed a shield over him as dragon flames leaped out at him. Even though the flames didn't touch him, the heat from the dragonfire blistered him.

Then the dragon was gone, and Seanchan leaned nonchalantly on his staff and said, "Well, Braken. What now?"

Braken stepped out from under the balcony and took a fresh grip on his staff. He began to chant in the Old Tongue:

> 'Ch alluoedd chan caddug d a gollwng
> R Kracken chan 'r dywyllwch byllu.

> Come you powers of darkness
> Come and release the Kracken from the fire pit.

A portal began to open between Braken and Seanchan. From the deep dark depths fire flickered, the flames orange, then yellow, then blood-red. The crowd shifted nervously, casting fearful looks as a murky shadow began to move within the flames, growing larger as it climbed upward from the deep pit.

Seanchan began to chant in the same tongue:

> Bod cerddedig 'ch alluoedd chan caddug
> Bwria baci i mewn i 'r annwfn
> Danau Chan a daethoch.

> Begone you powers of darkness
> I cast you back into the hell-fires
> From which you came.

The portal snapped shut and Braken staggered from Seanchan's force. Feebly he raised his staff as Seanchan began to roll a ball of blue flame.

"No you don't!" a voice snarled.

The Seekers' heads turned toward the voice and saw the black-haired man with a long scar down the right side of his face holding another man by the arm. A bow and arrow lay on the ground at his feet. The man grimly smiled and gripped the would-be shooter by the other biceps, raised him from the ground, and broke his back across his knee.

Instantly Tarin and Sirona were next to him, blades drawn threateningly.

"He was going to shoot at Seanchan," the man explained, wiping his hands across his leather pants.

"Bricriu!" Tarin snapped, and spun around looking for the Poison-tongue.

In the courtyard, Seanchan paused at the interruption, the ball of blue fire half-rolled. He glanced at the others and quirked an eyebrow. Braken straightened, and a black bolt of lightning sped from his staff toward Seanchan.

"Look out!" Lorgas cried.

Seanchan's attention snapped back to Braken. Automatically he threw the blue fire and quickly swept his staff around him, creating a shield that sparkled like beads of spring water in the sunlight. But he wasn't quick enough, and the black lightning exploded against the shield and burst around it in a black fire that covered Seanchan. The others strained their eyes to see Seanchan, but the black fire raged around him, then abruptly stopped.

And Seanchan was gone.

But not alone. The blue fire struck Braken, and a hideous and painful shriek came from him as his body swelled, then exploded. Gobbets of flesh and muscle rained down on the courtyard.

And Braken also was gone.

29

For a minute Seanchan looked around him, confused. He still held his staff, but he could see nothing in the darkness except for flames leaping high from a deep pit a scant few feet in front of him. Painful cries rose from the pit, causing the hairs on the back of his neck to tremble. Then he remembered the portal and Braken and its opening and being drawn into its vortex by a sudden hot wind before the portal collapsed in upon itself, trapping him inside.

He raised the staff and called out "Byrrcomin!" and a blue-white light began to glow from the head of his staff. He heard shuffling in the darkness and spun around to find the threat but saw nothing. He heard the scrape of nails upon rock, but he was alone.

"A fine state of affairs this," he murmured to himself. "Now what to do? What to do?"

He raised the light on his staff and peered around him. He was standing on a rocky path that wound its way around boulders and across small rifts from which tiny flames licked. The path ran on either side of him and he stood undecided about which way to go. He sighed and went to a rock and sat down, keeping a firm grip on his staff and the light.

"I wonder if this is in the bowels of Teach Duinn?" he said, remembering Donn the god of death and his island where all souls gathered before being assigned either to the Pit of the Damned or to a place of green fields and trees where they could live in peace and harmony. "Or is this the edge of the Great Rift?"

He shook his head and sighed deeply. "'Tis a fine mess this is, Seanchan. I didn't think Braken had it in him."

He remembered being startled by the would-be archer and the man who broke his concentration by grabbing the archer just before Braken unleashed the black lightning.

"So this is where I was drawn. Interesting. Now what am I going to do about it? Leave, of course, but which way?"

A shimmering golden light suddenly appeared, coming along the path toward him. His eyes narrowed and he stood, taking his staff in both hands, readying it in front of him.

The light stopped just short of his staff and slowly went away, leaving a battle-scarred figure in front of him. The man had black and silver hair and bold blue eyes. He was shorter than the average man but had brawny shoulders and wore a gray tunic bordered in three red stripes. A man of nobility, for certain, although his face was clean-shaven with a small scar on his left cheek. He wore black knee-high leather boots. His face broke into a smile.

"Seanchan, how good to see you," he said warmly.

Seanchan peered closely at him. "Do I know you?"

The figure broke into a merry laugh and said, "Have you forgotten your old friend so soon? Don't you remember the gay times we had in the Great Hall of the Red Branch?"

Awareness spawned in Seanchan's eyes.

"Cucullen! Is that you?" he asked. "What are you doing in this damned place?"

"Finding you," Cucullen said. "And to lead you out of here. I think you were considering the left path, weren't you?"

Seanchan nodded. "It rises slightly, while the right path seems to angle down."

"Then you would have gone down, for here to start up leads only down. That way is the way we will travel. Oh, don't worry," he added as Seanchan looked at the right path skeptically. "You will not be harmed. Although the way may be frightening at times. At least I don't *think* we shall have any trouble. These are wary times as you well know. Not all of Maliman's people have managed to be released from the Great Rift and we may encounter them along the way. Still it is the only way to travel."

"Then where am I?"

"On the edge of the Great Rift," the shade of Cucullen answered. "Come. It is time to go. Although I do not think we will have trouble, it is still not wise to remain in one place too long."

Seanchan rose and stepped close to Cucullen as he turned and led the way to the right. The trail wound gently down, circling around the pit, and Seanchan could see that although the pit was deep, there seemed to be levels to it with shades dancing in the light.

"Tell me," Cucullen asked. "How fares my son?"

"Well," Seanchan answered. "You would be proud of him. A lot of you is within him. Including the *riastradh*, the warp-spasm. He wields Caladbolg well, as only the son of Cucullen could. There is no fear in him. He rides your great Black."

Cucullen nodded, a pleased smile turning into deep dimples in his cheeks. "If Black accepts him then there would be no fear in him. He is well then?"

"For now," Seanchan said soberly. "But the warp-spasm takes its toll on him every time he uses it. He ages. Not much but enough."

Cucullen nodded. "He must learn to control it. That is hard to do but he must learn to control it. Otherwise, it will draw him into itself and there will come a time when the warp-spasm consumes him."

"Control it?" Seanchan asked. "It comes on its own in the fierce heat of battle. There is no control of it."

Cullen shook his head. "Yes, there is. But I did not learn that until it was too late and I began to age each time it came over me."

"Then what is the secret of the warp-spasm?"

Cucullen paused and turned to Seanchan. "Scathach, the Woman of Victory, can teach him. It would be wise to send him there."

"No, that is impossible. We cannot take him to Scathach. Not now. He is needed in Earthworld. Badly needed. Maliman grows stronger each day and we grow weaker each day we try to regain the Bladhm Caillis, the Chalice of Fire. If we do not retake the Chalice and return it to the Red Branch, there is little hope in uniting the kings and chieftains and forming an army that will be able to defeat Maliman and his armies."

Cucullen gave a grim smile. "You will not have to take him to Scathach, The Destroyer Who Strikes Fear. She is already on her way to Connacht from the Island of Shadows. Maeve promised Connacht's armies to be commanded by her. Manannan has sent his chariot to fetch her across the frothy seas. Ulster may follow Connacht's lead and join its army with that of Connacht under Schathach's lead. *But,*" he added in emphasis, "Maeve lives by whimsy. She may well refuse to allow Connacht's army to follow Scathach and keep it at home. Or she may decide to lead it herself. One must take Maeve's promises with a steady glass of wine. She may also see how she could work the threat of Maliman to her advantage. If the Red Branch, who are the closest to Maliman's fortress in the Mountains of Mourne, and others wage war against Maliman, their armies will be riddled with death. Then Maeve, with a whole Connacht army, will be able to easily take the other lands and kingdoms. No, you cannot rely upon Maeve to hold to her word. You should know that, Seanchan."

Seanchan's face became warm and he said sharply, "I do not need you to remind me of Maeve's maneuverings. I am quite aware that to trust her is to trust a mockingbird to build its own nest."

A smile again curved Cucullen's dimples. "Then what do you need me for?"

"To guide me out of these infernal regions," Seanchan snapped.

Cucullen laughed and gave a mock bow. "Then I shall."

He turned and began to walk along the downward path.

"I need to get out, not go farther into this pit," Seanchan said.

"To go down is to go up," Cucullen said over his shoulder. "And stay on the path and ignore what we encounter. This place is trickery above all things. Stay close."

The heat grew more and more fierce as they made their way down. When they rounded a bend in the path, Seanchan noticed several shades wandering back and forth aimlessly, their expressions vague and perplexed.

"What are these shades?' he asked.

"These are those who did not help others or make a decision," Cucullen answered. "They are not wanted in any world and are doomed to forever wander between various regions."

A figure suddenly stopped and stared at them, vacant eyes staring at Seanchan.

"I know that one," Seanchan said. "That is Baindo One-eye from the Red Branch. He always argued about any of Connor's decisions."

Cucullen nodded. "That he did. And so he must wander here."

"Cannot these shades ever leave this place?"

"No. Never. In a way, they are among the most damned, although their physical pain is much less than other places. Their pain is mental anguish, knowing why they are here but not knowing that there is no way out for them."

"Seanchan Duirgeal," the shade called. "Give me the direction out of here. I do not belong here among the rest of these misbegotten. Give me the path to green fields and soft breezes."

"I do not know that way," Seanchan answered. "I myself am lost here."

"Yet you are mortal," the shade replied. "Why are you here?"

But Seanchan did not answer, as he and Cucullen rounded another bend and dropped down another level. Here they encountered shades who cried in agony as flames continually burned their hands.

"These are thieves," Cucullen said before Seanchan could ask his question. "But they are not robbers or murderers. Their hands will forever burn for taking from others that which was not theirs to have."

"That is Ailell Quickhand," Seanchan said, pointing to one of the shades who waved his burning hands at them, begging them to stop.

"He stole from widows and orphans," Cucullen said. "Do not talk to these people, for they have wily tongues and will try to work their will upon you."

Obediently Seanchan averted his eyes and concentrated on the broad back of his guide.

Again they rounded a bend and Seanchan saw other shades crying in agony as flames consumed their legs.

"And these unfortunates, who are they?"

"These are the ones who stole horses and cattle and did not share their ill-gotten gains with their lords and lieges."

One shade ran near Seanchan, who recoiled automatically from the shade's sudden closeness.

"Seanchan!" the shade called miserably. "Tell Donn that this is not where I belong. What I took I took as my rightful gain. Willingly would I give it back if I could only be released from this place!"

"Fuad! I know you well," Seanchan said. "And I know that you never gave your lord his rightful share of your bounty. No, I will not ask Donn—if I ever meet him—to change your sentence. You belong here."

"Seanchan! Wait!"

But Seanchan and Cucullen did not pause in their trek and continued downward as the heat became nearly strong enough to blister flesh. Seanchan noticed that Cucullen seemed impervious to the heat, and he asked Cucullen why.

Cucullen smiled. "I do not belong here. I am not one of the

Great Rift. I live in the forests and grasslands where Cernunnos rules. There the waters are cool and sweet and the feasting rich and succulent."

"How much farther must we travel?" Seanchan asked. "This heat is bothersome."

"Not much longer. We will not travel to the lower regions, although you may look into the pit and see what lies there. Soon our path will turn up and we will come to the gateway that will lead back to Earthworld. Be patient."

Around the next bend, Seanchan saw shades running against the backs of others with swords, inflicting horrible wounds that left them writhing and screaming in pain until the fire seared their wounds and closed them.

"These are the cowards who ran in battle or who refused to fight fairly according to the Rules of Warfare when challenged." Cucullen's face twisted in distaste. "They are not the worst, however. The worst are taken below to the Great Burning."

"Boca!" Seanchan exclaimed. "I wondered what happened to him. He was one who came upon your back during the cattle raid on Cooley, I believe."

Cucullen nodded. "I was hard-pressed to kill him."

Yet another bend appeared, and after they rounded it, Seanchan saw shades screaming in pain as they tried to reach the shelter of a magnificent house that rested on a plateau above the fiery mire through which the shades struggled only to be cast back after narrowly failing to climb out of the mire.

"These are those who gave false hospitality," Cucullen said to Seanchan's unspoken question. "They will never reach that house, which promises Otherworld delights."

And here Seanchan saw Borach, who demanded that Fergus Mac Roich accept his hospitality, leaving Deirdre and the sons of Uisneach to fend for themselves as they made their way to the Red Branch, where they had been granted protection from Connor, who withdrew his pledge after they were in his hostel.

"You know that one," Cucullen said, pointing. "He is among the worst, for he used the Laws of Hospitality to force Fergus, who had granted Deirdre and the sons his great right arm for their protection, to stay for a feast in his hall, knowing full well that Fergus has a taboo placed upon him that does not allow him to refuse any feast when it is offered."

"A most despicable man," Seanchan said, watching as Borach managed to grab the edge of the pit only to have it crumble in his fist, casting him head over heels back into the fire, where his flesh began to blacken from the flames.

"Most despicable," Cucullen agreed. "As are the others. You would know them if there was time, but we must hurry, now, for we are close to where the path begins to go upward, and to go much farther down could prove treacherous."

Seanchan hesitated to look down into the pit and saw figures being beheaded only to have their heads grow back where the ones who gave false witness were punished; others having the flesh torn in strips from their bodies for betraying their lords; robbers who stole from their lord; and murderers who slit each other's throats and drank the blood to assuage their thirst.

And then, the one at the very bottom: Ragon Garg-Fuath, whose name meant "hatred for all." He had been cast out of the Pantheon by The Dagda after he led others in a war against the gods of the Pantheon. He then had formed the Cultas Dubasarlai, the Cult of Black Sorcerers, who formed all other evil beings. And now he could see the Black Sorcerers just above Ragon. Ragon roared and turned and twisted to escape, but the lower half of his body was frozen into the black ice at the bottom of the pit.

"Moggan, once one of the brethren who saw the evil Ragon created, turned against his brother, and cast the spell that keeps Ragon there. Try as he might, he cannot escape, as the spell has no beginning and no end and cannot be unraveled."

And then all disappeared from view as they rounded a corner and the path leaned steeply upward. Stones threatened to trip them up with every step. Calcium deposits showed in white streaks on the faces of stones and boulders. Somewhere a cataract roared, but Seanchan could not see it. Up higher, signs of skeletons of animals that dated back to the days of Tuan and the beginnings were etched into granite facings. The air became cooler as they went up, and the flames began to flicker, with green coloring the peaks.

"This is the place for warriors waiting to enter the green fields," Cucullen said, pausing on a small level piece of ground to allow Seanchan to catch his breath. "It is here that they wait to be called to Donn on Teach Duinn for judgment. Most who are here will be granted passage to the green fields. Although some will not make it. These are the ones who have tried to hide their past, and their punishment is the most severe. They are cast down into the black fire at the bottom of the Great Rift. One may murder but one who practices deceit and betrayal of this sort is considered the foulest of all the dead." He shuddered with memory of the place, and Seanchan wondered what punishment could so affect the shade of the Red Branch's greatest and famous warrior. But Cucullen refused to elaborate and turned to lead Seanchan farther up into the reaches of the pit.

"I do not know where we will come out," Cucullen warned. "That changes with the shifting of the Otherworld from day into night. Not all things are stationary; most exist in motion."

"I understand," Seanchan said. "I hope that it is not far from Cairpre's court."

Cucullen paused again and, frowning, said, "Cairpre's court? Is that where you came from?"

"A Druids' duel," Seanchan said. "I was close to being incinerated before I could block Braken's black lightning bolt."

"Braken, was it?" Cucullen asked, then laughed. "Well, Braken is here and it did not take long for Donn to throw him down into the deepest recesses of the pit. He languishes there, and if you wish to see him, you may look into this basin of water as a scrying place."

For the first time Seanchan noticed they had paused near a rock with a scooped-out top in the rough form of a water basin. The water was clear and cold and very blue, with silver clouds shifting at the bottom. Obediently he bent forward and focused upon the water. Murky shapes emerged, and then he saw Braken, his whole being burnt black, writhing in pain as lions and ravening wolves tore at his flesh, tearing off thick chunks only to have the flesh grow back over the wounds, which were again raked by the powerful claws and jaws of the beasts.

"He betrayed his oath, his *Druid* oath, which cannot be violated," Cucullen said firmly. "That is not tolerated here." He hesitated a moment, then added, "In some cases, the shade is destroyed and no remembrance of such a man exists. That is really the worst of all, I think. A man has his spirit, his soul, and to have it destroyed so there is nothing that is or was, I think, would be worse than what seems to be the worst. Honor is all that man has. To have that gone . . ." His voice trailed off. He shook his great mane of hair and turned again to the path and began to lead Seanchan upward.

Seanchan began to pant and his legs trembled as a great weight seemed to settle more and more upon his shoulders. At last, he was forced to pause and lean heavily upon his staff to keep from falling down.

"I . . . don't . . . know how much . . . I can bear," he stammered, striving to pull breath into his lungs.

"Coming out of such a place is very hard," Cucullen said sympathetically. He moved to Seanchan's side and wrapped a hard-muscled arm around Seanchan and lifted him upright from leaning on his staff. "Come. Let me bear your burden. I can carry you this way but I cannot carry all of you. That is not allowed here."

Seanchan nodded gratefully, gasping too much for speech. Cucullen's support eased the burden greatly, and he found that he could shamble forward with little effort. Yet there was still the hint of burden there and that kept his shoulders bowed.

After what seemed an eternity but was, he remembered later, only an hour or two, they came to a great granite slab that was a door. Cucullen eased him down on a stone carved into a chair. Seanchan sank down gratefully and drew a great, shaking breath.

"Here, you must exit yourself. The stone must be removed and that I cannot do. You must do it. The door leads to the Otherworld and this door you must open by yourself. I will wait, however, to be certain that nothing happens to you until you leave."

Seanchan studied the door. Above it was a legend carved deeply into the lintel. He nodded and straightened on the chair and pointed his staff at the door and intoned,

> *Archa agori at chyfaill*
> *Sy chyfaill at 'r dirio.*
>
> *I bid you open to a friend*
> *Who is a friend to the land.*

The great slab shuddered and then slowly began grinding as it opened. Spiderwebs were dislodged and spiders of a size that Seanchan had never seen scurried up the wall to disappear in the dark overhead.

Then the door was opened and a gray mist swirled beyond its threshold. Seanchan turned to Cucullen with a questioning look, and Cucullen said, "You must go through the mist alone. I cannot go. This must be done on your own. Farewell, my friend. It was good to see you again."

And Cucullen's shade slowly disappeared.

Seanchan drew a deep breath and rose, pulling himself upward by use of his staff. The load was unbearably painful. Slowly he forced his way forward and entered the mist. A soothing cool washed over him, and the load on his shoulders was suddenly lifted. He found himself on a green hillside beneath an apple tree fully leafed and bearing fragrant blossoms. The door began to close behind him, and he turned just in time to bid Cucullen farewell and call a quick thanks for his guidance. A lark landed in the apple tree and began singing. Seanchan sighed and made his way to the tree and sat beneath it, leaning back on a green swath, enjoying the day.

Then the warmth of the day made him drowsy and, closing his eyes, he slept deeply and well. When he awoke, a beautiful roan horse stood before him, waiting patiently.

"Well," Seanchan said. "And where did you come from?"

The roan tossed its mane and pawed the earth.

"I suspect that you come from Saingliau or someplace like that, didn't you? Like Cumac's Black?"

The roan vigorously nodded its head, and Seanchan chuckled.

"Well then, I am happy you have found me. I shall call you Gray-mount. Would that suit you?"

The horse nodded again and Seanchan said, "Then Graymount you shall be. Will you carry me?"

The roan immediately knelt, and Seanchan laughed in delight and mounted. The roan trotted away without Seanchan's nudging, heading toward the east.

30

The Seekers looked at each other, shaken. Across the way, Bricriu smiled evilly and Tarin flushed, drew his sword, and started across the courtyard toward Bricriu. The smile slipped from Bricriu's face and fear shone wetly in the perspiration that suddenly sluiced down his face. He turned and scurried away, looking fearfully over his shoulder at Tarin and the dark cloud that had settled over his features.

Sirona hurried to Tarin's side and grabbed him by his sword arm, stopping him.

"Don't!" she warned. "Remember he is protected. The Laws?"

Tarin stopped, his chest heaving. He shook his head and slid the rune-blade back in its sheath. He glared at Sirona and said, "I would say that he has near worn out his welcome. At least I would have him leave if this is my place."

Sirona shook her head. "That doesn't matter. As long as he is offered protection then he is safe. We can't touch him."

"Ahhh," Tarin said in disgust, and stalked away toward the Great Hall.

"It seems, good people, that the Druids' duel is a tie," Cairpre called from the balcony. "A bad conclusion. I am very disappointed in the outcome. But there is nothing for it, I suppose. Well"—he struggled to his feet, pulling his bulk up by gripping the iron railing around the balcony—"let us return to the Great Hall and be entertained by our storytellers and bards. This day"—he fanned his oily face with a square of linen—"is very hot and I am uncomfortable."

He turned and waddled away. The man who had stopped the would-be archer nudged his still form with a toe, then ordered two guards to take him away. The guards looked loath to do that but followed their orders, one taking the man by the shoulders, the other by the feet.

The man drew a deep breath and came over to the Seekers. He paused in front of them and said, "My name is Dathi. I regret what is happening here." He spat in disgust. "This court was not always this way. In the days of Diartin, Munster was great, a place to be feared if you were a raider or Sword-wanderer looking for spoils. But since Cairpre came to be king, the best of our warriors have left, leaving these fawning fools as protectors of the city and court."

The Seekers exchanged glances. Then Sirona said, "One man is not responsible for another's way. But this"—she looked around at the piles of refuse and garbage in the corners of the courtyard, the dog turds lying here and there, the dried puddles of vomit where drunken men had voided their stomachs from too much wine—"this is beneath contempt. This is not a fortress but a home for pleasure-seekers. I am surprised that it has not been taken by bandits and out-lawed Sword-wanderers."

Dathi shrugged and ran a hand over his black gray-flecked hair. "I think it is because it is far away from its borders. To cross the land to wage war against this fortress is not easy. And we would be warned long before any army would arrive at our walls. Of course"—he grimaced—"not that that would make any difference. A small band could take this place at the right moment."

"And the Dark Forces," Tarin said, then related how he had en-countered a vampire in the night. Dathi's face darkened.

"I suspected that something like that would be happening. Ma-liman knows the strong kings from the weak. It is only a matter of time before this place falls to his minions."

"You could leave," Cumac said. "Is there anything holding you here?"

"I have been the champion of this court for nearly twenty years. It has become my home, now, and I must guard my home the best that I can. Regardless of how it has fallen upon evil ways."

"To guard your home is not necessarily to remain here," Bern said. "Join us to bring the Chalice back to the Red Branch. With the Chalice safely out of Maliman's hands, you are protecting this place. You will earn the favor of the Red Branch and Connacht. Their armies will be obligated to help Munster if it is attacked."

Dathi scratched his head. "That makes sense. I grant you that. But I feel my place is here."

Cumac shrugged. "The offer is still there. Think about it. For now you do not have to make any decision about leaving, as Bricriu is still within these walls. And that is a problem, as our hands are tied. We must find a way of getting Bricriu outside the walls before we can get to him and the Chalice."

"There *might* be a way," Lorgas said suddenly. The others turned to look at him. He smiled in return.

"If the Laws prevent us from seizing him, then let us use the Laws to take him."

"How are we going to do that?" Cumac asked.

"If Bricriu is found guilty of theft, Cairpre would be within his right to send Bricriu away. Would he do that?" he asked Dathi.

"Why would Bricriu steal anything?" Bern asked. "He has what he wants right now. There is no reason for him to steal anything."

Lorgas grinned. "He won't. But it only has to *appear* that he has stolen something. Something that Cairpre values greatly."

"It might work," Dathi admitted. "Cairpre has a favorite bauble: a necklace of green emeralds. He wears it from time to time when kings meet."

"Can you get it?" Cumac asked.

"No, I think it would be better if Dathi is kept out of it. I'll get it," Bern said.

"Then you agree with Lorgas?" Cumac asked.

"I do."

Cumac looked at each of the Seekers in turn, then shrugged.

"Then we all are in agreement," he said.

"Where do I find this necklace?" Bern asked.

Dathi shrugged. "In Cairpre's room there is a heavy oaken door that leads to another room. It is kept locked all the time. But in there is where Cairpre keeps his most valued treasures. It will be difficult in getting to it, though, as his room is always guarded whether he is in it or not."

"That will not be too difficult," Bern said. He glanced at Lorgas. "Will it?"

Lorgas shook his head. "Leave this to Bern and me. This is work for elves."

"When you have it, take it immediately to Bricriu's room. Hide it where he will not see it but a serving wench will find it when she cleans his room."

"As good as done," Bern said, and the two elves walked off, their heads together, speaking softly.

"This should make Cairpre drive Bricriu from court. Cairpre does have a terrible temper when it arises. Which is not really often unless someone spills food or drink on him or a warrior earns his displeasure for something done that infuriates him."

"We shall see," Cumac said.

* * *

"shh," Lorgas whispered to Bern as they peeked around a corner of the hall leading to Cairpre's room. The hall was lit by flickering torches in heavy iron sconces fixed to the walls on each side. The space between the sconces was taken up by woven tapestries that displayed pictures of hunting and war and one wedding when an ancient king of Munster had taken the daughter of another king as his bride. No one remembered the name of the king or his wife anymore, as that had been lost in time centuries before. Now the tapestry showed moth holes and the once-gay colors were dingy and gray.

Down at the end of the hall two guards flanked the great door leading to Cairpre's room. The two elves considered them carefully, then pulled back from the corner. Bern touched the Bisuilglas on his shoulder, the sacred talisman of Rindale, the Hall of Warriors, where Ervalians gather when they are slain, and looked at Lorgas.

"The spell will only last a few minutes," Bern whispered. "I can slip through enchantments with it and hold them within the enchantment but you will have to be quick. I can only hold the magic of Earthworld so long."

Lorgas nodded grimly. "Five minutes?"

"No more," Bern cautioned. "The Bisuilglas was not meant for this, so I don't think I can hold it any longer than that. We will have to be back here by that time. If all goes well, the guards will not know what happened. Are you ready?"

Lorgas took several deep breaths and nodded.

Bern closed his eyes and chanted an ancient spell.

> *Ad 'r allu chan Rindale d'forth*
> *A canlyn 'm ewyllysia. Harneisia 'r allu*
> *Chan 'r briddo a ad 'm at basio*
> *Rhyddha chan 'm caseion chreuau.*

> *Let the power of Rindale come forth*
> *And follow my will. Harness the power*

Of the earth and allow me to pass
Free from my enemies' eyes.

A gold mist slowly built around Bern, and he hurried down around the corner down the hall, running toward the guards.

The guards looked in puzzlement at the mist but then froze in place as the mist came over and around them with Bern faintly visible before them.

Lorgas sprinted around the corner and down to the door. He opened the door and hurried into the room. The bed was huge and canopied, with red, white, green, and blue silks draped over the canopy. Rich carpets in greens and blues covered the floor, and the chairs gleamed blackly. A fire flickered in the fireplace. Next to the fireplace was a huge oak door. Lorgas hurried to it. The lock was massive but old and Lorgas's lips curved into a laugh as he took a hook he had made from an old iron poniard that afternoon. He slipped the hook into the lock and turned it twice. The tumblers slipped open and Lorgas entered the treasure room. Quickly he glanced around and immediately saw the emerald necklace spread on a square of black cloth. He grabbed it and hurried from the room, carefully leaving the door slightly ajar, then ran from the room. The gold mist was beginning to fade as he pulled the bedroom door shut behind him. He ran down the hall and around the corner and was joined seconds later by Bern, panting, his face pale with sweat.

"That was close," Bern whispered hoarsely. "I couldn't have held it much longer. Did you get it?"

Lorgas held up the necklace. Green lights sparkled from the facets of the stones and from the highly polished gold holding the stones in their settings.

"I decided against relying on a servant girl," he whispered to Bern as they hurried down the hall back toward their rooms. "That seemed to chancy to me. I left the door slightly ajar so Cairpre will see it when he retires for the night. Surely he'll check the room and will see that the necklace is missing. It was in plain view on a piece of black cloth. Not hard to miss. I think he'll be enraged and call for the entire fortress to be searched for it. The searchers will find it in Bricriu's room. I'll put it under his blankets at the foot of his bed. What do you think?"

Bern nodded. "Much better than relying on a serving wench who might be afraid to tell Cairpre that she found the necklace in Bricriu's room since Cairpre's temper has been known to flare from time to time."

Lorgas nodded. "I thought you'd agree. Now for Bricriu."

The Poisontongue's room was at the other end of the hall and unguarded. The elves ran down the hall and gingerly opened the door. The room was empty, although torches and the fire in the fireplace illuminated the room brightly.

"Hurry," Bern said. "I'll stand here."

Lorgas ran into the room and in a twinkling placed the necklace beneath the bedcovers and slipped out of the room.

The elves each took a deep breath and let it out slowly. Relief showed upon their faces. They patted each other on the shoulder, congratulating each other, and strolled down the hall to their rooms.

The entire fortress heard the shriek of rage at the midnight hour. Moments later, Cairpre stormed into the Great Hall shouting for his guards and for the doors to the halls and Great Hall to be barred and guarded.

Warriors and servants alike ran frantically to the Great Hall, pulling on clothes as they hurried. Cairpre stood on the dais, dressed in a snowy white sleeping shirt that could have been used as a tent. His eyes were nearly lost in rage in the suet of his face. His fat bobbled with indignation and servants cowered at the foot of the dais.

"Where is it?" he shouted, his face purpling. "Where is my emerald necklace? There is a thief here! Hunt him out! Now! Now! Now!"

Dathi strolled out in front of the warriors and stood on the bottom step of the dais, staring at Cairpre. His face was expressionless but stern and demanding, and Cairpre took an unconscious step backward impulsively.

"What are you shouting about?" Dathi said. "What brings on this unseemingly display from a king?"

Flecks of spittle appeared at the corners of Cairpre's mouth as he said, "The emerald necklace that has been in my family past knowing. Gone! Gone! A thief is here among us!"

"Serious charges, Cairpre. Serious to make uniform as if all here were guilty. Perhaps you misplaced it."

"I . . . did . . . not . . . misplace it! It is always in its place in my treasury! Always! Unless I'm wearing it!" He stamped his foot in anger, causing the fat on his chest to bounce nearly to his chin. "A thief is here and we will catch him! Tonight! You hear me? To-night!"

Dathi sighed and turned away from Cairpre and motioned to the nearest five warriors behind him.

"Each of you take five men and divide the search among you. Search all the rooms very carefully. The scullery, the kitchen, servants' quarters, the stable and livery. Everywhere!"

Obediently the five warriors turned and selected their five and dispersed after a moment spent dividing the search.

Deliberately Dathi motioned for a servant and ordered her to bring wine and cups for him and the Seekers who stood silently beside him, their faces a mirror of innocence. The other warriors grumbled and sat at the tables, heads held in their hands, talking, as servants brought them foaming goblets of ale and wine.

"He's losing it, he is," one grizzled veteran said quietly so Cairpre could not hear. "I've known it to be coming. A matter of time. A man gets that fat and the vapors start coming upon him. You listen and you'll hear his belly gurgling from here, I tell you."

"Aye," another answered. "That it is. And when he passes air, why the Great Hall reeks of it."

"I heard . . ."

"I saw . . ."

"You know . . ."

"Searching is worthless. The thief will be long gone by now."

"But if he's missing . . ."

". . . then we'll know who he is . . ."

"I was bedding a comely wench . . ."

Complaints went around the room, softly, causing a soft susurrus in the air, words fleeting quickly from lips to lips. The atmosphere was tense, but soon the ale loosened tongues and merriment began to break out, although somewhat subdued.

Bricriu sat by himself at the head of the table just below the dais upon which Cairpre, now sitting, fumed, fat fingers clutching a jeweled goblet from which he drank deeply while a nervous servant stood nearby, ready to refill it. His red-rimmed eyes glared over the Great Hall as his lips, thick as white slugs, moved in and out, muttering words that only he could hear.

Two hours passed. Then three. And midway in the fifth hour, a warrior came into the Great Hall and approached the dais, holding the emerald necklace in his hands. Cairpre grabbed it as if it would suddenly disappear in air if not in his hands. He caressed it, his eyes studying it carefully to assure him that nothing was missing and that the necklace had not been damaged. Then, sighing, he placed it around his neck and glared out at the searchers and the hall.

"Well and good," he said angrily. "But where was it found?"

The warrior shrugged and then said, "We found it in the room of Bricriu."

Bricriu blanched and leaped to his feet, shouting his denial.

"Impossible! If it was found there, then someone put it there!"

Nuad and Fergma immediately leaped to their feet, growling, their eyes fierce on Bricriu.

"Easy," Cumac said, dropping a hand to each back.

"And how would that happen?" Dathi growled, his eyebrows coming together, his eyes like anthracite as he studied Bricriu.

"I don't know! But I didn't take it!"

"We found it under the bedcovers at the foot of his bed," the warrior said. "We would have missed it except we searched twice since none of us found it the first time through. That is what has taken so long," he added apologetically, although he did not feel an apology was necessary except to try and placate Cairpre's rage.

Bricriu stood, mouth gulping like a fish, his face as white as beech ash.

Cairpre nodded at the warrior. Then his eyes shifted like a lizard's as he studied Bricriu.

"I . . . didn't steal it!" Bricriu stammered. "Why would I steal it when you have provided everything for me?"

"Perhaps because you wanted it?" Cairpre said, his face flushed scarlet with barely contained rage.

"Why? Why? I demand to know why!"

"Demand? Demand? In my court you *demand*? No one demands anything of me! I am king! *I* demand! Not you!"

"No, no. I meant nothing by my words," Bricriu hastened to explain. "But . . ."

"No 'but's!" Cairpre interrupted. "Why was my necklace found in your room if you did not put it there!"

"I don't know! I don't know!" Bricriu wailed, his hands running through his hair. His eyes fell upon the Seekers and he pointed a trembling finger at them as he shouted, "They stole it! They stole it!"

"And why," Cairpre purred dangerously, "would they do that?"

"To . . . to discredit me in your eyes," Bricriu said. "They would do anything to harm me."

"But theft?" Cumac asked, stepping forward. "We are here by your indulgence, Cairpre. As is Bricriu. Why would we endanger that? None of us has anything to want or to expect other than our quest to return the Bladhm Caillis to its rightful place. To steal anything would violate the Laws of Hospitality and you would send us from your fortress. We would be away from what we seek. No, I can speak and say that the theft of your necklace would not benefit us. And would we be so foolish as to put it in another's room if we stole it? No. Likely not."

Well, Cumac said quietly to himself, it isn't *exactly* a lie. I did not say that we did not steal it. Not exactly.

"What say you to that, Bricriu?" Cairpre asked, turning his attention to the Poisontongue.

"Lies! All lies! I did not take it!" A crafty look came into Bricriu's eyes. "And when, I ask, would I have been able to steal it? You have guards always at the door to your rooms so I could not have passed by without them knowing."

Cairpre turned to the guards, who waited at the foot of the dais, ashen-faced.

"Did anyone go by you?" he demanded.

"No. No one," one of the guards said, shaking his head vehemently. "The theft must have taken place when others were on duty."

"Unlikely," Cairpre grunted. A light gleamed in his eyes as he turned back to Bricriu. "And as to when you could have taken it, you will remember that I let you look upon the treasures when you first came here. It would have been a small matter for a thief as skilled as you—after all, you *did* steal the Bladhm Caillis from the Red Branch—to slip it in your tunic sometime before we left the room. I have not been back in the room since then. That leaves only you."

"But . . . but . . ." Bricriu stammered.

"No 'but's. You have stolen from me. From Munster, as this"—he fondled the necklace—"is one of Munster's dearest treasures, handed down from king to king since time known. I will tolerate a lot under the Laws of Hospitality, but thievery cancels the Laws and their protection. However, I will not have you punished. I will not have you slain. Instead, you are banished from my court and from Munster. You have three days from now to leave Munster's borders. If you are found within our borders after that, you will be beheaded and your body buried in the sands of the sea at low tide, your bowels taken from you and burnt to ash and that ash thrown to the winds that no more memory of you will exist. You will be gone from my court by first light. However, I will not allow the Seekers to leave until tomorrow's gloaming to satisfy the intent of the Laws of Hospitality. I would suggest that you leave as quickly as you can. Dathi, you will govern his departure."

Dathi nodded and turned to Bricriu. "His Highness, Cairpre, has directed that you leave the safety of this fortress forthwith. Under his direction, I will escort you to the outer gates in two hours. Make ready."

He turned on his heel and winked at the Seekers before striding forcefully from the Great Hall.

Bricriu glared at the Seekers and said, "You are responsible for this. You! I will not forget this!"

"I hope you don't," Tarin said coldly. "I am looking forward to making your acquaintance on the field." He patted the hilt of the rune-blade and, turning on his heel, led the Seekers from the Great Hall as Bricriu stood, fuming for a moment, before realization dawned upon him. Hastily, he hurried from the Hall, going toward his room.

31

A gray overcast day showed itself when The Dagda called the gods and goddesses to a forum. In the far northeast, flashes of red fire appeared from Maliman's forges and heavy black smoke hung overhead. Lightning crackled and thunder boomed, but it did not rain, and The Dagda knew that Maliman had reached his full strength and was rebuilding his armies from Sword-wanderers and bandits and outlaws who had sworn their allegiance to him along with hobgoblins, goblins,

Deag-duls, and Black Baggots. The Grayshawls had left when the final seal broke holding them captive in the Great Rift, releasing them and the last of the Nightshades. Warggads and Truacs had already left the Great Rift, and now the battle for Earthworld was beginning to make itself felt in the Otherworld.

The Dagda rose, stroking his long, gray beard, and studying the others, seated in a semicircle in front of him. His eyes were tired and appeared bruised, but his robes were clean and there was still the hint of iron in his stance.

"My friends," he began. "You all know that things are not going well in the Earthworld. We can see the result in our world as well. Maliman's forges are working night and day to produce weapons for the mighty army he is building. Most of Maliman's followers have escaped the Great Rift, with only a few still being held in its greatest depth. I fear, however, that they too will eventually be freed. Ragon Garg-Fuath may also escape, although I do not think we have to worry about that at present."

Still the mention of Ragon Garg-Fuath's name caused a stir among the gods and goddesses. He had been exiled to an island in the Western Seas hidden by enchantment. His name meant "hatred for all." He had been cast out of the Pantheon of Gods by The Dagda for his excessive pride, which made him desire to be as strong as The Dagda. A great war broke out in the Pantheon of Gods, and after Ragon and his forces were defeated and exiled, he eventually formed the Cultas Dubasarlai, the Cult of Black Sorcerers. This cult formed the goblins, hobgoblins, Grayshawls, Nightshades, werewolves, and ogres to torment man. Eventually, Ragon's Black Sorcerers managed to escape from Ifreann, an enchanted island in the Sea of Ice, along with the spirit of Ragon. However, all were then defeated by Moggan, who exiled them once again to Ifreann, this time casting Ragon into the very depths of the Great Rift, where Ragon had been imprisoned with the lower half of his body frozen into the black ice and fire licking about his flesh while he furiously tried to escape.

The Dagda raised his hands, calling for quiet, and when the hubbub ceased, he spoke, saying, "As I said: We do not have to worry about that now and should not. There is worry enough for Mali-man. I believe that we should begin preparations for war. I hope that we will not have to go to war, but it is wiser to be ready if we have to than to fumble and bumble our way into readiness if war does break out."

Lugh stirred himself and rose, saying, "Are you thinking that we may have to join forces with the armies of Earthworld?"

The Dagda hesitated, then said quietly, "Yes. We may have to. If Maliman manages to control Earthworld then he will be here next. You can already see his presence is making itself felt."

He pointed to the north. Automatically the others turned to look at the fire, lightning, and black cloud.

"We have had bad days for over a week now," The Dagda contin-ued, "and the rain that does fall upon our trees and fields carries a bitterness with it that is turning the leaves and grasses brown."

"Then," Lugh said slowly, "I say that we should ready ourselves for fighting. If we don't have to fight, then so much the better. But don't you think that one of us should go to help the Seekers?"

The Dagda pulled furiously at his beard for a moment, then said, "Not to help. We must not stray into the affairs of men just yet. However, we also have the Ard-ri to think about. He is being well cared for and loved by two mortals in Callyberry. I think it would be wise if we sent one of ours to be there if trouble or Mali-man finds him."

"I'll go," Lugh said. Golden light began to shine about him.

"No," The Dagda said. "I think it should be a woman. A warrior will only draw attention to Callyberry. Especially one of your de-meanor, Lugh. I mean no offense but secrecy is our greatest ally at the moment."

"Then I'll go," Fand said, rising, and shaking her golden tresses. "My son, Cumac, is already in Earthworld and I would feel better, now, if I were too."

"You will have to disguise yourself," The Dagda said. "You will have to leave your jewels and finery behind and take on the guise of a serving woman. You must make yourself plain and I do not think it wise if you were to tell the husband and wife who are keeping the babe safe who you are. They might begin to treat you as a god and not a mortal."

"I understand," Fand said.

"But I charge you, Lugh, to be ready to come to her aid if needed. There may come a time when your mighty arm is needed to help protect the Ard-ri."

"I'll keep ready," Lugh promised, looking at Fand.

"Good. Then we'll turn our attention to the Otherworld. Goibniu, you will gather those you need and put your forge to use making weapons for us."

The smith god nodded and rubbed a callused finger alongside his nose. His face had been burnt nearly black from working at his forge, and his shoulders were heavy with muscle from swinging his hammers.

"More than me is needed, I'm reckoning," he growled. "I have need of others to work the bellows and to keep the fires hot. Boand," he said, addressing the river goddess, "I'll have need of your waters to quench the iron." She nodded her agreement. "Donn, I shall need ore from the great depths beneath your island." The god of death acknowledged Goibniu's words. "And there will be others. I'll let you know when I need you. Remember, though. I give the orders and you will follow them. I don't have time to play namby word games with you."

"We all know you are blunt-spoken," Dianchect, the Healer, said.

"You, Dianchect," The Dagda said. "Ready your herbs and healing powders. Make yourself ready for anything."

"I shall," Dianchect said.

"Now, I suggest we all think about what else needs to be done. We shall meet again within the week."

Slowly the gods and goddesses left, talking to each other about what they might be able to contribute toward building the army that The Dagda had called for. Manannan Mac Lir, the sea god and husband to Fand, caught up with her and said, "You will see Cumac when you are in Earthworld?"

Fand nodded. "Yes. The Seekers must be told what is happening so there will be no surprises."

"I don't think that wise," Manannan said. "It would be better if men do not know what is happening here. Otherwise they may begin to think that we will be there to help them out of any difficulty. They must not know that we are making ready here in the Otherworld lest they grow lax and reckless."

"Cumac is my son," Fand said.

"Yes, but you sent him into Earthworld to return the Chalice to its rightful place. He has done well in his endeavors. Leave him be."

"You cannot order me!" she said furiously.

"Yes," Manannan said sharply. "I can. And you will do what I wish. Now, there's an end to it. See that you follow my wishes."

He strode away to where his chariot and white horses waited and, mounting the chariot, drove the team toward the distant sea.

Fand watched him go, seething, then said softly, "We shall see, husband. We shall see."

32

Fedelm awoke with a start, staring into a pitch-blende night. What had awakened her? She lay silently, straining to pierce the silence around her, searching for the sound or whatever had come to her in her sleep.

"Fedelm."

A hoarse whisper came and she craned her neck, looking behind her. A faint light appeared in the darkness with a shadow hovering within it. The shadow seemed to be staring at her, beckoning her to call to it. Still she hesitated, feeling around her for her weapons, but then the past came rushing back to her and she remembered being brought here to the Cave of Tuan by Cathlon and that her weapons were elsewhere. She drew her hands back to her side and silently sat up, her attention steady on the shadow and light.

"Fedelm of the Sidhe." The whisper came again, this time firmer and demanding an answer.

"Name yourself," she said, readying herself for whatever might come her way.

"No names. Or have you forgotten already?"

"I haven't forgotten. But names you once had you still have. Call yourself by that instead of 'noname.'"

A chuckle came from the shade. "We can call ourselves anything. But we do not. Our names mean nothing anymore and in some instances meant nothing when we lived and walked the earth. Here, we are what you see, nothing more."

"I don't believe that," Fedelm said flatly. "You remember being men. That is with you. Even as shadows you exist. So what do I call you?"

The shade remained silent for a long moment, and Fedelm feared that she had lost it. The silence deepened, but she stubbornly held her tongue, waiting for the shade to speak. At last words came from it.

"I was once a man. But I refused to serve my lord or any other. My sword arm was great and I fought many duels. But only for myself; never for anyone else. Now I walk in the shadows in this valley, doomed, condemned by what I had been and what I had never become. To speak my name is to recognize what I had been. Now I am among the forgotten."

"Then you serve Maliman?"

A harsh laugh came. "I serve no one. Least of all that sorcerer, that rim-walker."

"Then by not serving you serve," she said. "Acknowledge that and earn your peace."

Another long silence fell between them. The light flickered and nearly went out, taking the shade with it. But then it brightened a little and the shade said, "Words. Only words. Here, in this valley, I live among others who are like me. You risk much by coming here."

"I had little choice," she said. "I was brought here by Cathlon from the Dreamworld when others were seeking me. I have no weapons with me. Nothing to defend myself with other than my own hands."

"No arms?"

The response carried real wonder with it, and Fedelm responded, saying, "I told you. Nothing. I am as you perceive me."

Again a long silence came between them, then a sigh like a wind coursing through pine trees.

"At the back of this cave you will find weapons for you. Take the right hand of the fork you will come to. There you will find what you need."

"I thank you. And you? What about you?"

"Doomed. Doomed."

Boldly Fedelm asked, "Then serve man, not Maliman. Join with us."

"That is not for me to say," the shade replied. "Here I am; here I stay. To ask more of me is to endanger yourself. Do not go farther into the valley. There you will come to your death. Much evil exists deeper in the valley. Evil that goes beyond what you have experienced before."

"How do you know what I have faced?"

A quiet chuckle and the words, "All things are all things. We hear, but we cannot act. Here, all hope is abandoned. You should take the weapons I have offered and leave. But do not leave until the dark of the night has passed and the lark sings. A nightingale's song is a death song. It awakens what lies in the deep."

"I shall wait here," Fedelm said firmly. "Unless my friends manage to wrest the Chalice from Bricriu, and then I will leave to join them. Otherwise, I will remain here and stop him when he comes."

"*If* he comes," the shade said.

Then the light flared, and in the sudden burst of illumination, the shade disappeared. Yet the light still burned, drawing Fedelm deeper into the cave.

She moved forward warily, her eyes casting from side to side, searching for danger.

Deeper and deeper she went, winding her way through the cave until she came to the fork. She took the right arm and that again led her deeper and deeper until she at last came to a pool of stagnant and black water. The light hovered over the pool, seeming to beckon to her.

"Am I to enter the pool?" she asked.

The light flickered and turned to something resembling a spear, the head pointing down into the pool. A faint white light seemed to glow within the depths of the pool, and Fedelm breathed deeply three times, then entered the pool in a clean dive that neatly split the water.

A numbing cold swept over her but she clamped her jaws tighter and swam down and down toward the light. Dimly she saw the opening of a tunnel and entered it. The light seemed to pull her upward and she followed it, her lungs aching for breath. At last she broke the surface of the water and pulled herself up on a broad ledge. She breathed deeply, pulling dry air into her lungs as she lay gasping on the edge of the ledge. When her breathing slowed, she stood and looked about her uncertainly.

Black dripstones hung from the ceiling. The floor of the ledge seemed wet and slick beneath her feet. Tiny crystals blinked from the walls, lending light to the gloom. Something sinister seemed to move in the darkness, and she looked toward the sound fearfully, but saw nothing.

Then she saw a pile of weapons and rare gems and gold at the far reach of the ledge. She walked to it and studied the pile carefully.

The weapons were old and some rusting. Silver was tarnished and the gold had a dull sheen to it. Bows without strings leaned against the wall and rotting quivers filled with arrows with moldy fletching hung on pegs. All in all it looked like a refuse heap for cast-off weapons. Then a silver light glowed around a long slender black box and she crossed to it, knelt, and opened it.

A black sword with a silver guard and pommel rested within the box. The blade was black as obsidian but of steel with strange symbols worked into the blade. The pommel was a silver knob and the grip tightly wrapped black leather. The scabbard to the sword rested on the inside lid of the box, also wrought in silver and black leather.

Gingerly she ran her finger along the blade, feeling the power of the blade pulse through her finger and into the palm of her hand. It was a large blade—nearly four feet in length—but when she lifted it from its bed, the sword fitted itself into her hand as if it had been crafted for it. She swung it and a strange song came from the blade as it cut through the air. She took the scabbard from the lid and sheathed the sword and swung it over her shoulder. At first it hung loosely; then, as if ordered by an unseen command, it fitted itself to her, nestling firmly but lightly over her shoulder and back.

A matching knife and sheath on a black leather belt showed in the bottom of the box, and she lifted it free and belted it around her waist. As the sword had to her shoulder, the belt fitted itself to her waist, although when she first tried to buckle it, it seemed meant for a large man.

"Strange," she muttered. "Very strange."

Then the light shifted to the wall and she saw a black bow gleaming from its hooks and a black quiver filled with black arrows hanging from a peg. She came closer and studied the curious design wrought in finely figured silver letters down the curve of the bow and along the side of the quiver.

She took the bow and drew it. The draw was effortless, yet she felt great power in the tension of the bow. She lowered the bow and took the quiver and draped it over her other shoulder. It fitted itself to her the way the other weapons had. She slipped the bow into a sheath made for it along the side of the quiver.

Then the sound came again, nearer this time, and she spun around, searching for the source.

A figure, much like that of a man but not, crouched on two legs, the knuckles of what passed for hands resting on the floor in front of it. It looked covered with armored scales molded over lumps the size of melons. Its shoulders were massive, and the muscles bulked large like hogsheads. Black marble eyes stared at her. Two holes in the middle of the face passed for a nose, while thin lips revealed large fangs as it growled. No hair grew on the monster, which appeared covered with a green fungus. Its fetid breath seemed to fill the air, causing Fedelm to gag.

Her arm whipped over her shoulder, seizing the handle of the blade and drawing it.

"Welllcommmme," the figure growled. "Weeee haaaavvvvve beeeen waaaaaaitinnnng foooorrrrr lllllloooonnnnggg tiiiiiiimm-mme. Cooooommmmme heeeerrrreee, mmmmmyyyyy mmmm-moooorrrrssssellllll. I hunnnnnngggggeeeerrrr."

"Hunger be damned," Fedelm said. "Come, wretch! Earn your meal! If you can!"

"Iiiiitttt bbbbbbaaaaaaddddd," the monster said. "Cccccccoo-ooooommmmmmmeeee mmmmeee ssssssssuuuuuuuppppppp-eeeerrrrr."

Suddenly it gave a leap, howling as it came through the air toward Fedelm.

Fedelm ducked under the leap and spun around to face it as it landed and spun around to leap again.

Again Fedelm ducked and this time swung the blade at the underbelly of the beast as it passed overhead. A large shriek came from the monster. It landed and this time seized a rusted sword from the pile and rushed at Fedelm, swinging the blade fiercely as curses bubbled from its hideous gash of a mouth.

Fedelm met the monster's blade. The swords rang together, the force of the monster's swing so fierce that it nearly tore the sword from Fedelm's hands. Grimly she parried, cutting again across the monster's chest.

A shriek sent fear sweeping over Fedelm, but she ignored it, slid her blade across the monster's blade, then swung with all her strength at the monster's neck. The monster caught Fedelm's blade in one hand as it swung its sword again at Fedelm.

Fedelm leaped backward, drawing her blade from the monster's grasp. Stubs of what appeared to be fingers flew through the air, and green blood spurted from the wounds.

Then the monster rushed, catching her on a backswing, crushing her to the floor. The breath whooshed from Fedelm's lungs as her sword slipped from her grasp. Saliva dripped from the monster's mouth as it tried to lower its head to bite Fedelm. Desperately she put the heel of her hand against the monster's forehead, pushing its head back and away. The monster gripped Fedelm by the throat with its whole hand and began to squeeze. Black dots swam in Fedelm's vision, and she tasted brass at the back of her throat as she drew her legs up under the monster and tried to push it off her. But the weight of the monster was too much, and slowly Fedelm grew faint.

She strained against the monster's bulk and stabbed stiffened fingers into the monster's eyes, feeling the jell roll under her fingers.

The monster screamed in pain and fell away from Fedelm, clawing at its face.

Fedelm gasped and rolled weakly away. Her hand fell onto the hilt of the sword. She stood, wobbling on her feet, then gritted her teeth and swung the sword with both hands. The blade sliced cleanly through the monster's neck, and its head bounced away as green blood fountained upward. It stood, wavering for a moment, then fell backward with a crash that tumbled plates and gold and gems from the pile. Its legs twisted in pain for a moment, then stilled. A long sigh swept through the cavern and then—nothing.

Fedelm stood gasping, leaning on the sword, her fingers gingerly pressing against her neck. She coughed and spat, then stood erect and slid the sword back into its scabbard.

"Enough," she croaked. She walked to the water's edge, drew great breaths again into her lungs, and leaped into the water, reswimming the way to the top of the pool, where she pulled herself out onto the floor of the cave.

She lay, panting, weak, hurting for many minutes before stumbling to her feet. The glow appeared in front of her again, and she followed it as it brought her back up to the entrance of the cave. She collapsed on the floor, slipping her new weapons from her.

"You have done well."

She raised her head and saw the now-familiar shade before her. She grimaced. "I am lucky."

"Yes, you are," the shade said. "More than you realize."

"What was that?" she asked, gesturing toward the back of the cave.

"A thing from before time. She was the mother of all evil. That which haunts the earth now came in the beginning from Her loins."

"Thank the gods that I had this sword."

"Yes. Thank the gods. But that sword was not made by man, for no weapon made by man could have slain Her. Your sword was made by the father of Goibniu, the smith of the gods, the bow and arrows by Goibniu's mother, Nemain. These weapons have been given to you, but it is up to you how you use them. Be wise. Otherwise you will fail and become one like us. Being from the Sidhe does not protect you here. Here you are no more than any other."

"I understand. I think," Fedelm said.

"See that you do. The strength of your weapons is the strength that is within you. The weapons will draw upon that strength. They were made so. They answer to their owner either good or evil. Wield them well."

"I thank you."

A quiet chuckle came from the shade. "Thank yourself. I only led you to them."

"For that I thank you."

But the shade did not reply and slowly slipped from view. Fedelm turned toward the cave's entrance and saw stars shining brightly overhead as if fire diamonds had been pasted against a black mantle.

She lay down and took a deep, painful breath. Then her eyes became heavy and she slept.

33

Stealthily Bricriu crept from his rooms, carrying
the Chalice in its bag on one shoulder, another
bag with his belongings over the other. He held
his sword in his hand. Black eyes darted from
shadow to shadow as he made his way through
the dark in the Great Hall and through the
night to the stables. He paused for a moment
before his eyes steadied on the horses belonging
to the Seekers. A pair of fine chestnuts stood in

a stall next to a great black that eyed him with malice, lips curled back from white teeth.

Bricriu grinned to himself as he made his way to one of the chestnuts and studied its lines. Perfect, he thought. You will take me safely away. And that will leave one of the Seekers without horse.

He reached for the saddle hanging on the chestnut's railing, then froze as a voice cut through the darkness around him.

"Take it. That will make you a thief again."

He spun around and saw Tarin leaning against a post, his face a frozen mask, his eyes gleaming. Fear laced through Bricriu's bowels, and he clenched his buttocks together to keep from voiding.

Slowly Tarin drew his sword, the rune-blade rasping from its scabbard so loudly that Bricriu thought it must awaken the entire court. Tarin rested the point on the ground in front of him.

"I thought you would be sneaking away, a thief in the night," Tarin said. "Cairpre has given you a day away. But I could kill you now as a thief. That chestnut belongs to me. His name is Borun."

The chestnut flung his head up on hearing his name. He stomped his hooves and snorted and turned toward Bricriu, and the Poisontongue felt water running through his bowels as the horse stared at him.

"The Laws . . ." he stammered, but Tarin cut him off.

"They do not apply now. A theft from me is not a theft from Cairpre or his court. I do not grant you leave. Saddle Borun. If you can," he taunted.

Bricriu seized the bag containing the Chalice to his breast, holding his sword out in front of him as he backed away. Tarin grinned and followed him, raising his sword, tracing lazy patterns through the air.

"I have been given the right to leave in peace," Bricriu said fearfully.

"Then you must leave on the horse you rode in on," Tarin said. "Any other and you will die. Legally, I might add. Not even Cairpre can save you from *that*!"

"I have been promised safe leave!" Bricriu said, his voice shrill. He waved his sword in front of him.

"That," Tarin said, nodding at Bricriu's sword, "I could take as a threat and defend myself against you."

Immediately Bricriu lowered his sword.

"I will give you no reason to stop me," he said. He slipped his sword into its sheath. "That"—he pointed behind Tarin—"is my horse. I will take him and leave."

"Take him," Tarin said carelessly, making no move to stand aside.

Gingerly Bricriu made his way around Tarin and to his horse. He placed his bags on the ground near a gaunt horse and took his saddle from the railing beside the horse. Quickly he saddled and fitted the bridle then gathered his bags and mounted the horse. He watched Tarin carefully as he rode the horse from the stable.

"We will be meeting again. Soon," Tarin said. "Always watch over your shoulder. Sometime I will be there."

Bricriu kicked his horse into a trot and turned its head downhill toward the main gate, casting fearful glances over his shoulder until he rounded a corner and disappeared from view.

Tarin spat and sheathed his sword and left the stable. Suddenly he stopped, hand on the hilt of his sword. He stared into the shadows and exclaimed, "You! Show yourself!"

Dathi stepped out of the shadows. "I saw you leave and thought to follow you in case you decided to take it upon yourself to rid us of the trouble of Bricriu. You know that he has been granted safe passage."

"In most things, yes," Tarin said, his hand dropping from his sword. "But there was the chance that he would try to better his mount and that would have left him to me."

"Perhaps," Dathi said. "But I would have been forced to stop you. Cairpre granted him freedom to leave and I won't allow a splotch upon the name of Munster despite the worthlessness of the king."

Tarin smiled mirthlessly. "And do you think you could have stopped me, Master Swordsman?"

Dathi shook his head and said, "I would not like to, but there is the question of honor."

"Yes," Tarin said mockingly. "The question of honor. Misplaced as

BRIAN CULLEN

it is, always the question of honor. But I don't think you would be wise to cross swords with me. Especially for the likes of Bricriu."

"As it is, I won't have to. Bricriu is gone," Dathi said. "I know who you are, Tarin. And what you are. I feel no need to cross blades with you unless I am driven to it."

"Yes. As you say: lucky."

Dathi hesitated, then shrugged and said, "Since everything is now as it should be, what would you say to a glass or two of wine before retiring?"

Tarin smiled grimly, then laughed and said, "Why not? We'll drink to what luckily wasn't."

He clapped Dathi on the shoulder and, together, the pair turned and walked back to the Great Hall.

MORNING rose gray, and cold rain fell, turning the town streets into mush. Cumac knew that the road leading away from Cairpre's court would be a quagmire. Yet the Seekers refused to stay another day and quickly readied themselves for travel before Cairpre's court awakened. Dathi, however, waited for them at the stables, his horse ready, carrying a small pack. A gray cloak was slung around his shoulders, with his sword hilt angled over his right shoulder.

"I see you are ready," Tarin said.

"I decided that I would like to go with you," Dathi answered. He made a gesture of disgust, loathing showing in his face above his gray beard. "This place is a fool's playground, nothing more."

"You are Cairpre's champion," Cumac said pointedly.

Dathi shrugged his shoulders in irritation. "Champion of what? I have decided that there is no honor left here. Let Cairpre choose one of those fawning prigs as his new warrior. I'm done with it."

"Then you are welcome," Sirona said. She looked at the others sternly.

"We can use new company," Lorgas said, looking sideways at Bern. "I'm tired of the same old stories. New blood is needed, I say."

"What would you know of new stories, half-wit? Everything is new to you a half-hour after you hear it," Bern said scathingly.

"At least I have stories to tell," Lorgas rebutted. "City elves know little except the doings of court."

"What . . . what . . ." Bern sputtered.

"We're wasting time," Cumac said. "Tarin, take the lead."

Tarin nodded and led the way out of the fortress.

The town below the fortress was gloomy and appeared abandoned as they rode through it, huddled deep within their cloaks but determined to catch Bricriu. They had not been this close to him away from a fortress in a long time, and the road he had seemingly taken led toward the Valley of Shadows. They missed the foresight of Seanchan and Fedelm, but Tarin was wise in following others and was certain that this was the road that Bricriu had taken. The other roads led back toward the north, and there was nothing in that direction for him, knowing as he did that Connacht would block him from its borders or seize him and throw him in a cell, given Maeve's pronouncement that if Cumac survived the challenge in the Cave of Cruachan she would lift the Laws that allowed Bricriu to stay safely in Cruachan Ai. It had been a hard challenge, but Cumac had defeated the Cruachan lions and Bricriu had little choice but to flee Maeve's fortress.

The road they had taken meandered around the southeastern part of Cairpre's land, skirting marshes and the lowlands, but it was slow going with the rain and deep mud and slop of the road; yet they were comforted in knowing that Bricriu too had the same difficulties in traveling that they were experiencing. And they were better mounted on fresh horses.

Once they thought they saw Bricriu going over a high ridge only a few miles in front of them and lifted their horses into a lope, but when they topped the ridge, they saw a forest below them and the road wound into the forest.

Tarin shook his head. "That is Craymore Forest. A dangerous place. We will have to keep on our guard when we are in it."

"The wolfhounds will warn us of what we cannot see," Cumac said grimly as they watched them course back and forth in front of them, oblivious of the rain, always searching for what might be in front of them.

"The rain makes it more difficult to scent danger," Sirona observed as she watched Nuad and Fergma work the land in front of them.

"Not that much, I'm thinking," Bern said. "There is a bit of magic to those wolfhounds. They are not like others."

"Bern is right," Lorgas agreed. "If there is something ahead of us, they will find it. Of that I am certain."

The Seekers nudged their horses and rode down the ridge to the edge of the forest where the wolfhounds sat, waiting on them. The forest looked dark green and gloomy, oak and ash trees grown so close together that they formed a canopy overhead that kept the rain from falling upon them, although water dripped from the branches and leaves. Beneath the trees dead leaves lay, giving off the scent of tannic. Gray squirrels leaped from branch to branch, and ravens perched on the branches, beadily eyeing them as they passed. Sirona rode uncomfortably beneath their gaze.

"I don't like them," she said firmly. "They look as if they are watchers for someone or something ahead of us."

"Maybe they are," Tarin said indifferently. "But there is nothing for it. We must go this way. What lies ahead, lies ahead. To dwell on it accomplishes nothing. Ride wary but do not let the unknown weigh upon your shoulders."

"I'm afraid of no one," Sirona said tautly.

"I know," Tarin answered.

"I think she's right," Dathi said. "One or two ravens I would ignore. But there are many here. I think they serve someone."

"Maliman?" Lorgas asked.

Dathi shook his head. "Maybe. But I don't think so. I think they serve someone or something ahead of us."

Cumac looked at the wolfhounds trotting down the road in front of them. "Nuad and Fergma sense nothing."

"Still there is something, I'm thinking," Dathi answered.

They rode in silence after that exchange, each lost in his or her thoughts. The road turned to a trail that forced them to travel single-file. Nervously Sirona and Dathi fingered their weapons, reaching over their shoulders to make certain their swords were loose in their sheaths, touching their knives around their waists to affirm that the knives hung properly for quick use.

Midafternoon came before the Seekers saw anything other than the squirrels and ravens. A small clearing opened up in front of them. In the center of the clearing stood a woodcutter's hut. Gray smoke curled from the stone chimney and furled down around the chimney and hut.

The wolfhounds paused, ears perked, low growls coming from their throats.

The Seekers drew rein and spread out on either side of the wolfhounds. Cumac's Dragonstone pulsed red and black at his shoulder. Tarin glanced at it and silently drew his rune-blade. The others quickly drew their weapons and sat warily upon their horses.

"The wolfhounds do not like this place," Sirona said softly, her eyes scanning the forest across the clearing from them.

"I don't like it either," Bern said.

"Nor I," Lorgas said.

"Nor I," Dathi added. "There is something gnawing at me here. Something isn't right about this place." He took a deep breath. "It has the stench of something dead. Or nearly dead. Gangrenous. Like a battlefield turning."

Tarin ignored the others and gigged Borun, his chestnut, forward, riding warily as he approached the hut. The others spread out behind him, casting looks hither and thither for danger.

"Hallo the house," Tarin called.

Immediately a dog began barking from inside and Nuad and Fergma crouched, threatening growls rising in their throats.

After a moment, the door opened and a huge man stepped out, pausing under the eaves. He eyed the Seekers suspiciously.

"Who are you and what do you want?" he asked rudely. His unruly black hair hung to his shoulders and low over his brow, nearly touching his thick eyebrows, which drew together in a frown. His black eyes were unfriendly. His beard was ragged and unkempt. His shoulders were so heavily muscled that they forced him into a slight stoop. He wore a wool jerkin and leggings, his boots cross-laced up his calves.

"Did a rider come past here? Black-garbed with a sour expression on his face?"

"Not many ride this trail," the man growled. He looked at the wolfhounds. "Your dogs are unfriendly."

"No more than yours," Tarin said coldly. "And put a civil tongue in your head. This is no way to greet travelers."

A leer showed as the man's lips turned up. "The way I greet others is my business. A man rested here for a few hours before moving on. He might have been the one you seek."

"How long ago?" Cumac demanded.

The man shrugged. "Time means nothing here. Three or four hours. But he won't be far. The forest becomes hard going ahead."

"Nevertheless we should ride after him," Sirona said, wheeling Bain around in a half-circle.

"Suit yourselves," the man said, shrugging. "Makes no difference to me. But night is coming and here it comes hard and fast. You won't get far in the dark. Ain't much ahead either. Your man will make a cold camp, that's certain."

"Then we claim shelter under the Laws," Cumac said.

The man laughed mockingly. "Who am I to care about the Laws? I am Congal the Woodcutter. There are no laws here 'cept what I make."

"We are the Seekers," Cumac said. He introduced the others as Congal shook his head.

"Well, can't say I haven't heard of you and him that's ahead with that bag he keeps at hand. I expect that is the thing you're after. Makes no difference to me one way or druther. Now, I say again: What do you want here?"

Cumac looked at the others, then glanced up at the sky. True to Congal's words, dark clouds were gathering, heavy with rain, with night closing fast on their heels.

"I think we'd be better off stopping here," he said to the others. "What do you say?"

"Might be better if we dry out and leave early morn," Dathi said. "Bricriu won't be traveling in this. He'll hold up somewhere, I'm thinking. Only a fool would guess his way in the dark and whatever he may be and isn't, Bricriu's no fool."

"Settled then," Tarin said, and swung down from his horse.

"Here now," Congal demanded. "What do you think you're doing now?"

"Spending the night," Tarin said, walking toward the man. "We'll pay for you hospitality that won't be freely given. Rest assured you'll be out nothing."

"Can't stand rudeness," Lorgas said, swinging down. "For a pebble I'd split your head for you and feed you to the ravens."

"You'll not get a feast here," Congal warned. "This is a poor man's home. Got some bread and ale. Maybe some honey. Wait here and I'll make ready for you."

"And maybe some meat, I'm thinking," Lorgas said. "Leastways that's what I'm smelling. A haunch of venison roasting over the fire."

He pushed passed Congal, carrying his ax in hand, and entered the hut, stomping his feet and shaking the rainwater from his cloak. He ignored the hound growling and strode purposefully to the fire, spreading his hands to the warmth. Above the fire, the haunch of venison roasted on a soot-blackened spit, grease dripping into the fire, causing tiny blue flames to snap and crackle.

"After you," Tarin said coldly, pointing the way through the doorway with the rune-blade. "And shut your hound up. He's making ours nervous and he's no challenge for either one of them."

The man grumbled but called out for the hound to be quiet, then turned and led the rest of the Seekers into the hut.

Inside, cobwebs hung from the ceiling and in the corners tiny spiders ran up and down the walls. The floor was hard-packed dirt. A plain wooden table bearing old grease splotches stood in the center of the room, sided by wooden benches. In one corner was a willow bed, blankets carelessly tossed upon them. Dust lay everywhere, and above all was the smell of ruin.

"By the gods," Dathi swore. "Don't you clean, man?"

"What for?" Congal growled. "Only get dirty again."

He crossed to a cupboard and pulled out wooden platters that appeared to have been at least wiped, if carelessly, and wooden mugs. He slapped them on the table and went back to the cupboard and brought bread and a jug of sour ale to the table. A pot of honey followed and, to the surprise of the Seekers, it was good honey with a light rose scent and taste.

"There. That's all. If it ain't good enough, go hungry for all I care," he said.

"And there's this," Lorgas said, lifting the venison from the fire and dropping it on a platter in the middle of the table.

"You'd take food from a man's mouth?" whined Congal.

"No. But neither will you refuse us. Especially since we're willing to pay," Bern said, taking his knife and cutting a generous slice of venison and transferring it to his platter. "You think we'd give a gold coin for bread and sour ale?"

"A gold coin?" Congal asked, a crafty glint coming into his eyes. "You'll give a gold coin for food and drink?"

"That we will," Sirona said. "But put a civil tongue in your mouth or you'll get nothing. And lay out a pallet for all of us. No ticky ones," she warned. "Or with fleas. You can keep them for yourself, seeing as how you must think of them as friends." She looked around significantly.

"I can only give you what I've got," Congal said. "Leastways the blankets might be all right seeing as to how I've kept them in cedar for the past few months. Maybe it's been a year," he added, frowning. Then he shrugged. "Time passes and there's no meaning to it or its passing. You'll have to make do or go without."

Bern sighed and shook his head. "Reckon we'll have to. Although damn me if I can understand how a man chooses to live this way. Defies all logic."

"I'll care for the horses," Dathi said, rising.

"I'll help you," Cumac said, following the warrior out the door.

LORGAS came awake suddenly, his eyes staring into the feeble light cast by glowing embers from the fireplace into the hut. He frowned. What had awakened him? Something. A low growl, barely heard, came from the throat of Nuad.

Lorgas raised his head cautiously, his fingers closing around the haft of his ax lying beside him. A shadow moved over Tarin. Light sparkled from a long knife in its hand.

With a warning shout, Lorgas leaped to his feet, swinging his ax overhead. He turned the haft in his hand and the flat of the blade struck Congal square in the face, sending him tumbling away from the Seekers.

Congal's hound snarled and leaped at Lorgas as the others jumped to their feet, swords drawn, looking around for the danger.

Fergma leaped past them, huge jaws grabbing the hound around the neck. Fergma gave a massive shake of his head, snapping the hound's spine. He opened his mouth and the hound dropped lifelessly to the floor.

"What's going on here?" Cumac demanded.

Lorgas pointed his ax at Congal, now recovered from Lorgas's blow, squatting, ready to leap, knife still in hand.

"He was going to cut your throat, Tarin."

"Why?" Tarin asked, his eyes smoldering.

The man shrugged. "For your purses. What else? Gold is hard to come by in the forest."

Then without warning he leaped forward, swinging his knife in a murderous arc. But the blow never landed as Lorgas stepped forward and beheaded Congal with a mighty swing of his ax.

Congal's head bounced twice, then rolled into a far corner of the hut, where it rested, facing them.

"A good ending to a bad beginning, I think," Bern said, sheathing his sword.

The others murmured agreement, following suit.

Then a dry chuckle came from the corner. They whirled and looked at the head of Congal, sneering at them.

"An end? All beginnings come from ends. This is only another beginning for you."

"Wizardry!" Tarin said sharply.

"Speak, foul being! What are you? Maliman's agent?" Cumac demanded.

"I am Congal. As I told you. When Ragon and Maliman and his others were cast into the Great Rift, I alone escaped. At least, I think I was the only one. I came here and live like this and have remained here. Few dare to pass my way, as the trail leads only to the Valley of Shadows. Only the unwary come here!"

"Before what were you?"

"Ah. Well, I was one of the Cultas Dubasarlai, the Black Sorcerers, who were not allowed into the Otherworld as we followed Ragon Garg-Fuath and then Maliman. Now you are here and starting a new beginning—as I said before."

"And what might that be?" Sirona demanded.

Another chuckle came from Congal's head. "Much lies ahead of you before you reach the Valley of Shadows, for there you are going for all your denying. You may die before you reach the valley but know this: That you will die if you go through the valley."

"If that is where Bricriu has gone then that is where we go as well," Tarin said.

"He bears the Chalice. He'll pass through with little difficulty. But you will not. Much awaits you."

"And what might that be?" Cumac demanded.

"Much."

Congal's face broke into an evil smile.

"Light is graying over the trees," Dathi said. "I think it's best we be riding. Rain's stopped but it could come again. And soon."

"All right," Tarin said.

"Don't forget the gold coin you promised," the head spoke. "Leave it on the table. I'll get it by and by." His eyes rolled to where his headless body sprawled on the floor. "It'll take time but I'll join the other half in a while."

"Will you indeed?" Dathi asked softly. He crossed to the head and lifted it by its hair. Congal complained loudly as Dathi set the head atop the cupboard. "That should keep you awhile. And as for your body"—he turned to the others—"would we be civilized if we didn't give it a decent burial?"

"No!" Congal shrieked. "Leave us alone! Go! We cannot harm you further!"

"But what about other travelers who happen this way?" Bern asked. He looked at the others. "Dathi's right. Won't take much to bury it. I say do it away from here, though. In the forest. We can pile leaves and such over it."

"No! No! No!"

"Take it then and good riddance," Tarin said. He threw a gold coin on the table. It spun on its edge briefly, then fell over. "To keep our promise," he said to the head. He glanced at the others. "Ready?"

Bern and Lorgas looked at each other and nodded, then picked up the body and left the hut as Congal continued to shriek and curse them. The carried it across the clearing and a short distance into the forest, then laid it behind a large oak and covered it with leaves and branches.

"You know the animals will get him, don't you? Wolves and such and goblins and hobgoblins if any are in this forest, and I would be surprised if there weren't," Lorgas said.

"More likely Truacs and Merrows," Bern said. "Since the opening of the Great Rift I'm thinking that all has been released upon the earth." He nodded at the forest around them. "And this place strikes me as a place they would come to live. Them and others. I don't think we have to worry long about Congal."

Lorgas nodded in agreement, and the two elves made their way back to the hut. Dathi had saddled their horses and made ready. The Seekers mounted and rode to where the trail again entered the forest and again continued their pursuit.

34

The Seekers quickened their pace, trying to escape the forest before nightfall, but the trail twisted and turned back on itself so much that direction was lost. Yet they knew that as long as they stayed on the trail it would eventually leave the forest. But to go off the trail, Bern said to the others, would lead only to trouble, for who knew what else lived in this forest? Nothing good—not even the squirrels. He swore as one dropped an acorn on his head. Or threw it, for it did smart and the others laughed as he scowled up into the trees, searching for the squirrel, and rubbing the spot where the acorn had landed.

There was no gloaming. There was day, and then night fell so quickly that it seemed the very sun had been extinguished by a vast candle-snuffer. They were forced to stop and gather dead wood to build a fire. They stayed on the trail and huddled around the fire as Cumac took bread and dried meat from one of the bags and divided it evenly among the Seekers.

"We have only water," he said somewhat apologetically.

"Ah well," Lorgas sighed. "There's nothing for it, so little will come of complaining."

"Look at it like this," Dathi said, nibbling on his bread. "Soon we shall be out of the forest and then we will undoubtedly find a place where we can eat and drink properly."

"None too soon for me," Lorgas said.

They ate in silence for a long moment; then Sirona suddenly straightened, pointing into the darkness.

"What's that?" she said.

The others turned and saw red eyes staring at them. Then other red eyes appeared around them.

"I don't know," Cumac said.

Bern threw a large dead branch on the fire. The flames leaped higher, casting light into the darkness. Automatically Dathi looked overhead and saw the immediate danger: giant spiders sliding down from filaments. Red hourglasses showed on their bellies.

"Spiders! Giant spiders!" Dathi yelled, drawing his sword. He swung at one, splitting it nearly in half. The spider shrieked and fell to the ground, writhing in its death throes, foul-smelling black blood spilling onto the ground.

The others leaped to their feet, drawing their swords. Lorgas roared and swung his ax, cutting off another spider's head. Black blood spurted, but he leaped back away from it and ducked as one of the spiders hissed and spat at the elf. The poison struck a hazel-bush behind Lorgas. Its branches twisted in agony and its leaves curled brown.

The elf grimaced and dodged the legs of a spider still dangling from its filament. His ax split the spider's head in half.

"Watch for them to spit!" Lorgas yelled. "It's poison!"

The others heard and dodged and ducked as streams of poison were spat at them. Swords flashed and sang as the Seekers slashed at the spiders threatening to overrun their defense.

A spider leg flashed out, striking Tarin in the chest. He staggered backward and nearly fell but managed to get the rune-blade in front of him as the spider squealed and triumphantly leaped forward. But Tarin suddenly squatted and as the spider flew over him, Tarin stabbed with his blade through where the red hourglass came together, into the spider's stomach, and leaped away as the black blood poured out and the spider screamed and curled its legs around the hurt in its belly.

Cumac found himself heavily beset by three spiders, Caladbolg singing in a rainbow's bright colors as he blocked first one then the others. One spider jabbed a foreleg at Cumac, but he leaped out of the way, severing the leg with one blow from Caladbolg. Still Cumac was being slowly forced across the trail away from the light until Sirona came to his aid. Together they stood back-to-back, swords flashing redly as they sliced through spider after spider.

Dathi drew his wooden-handled knife from its sheath on his belt and threw it across the fire and struck between the eyes a spider trying to come up behind Tarin.

Lorgas and Bern stood back-to-back as well, slashing and hacking as the spiders came toward them.

But there were too many spiders and the Seekers knew in their hearts that they would not be able to battle forever against them. Still they battled on, slashing and stabbing and hacking as the relentless horde threatened to swarm over them time and time again.

Then suddenly a bright white light seared over the trail, striking spiders and turning them immediately to ash.

The remaining spiders squealed in fear and scrambled back into the darkness and the trees.

The Seekers bent over, panting, their arms trembling from the sudden battle.

"What was . . . that?" Sirona gasped.

"I don't know," Cumac answered. "But it was timely. We were about done and I can think of no worse death than being wrapped in a spider's web, waiting for the spider to get hungry."

"It appears you were hard-pressed," a voice said from the darkness of the trail ahead.

Instantly the Seekers straightened, swords and ax held ready.

"Show yourself!" Tarin demanded.

A quiet laugh came, and then a figure, dressed in gray and white robes with three gold threads on the hem, flowing white hair falling over his shoulders and white beard dropping down upon his chest, stepped from the darkness and leaned upon his staff. A roan horse stood quietly behind him.

"Seanchan!" Cumac gasped, lowering his blade.

The others stared wonderingly at Seanchan, then put up their weapons and gathered around the Druid, greeting him with nods and pats and big smiles.

"You've returned," Lorgas said.

"Obviously," Seanchan said.

"Where have you been?" Sirona asked.

Seanchan shook his head. "In darkness and light and fire. In the Great Rift and out again. And wiser for my travel. A place not meant for men yet men are there awaiting punishment and being punished for their wrongdoings in this world."

"We thought you were gone after Braken threw his spell at you."

"I was gone and nearly forever. But a guide led me out of the pit. Your father, Cumac."

Cumac flinched and stared at the Druid. "My father?"

"Well, his shade actually," Seanchan amended. "But as hale and hearty as he was at his best. He does not reside in that fearful pit but in the green fields and forests guarded by Cernunnos. A sylvan place for those who have earned that right in Earthworld by selfless acts."

"Did you see Fedelm?" Cumac asked.

"No," Seanchan said, shaking his head. "But I believe I know where she is: the Valley of Shadows, in Tuan's cave."

"That does not bode well," Tarin said grimly.

"Cathlon, a Dream Guardian, is with her," Seanchan replied. "At least I *think* he is with her. If not, then he is not far. He will help watch over her."

"How do you know?" Dathi asked.

Seanchan smiled softly and stroked his beard. "I do not know. I *feel*, though. The woods speak to me on occasion—well, at least the oak trees—and from them I sense that she is there."

"Tuan's cave? What is that?" Dathi asked.

"Tuan was the first to come to Erin. He is the sole survivor of the Great Flood that cleansed the earth. He has the ability to shape-shift and exist on land, in the sea, and upon the air. He is the sole survivor of the race of Partholonians and the plague that killed all of them. He sometimes appears as a stag, a boar, or an eagle. We'll have someone sing the Song of Tuan for you if we can find the right bard," Cumac said. "How long will we remain in this forest?"

"We will leave the forest at noontime, when the sun is at its meridian height," Seanchan said. "Then we shall rest until the following morning, when we shall enter the Valley of Shadows."

"Is there no way around?" Tarin asked.

"There is. But the trail is longer—much longer—and leads through the Dismal Swamp. No, I think we shall have to make our way through the Valley of Shadows."

"Ah me," Lorgas said mournfully, leaning on his ax. "The way never gets easier, does it?"

"No," Seanchan said. "And before this is over, I think it will become more and more difficult. Hopefully, we will catch Bricriu in the Valley of Shadows. Hopefully. But he does carry the Chalice of Fire and that will help protect him as he travels. Which is one of the reasons why we haven't caught him yet. We are forced to stop and fight against whatever besets us while he slips by. The Chalice surrounds him with a mist and within that mist whatever lies in wait sees a herd of deer and no Bricriu. Another thing I learned while in the pit," he added grimly.

"By the gods!" Bern swore. "I cannot believe the Chalice will protect Bricriu."

"It doesn't," Seanchan said. "But it does protect itself and Bricriu holds it so Bricriu too is protected. Now, I think we should get some rest and leave early in the morn."

"Would you eat?" Lorgas blurted.

The others laughed.

"Good Lorgas," Seanchan said. "Always the stomach, eh? Yes, I will have a bit of bread and a bit of meat. But first . . ."

Slowly he moved his staff in a circle, intoning:

> *Briddo, am-dro, a danio*
> *Brennau, berthi a 'n goediog ddeildy*
> *Arail ni bydew hon da nos*
> *A cadw ni 'n ddihangol chan adwyth s drem.*

> *Earth, wind, and fire*
> *Trees, bushes, and wooded bower*
> *Guard us well this good night*
> *And keep us safe from evil's sight.*

A golden light flickered in a circle around them and held strong while overhead the trees came tightly together in a seamless roof. The bushes around them rattled their branches and interwove their branches with one another, forming a thick wall around the Seekers.

"There," Seanchan said with satisfaction. "We should be safe for the rest of the night."

The Seekers sighed with relief and curled up in their cloaks, keeping their swords and ax well at hand. But Seanchan's spell held, and they slept soundless and dreamless for the rest of the night.

35

Gray light greeted them at dawn with a fine
mist hanging in the air—a "soft day," they
would have called it except the air was dank
and sour and they were still in the forest and
knew that the Valley of Shadows lay shortly
ahead of them. They gathered their gear and ate
a quick and cold breakfast before mounting and
taking once again to the trail, this time with
Seanchan leading on his roan. Cumac noticed
that Black kept edging forward to be close to

the roan and smiled to himself. Obviously Black knew something that he didn't.

They heard movement in the brush on either side of the trail as they rode along it, and once Tarin thought he saw yellow eyes gleaming, but when he turned in his saddle to look at them, they disappeared with a quick rustle as of wolves or large hounds running, and when he glanced ahead to where Nuad and Fergma trotted, seemingly unconcerned, he gave up the sighting as a careful imagination at work.

By noon they left the forest and found themselves at the edge of a gray field that stretched toward a pair of mountains that Seanchan identified as the Paps of Anu. There a gray cloud hovered over a pass next to the mountains. Seanchan pointed at the pass and said, "There lies the Valley of Shadows. It seems close but is a good day's ride from here. I think we would be better off making our way halfway across this plain and camp before riding to the pass. Far better, I think, to enter the pass at noon, when the sun has a chance to light the way through the pass, than to come upon it in the early morning or early night."

"Will Bricriu camp as well?" Cumac asked.

Seanchan shrugged. "If he has any sense at all he will. I reckon he's only about eight or nine hours ahead of us, which means he might chance camping at the beginning of the valley before attempting to go through it."

"If Bricriu can do that," growled Lorgas, "then I think we should get as close as we can before nightfall. Hang this camping early. We *might* come close enough to Bricriu to see his fire if we ride to nightfall and then we'll have a beacon to follow. We might catch him before he enters the valley and then we won't have to put up with any of its nonsense."

"Oh make no mistake," Seanchan said. "There is no nonsense in that valley. None at all. Even the very ground can be treacherous."

"Our task is to catch Bricriu," Bern said. "I agree with Lorgas: Let us travel as far as we can and if we can see Bricriu's fire, then I say we ride to it regardless how close it is to the valley. If we get to him before he goes into the valley then we will have him and the Chalice and the valley be hanged. We can always find a way around it then."

"Let Cumac decide," Seanchan said. "He was the first chosen for this band. He should have the choice."

Expectant eyes turned to Cumac, who fidgeted for a moment, then said, "I have to agree with the others. Let us travel as far as we can before making camp. We may get lucky enough to find Bricriu's fire and then we have him."

Seanchan sighed and bowed his head for a moment then said, "As you wish. But we dare not waste time, then. Let us go."

Resolutely he pressed his knees against the sides of Graymount and rode out upon the plain, following the questing wolfhounds.

ᴅᴀʀᴋ had fallen fully when Seanchan at last reined in Graymount and said, "This, I think, is as far as we dare to go in the dark. And it is a goodly piece farther than I wanted. I cannot see Bricriu's fire, so I suggest we make camp here in this hollow and leave at first light. Plenty of deadwood is around, so we won't have to search far for firewood, and here our fire will be unseen, as it will be sheltered by the hollow."

"All right," Cumac said, slipping from the back of Black. "We'll stop. I know you did not want to do this, Seanchan, but I think it was worth the effort to try."

"Oh I don't mind the distance," Seanchan said. "It is what the night might bring being this close to the valley that worries me. Let's get that fire going. A goodly blaze may discourage night creatures from attacking us. Light is always a good friend in darkness."

The elves dropped from their horses and began to collect wood. Soon a fire flickered cheerfully against the night, and Cumac laid out bread and cheese and slices of cold mutton for their supper. No complaints came this time about the fare, as all were tired and hungry. Soon the meal had disappeared, and the Seekers lay back upon their blankets with their cloaks covering them.

"I'll take first watch," Tarin said. "Who will take second?"

"I will," Dathi said.

"Awaken me when it is time," Cumac said.

"And me after," Sirona said.

"We will take the last quarter together," Lorgas said. He looked at Bern. "What say you to that?"

"Agreed," Bern said wearily, rolling himself into his cloak. He yawned. "In the meantime, I'm sleeping. You do what you want."

Within seconds, a soft snore slipped from Bern's cocoon. Seanchan chuckled. "Well, that is promising." He yawned. "I think I'll follow him into Dreamworld. Maybe I can learn something there."

The others fell asleep along with him while Tarin placed a log on the fire to keep it burning fully. Slowly the hollow warmed. Tarin fought to keep his eyes from closing, and wished that he had waited for someone else to volunteer for the first watch. But then he contented himself by remembering that he would have the longest period of continuous sleep when his watch was over.

He stood and paced around the fire, working his shoulders to loosen them. He took a small bottle of water and splashed some on his face, scrubbing it briskly.

And then he heard Black snorting angrily and quickly drew his sword as he walked to the side of the horse. He placed his hand upon Black's neck and asked, "What is it, big fellow? Something out there that you don't like?"

Black shifted his hooves and jerked his head up and down and around, anger showing in his eyes.

Graymount moved next to him, and shifted her hooves angrily as if stomping the grass and ground to make for firmer footing. Then the chestnuts Bain and Borun joined them, facing the other way, angry rumblings coming from their throats.

Across the fire, the wolfhounds leaped up and turned to the darkness, hackles raised, and warning growls coming loudly from their throats.

"All right," Tarin whispered, clutching the haft of the runeblade. "Let us make ready."

Quickly and quietly he made his way among the sleeping Seekers, shaking them awake.

"Something is coming," he said as Lorgas started to complain.

Immediately Lorgas was on his feet, ax in both hands, staring around into the darkness.

Seanchan strode to the fire while the others formed a circle around him.

"What is it?" Cumac whispered.

"I don't know," Tarin whispered back. "But the horses and the hounds do. Look at them."

Now the animals were staring intently into the darkness. The wolfhounds crouched, ready to leap, lips drawn back as snarls rolled from their muzzles.

Then an angry scream came from Black and he reared on his hind legs, slashing the dark with his forelegs. Graymount quickly followed, screams coming from her throat as well, and the wolfhounds launched themselves at shadowy beings that suddenly appeared at the edge of light.

"Nightshades and sumaires!" Seanchan shouted. Fire erupted from the end of his staff, and balls of red flame were flung out into the darkness, followed by screams of pain from what they struck.

Then sumaires, mounted on Memans, cannibalistic black horses, charged into the firelight. They were followed immediately by Nightshades, ancient warriors who once followed Ragon, upon steeds of the night. Flowing black cloaks over gray cloth that appeared to be winding sheets spread out behind them. Firelight reflected like diamonds from the black blades of their swords held by black steel gauntleted hands.

Tarin ducked under a Meman's head and leaped to behead a sumaire riding down upon him and immediately rolled under the hooves of another and leaped to his feet, the rune-blade slicing through the sumaire's middle, cutting it to the backbone. The Meman spun on its hooves and attacked Tarin, but Black, screaming his challenge, crashed into the side of the Meman, knocking it into the fire and trampling it with his hooves.

Sirona's sword danced and swung in her hands, beheading sumaires and stabbing Menans in their neck. A Nightshade came out of the darkness toward her, but Nuad flashed by her in a blur and tumbled the Nightshade from his horse. Nuad's jaws immediately closed on the Nightshade's throat, ripping it apart. Blood fountained into the night, but Nuad had already left the Nightshade and had leaped upon the back of another Nightshade's horse, powerful jaws crunching through the Nightshade's neck.

A sumaire and a Nightshade came after Cumac, but he waited calmly for them and when they came together before reaching him, he gave a war cry and the warp-spasm came fast upon him. He gave a salmon-leap and while he passed overhead of the sumaire and Nightshade, Caladbolg blurred in his hands and the riders rode on a few more strides before tumbling from their horses, sliced in half. Immediately Cumac roared his battle cry and rushed the attackers in a fury that blurred and appeared ghostlike as he deftly dodged blades and horses' hooves, killing here and there with a savagery that awed those around him.

Dathi leaped to put his back against Tarin and Sirona, forming a threesome that fought grimly, meeting horseman after horseman with blades that flashed like a steel curtain, while Lorgas and Bern stood back-to-back, hacking and slicing at whatever appeared in front of them. A Meman slipped past an ax-swing by Lorgas, tearing his shoulder as it passed. Lorgas staggered, then came grimly to his feet, ignoring the pain and the blood flowing from his shoulder. He hacked a sumaire with such power that the sumaire was nearly cut in half and fell from his mount. Lorgas spun on his heel and cut away the Meman's hind legs as it tried to gallop by, and the horse fell screaming in pain to the ground. It tried again and again to rise, but couldn't.

Bern felt Lorgas stagger and renewed his fight, moving grimly in a semicircle to keep as many of the enemy from Lorgas as he could. The Bisuilglas gleamed and pulsed on his shoulder, lending its strength and wisdom to Bern's fight. Bern's sword seemed to take on a life of its own as the blade blurred in the air, slicing and cutting with a wild vengeance.

A sumaire tried to ride upon Seanchan but was met by a ball of fire that ignited upon striking him in the chest. The ball broke apart and flames leaped upon the sumaire and ran down to wrap the Meman in flames.

Screams of pain and fury echoed through the night as the enemy rode down again and again upon the Seekers. Then Dathi staggered as a Nightshade sword sliced into his shoulder, but the warrior recovered quickly and resumed his attack, slaying the Nightshade who had wounded him with a single thrust that went through the Nightshade's body. Grimly the warrior continued to battle, although the wound was telling upon him. He fell to a knee but quickly rose, swinging his great sword with a renewed fury.

Then as suddenly as the attack came, it was over, and the Seekers stood, panting, around the fire.

"Anyone hurt?" Seanchan asked. Then he saw Lorgas on one knee with Bern trying to stanch the flow of blood, and Dathi, where Tarin and Sirona pressed compresses against the wide-opened wound.

Immediately Seanchan crossed to Dathi and motioned for Tarin and Sirona to stand and let him attend to Dathi. Seanchan knelt and used both hands to press the edges of the wound together. He spoke in a strange language and the edges of the wound closed. Dathi lay white-faced and shaken, and Tarin grabbed a cloak and quickly covered him as Seanchan rose and went to Lorgas.

"It's not so bad," Lorgas said gamely.

"Bad enough," Bern said. "It's your drinking arm."

"Ahhh nuts," Lorgas said disgustedly. Then, hopefully, "Can you heal it, Seanchan?"

"Let's see," Seanchan said. He took a look at the wound. Already a green tinge was showing around the edges of the wound. The elf looked hot and feverish, his eyes bright.

> *Datha m'abet n turso*
> *Mit an bak n muso.*

> *Heal this wound and make it*
> *The way back as it once was.*

A light blue smoke flickered up from the wound, and Lorgas gasped as the healing flame seared the wound, then closed it. Sweat popped out on the face of Lorgas, and he groaned in pain.

"Keep water in him," Seanchan said to Bern. "The healing will dry him."

Bern nodded and quickly collected his and Lorgas's water bottles and lifted the elf's head, allowing a small trickle to slip past dry lips.

"Where's Cumac?" Seanchan asked, looking around the fire.

The others shook their heads.

"The last I saw him he was in the warp-spasm and running into the dark with that salmon-leap of his," Tarin said. "I don't know what happened after that."

"I haven't seen him," Sirona said.

"Nor I," answered Dathi through clenched teeth.

"Ah me," Seanchan said, passing a hand over his eyes and leaning tiredly upon his staff. "Well, I'd better see if I can find him."

He took a firm grip on his staff, a deep breath, then went into the darkness, a tiny ball of light showing him the way.

"I hope he finds Cumac," Sirona said, watching the Druid go.

"So do we all," Tarin said. The others chorused their agreement.

SEANCHAN did not have far to go. A hundred feet outside the rim of the firelight he found Cumac on all fours, gasping for air, the warp-spasm gone. Quickly Seanchan felt his forehead, then jerked his hand back, burning.

> *Ath bentoine ne' sien arhth beath*
> *A'betain ma tien sa cublea.*
>
> *I summon fire, air, and water*
> *To aid this man in his need.*

A fire flickered in the air, creating a cloud above Cumac, and water poured from the cloud over the warrior, cooling him. He sighed deeply, then rose shakily and tried to smile at Seanchan.

"That was close," he said. "Very close. I had to fight to bring myself back."

Seanchan looked at him closely. "But you *did* bring yourself back? The warp-spasm didn't leave on its own?"

Cumac shook his head. "No, I willed it away."

"Then," Seanchan said, grinning and slapping Cumac on his shoulder, staggering him. "Then you are beginning to be able to control it. At least this is a beginning."

"A beginning. Yes," Cumac said. "But I hope it becomes easier."

"With need. And with practice," Seanchan said. He turned and led Cumac back to the others.

Black and Graymount came in from the darkness, spattered with blood. The wolfhounds followed and sat down together, taking turns to clean the other.

"I would say we were very fortunate," Seanchan said. "Not, I add, that I am surprised about what happened this close to the valley. I warned you all, but that's not here or there. We made it through and I think we'll be safe for the night. Now, let us sleep. Black and Graymount and Nuad and Fergma will watch for us."

Gratefully the Seekers tumbled into their blankets, stretching knotted limbs, and falling into dreamless sleep.

36

The day rose with a gray sheet laced with black ribbons across the sky. The Seekers walked out of the hollow and stared at the valley near them. Fog swirled within the valley, and a coldness fell over the Seekers. They did not see Bricriu.

"So that is where we are going," Sirona said.

"Yes," Seanchan said grimly. "And I wish we weren't. I know what awaits us in that valley and I do not like it."

"Well, what are we waiting for," Lorgas

demanded. He shook his shoulders and tested his wounded shoulder. A short bite of pain came, but nothing that bothered the elf. "We have to go into it anyway, so let's go. The sooner we go the sooner we are through it."

"I agree," Cumac said. His face looked wan, and tired circles rimmed his eyes, but he still stood straight and tall and a battle light shone from his eyes.

Seanchan shrugged. "There is wisdom to your words. Saddle up. We leave now."

The Seekers went down to their horses and quickly rolled their blankets and slipped on their cloaks. Within the quarter-hour they were ready to go.

Nuad and Fergma took the lead and trotted toward the valley's mouth with Seanchan and Cumac riding side by side behind them.

"Ride wary," Seanchan called back to Dathi and Tarin immediately behind him. Sirona followed them with the elves riding together behind her. Dathi turned and relayed the message and then rode up beside Seanchan on the Druid's other side.

"What all can we expect there?" he said pointing.

"Everything. Anything," Seanchan answered. "But most of all, the shadows. Light is all that will combat them, and I hope I have enough strength to keep them at bay," he added grimly. "We cannot tarry in that valley, for I know not how long I can last. The rest of you shall have to attend to whatever comes our way. I will not be able to help."

"Perhaps cairnfire?" Cumac asked.

Seanchan turned in his saddle to say, "No. Most definitely not cairnfire. That valley is bewitched, and I do not know how the cairnfire will affect shadows that are all that's left of what was once alive."

They came to the mouth of the valley and paused for a moment. The pass was narrow, but two and sometimes three would be able to ride abreast easily with room to spare. Seanchan looked around at the others and asked, "Well, is everyone ready?"

The others murmured their agreement and Seanchan turned, took a deep breath, and led the Seekers into the valley.

Immediately the fog closed around them, and they could feel

the clammy tendrils of fog clinging to them. Strange sounds filtered through the fog and mist, and the Seekers unconsciously took their weapons from their sheaths and rode with them in hand.

Then an eerie silence fell upon them and the silence fell heavily upon their ears. They strained, trying to hear something, but no sound came to them and they huddled closer together, each watching warily not to be surprised.

Then wraithlike figures appeared in front, behind, and on each side of them. Seanchan shouted a warning and then light blazed from his staff. The figures disappeared, falling back and away from the Seekers. But then other figures appeared and the Seekers felt their hearts grow cold.

Goblins, hobgoblins, Deag-duls, sumaires, and Truacs appeared, and then the attack was on, with the Seekers forming a loose ring around Seanchan, who held the light steady with his staff.

The goblins came first, screaming and yelling as they fell onto the Seekers, who grimly drove them away, slaying them. Black gouts of blood flew everywhere, slopping onto the Seekers and their horses. Then came the hobgoblins, sliding craftily in from the side, but Sirona and Tarin and Dathi turned to meet them with flashing swords and battle roars that echoed off the sides of the valley and into the mist.

Again the warp-spasm fell over Cumac. One eye bulged out while the other shrunk to the size of a needle. His bones twisted and cracked and muscles bulged. He opened his throat and his shout was like a bodhran beating in his throat, freezing the attackers momentarily, allowing him to leap into their midst, Caladbolg singing wildly as Cumac attacked recklessly, heedless of the others, savage cries coming from him as figure after figure fell before him.

Then a shrill yell came and a figure leaped down from on high to stand next to Seanchan.

Fedelm.

Arrow after arrow sped from her bow, each shaft finding its target.

"About time you came," Tarin shouted.

She flashed a quick grin at him, then leaped upon a boulder near Seanchan to gain extra height. The arrows kept speeding from the never-emptying quiver.

The sight of Fedelm gave renewed strength to the Seekers as they fought grimly like fiends possessed.

Another figure dropped in beside Seanchan.

Cathlon.

"You look as if you could use some help," he said, drawing his sword. "So here I am."

"Welcome. Most welcome," Seanchan said.

Cathlon grinned and leaped upon the boulder to guard Fedelm's back as she continued to find marks for her arrows.

Black blood mixed with red rolled in a small flood around the Seekers as they grimly fought. But the numbers began to tell upon the Seekers and they began to be driven back with Seanchan as the center.

Then a hollow voice called.

"Do not spread the light too far, Seanchan! We are here for you."

And shadows appeared just beyond the light, weapons in hands, falling upon the enemy shadows, shattering the air with gleeful shouts, as they leaped toward other shadows.

"Move forward!" the voice called again. "Move forward! We shall take the rear!"

"Who are you?" Seanchan yelled.

"Those seeking a second chance to regain their honor!" the voice called back. "I am Bocha!"

"The former king," Seanchan said. Sweat was beginning to flow down his face as he fought to keep the light. "Welcome!" he shouted.

"Press on! Press on!" Bocha shouted.

The shadows spilled on, then rolled over other shadows, driving them screaming into the edges of light. Then the shadows fell over the goblins and hobgoblins, which shrieked and, turning, ran from the battle, scurrying up the walls of the valley and disappearing into caves.

Yet the Nightshades and Truacs and sumaires fought on, grimly trying to close the circle to where the Seekers would have no room to swing their weapons.

Then a sumaire leaped into the circle and swung its sword at Sirona's back. Dathi gave a warning shout and leaped in to block the blade. The blade struck Dathi's sword and slipped down, slicing into Dathi. The old warrior staggered, then renewed his attack upon the sumaire. Sparks flew from their blades and then a loud scream came from the sumaire's throat as Dathi brought a slice down upon the Sumaire's throat, severing him to the bottom of his belly. Intestines rolled out and blood sprayed over all.

Then the Seekers began to move down the valley, slowly at first, then faster as the enemy turned more and more to fight with the shadows that were behind them.

Then the Seekers were at the end of the valley and ran out from the mist. Some Truacs followed them but were instantly slain by Sirona and Tarin. Cumac emerged from the mist, covered with blood, the warp-spasm slowly leaving him. Fedelm and Cathlon came next. And then Dathi, staggering from his wound.

Blood seeped from his lips as he grinned at the Seekers.

"I thank you for my life," Sirona said formally, reaching to help him.

"It's been a good day," he gasped. "A good day."

"Let me help," Seanchan said, coming to his side.

But Dathi shook his head. "I feel the presence of Donn. There is nothing you can do for me now. I thank you for letting me come . . . with . . . you."

His sword fell from his hand and he pitched forward. Sirona caught him and laid him gently upon the ground. She closed his eyes and took a cloth from her bag and a water bottle and began cleaning him. Tears showed in the corners of her eyes, but sobs never came from her throat.

Tarin came forward to help, but she shook her head and told him that this was something she wanted to do by herself, and the others left her to her task.

Fedelm turned to Cathlon and smiled.

"I see you found some weapons," Cathlon said.

"I did," she said. "With the help of a shade."

"Those weapons were not made by men, you know," Cathlon said. "They come from a time when there were giants upon the earth."

"I know," Fedelm said. "And thank you."

Cathlon nodded and smiled. "My time here is finished. I must return to Dreamworld."

"Before you go," Seanchan said, "can you tell us about Bricriu?"

Cathlon grimaced. "He slipped through the valley unharmed at night with the help of the Chalice. He is now a good day ahead of you. Take the road along the coast and follow it north. And good luck."

"Thank you," Seanchan said as Cathlon slowly disappeared. "You were most needed."

Then Seanchan turned to the valley and shouted, "Bocha! You have earned your honor this day."

"Or night as it may be here in the Valley of Shadows," Bocha shouted back. "But we thank you, Seanchan Duirgeal! May the gods watch your steps!"

The mist swirled, then rolled back in upon itself into the valley.

Cumac sighed and leaned on the hilt of his sword and said, "Now what do we do?"

"We must get away from here as far as we can travel. It is still not safe here, especially when night falls upon us. The enemy will come again upon us then."

"What now?" Tarin asked. "We have missed Bricriu. He is headed north toward Maliman now."

"We must not lose hope," Bern said. "Wherever good men and elves gather, there is hope."

"And women," Sirona said.

"And women," Bern added.

"Will we ever catch Bricriu Poisontongue?" Cumac asked.

"Eventually," Seanchan said. "Eventually."

"Then let us move away from this wretched valley," Sirona said.

And so the Seekers, with heavy hearts, wearily mounted their horses and, led once again by the wolfhounds Nuad and Fergma, rode away from the valley, continuing their search for the Chalice of Fire, turning upon the road leading up north to the Mountains of Mourne.